THE VALOR OF PERSEUS

TAPESTRY OF FATE
BOOK 2

MATT LARKIN

INCANDESCENT PHOENIX BOOKS

The Valors of Perseus: Eschaton Cycle
Tapestry of Fate Book 2
MATT LARKIN
Editors: Sarah Chorn, Regina Dowling
Cover: Felix Ortiz, Shawn T. King
Map: Francesca Baerald

Incandescent Phoenix Books
mattlarkinbooks.com

TITAN ERA
OKEANUS
THULE
HYPERBOREA
KELTIA
ILLYRIS
SALON
RASSENIA
MNEMOSYNIA
THRINAKIA
OLMECATL
TARTESSOS
KARKHEDON
KARTH
KEMET
MEMPHIS
TIWANAKU
TIWANAKU
INUMIDEN
OSIRION
THE GREAT VELDT
KUSH
KONGO JUNGLE
HY-BRASIL
KGALAGADI DESERT
AZANIA

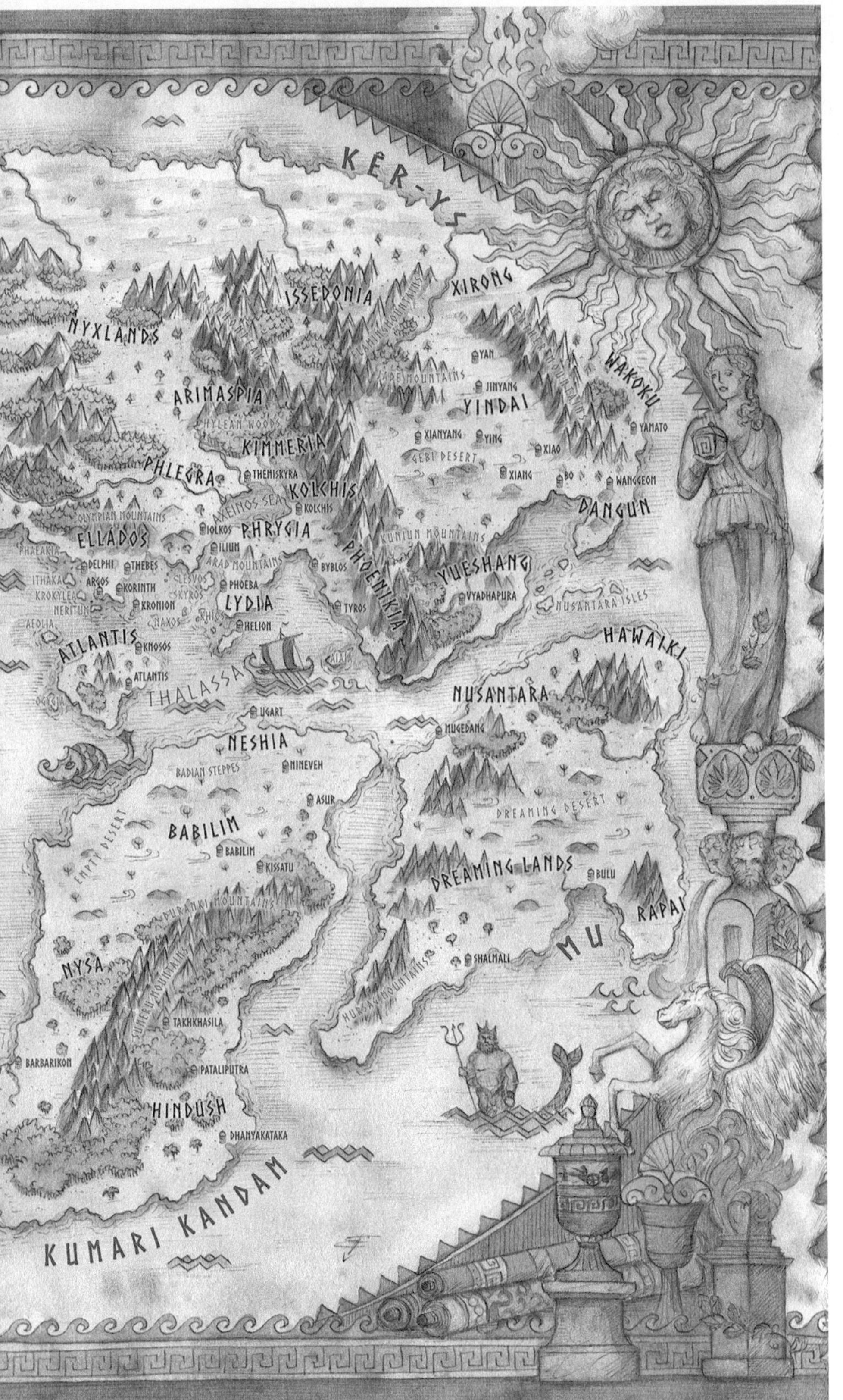

KER-YS
XIRONG
ISSEDONIA
NYXLANDS
YAN
WAKOKU
ARIMASPIA
JINYANG
YINDAI
YAMATO
HYLEAN WOODS
KIMMERIA
XIANYANG
YING
XIAO
PHLEGRA
GEBI DESERT
THEMISKYRA
XIANG
BO
WANGGEOM
KOLCHIS
OLYMPIAN MOUNTAINS
AXEINOS SEA
KOLCHIS
DANGUN
ELLADOS
IOLKOS
PHRYGIA
KUNLUN MOUNTAINS
PHAEAKIA
ILIUM
ARAD MOUNTAINS
DELPHI
THEBES
BYBLOS
PHOENIKIA
YUESHANG
ITHAKA
ARGOS
SLESVOS
KROKYLEA
KORINTH
SKYROS
PHOEBA
VYADHAPURA
NERITUM
KRONION
LYDIA
NAXOS
KHIOS
TYROS
NUSANTARA ISLES
AEOLIA
HELION
ATLANTIS
KNOSOS
HAWAIKI
ATLANTIS
THALASSA
OGYGIA
UGART
NUSANTARA
NESHIA
MUGEDANG
BADIAN STEPPES
NINEVEH
ASUR
DREAMING DESERT
BABILIM
EMPTY DESERT
BABILIM
DREAMING LANDS
BULU
KISSATU
RAPAI
DURANKI MOUNTAINS
MU
NYSA
SHALMALI
SUMERU MOUNTAINS
TAKHKHASILA
HUMAN MOUNTAINS
BARBARIKON
PATALIPUTRA
HINDUSH
DHANYAKATAKA
KUMARI KANDAM

THE WHISPER

It starts with a whisper, a haunting intimation of a World askew. That we are, in the end, caught in a death spiral, time nearly played out, whilst entropy tugs ever harder upon the Wheel of Fate.

Looking now into the dying embers, we at last apprehend Truth, and in it the revelation that the vaunted tales of old were not what we thought ... And neither, in fact, were we.

For if we have lived before, might not all we've dreamt be but our souls' memories of Worlds become dust ...

A QUICK NOTE

For full colour, higher-res maps, character lists, location overviews, and glossaries, check out the bonus resources here: https://tinyurl.com/hw52dzss

And if you liked this book, be sure to check out my offer for a free novella at the end.

PROLOGUE

2387 Golden Age

Kronos had built his city of Kronion into a thriving metropolis that would survive even the fall of its founder. There was a part of Prometheus, as he climbed toward the acropolis, that twisted up in knots knowing his erstwhile friend would soon suffer agonies Prometheus would not have wished upon his enemies.

Was Kronos to be yet one more sacrifice upon the altar of Ananke? He would find himself defeated and broken, cast into torment in Tartarus, and Prometheus would not lift a hand to stop it. Would, in fact, contribute to it. Because, if there was a hope of averting the culmination of Fate, it lay in the gambit Prometheus set in motion long ago. A play so desperate, so audacious, he dared to believe neither the Fates nor the forces of Khaos would be able to predict or avert it.

But for it to work, the Wheel of Fate must spin and spin, until its final moment. The cycle must continue and history, forever merciless, must endure.

So, after mopping sweat from his brow, he made his way into Kronos's palace in the acropolis. The servants knew him here and brought him to see the king in his private chambers. Kronos sat almost buried in a sea of papyrus scrolls, furiously sketching out notes.

A glance told Prometheus enough. The man still sought his vain means of subverting Ananke. He would try and try, as he had even in Eras past, and he would fail. Neither the Fates nor their tapestry were easily undone.

"It's funny, yes?" Kronos asked, offering Prometheus only a brief glance. "They call it the Time of Nyx. As if the whole of it was defined by her."

"Nigh enough."

Now Kronos did favour him with a longer, appraising look. "You intimate that naught achieved in the whole of Vulgeth mattered? That all that came before was the expanse of the night that swallowed it? And even in the Eras before *that*?" Kronos scoffed. "No, you don't believe that."

Prometheus settled himself upon the floor in front of Kronos, legs crossed. "I hear Raziel calls himself Enki now."

"Not going to answer me?" Kronos dropped the papyrus he held and set down his stylus. "Always with the evasions, eh?" The other man's face darkened. "Why is it that, no matter how much time passes, no matter how oft I extend my hand, I can never win back your trust? What, because I did not believe the unbelievable without proof?" The man's voice had risen almost to a shout. "Because I did not apprehend the Ontos until I caught some glimpse of it for myself? Is that so very great a crime, *brother*?"

Prometheus offered him a sad smile. It was worse, of course, because Kronos had a point. To condemn his former brethren for eternity for a mistake made in ignorance was petty of Prometheus, and he knew it. But then, it was not just condemnation for their errors, but out of necessity. That was Ananke, the real Ananke. The reality that, whatever he might will, causal chains bound his hands, and always would.

And for those who could glimpse the future, those chains became far more complex—far more damning—than the forces that determined the decisions of other men. Just as Kronos's own Oracle Mirrors had ensured his damnation and led him to make choices that would resonate through eternity.

Just as Prometheus's vision in the flames had shown him what Zeus would do.

Prometheus could not spare Kronos his Fate, and any forgiveness he offered the man would be a mockery of the word.

"Such times are long past," Prometheus said. "And I am sitting here now, am I not?"

Kronos once more snatched the papyrus he'd been recording on, now pushing it toward Prometheus. "The others are gone now, my friend. It's just you and I, but now that we know the Ontos, there has to be some way to break the Wheel of Fate."

Oh, but they *needed* the Wheel of Fate. Breaking it could not be allowed until his gambit had played out. He tried to keep the thought from his face, but Kronos must have seen something there.

Prometheus glanced over the notes Kronos had handed him. Oblique references to the Tablet, the Box, and the Chambers. Connections made to the Destroyer, yes, but maybe not the right connections. Kronos circled answers so close and yet forever obfuscated from him.

"Is that not the purpose behind the Tablet of Destiny?" the Titan King blurted at Prometheus. There was a frenzy in him now, and Prometheus had to wonder just what, exactly, Kronos had beheld in the Oracle Mirrors beneath Vulgeth long ago. Or perhaps in the days that followed, after moving the mirrors to the tainted peak of Olympus. Either way, something he had seen in his future had scoured him to the pith and redoubled his desperation to free himself of Ananke.

"Something like that," Prometheus admitted, though Kronos did not understand so much of the Tablet as he thought. Nor would Prometheus dare ever voice the whole of his play aloud and risk the Moirai or others hearing of it. "But destiny is not always quite what we think. Besides, I have my own Oracular Sight, as well you know."

"As if it has helped us much of late."

No, and it would harm. The vision he'd beheld in the flames whilst training Hestia had been too clear, and the time had come.

"Enough to see perfidy in your very halls." Brought in, on some level, by Prometheus himself. But the Fates would have their tapestry, and Prometheus was but their avatar.

Kronos blanched. The king remained paranoid. Twisted—as was Prometheus, as were all Men—by the past. Kronos had watched in the so-called Time of Nyx when all he'd built had come crashing down around him. When the Cabal had faltered and broken, and darkness had threatened to swallow the cosmos, because he had been too blind to threats within his midst. No one who had beheld Nyx in her awful grandeur was ever the same.

It would not take much, now, to send so tormented a man digging for traitors, desperate to avert any such end again.

"What perfidy?"

It was too late to back away now. It had always been too late. "Pyromantic visions are not always literal ..." Though this one surely was. He had seen what he had seen.

"What?" demanded Kronos.

"A prophecy that one son will slay the other."

Now, Kronos was on his feet, shaking his head in vain denial. Prometheus would try to assuage his guilt for this by reminding himself he did not cause Zeus's actions. Even if he now played upon Kronos's fears to ensure the man found out about the crimes, Prometheus was not actually starting this war.

But the vision told him what must impend. Sometimes, all Prometheus could do was stoke the flame. Keep the Wheels turning.

Was it because Kronos had failed him eons ago, when Prometheus needed him? Prometheus hoped not. He would blame Ananke, because he could not stand the thought he would so damn a man for an honest mistake. Still, his reasons mattered only to him, he supposed.

Ananke held them all.

And however much he might wish otherwise, Kronos had never been the one to challenge Fate.

PART I

Consequently, we cannot help but believe we have reached the last of the Ages, for how much farther might Man yet fall? The Age of Heroes that my colleagues call the Bronze Age, that ended with the fall of Ilium, even as the Titanomachy ended the Golden Age, and the Gigantomachy ended the Silver Age. Every Age ended by cataclysmic war, and we are forever left lesser than what has come before. And now, in times of unending turmoil and strife, I shudder to think what final war will extinguish this world.
— Kleio, Analects of the Muses

1

PANDORA

400 Dark Age

*B*rizo's fall from Taygete's Bridge heralded the doom of Atlantis. With her death, the whole of the island came apart in dust and crashing stone, in cacophony and the roaring collapse of dreams. All around Pandora, the world began to falter, colossal waves racing over the dying polis while a furious storm raged over the distant mountains.

With a shriek, Pandora fell a half-dozen feet to where a flagstone had settled below street level.

Oh, fuck. Not like this! Not like this, after everything!

A woman wearing a crimson khiton hopped down beside her, offering a hand. Pandora grasped it and was hefted to her feet. She met the other woman's gaze.

It was *her*. She was looking in a mirror at another Pandora.

And the other Pandora held the Box in her free hand. "We don't have much time."

Despite the tumbling panoply of destruction unfolding around her, Pandora could do naught save stare at herself in incomprehension. Her mind refused to parse what she was seeing, and all she managed was an inarticulate moan at the other Pandora.

The woman grabbed her arm. "I know, I know. I remember what it was like. Try to focus, though." She squeezed, tight enough to jolt Pandora from her daze. "Focus, Pandora. You're trying to save Prometheus, yes? Only a son of Zeus will be able to set him free. You understand? A son of Zeus." She waited for Pandora to nod, though the stupor had not quite passed. But the other woman pressed the Box back into Pandora's hand. "I've set this for you, all you have to do is open it."

Pandora accepted the puzzle box, glancing at it, then back up at the other Pandora who had released her and cast a sudden glance at the chaos unfolding around her, gaze lingering a moment on the storm raging on Mount Evenor. "Go, Pandora."

Feeling the fool, Pandora nodded at herself, then searched for the clasp to pop the top of the Box and go wherever she was sending herself.

"Oh, wait!" the other Pandora blurted even as Pandora pressed the button. "You must convince Nike to fight alongside Zeus, against Kronos, or Pyrrha will die!"

Wait, what? Nike?

Pandora's ears popped and light bent backwards, even as the city continued to pitch inward about itself.

THE WHOLE of her World shifted, and not just from the Box, though its vertiginous waves had her tumbling to her knees and pitching into the dirt. No, it was as though the foundations of her reality had imploded, throwing into question all intuited sense of causality, leaving her in a maelstrom of doubt.

Focus. Focus on the present moment for now.

Groaning, Pandora pushed herself up on her elbows. It had been slightly easier than last time, she supposed.

The ground beneath her had stilled, no longer rising and falling like a storm-tossed sea. That also counted as an improvement.

Based on the sun, it was nigh to noon, and she knelt upon a hill, blinking at an expanse of mountains that stretched up in the distance. The Olympian Mountains? Far off, she could just make out the eternal storm that raged above Olympus itself.

Gods, her mouth tasted foul, and her body ached, both from being hurled to the stones and from the bruising of her mind the other Pandora had delivered. That was so ... She had seemed so different, as if seeing the World from some angle Pandora could not conceive of, and yet, if she was to be believed, that moment would lie in Pandora's own future.

Trying to wrap her thoughts around it returned the sense of vertigo, and Pandora decided it best to remain upon her knees for a moment more, drawing in deep breaths. It was an enticing puzzle, yes, but one she was so deep in the midst of that it could consume her, drown her in a turbulent sea of unanswered questions.

In front of her lay the Box, and slowly, almost painfully, she felt her gaze drawn to it. *What* had she opened with this thing? What utter madness had she unleashed?

Part of her wanted to weep, but instead, she found herself seized by a burst of hysteric laughter at the sheer preposterousness of what had befallen her. What still *would* befall her, in the days to come. Unless she could change the future and come back to the same paradox that had led Prometheus to ensure the timeline remained unchanged so Pyrrha could be born. If she took steps that prevented her future self from saving her past self, wouldn't she already be dead?

Actually, there *were* tears moistening her eyes, even while she knelt there, giggling. Giving over to it, Pandora pitched onto her side, wrapping her body around the Box, and letting the fit pass. It was too much.

Ananke was too much. An ouroboros, a serpent consuming its own tail, encircling the cosmos in its constricting coils. With every passing instant, with each deepening of her understanding, the ouroboros grew tighter, until the very life would seep out of her.

And Pandora could not but weep at the futility of finding a way free.

When at last she had composed herself, she rose and descended the hill, pausing at a packed dirt road that ran the length of the mountains. Indeed, this could well be the very track she and Prometheus had followed from Delphi to Olympus, and if so, Delphi lay to the west.

Perhaps the Oracle there—was there even an Oracle at this time? —could help her figure out how to find a son of Zeus. The other Pandora had neglected to provide a name, either because she had been so distracted by whatever else she was looking for at the time, or because she trusted Pandora to figure it out. Perhaps the latter if all of this had already happened to the other woman.

So, she would have sent her to a time and place close enough to find whomever she needed to save Prometheus, or at least, Pandora would have to assume so. "All right then," she mumbled and set off down the road, toward Delphi.

She would find the son of Zeus, convince him to help her, even against his father's wishes, and rescue Prometheus from Tartarus. Once all that was done, she could see about attending to the rest of the future.

And the Moirai—had they indeed woven this obscene procession of Fate—could go fuck themselves.

ON THE PERIPHERY OF DELPHI, a small stream of pilgrims flowed toward an arch cut into the mountainside, which, Pandora assumed, must be the famed cave of the Oracle. Though Apollon himself ruled both the Oracles and this city, tales said he was rarely in residence, preferring to spend his time in Olympus. Or, perhaps, Zeus encouraged Helios's golden son to remain where he could keep an eye on him.

Either way, a mortal Oracle most oft offered the pronouncements, and if Pandora was very lucky, perhaps she could help her as well. She joined the queue of pilgrims, suddenly self-conscious of the dusty state of her peplos. Her garment had come from the Golden Age, then been splatted with mud and dust from the fall of Atlantis. And now she prepared to enter the Oracle's cave in an unknown time.

Even with her brushing off the clothes, none of the others seemed to pay her any mind, so caught up in their own pressing issues. She imagined them pondering over just how to phrase their questions, over just what mattered the most. Wrapt within the crushing weight of one's future, one might easily overlook oddities in the present.

The queue flowed slowly, a hiccupping stream, really, giving Pandora too much time to imagine what went on within. A pair of guards allowed one person in at a time, and each pilgrim would vanish for but a few moments sometimes, or sometimes for so long Pandora's feet began to ache from standing in one spot. Some of those who emerged beamed, some looked bemused, and more than one came out shaking their head, eyes haunted, ill-pleased with whatever prophecy had been offered up to them.

The day began to wane, and evening closed in. Would they turn her away and tell her to come back tomorrow? That fear crept up on her, over and over, as the afternoon set and gloaming settled. But when the last pilgrim emerged, the guards waved her in as well.

"Make it fast," the elder one snapped at her as she passed. "Time for wine and soup."

Yes, and Pandora could have done with both at this point. Would the guard have cared had she mentioned someone she loved languished in Tartarus in eternal torment and the Oracle's words might lead to his salvation? Probably not.

What was utter torment for a stranger when compared to the lure of a hot meal for oneself? Those unperceived occupied a kind of non-reality for most people, abstractions without substance, thus afforded empathy only in the abstract.

The archway led into a hexagonal chamber with multiple tunnels branching away. As only one was lit, Pandora followed it to find the

Oracle in a steam-drenched chamber. The girl was younger than she'd have suspected, maybe only sixteen or seventeen. Her eyes flitted about unfocused, and she swayed where she sat, ever so slightly. Was the girl drunk? The steam was wafting up through grates in the floor just behind the Oracle.

No, perhaps not drunk. Maybe there was some hallucinogenic compound in the steam she breathed. Once, lounging in their cottage, Prometheus had told her that many Oracles relied upon mind-altering substances to help them access their gifts.

"So it goes," the girl moaned. "When the once obstinate foundations dance like water, and the tide rises without fall. The sweeping groan of a firmament stretched too thin, even as the Storm Lord claims an evanescent throne."

Frowning, Pandora knelt before the Oracle, uncertain what to even say to that. Did the Oracle offer a puzzle, or was her mind so addled by the fumes that she spewed nonsense everyone took for wisdom? Even a few breaths of these vapours left Pandora's head light, and a slight vertigo claimed her.

The girl herself reclined in a pose Pandora would have used in her former life as hetaira to entice her clients, though she suspected the Oracle was too far inebriated to be intentionally provocative. Still, sweat made the girl's thin khiton cling to her flesh, and she had her knees apart in a pose that must have driven men to distraction. She supposed the Oracle's status as Apollon's chosen protected her from anyone making unwanted advances upon her. Oh ... or perhaps anyone, save Apollon himself. Was that why the Oracles were always female?

Eh. The vapours *were* affecting her, and her mind was wandering. "I haven't gotten to ask my question yet," she said.

"And still answers unfold, blooming like flower petals when the spring at last arrives. You will find yourself bereft, adrift in a sea of misremembered dreams, until that stuff of you becomes motes of light blinked away."

Pandora shifted. It was too warm here and sweat had begun to dribble down the back of her neck. "Uh huh. Tell me where I can find the son of Zeus who might help me free Prometheus."

"In distress, one most oft finds those capable of greatness."

Ostensibly profound and utterly meaningless. What else should she expect? "I was rather hoping for a name and location."

"I have no names for you ... and you are out of time."

"What, that's it? That's all you have for me?" She had stood in a queue all afternoon for this? With a groan, Pandora rose, shaking her head and making her way back out of the tunnels.

The older guard grunted when she passed. "Finally. Hope you got what you wanted."

Not bothering to answer, Pandora made her way toward the hill where the polis of Delphi sat. With luck, she'd make it up there before they shut the gates and be able to find lodging with some kind stranger. Or, if needs be, she had some few drachmae, though not from this time.

Not from ... they were out of time ...

Pandora's sandals caught on the dirt, and she stumbled before turning to look back at the Oracle's cave. The girl had said she was 'out of time.' Had she *known*? Had the child apprehended far more than she seemed to, or was her parting line merely the dismissal it had seemed?

If the former, perhaps all of the Oracle's words held some import. Resuming her plodding trek up the hill, Pandora ran them over in her mind, round and round. Storm Lord? Was that Zeus? If so, her claim he would sit an evanescent throne seemed to imply even his reign upon Olympus would not last overlong in the greater scope of history.

That, at least, offered Pandora some small comfort.

Still, she had not found what she had come looking for. She needed Zeus's son to help her save Prometheus, and it seemed she was going to have to find him herself.

2

———

HEKATE

225 Golden Age

For years, Hekate had lingered in Phoeba, studying under the reluctant tutelage of the Titan Phoebe, and ever feeling too seen by the woman's husband, the Oracle Koios. But every student must reach a point in which they recognise a teacher has little more to offer, either through recalcitrance or having brushed up against the brink of their own ability. Besides, Artemis had long since wearied of tarrying in one place, and Hekate could not deny her friend.

Thus, they had set sail to Phoenikia and landed in Byblos, a city legend claimed Kronos had raised out of the Time of Nyx. While Artemis busied herself with tariffs for the harbourmaster, Hekate didn't bother trying not to gawk at the timeless wonder that unfolded before her. Of a certainty, the harbour reeked of brine and fish the same as any other, but beyond lay the great stones of the wall that had protected Byblos since before time began.

When they made toward the gate, Hekate paused to trace her

fingers over the surface, heedless of the way Artemis stared, eyebrow quirked. This place seeped in history, and history had its own power, compounded down through the ages, as if the souls of everyone who lived and died here had imprinted upon the land. How much blood had stained these stones over the passing of ages? Rain may have washed the surface clean, but Hekate could feel the stains run deeper, like wounds that never quite healed.

Beyond the walls, they passed by a spring sunk down into a crater, and she fancied it, too, had a power of its own. Already, the gloaming closed in around them, enlivening the mysteries of this place, quickening its energies. Night was her time, even as Enodia had promised. With the deepening of shadows, the Mortal Realm seemed to grow closer to the Penumbra.

It was not just Thoth, the favoured Primordial to whom Phoebe and Artemis had sacrificed so oft, though the Elder God of the Moon did revel in the night sky. No, it was as if all the worlds of the Spirit Realm—save perhaps that of Sun—brushed against the Veil as the light dimmed.

"We could wait until the morn," Artemis offered. "I'm certain we can find lodging in the city."

Hekate favoured her friend with a withering look. Enodia had trained with the Circle of Goetic Mysteries, as had Phoebe and the famed Morpheus. Even Artemis's own father Helion was a member. All the great workers of the Art Hekate had ever heard of had learnt their craft in the Lodge of Whispers set within the heart of this very city. "I've waited long enough to learn the greater arcana. I'd not delay another hour, given the choice."

"Mmm." Artemis bit her lip, then shrugged. "So be it." She paused long enough to buy an oil lamp, before pushing on.

The huntress guided Hekate deeper into the ancient city. Within every alley, shadows danced, and the currents of the Penumbra whispered to Hekate, though she refrained from embracing the Sight and looking directly beyond the Veil. Countless shades must flit about such a place, and Hekate had no time for their self-absorbed lamentations.

They came to an inner wall, lower and thinner than the defensive barrier yet cut from similar grey stones. It demarcated the boundary of the ancient necropolis nestled at the very heart of Byblos. How many generations of dead lay entombed behind this wall? A hundred? A thousand? Or did the procession of the deceased carry on without limit, vanishing into the same oblivion that claimed their souls? A burnished gate cordoned off the city of the dead, and Artemis paused at the threshold, peering through the grating as if expecting to see something dire lurking in the tenebrous expanse beyond.

The grate itself had been wrought to look like a hedge of thorns, spikes twisting back upon themselves. Or pointed, slightly inward, toward the graves.

"The Circle could have picked a more hospitable place to set up their lodge," Artemis complained. Perhaps the huntress wanted Hekate to demure, to say they could return in the morn after all.

"I didn't think you, disciple of the Moon, one to fear the night," Hekate said, grasping the gate herself and shoving it. The door swung inward with a squeal of tired hinges, thorns scraping over dirt and rock below.

"It's not the Moon that ought to concern us," Artemis said, following just behind Hekate.

As Hekate stepped through the gate, the sense of having pushed into another world seized her. A slight chill seeped into the air, followed by a wind that, Hekate thought, the wall ought to have cut down more. It ruffled her peplos, evoking a shiver. Hints of mist without apparent source wafted among the grave markers, obscuring vision, though she could make out hints of those markers stretching on an on beyond the vapours.

Had the Penumbra itself begun to bleed into this space? Hekate had to admit to a fluttering in her gut at such a thought. Her tentative steps forward lacked the confidence she should have projected ... but maybe Artemis had the right of it. There was a darkness beyond mere night that infected the Mortal Realm here. A creeping insidiousness that had her throat closing up and her fists clenching at her sides, even as her sandals slapped upon the cobbled path forward.

A hint of a moan carried on the wind, a susurration playing out over her shoulder but dissipating if she sought its source. She could embrace the Sight now and *know* what lurked out there, but something held her back. A nameless dread that grew riper with each passing instant. The Elder Gods alone knew how many shades dwelt within these walls. Shades, and worse, darker things.

Something traced along her forearm, like a fingernail brushing over her, enough to scatter the hairs on her arm. Hekate gritted her teeth and stole a glance back at Artemis. If she looked ... if she peered through the window, she brought her soul closer to whatever now reached for her.

Artemis snatched her hand and yanked her forward, fear lending speed to the other Titan's steps where it had stolen Hekate's momentum. Neither seemed able to speak, as if they were stuck in a miasma of dread and despair.

Even knowing it was the polluting effects of the Penumbra affecting her, knowing she was a necromancer and could have worked the Art to try to command some few of these ghosts, Hekate still could not shake the sense of impotence that had claimed her. It took all her will to continue forward, passing more and more of the grave markers. They became not names nor even people, but claws jutting up through the mist, beckoning the living fool enough to tread into this place.

Then beyond, darker shapes formed in the vapours. A field of obelisks piercing the night, rimming a rocky hill. Her heart hammered as they approached the ridge. An archway was cut into it, sealed by double sandstone doors, these engraved with the twisting geometric patterns of the Art and wards that served to hold back unwelcome eidolons. Perhaps that was the only way the sorcerers could stand to dwell in such a place as this.

The Titan threw her weight against one of the doors and it creaked on unseen hinges, stone grinding upon stone as it gave way to her momentous strength. As it cracked open, welcome lamplight spilled out from the threshold, though it failed to illuminate the dark of the necropolis, as if even light was turned back by the darkness that had taken hold here.

Following Artemis, Hekate ducked into the blessed hints of brightness. A tunnel bored into the hill, sloping downward ever so slightly. Oil flames hung from bronze chains suspended from the ceiling on either side of the hall, though spaced far enough apart they created dancing rivers of shadow rather than banished the gloom.

Lamp out in front of her, Artemis pushed forward. They had made their way further but a few moments when a girl stepped up to bar their path. She had pitch-black hair and dark grey eyes. Most striking, however, was a spiralling tattoo upon her cheek. "You have come to enter the Circle."

"I am Artemis, daughter of Helion," Hekate's friend said before she could answer. "Is my father present?"

"He is," the girl answered. "I am Oizys, novitiate of the Outer Circle. I will take you to the lodge." The sorceress fixed Hekate with a discerning look that lingered longer than it ought to have, but she said naught more.

Oizys guided them through the rest of the tunnel and into a colonnaded vestibule bedecked with couches and throw pillows. A trio of braziers basked the high-ceiling chamber in warmth and light, which, while welcome, felt jarring after the chill and gloom that encompassed this place. Sitting about the room were perhaps ten men and women. A few studied scrolls, one scratched away with a quill, and others reclined in murmured conversations, goblets sloshing with red wine.

Among those reclined a golden-eyed Titan, a head taller than any other, who started upon seeing Artemis. "Daughter," he said, rising stiffly and handing his cup to a woman who remained sitting. "What are you doing here?"

"Isn't it obvious?" Artemis said, and Hekate could have sworn she could actually see the tension strung between them. "I've come to learn the greater mysteries at long last, Father." Artemis said that last almost as a challenge and Helios glowered, eyes glinting in the firelight.

"What makes you think the Circle seeks new members?"

"Oh, come off it," a woman said, stepping out from a chamber beyond this one. Her hood was up, but Hekate thought she too had golden eyes, which meant perhaps some relation to Helios. And some distant relation to Hekate, for that matter. "The Outer Circle has space for two more novitiates, and in walk two seeking the positions. Praise the Moirai and move on."

Helios grunted in assent—or frustration—but beckoned his daughter to follow.

"Keuthonymos," the woman said, "induct our new recruit."

The flaxen-haired young man with the quill immediately scrambled to his feet. "Yes, mistress." He scurried to Hekate's side, snatched her hand, and pulled her away from the vestibule, down another hall. "I am Keuthonymos of Hyperborea, though everyone here calls me Keuthos. I'm, uh, the newest member of the Circle, but if you have any questions, I'd be happy to assist in any way I am able."

Hekate raised a brow, gaze darting to where he still held her hand. The young man abruptly dropped it, blushing. "Forgive me, I ... My enthusiasm may have gotten the best of me."

Well, Hekate could empathise with that problem. "Where are you taking me?"

"To see the grand library, of course." Keuthos guided her down the hall to a bronze-banded door engraved with further wards. He slid it open slowly. At first, she thought him nervous, but when she spied two more sorceresses studying scrolls in the library, she began to suspect him merely trying to avoid disturbing them.

Within the room lay shelf after shelf of rolled papyrus, each stuck into its own alcove. Some had cases, some were loose. All were kept well away from the oil lamps set in the centre of the room. Beyond them, upon a pedestal, rested a bound tome of countless pages. Finding herself drawn to it, Hekate paced over. It was like a hundred papyrus scrolls packed into a single container, and never had she seen or imagined its like. A rose-gold chain connected it to the stone pedestal.

"The Circle's prized possession," Keuthos said. "A book from the Time of Nyx, left to us by our founders Damkina and Enki. The Sefer Raziel is said to be written by the greatest scholar of arcana in all history, but we have yet to decode it."

"What about your founders?" Hekate asked, gingerly brushing her fingers along the leathery cover. When Keuthos didn't object, she opened the tome. Within lay inscriptions written in a foreign tongue, along with numerous diagrams and what she had to assume where Supernal glyphs. A book for understanding the cosmos. For *mastering* the cosmos.

"Enki left the Circle long ago. Some say he wanders the world aimlessly, his will broken by what he found inside that book. Damkina rarely visits us anymore, and some speculate she will leave us as well. Though you met her tonight—it was she who instructed me to induct you. If she understands the tome, she does not share that with the other members of the Circle."

"She doesn't understand it," one of the sorceresses snapped, rising. "No one does."

Keuthos bowed to her. "Deino."

Upon closer examination, both Deino and the other sorceress had the same grey eyes and spiral tattoos as Oizys. Sisters?

The young sorceress ignored Keuthos, raising her chin to Hekate. "Who's this flame-haired wench? You're not meant to make withdrawals from the brothel, novitiate."

Oh. Maybe these sisters were kin to Hera. Hekate allowed a knowing smirk to spread across her face. There were times, when facing such obnoxiousness, when the greatest insult imaginable was to refuse to be insulted. If needs be, Hekate could always arrange to have a serpent slither up Deino's bowels later. For the moment, she just kept that smile plastered upon her face until the other woman squirmed and moved off to rejoin her sister.

"Inner Circle?" Hekate asked Keuthos as they left the library.

"The grey sisters? No, not yet, though speculation holds one or two of them might advance soon."

"Only two?"

Keuthos glanced at her, face stern. "The Circle has a maximum of nine members in the Inner Circle and nine in the Outer. At present, there are but two spaces in the Inner Circle vacant, though if Deino is correct and Damkina truly abandons us, it would free a position on the Inner. Speculation also holds that Phoebe might step down. It could go various ways."

He guided her back toward the main vestibule but walked its circumference to another hall. "These are private chambers for members. The one at the end is vacant, so you can claim it for sleeping."

Hekate cracked open the door in question. The room was plain, naught save a wash basin and a mat on the floor, but given that expansive library, she didn't expect to spend much time in a personal chamber anyway.

"Uh, hmm ..." Keuthos cleared his throat. "You came at an interesting time. We're preparing for the, um ... Sea of Oneness, soon."

"Sea of Oneness?" she asked.

He blushed so furiously she imagined him bursting into flame right in front of her. "We, uh ... share knowledge through ... shared ..."

Oh. Hekate folded her arms over her chest. "It's an orgy." Gaia, he couldn't stop staring at his sandals. "Keuthos, if you want to invite a girl to an orgy, you should be able to look her in the eye."

The Hyperborean scratched at his hair. "Sorry. I shouldn't have said aught, I just ... Well, you might hear ..."

Hekate supposed she ought to have some mercy before the boy died of embarrassment. He'd probably wind up haunting her if he did, and then she'd never hear the end of it. "Well, I've heard it's the most effective way to gain insights into the arcana."

"Hmm, especially if you can get one of the Inner Circle members to, ah ..." Climax? Gaia's expanse, it was all she could do not to burst out laughing at his shyness. "We're calling up Dagon, the greatest patron of our order. Sometimes—I mean I heard—sometimes he imparts great wisdom if he's pleased."

"Well," Hekate said. "Let's not disappoint him."

THE POETRY of flesh carried within it a microcosm of all the cosmos. Or so it seemed to Hekate, writhing in the twisting mesh of nigh a score of bodies. The chorus of their moans and grinding reverberated through the vestibule, a clarion thinning the Veil in its own way. Each spasming release of energy a sacrifice to forces beyond the world, calling forth unfathomable power of eldritch import.

Dagon, a god of the deep, Herald of Tiamat, the Primordial of the Seas. His webbed fingers seemed to brush over her mind with each fervid gyration of her hips. So many bodies, and she swore she must have tasted them all, with mouth and nethers, with fingers grasping and stroking. With shared breath into the aptly named Sea of Oneness.

It was Helion inside her now, hints of sunlight seeming to gleam in his eyes as she ground atop him. His warmth exploded inside her, hotter than most. Her mind reeled, scattering, adrift within the sea and the cosmos both, as though wandering her dreams whilst half-awake.

WHEN THE MOON ROSE, so did she, grimoire in hand. To draw the spirit's attention, she dug its glyph in the sand, a trough that would serve to bring it closer though offer no assistance in commanding it. Then, rising and taking a few steadying breaths, she began the incantation to evoke a Storm spirit.

Supernal words once more reverberated inside her mind and sent her soul shuddering in a blurring of dread and ecstasy. The world-rending power of it rushed through her, even as she embraced the Sight. Color and warmth bled from the world, and she beheld the desolate shadowscape of *the Penumbra. Here, nether winds already whistled about her, but they failed to stir the sands of the Mortal Realm.*

At first. Then, a whisk set the desert twisting in a dozen whorls. The howling intensified, reaching into both Realms. In the Etheric sky, iridescent lightning crackled overhead, offering hints of colour in the otherwise blue-green Penumbra. The winds became a gale, whipping the desert into a frenzy that spun about her like a maelstrom. The sands lacerated her exposed arms and legs, but Hekate forced herself to ignore the pain—she could not afford to direct Pneuma to suppress it—to continue her incantation.

The spirit drew nigh, and she could not falter now. It came, plunging through the firmament, feathers coruscating with lightning as it plummeted to crash down before her, an avian mockery of a woman. The harpy landed in a crouch, taloned feet digging rivets in the sand as it slowly rose, head cocked too far to the side while its onyx eyes remained locked upon Hekate's face and soul. Blood dripped from rubescent wings as the spirit spread them overhead.

HANDS STROKED her face and breasts and hips, and a presence filled her insides and wormed its way into her mind. Morpheus's hypnotic eyes seized her soul, lulling her down, deeper into the maze of living dreams. Non-realities unfolded around the vestibule in shadowy panoply, teasing out obscure intimations, in warnings of dread and echoes of voices yet to be heard.

THE GREAT THRONG *had gathered before the cyclopean walls of Ilium, Menoetius standing a full head above the rest of his forces, clad in full battle panoply, his breastplate glinting in the morning light. The Titan lord strode forward, his ranks parting around him like the sea around a ship, clanking his long spear across his bronze-banded shield.*

His burnished helm concealed all but his eyes, but still, Hekate saw the challenge there, even before he pointed his lance at Zeus, his throng unleashing a collective whoop in time with his movement.

Her gaze fell on the prince beside her, a malevolent smirk curling his lips as his eyes clouded. The air grew pungent, crackling with energies that had the hair on Hekate's arms standing on end. A clean taste filled her mouth as Zeus thrust his arms skyward, his sudden cackle so rabid as to silence both armies, drawing all eyes upon him.

They could not know, though Hekate's gaze rose to the gathering dark above, the roiling clouds, the fulgurations that coruscated among them in forewarning of what impended. A bellow escaped Zeus, primal and mad, melding into the roar of thunder that, at once, issued from the storm above and the chest of the Titan at Hekate's side. Instinct had her falling back, away from him.

Menoetius must have apprehended the danger at last, for the Titan lord charged forward, sandals slapping stone, spear primed to impale Zeus. He made it a dozen steps before the blinding effulgence ripped down from the firmament, a streak of such bitter whiteness it sent afterimages skittering over Hekate's vision.

The blast of lightning streamed into the Titan, and he jerked to a stop, seized by convulsions. The galvanic river did not abate, but continued to flow into Menoetius, leaping in arcing chains into his forces. Waves of acrid stench washed over Hekate, the scents of charred flesh as Man and Titan cooked beneath the current of Zeus's power.

WITHIN THE VESTIBULE, just beyond the mountain of flesh, the rising sense of an obscene presence. Cosmic and momentous, utterly alien. And ravenous with insatiable cravings for things unnamed. Borne up by salacious waves, it rose.

In her mind's eye, she saw the webbed fingers, the opalescent eyes, the flapping gills. Not like the mer she had seen in Thebes, no. This was something monstrous, more fish than man, squamous and caked in barnacles. Its clammy grasp settled around her ankles and yanked her downward, through the others who lay beneath her, through the floor, and into caliginous watery depths.

Hekate flailed as icy water surged into her lungs, but she had naught to grab unto. The world had become submerged, with all sense of a surface shrouded. Dagon yanked her close, forced her to gaze into those alien eyes as he took her, joining the orgy with lurching thrusts of his cold, scaled member.

Absolute terror forced down any sense of disgust that had begun to rise. The agony of drowning seized her. Her lungs shuddered and felt apt to explode. The whole of her existence condensed, left Hekate desperately wishing she had never looked into the dark. Reaching for hands of parents whom she had left so far behind.

Wishing anyone could ... save her. Please, someone *save* her!

Then she was drifting loose, her corpse floating in a watery underworld, her soul somehow yet trapped within her drowned body. Still seeing with dead eyes, peering into the lightless expanses of the cavern far below. A pulse thrummed through the water, powerful beyond measuring, slow and rhythmic.

Was that ... a heartbeat?

Hekate wanted to weep, but the dead had no tears. Only abject horror, forced to bear witness to realities the mortal mind was not meant to fathom.

There, in the uttermost depths of the cosmos, something mountainous writhed. Cephalopodic tendrils vast enough to crush cities like walnuts ... Wriggling expanses of muscle and terror. An alien consciousness closed around her, found her, penetrating her to the pith. It judged her a mote of dust, offensive but inconsequential.

A sea of incandescence opened beneath her; an eye so immense civilisations could have fallen within it. And it saw her. The spilling radiance adumbrated hints of the colossal monstrosity lurking beneath the world, something neither quite draconic nor squid, but some foul amalgamation of all benthic life.

Hekate's scream threatened to rip her body apart. To shred her soul from the unspeakable horror of looking into such limitless puissance. Her mind cracked at the seams, and all she was began to billow forth, untethered.

"HEKATE!" A distant name, shouted as if from behind a silk curtain. A thought that attached to naught, adrift.

"Hekate, come back!"

A sharp slap that abruptly faded, leaving only stinging, and warmth as two hands pressed upon her cheeks.

Then, yanked violently from alien perceptions, Hekate lurched forward, retching up a torrent of seawater that had filled her lungs. She collapsed into Keuthos's arms and he held her close, rubbing her bare back. The heat of him seeped into her, slowly forcing unwelcome life back, even as her mind reeled, struggling to hold itself within a petty mortal form once again.

Memory.

It bombarded her, choked her, drawing forth an inarticulate wail, for she was beyond words. A moan, not of pleasure, but of anguish she could never express.

Someone pried Keuthos away from her and jerked Hekate upward by her forearms. This was … Morpheus.

The oneiromancer peered deep into Hekate's eyes, giving her the sensation of something flensing away all the illusions of herself she projected to glimpse her raw, broken soul. She was naked already, but his gaze left her feeling more unclad than ever before. "She remains," Morpheus said. "Or most of her does. Some piece may have been siphoned off by the brush with the infinite."

"She lost some part of herself?" Keuthos said, voice so aghast that, had she been able to form more thought than horror, Hekate might have laughed.

Morpheus rolled his eyes, releasing Hekate and allowing her to slide back onto a floor slick with human fluids. "Did you think the Art would come without cost? Did you think you glimpse fragments of Truth and remain unaltered by such? There is a cost, novitiate, to all secrets beyond the ken of Man. If you glean naught else from your time here, best take that lesson to heart."

Numbness seized Hekate, and she wrapt her arms around her knees. She knew she ought to climb to her feet, wash off the filth, and find her chambers. But the thought of moving—much less venturing alone into the dark or risk the nebulous shadowscapes of dream—opened a hollow inside her gut deep enough to swallow her whole.

"I could have died ..." she rasped, not even certain how to feel.

Morpheus chuckled. "As if that ought to be a sorcerer's greatest fear." The oneiromancer knelt and pushed his forefinger between her brows. "You ought to know better than that by now." A pause, and the expression on his face might have been pity or sadism, she could not judge. "Sweet dreams, little Hekate."

Only when he had left did Hekate see the pools of blood welling in the vestibule. Someone had thrown a sheet over a body, though it had already soaked through and turned crimson. A half dozen members of the Circle stood about, ashen-faced and red-eyed.

When Hekate turned to Keuthos seeking answers, he offered a single word. "Artemis."

3

PANDORA

623 Bronze Age

Zeus had two Olympian sons. The elder, Ares, was his son by Hera, his wife. The other, the only of Zeus's bastards with enough power to be elevated to the position, was born to the Pleiad Maia. His innumerable other bastards were usually considered demigods. While it was possible the other Pandora had meant Ares or Hermes might help her save Prometheus, Pandora found it monumentally unlikely she'd sway an Olympian to her cause. Thus, she had to assume she needed a demigod or lesser Titan.

She'd found lodging with a Heliad family who had seen her golden eyes and declared her a distant cousin to them, offering her guest-friendship. The patriarch, Hilarion, welcomed her to his hearth and ordered his teenage daughter, Melitta, to serve Pandora dinner. The girl laid out a blanket by the hearth, then brought her a bowl of vegetable stew.

After the tumult that had washed over first ancient Thebes and then Atlantis, Pandora could not even say how long it had been since she had last eaten, and she inhaled the first bowl. Melitta, the kind soul, refilled it without forcing Pandora to beg for a second serving. This time, Pandora savoured the soothing warmth of it, pausing to taste and enjoy.

"You seem famished," the girl said. The young woman might have been fourteen. Her hair was the colour of flame, like so many Heliads, and fell in light curls around her face. Mostlike, her father had already begun the process of bargaining with another man to marry her off, haggling for her dowry as if Melitta were a donkey sold at market.

"I feel like I haven't eaten in a thousand years," Pandora said around a mouthful of carrot.

Melitta quirked a strange smile. "Odd thing to say."

Actually, Pandora had no idea what century she was even in but posing such a question without seeming a madwoman presented an interesting challenge. "Where's your mother?" she asked instead, biding her time.

The girl's smile slipped. "Passed last winter. Our mourning only ended a month back, in fact. If you'd come then, you'd have found shut doors, I'm afraid."

"I'm so sorry for your loss." And had she now stumbled into a home with a father seeking a new mother for his daughter? Pandora would need to tread with care to keep anyone from getting the wrong idea, but neither could she afford to turn away hospitality when offered. Or maybe the answer was simple enough. "I've actually become separated from my husband and I'm seeking after him as well." Prometheus might not have ever married her, but what they shared was close enough it didn't feel like a lie. "The Oracle told me a demigod would help me find him."

Well, that one was a lie, of course.

Melitta's eyes widened. "A demigod?" She gnawed on her lip. "Papa told me, rumour claims King Proitos hosts a demigod now, in his palace."

Proitos. Not a name she knew.

"He's king here in Delphi?"

Now the girl cocked her head like Pandora was drunk. "Obviously."

Obviously. "And the name of the demigod?"

"Well, as I said, we've just come out of mourning, so I don't think Papa's gone to call on the king since then. That being the case, I can't rightly say who resides in the palace at the moment."

Even so, it was a place to start.

AT NIGHT, when Hilarion and Melitta slept, Pandora found herself sitting by the hearth, turning the Box over and over in her hands. This thing, this puzzle had unleashed the ouroboros that slithered round the World, hadn't it? It had given her both Pyrrha and Prometheus with one turn of its gears, only to steal them away with the next.

With every shifting panel and gyration, she came both closer and farther from the life she sought. But then, that was how a puzzle box worked: sometimes you had to undo parts already solved in order to close in upon the solution.

Was this device then a burden or blessing? And did Pandora herself bear culpability for the chaos it wrought, the madness of the ouroboros's circles?

Despite her fatigue, sleep came hard.

KING PROITOS'S estate sat beneath the acropolis, surrounded by a wall just a hair taller than Pandora herself. She waited until the afternoon, when the gates were thrown wide and the palace seemed inviting, before presenting herself to the guards.

Asking around the polis had provided some few answers. Proitos was one of the two sons of the old King Abas, himself a Tethid descendant of Io. His branch of the line had come from Phoenikia long ages back, which meant, among other things, that Pandora had reached a time some centuries after her own.

His guest was Bellerophon, a demigod, though rumour diverged as to exactly which Titan had sired him, with the father ranging from Zeus himself, to Poseidon, to Glaukos, the demigod son of Merope and Sisyphus. That last name had Pandora's lip curling in disdain at the memory of a man Kelaino had forced her to *attend to*.

Either way, while Proitos was a Tethid, Pandora trusted in her eyes to pass her off as aristos, and thus earn her an audience. "The Heliad Pandora here to call upon King Proitos," she proclaimed with feigned haughtiness that would have done Kelaino herself proud.

The pair of house guards looked her up and down before one summoned the steward, who examined her with equal rigour. "The purpose of this visit?" he asked. Pandora had to admit, he pulled off aristocratic disdain better than she could.

"Does an aristos need a purpose to call upon her fellows?" Pandora asked.

From the look on his face, the steward was about to point out that aristocratic *women* did not go about unaccompanied anywhere, much less calling upon kings.

"Give over, Paramonos," someone called from just inside the palace. "She's clearly got divine blood and—one would imagine—a good reason for calling on the king. Let him decide if it's worthy, yes?"

The steward immediately bowed to the speaker, who strode forward and offered Pandora his arm. Her intercessor was a Tethid himself, with hair dark as her own—though his was scraggly and curled, including his beard—and eyes blue as the sea.

She accepted his offered hand and he led her inside the palace.

"Pandora, did you say?" he asked.

"I did."

"What a lovely name. I am Bellerophon, out of Korinth, though I've been dwelling here in Delphi for a time already."

Bellerophon, himself. Could he be the one she needed? He led her through frescoed halls and into a sun-dappled courtyard where he bid her sit upon a bench beneath a cypress tree.

"What brings you to Delphi, then?" she asked. "The Oracle?"

Bellerophon's visage darkened so quickly Pandora almost winced. "Hmm. Is that not already the talk of the town?"

"I've heard your name, only," she said. "And that you're a son of Zeus," she quickly amended.

"Heh. No, Poseidon, though raised by Glaucus of Korinth, at least until I quarrelled with his real son." The demigod sank down beside her, his posture filling in the missing pieces of his tale.

"You killed your foster brother and went into exile for the crime."

A grunt, and a sharp look at her for having deduced his past with such ease. "I could hardly remain in Korinth, even had my foster father not cast me out." The man turned to look at her. "But Proitos offered me pardon and shelter, and for that I remain ever grateful."

A sad tale, but if he wasn't Zeus's blood, he wasn't the demigod she needed. She nodded slowly with Bellerophon's story, his gaze heavy upon her. What were the odds one demigod would know another? "I have a prophecy that tells me only a demigod son of Zeus can help me save my husband from a dark fate." The lie had served well enough with Melitta, perhaps it was worth keeping the same story. "Do you know of such a man?"

Bellerophon scratched at his beard before pushing off the bench. "Eh, well, not personally, though the king mentioned tale of one. I'll announce you and perhaps he will share the story himself."

"Thank you."

✿

PROITOS KEPT her waiting in the courtyard until the evening, when at last the steward appeared and called her for a supper taken with several women from the household, including the queen, Stheneboea, whose stern gaze never lifted from Pandora. Through probing small talk, Pandora decided she was six or seven centuries after her own time, with the Muses having termed the years following another great war the Bronze Age. Of the war, it seemed Gigantes had led an assault on Olympus itself.

An assault that had, sadly, failed.

And she was hundreds of years into the future, adrift in history, as if the ambit of time was some monstrous squall that could swallow her whole. If it did, if she vanished forever, would anyone know to grieve for her?

Pandora filed away the pieces of history in her mind for further examination, afraid to press her questions too far. She couldn't imagine Stheneboea or anyone else might guess her a time traveler, but neither did she want anyone more suspicious of her than they already seemed. And the queen certainly appeared apprehensive toward her, though why, Pandora had not quite worked out. Did Stheneboea imagine Pandora might have some designs upon her husband?

"You are a friend of Bellerophon?" Stheneboea asked once they had eaten and the house slaves brought out the wine in painted amphorae.

"Not really," Pandora admitted, accepting a goblet offered to her by a slave with a nod.

Stheneboea's frown deepened, perhaps at Pandora acknowledging the slave or perhaps at how she'd come to be here, if not a friend of Bellerophon. "But you knew him?"

"By reputation," Pandora said, eyeing the queen over her wine. The woman's eyes wanted to pry inside Pandora's mind, she knew, but Stheneboea seemed to lack the insight to read her, Fates-be-praised.

After supper, the king summoned her, not into his throne room, but into a more intimate lounge lined with low divans and decorated with plants she thought native to the southern reaches of the peninsula. Amid them, the blooming daphne flowers, their scent instantly bringing her back to the Aviary. To happier memories upon Ogygia that left Pandora wistful, barely restraining the urge to hug herself as tingling joy and agony shot along her limbs.

It was the *reason*, the source of her pain, and every reminder of it only strengthened her, forging her resolve like beaten bronze.

Though high windows let in moonlight, most of the illumination came from a pair of braziers. Their flames cast dancing shadows upon King Proitos, who reclined upon one of the couches. Given his youthful wife, he appeared older than Pandora would have expected, tinges of grey speckling his beard visible even in the dim light.

"Bellerophon tells me you wish to hear of Perseus, and, you know, I find few pastimes more relaxing than an evening of storytelling." He paused to take up an amphora and pour two bowls of wine, motioning for Pandora to take one. Did he know his queen had already plied her with several cups of the stuff?

She took up a bowl anyway, then settled down on the nearest divan, leaning upon the armrest to gaze at the king. "Stories ascribe meaning to our lives," she said. "We see the depths of our own souls reflected in the struggles of others."

The king raised his bowl in salute. "Indeed, indeed." He sipped, and she did the same. "Well, hmm. Where should I begin? With my brother, of course, the king of Argos. You see, that should have been my throne, but that is perhaps another story. My brother Akrisios became king of Argos and, when he married—after a time—he came here and consulted the Oracle to ask about when he would have a son."

For some reason, the thought brought up snickers in the king, and he took another swig. "Well, she told him, rather, that his own daughter would birth a son who would prove his undoing. Heh. My brother, kindly soul he is, he took his daughter Danaë and built a bronze hold underground and locked her inside, no doubt thinking not a soul would have access to her, uh ..." The king cleared his throat. "Hmm. The place was set inside a cliffside, and her only view of the outside came from a window that overlooked a precipitous fall to the rocks that jutted from the sea far below. Perhaps he hoped she would jump and solve the problem. Maybe he'd have killed her himself, but we all know how the Olympians feel about slaying one's kin."

Pandora quirked a brow. Had not Zeus damned his own father into the depths of Tartarus centuries before doing so to Prometheus? But it would be difficult to challenge Proitos's claim without revealing more about herself, and besides, that Zeus would prove a hypocrite little surprised her. Hypocrisy was the least of his crimes.

"You know, when she got with child, my brother insisted I had somehow snuck in and seduced Danaë?" The king chuckled, shaking his head ruefully, clearly wishing that was the case. "No, but the girl claimed Zeus had come in through the window, radiant as a golden light, and lain with her." The king paused for more wine. "If one had asked me, I'd have assumed it was one of the men Akrisios set to guard her door, and I told him as much when he accused me. But the girl persisted in her claims Zeus had come to her.

"So kind, pious Akrisios can't kill his daughter, and he sure as Hades can't kill a child that *might* have Zeus's blood in him. So, when the babe is born, and it's a boy, he has the both of them locked in a chest and thrown into the sea. 'Oh, it wasn't my hand that killed them,' or I imagine this is what he'd tell Zeus if the King of Olympus ever showed up demanding to know what happened." Pandora rather suspected such a tepid defence would only further enrage Zeus should he deign to care about his offspring. And her stomach churned at the thought of a man so abandoning his own daughter. To cast her off as unwanted ... "Akrisios, he says, well, let Poseidon carry them where he wills." Proitos snickered. "Maybe he did. Because I learnt not so long ago that the chest washed up on the shores of Neritum."

A small island off the coast of Argos. Pandora set aside her wine bowl, having had but a few sips. "Does Akrisios know this?"

Proitos grinned. "I rather imagine he thinks them both dead for two decades. No, word is, the boy was raised by the petty kings of the island, Diktys and Polydektes, the former of which married Danaë and claimed Perseus as his own."

"Then how do you know he's Zeus's son at all?"

"What, besides Danaë not concealing her identity?" A chuckle. "Let me tell you, if the boy has brains, he didn't get it from her. No, but this Perseus has Titan speed and strength, or so the tale tells it. Word came he fought off half a dozen village boys three years his senior, or more, and they could barely land a blow. Which is how we even got to hear about it. They say he's fast as a mountain gale."

Pandora folded her hands in her lap giving Proitos an appraising look. Was that it, or had the king bribed or threatened the Oracle for news about his brother's fate? "I should like to meet this Perseus, then." If he truly had Titan Pneumatikoi, that seemed to mean he was indeed a demigod, lending credence to his mother's claim Zeus had spawned him on her. Pandora noted Proitos's tale never mentioned whether Danaë had welcomed the embrace of the Olympian. Perhaps the king thought such things as irrelevant as Zeus did.

"Hmm, I can arrange a ship to sail for the island in day or two, I think," the king said, sloshing more wine in his bowl. "Though, the merchant captains are like to want to stop in Argos on the way." Now, Proitos looked up and winked with heavy lidded eyes. "Wish I could see Akrisios's face when he learns his grandson yet lives."

"I appreciate your hospitality and your help reaching the island." What exactly had passed between the two brothers to inspire such animosity? Proitos felt denied his birthright, yes, but was it mere lust for power that had riven the brothers? More to the point, would Proitos's enmity mean the king might have told her such things for his own reasons?

But the king said little more of his brother, instead calling for another amphora of wine and bidding Pandora to grant him news of whatever land she had last passed through. And wouldn't that be interesting? *At some point in the future the whole of Atlantis seems poised to sink beneath the sea, though I cannot say what year, exactly.*

Rather, Pandora claimed to have merely passed through villages of late, no place of consequence, and the king, well into his cups, seemed to take it at that.

As Pandora was rising to leave, Stheneboea came bursting into the lounge, her khiton disheveled and her face red. The woman huffed, eyes glancing over Pandora as though she was not even there.

"My queen?" Proitos asked, swaying a little when he stood. "What happened?"

"Your *guest* has tried to force himself upon me!"

What, Bellerophon? Pandora blanched in disbelief.

The king took a moment more, before roaring for his guards.

4

ARTEMIS

225 Golden Age

In the throes of a reality-warping orgy, Artemis felt something primal brush against her soul. A touch, rough yet caressing, that, though alien, she found herself welcoming in. The writhing sea of flesh melted away and she found herself walking, naked and dripping with sweat and other fluids, through a hypnagogic forest that itself bent and flowed around her. The trees arched as though caught in the midst of their own prurient encounters, the ground beneath her bare feet warm and heaving.

From the boughs, countless pairs of gleaming yellow eyes watched her slapping footfalls. A cacophony of animal cries filled the night, a burbling, chirping, croaking chorus somehow both familiar and alien.

Artemis saw naught save eyes, however, and found herself pushing ever forward. She could not have said quite what guided her steps, but her feet moved of their own accord, climbing a slope toward a rocky precipice. The stone now beneath her lacked the warmth of the forest loam, and Artemis shuddered but could not stop. Not until she reached the terminus and stood looking up in the sky. Where the moon ought to have graced the heavens instead loomed an aquamarine orb above her: Gaia, the Earth itself.

Because she stood upon the moon.

The revelation sent her to her knees, gasping, reeling. Her heaving breaths drew in the purest of Moon-tinged Pneuma, the very essence of Thoth whom she had so long praised. The Primordial's presence saturated every blade of grass, every tree, every stone of this reality, leaving little doubt the energies they had called up in the Sea of Oneness had driven her soul into the Spirit Realm.

Artemis rolled over, staring back the way she'd come, so flush with Moon Pneuma her senses felt apt to burst from her, take on a life of their own. Perhaps that was how she heard the slow, plodding footfalls of the immense brown bear that had begun to ascend the same slope she had climbed. On meeting her gaze, the creature reared up on hind legs, bringing its height to more than twice her own. She averted her gaze and froze, desperate to offer no further challenge, even as her heart pounded against her ribs and cold sweat ran between her shoulder blades.

With a huff, the bear plopped back onto all fours, then lumbered closer. So close, its hot breath ruffled her hair and the earthy stench of it filled her lungs. A low rumble built in its chest, a hint of a growl that could have become a roar if she displeased it in the least. Which meant she clenched her fists and tried not to whimper.

It waited for her, she realised of a sudden. Thus, despite her trepidation, she found herself with no choice save to look back at the bear. The animal before her embodied perfection, as if all bears had sprung from her, as if the sum of her exceeded even her enormous form, radiating out from this world into all others.

Looking upon her glory, Artemis gasped.

The Bear Queen opened her maw, baring teeth like knives, lunging at her face with sudden redness.

&

A CORPSE WAS in her mouth, limp and salty, its essence fled. She flung the body aside, blinking as she recognised the rent and bloodied mess of Inanna.

She had killed a member of the Inner Circle.

And looking down at herself, at the brown-furred paws caked in blood, she realised she had killed her *as a bear*. The spirit had latched onto her soul and made her—

The shriek assaulted her, joined an instant later by another and another, as half the Lodge of Whispers—those not too far gone with sorcerous hallucinations of their own—screamed, backing away. Some retched, some cursed, and one flung shards of piercing ice at her. Chilling blades lanced her side.

Her vision went red, and next she knew, she stood upon her hind legs, roaring in all-consuming rage. Absolute, mind-devouring fury had her, her only thought to crush and rend those who had harmed her.

More shrieks now, and blood, her claws shredding flesh, her paws sending men and women sprawling. Her bounds carried her across the chamber with unstoppable force. Her slap shattered bones.

Her wrath would have swallowed the whole of this cave temple.

"Stop!" A man screamed, arms spread wide, perhaps to keep her from the rest of the Circle, or to keep them from her. "Stop! It's my daughter!"

His scent, so familiar. Father ...? Her father, Helios, a member of the Circle ...

"Go," he rasped, looking to her. "Go. Be gone from here, Artemis."

Artemis. Her name ...

If the Titan had looked at her with wrath of his own, she'd have crushed him with one mighty swipe of her paw. But the man, her father, had only imploring desperation writ upon his visage. A desire to protect her.

Something in her broke beneath that need, and she turned,

bounding down the tunnel. She hit the double doors with her shoulders, and they burst open, sending her skidding into the necropolis. Allowing herself only a moment to gather her senses, she then took off once more, racing past grave markers to the bronze grate leading from this place. This too she crashed through, its thorns tearing her flesh, then bounded down the main street, out of this accursed human place and roil of stenches.

More screams, and someone stood before her, waving a spear in vain threat. She rose upon her hind legs, her claws splintering the spear and the man alike, his broken, bloody corpse cast aside like kindling. Then onward, on and on, out of here.

Away, away, toward the beckoning mountains and their blessed woods.

ARTEMIS AWAKENED to the glare of a hateful sun scorching her retinas. Its rays, never much welcome, now felt like spears flung down from Hyperion's vaunted perch, lancing through her muscles and sapping them of strength. The whole of her, from her shins to her shoulders, ached as though she'd taken a beating from a Cyclops.

Only when she pushed herself up did she realise she was naked save for a splattering of dried blood and a plaster of leaves and mud coating her. What in the dark of Nyx had happened to her?

An image, a hint of gnashing teeth and rending claws, flitted through her mind. Without further warning, her stomach heaved and she retched, spewing out half-digested chunks that ... might have included bones from a human hand. Moaning, Artemis pulled away, careful not to examine the former contents of her stomach any deeper.

A bear.

In tales her grandmother had told, some few Men roamed the wilds, their souls torn between Man and beast. Shifters, who became wolves or spiders or ... bears. The Circle had meant to call up the power of Dagon, but, perhaps because of her own affinity for Thoth, Artemis had managed to get her soul drawn to the Moon in the process. Once they had opened the door, she had fallen right through, and now …

Now she'd killed someone. The thought sat heavy in her empty gut. In truth, Artemis had slain a great many foes in battle, but never had she mauled and *eaten* one. Consuming Man-flesh turned Titans into Gigantes. How many had she had? How much did it even take for a Titan to begin to transmogrify, their outward appearance morphing to reflect their monstrous appetites? She didn't know, but if she didn't want to find out, she needed whatever spirit had gotten inside her exorcised without delay.

And Artemis, though she'd had slight training with the Circle, could not perform such a complex invocation herself.

The chills that wracked her as she made her trudging way down the mountain and back toward Byblos, had naught to do with her nakedness.

HER SENSES HAD BECOME MORE acute without even the need for flowing Pneuma into Perspicacity now. She could smell and hear things far away, even while animal instinct seemed to crane her neck around of its own accord. Thus did she find her father and Hekate tromping through the mountains, the latter making a poor attempt to follow the trail Artemis must have left the night before.

"You didn't take to the tracking lessons I imparted half so well as I might have hoped," Artemis grumbled.

Her father, golden eyes glinting, moved in to hand her a folded himation. He kept a careful distance from her, as if she might assault him even while in human form. With a glower, Artemis took the proffered bundle, wrapt it around herself, and fixed her gaze upon him.

"You knew I'd have no clothing."

Her father folded his arms across his chest and took a step backward. Perhaps his nervousness had betrayed him, or perhaps he wanted to give her space. His scent was awash in strange fragrances that might have indicated emotion, but everything felt different now than it had through Pneumatikoi, and Artemis could not say for certain what the Titan lord thought. "You're not the first to fall victim to this curse."

"Curse?"

"Blessing, some might have called it, those who welcome the savagery. Tales claim, in the Time of Nyx, such creatures as you have become ran rampant, preying upon Men with Otherworldly powers."

Clucking her tongue, Hekate stepped around her father and drew Artemis into a warm embrace. With her heightened senses, the woman's scent had also become all the stronger, and Artemis could feel the pulse of her heart beneath her flesh.

"Get it out of me," Artemis growled, squirming free of Hekate's grasp. She hated the timbre of her voice, how it vacillated between melancholy and rage, making so plain her desperation.

Hekate's face fell, already shaking her head. "A Moon spirit is different from other eidolons, Artemis. It doesn't possess you; it fuses with your soul. I can't ... No one can extract such an entity from a host without killing the host. It would shred your own soul to pieces. I just, that's not ..." Still shaking her head like a useless, craven wretch.

Red filled Artemis's sight, a sudden overheating rage narrowing her vision, choking her thoughts. Not knowing she meant to, she seized Hekate and flung her to the ground. "You did this! You insisted on joining the Circle, on delving their secrets! On worming our way into arcana not meant for this world!"

Hekate didn't try to rise, just sat there, raised hand trembling. "Artemis ..."

An unbidden snarl escaped Artemis, and she whirled on her father. The look on his face made plain he, too, had no answers for her. "Feckless miscreants, the whole of the Circle." She spat at his feet, not above a moment of glee as disdain creased his features.

Yes, let her at last *earn* his scorn. After long years, she had become the wretched thing he'd always seen in her.

"Artemis!" Hekate cried.

But Artemis flooded Pneuma into Alacrity. Combined with the bear strength of her limbs, her strides carried her away from the others with a speed they could never match. On and on she ran, back toward the mountains. Toward a life in the wild.

The only life a beast like her could hope for.

5

KIRKE

1587 Silver Age

Two years had passed since Kirke had returned from Kronion to Helion, and in the intervening time she had built a new alchemy lab. Working under her father's nose carried its risks, but this place had been home for so long, Kirke could think of nowhere better to go after Athene had banished her here. Nowhere to feel more comfortable, more certain of herself.

Her falling out with Kalypso meant Ogygia held little welcome, and the disaster with Pikus meant it best to avoid the western Thalassa. So, she holed up in her small estate beneath the acropolis, turned her wine cellar into an alchemy lab, and set about ceaseless study into what had gone wrong with the draught she'd given the Mnemosynian prince. Never had she imagined it might cause such a transmogrification of his flesh—never had she guessed Nectar *could* achieve such results.

Sometimes, when Kirke closed her eyes, she saw again the horrific popping of bone and muscle, the man becoming a woodpecker. Horror, yes, and awe. Transformative potions held fathomless potential if she could understand just how the Nectar—or the moly in it—had interacted with the other ingredients.

Bending over the table, heating a ceramic beaker, a bead of sweat ran from her brow into her eyes, and she scrubbed at them with the back of her hand. For long years, Kirke and Kalypso had sought after a means of using Nectar to grant Men and Nymphs the power of Titans. But if she could harness transformation, perhaps they had a whole other weapon available to them, one which no one had ever conceived.

Kirke poured a single drop from the beaker into a greater bowl of powdered moly and other reagents, then set to mixing them. Mother had told her that, in the Time of Nyx, were-beasts—Men fused with Moon spirits—wreaked havoc across the land. Few remained now, though Kirke's half-sister Artemis was among their number. Could that sort of power lie quiescent within the Nectar?

As she reached for another phial, a rapping sounded upon the door to the house above. Kirke sighed, setting aside the alchemical work, and grabbing a towel to clean herself up. Visitors did not oft grace her doorstep—Hyperion be praised—but if her father had sent someone, she couldn't well ignore him.

Indeed, outside she found a messenger in Father's livery shifting his weight from foot to foot, though he swept a respectful bow the moment she opened the door. "My lady Kirke," the man said as he rose, pulling a rolled papyrus scroll from his satchel. "Lord Helios bids me inform you that your sister shall wed in a fortnight."

Yeah, *which one*, Kirke considered asking. Her father had oh-so-many children, legitimate or otherwise, as if he sought to disprove the theory that Ambrosia reduced fertility. Instead, she accepted the scroll and unfurled it.

Pasiphaë would wed Minos, son of Zeus and Europa, on the eve of the next full moon.

Kirke sucked air between her teeth, knowing she should, no doubt, offer a response and that *why-the-fuck-is-she-marrying-Zeus's-*

bastard was probably not the correct one. Because, yeah, courtiers tended to blanch at that sort of thing.

"I'll be there," she said. That had to be the right answer because uttering it felt like nursing a rabid goat.

FOLLOWING Father's split with Leto, he had married Tethys's daughter, Perse, in a move Kirke assumed was meant to reaffirm Father's loyalty to Zeus. The Nymph had born him two children, Pasiphaë and Aeëtes.

Given that their mother had the charm of a bull with a rat gnawing on its stones—making her an improvement over Leto, of course—Kirke had made little effort to get to know either sibling in their youth. Over the years, though, a slow adoration had developed, bringing her closer to them than any of the rest of the Heliads.

Which meant, Kirke supposed, she ought to call on her sister and congratulate her. Father's gold-plated palace lay atop a mountain at the heart of Helios, glittering in the late morning light with enough splendour Kirke found herself in desperate want of an amphora of wine. Drink helped take the edge off headaches induced from blinding light and family interactions.

When she at last reached the summit, sweaty and parched, a slave took her to her sister's chambers within the gleaming halls. They passed frescoes painted with exotic details about Father's supposed glory now, even a mosaic depicting the lost glory days of the Golden Age. Sometimes Kirke thought Father coped with his diminished status by pretending it had never happened. He brushed over having bent his knee to Zeus, choosing instead to act as though he yet remained one of the rulers of the world, instead of a mere halo around a grander sun.

On the way, they passed Ixion, a captain in Father's guard, who nodded to her with his usual sternness. Kirke was moderately certain someone had implanted an orichalcum rod up the man's rectum and run it all the way to his skull so as to avoid any risk of having a guard captain who might smile. To compensate, Kirke beamed at him. One had to love seeing him squirm, struggling to keep a straight face.

In her chambers, Pasiphaë reclined upon a divan out on her balcony, popping grapes into her mouth while another slave fanned her with a palm leaf.

"Fetch us something to drink," Kirke ordered the slave, who rushed off once his mistress nodded.

Pasiphaë quirked a smile at Kirke, coy perhaps, but still not hiding her joy at seeing her older sister.

"You seem in a fair mood," Kirke said, shoving aside her sister's feet so she could settle upon the divan's end. "Yeah, if I didn't know better, I'd be thinking to myself you welcomed marriage to one of Zeus's kin. But I know better because that'd be absurd."

Her sister snickered. "A son of the king of the world, himself also a king who happens to rule Knosós? Why shouldn't I celebrate?"

Hmm. So no ill will in the least for the tyrant king who had usurped their father's power. But then, Pasiphaë's mother had not married Father until the last days of the Titanomachy, so her children had never known a world where Father had reigned. If not for Zeus's interference, they'd never have been born.

Still, Pasiphaë, a Nymph, did share enough of Kirke's frustrations with their lot that, in a fit of melancholy on returning here, Kirke had admitted to her that she had brewed the Nectar. Had told her that she had dreamed of giving Nymphs the powers of true Titans.

"A fine dream," Pasiphaë had said, "but just a dream. You can never tell anyone what you've done," the girl had warned. "Father would not shelter you, not from that." Not from Zeus, she had meant, knowing full well the king pressed his sandal heavy upon Helion's throat and need now but squeeze.

Oh, but then the girl's perspective changed when presented with the chance to wed into the royal line. A chance at power, even vicariously through the reign of a demigod husband, had sparked within her sister desires Kirke had seen all too oft over the long ages of her life.

Kirke reached over to place a hand upon Pasiphaë's knee. "Io was one of my closest friends." She didn't mention that Europa, Minos's mother, was one of Io's descendants, *also* raped by Zeus like her ancestress.

Scoffing, Pasiphaë rolled her eyes. "That was two hundred years back." Well, Europa less than forty years ago. "And anyway, Minos is not his father. Am I to judge a man based on the circumstances of his birth?"

Was that a jab at Kirke being Helios's bastard child with Hekate? Kirke chose to let it slide and give the girl the benefit of the doubt. At least on that point. "Are you not marrying him *because* those circumstances make him kin to the king?"

"Which means I am securing the position of our family by winning Zeus's mercurial favour." Huh. Perhaps Pasiphaë was more astute in all this than Kirke had given her credit for. "And what do you think would happen should I back out now, after Father has agreed?"

A point, she had to concede.

"Be careful, then, little sister," Kirke warned her. "Do not trust any of Zeus's brood."

When the slave returned with the wine, Kirke drank deep, shifting her tone to naught save praises and congratulations, and discussions of finery and plans for the impending ceremonies. Even slaves owned by their father could be bought by the Olympians, and Kirke would not risk drawing ears or eyes upon herself.

She could afford no chances.

WHEN THE WEDDING ARRIVED, Kirke attended in her finest peplos, her auburn hair woven into an intricate loop. While she might not have relished her sister marrying Zeus's spawn, she'd not miss such a function. How often did she get the chance to mingle and meet others, and besides, the palace fair overflowed with Titans and Nymphs and demigods from around the Thalassa. Sure, most only attended to avoid risking any semblance of slight toward the King of Olympus, but they came, nonetheless.

Winking at some men gawping at her, Kirke sashayed her way around her father's palace. No sign of Zeus himself, and thank Hyperion for that. The gathered throng needn't have worried about the king's displeasure, given that he cared for Minos only insofar as his son's welfare impacted his own image. Or perhaps he'd waylaid himself having found a damsel, peasant, or small animal to torment. If Zeus liked bringing the mighty low, he *loved* grinding the already low into the dirt.

For Father, though, she couldn't help but feel a twinge of pity. Given the fresh tapestries, the plethora of flute girls, the fountains of wine ... Father had gone out of his way to impress. Maybe word would get back to Zeus, maybe it wouldn't. But if Father had hoped to win Zeus's favour with the ostentatious display, Kirke suspected he was like to find only disappointment.

Though he nodded at her from his throne, Father didn't deign to speak to her. Little matter. Kirke hadn't donned her finery and golden jewellery to impress him. Instead, she scanned the crowd, swishing a goblet of wine as she walked, taking in the multitudes who had flocked to Helion for this event.

While her twin Apollon stood in the centre of the hall, soaking up attention from men and women alike, Artemis slunk in the shadows, looking so discomfited, Kirke could only assume Father had demanded she attend. Kirke's half-sister plucked at her peplos, having no idea how to wear it, shifting and squirming in a way that had a smirk creeping upon Kirke's face. Neither of Leto's brats had shown Kirke much affection, but Artemis was worse. Their Father's decline fell at her feet, and Kirke could not forgive that. If not for her, maybe the Ouranid League would not have fallen, the Golden Age not having ended.

She would never understand what had possessed the twins to side with Zeus.

In the lounge beyond the throne room, Hestia reclined by the hearth, staring into it as though it whispered secrets to her. Perhaps it did. Hestia glanced up, and Kirke followed her gaze, stifling a bout of shock as Zeus paraded through the room—the king's eyes briefly roaming over Kirke's body—the Nymph Themisto on his arm. Zeus escorted her off to some side room, his intent for Themisto clear as Thoth's full moon now rising.

Here he was after all, and it seemed Kirke's praise for Hyperion had been premature. Which meant the Sun could go jump in the sea. Grimacing, she moved on, spotting Mother out in the balcony, another woman beside her. Kirke made it only to the threshold when Athene, standing beside Mother, turned back, a dispassionate gaze on her face as she met Kirke's eyes.

A sudden flush ran through Kirke, a reminder of what she'd done in Kronion, what she might have cost her half-sister. A mistake she could not amend.

Yeah, maybe not tonight, then.

Kirke had only just returned to the throne room when her aunt Eos sauntered over, drawing her aside with a firm hand upon her elbow.

"Don't you look a vision of the sun itself," Eos cooed, clucking her tongue at Kirke's ensemble. As her father's sister, Eos had, on occasion, offered what little maternal care Kirke had received in her childhood. That the woman hadn't seemed to realise Kirke had grown up thirty-eight *centuries* later might have somewhat spoiled Kirke's gratitude for that. Maybe. "I cannot fathom how you've not yet managed to find yourself a husband, niece." Another cluck of that tongue, like the most judgmental chicken in history. "You have the figure for it, but I swear, everyone from here to Rassenia must have heard about your ... temperament."

Kirke flinched, more at the reminder of Pikus's homeland than Eos's condemnation of her independence. Yes, Titan males wanted a wife who would lurk by their side in silence, warm their beds, and stroke their egos, amongst other things. Witches who could intrude in on their dreams or brew potions to do unspeakable things did not fit into their conceptions of desirable wives.

"Yeah, you know, ahem. My reputation is all ... Yeah." Kirke shrugged. "But I hear they haven't heard of me yet in Neshia. I mean, I asked around, and everyone was like, 'no, we have no idea who you are, Kirke,' so there's that. Actually, huh." She pointed over in a random direction. "I think I see a potential future maybe-husband-material-man over that way, toward the, uh ... trout. Trout's great for catching men. So."

Extricating her arm from Eos's grip, Kirke darted into the crowd. If she could weave in and out of the people with enough delicacy, maybe Eos would lose track of her. If not, Kirke could slap a few random arses. The commotion would cause enough distraction to escape.

As it turned out, that didn't prove necessary, and Kirke made her way back outside, until she could just make out the Colossus straddling the harbour, limned with moonlight and standing testament to Father's true passion: making certain the world knew the sun shined out of his crotch. She leaned against the balustrade with a huff.

Why had she even come? She'd been looking forward to this, to seeing people, but she never knew what to do with ... people ... when she found them. Was this Mother's fault, for having turned from her as a babe? Was Kirke herself just broken?

"There's my big sister," Aeëtes said, sometime later.

Pasiphaë's younger brother grinned at her with that I-want-something-from-you grin of his. Yeah, that one Kirke saw coming from ten leagues away and still couldn't save herself from because it was always like this incoming tide while she remained rooted in place, waiting to drown.

Unable to stop her own indulgent smile, she patted his hand where he rested it beside hers. "What now? I'm not doing another of those cleansing potions, Aeëtes. Sometimes you just have to change your diet."

He waved that away. "There's uh, this Nymph here at the party."

"Yeah, it's like we just pop into existence whenever men have an itch."

Caught in the throes of his excitement, Aeëtes seemed to miss her tone. "She's just, she's beautiful, Kirke."

"Of course she is."

"And ... I ..."

"You need my help getting her into your bed." Kirke withdrew her hand from his and rubbed her face. It shouldn't surprise her. Everyone was drunk, half of them giddy with Ambrosia—or maybe even the latest batches of her Nectar. Why should Aeëtes prove different? "A love potion."

"I ..." Aeëtes cleared his throat. "I was hoping to marry Idyia. I mean, a love potion might do for it, but I thought if you talked to her on my behalf. I could ask Father to arrange it, but it would become more a business transaction than aught else, and I ..."

Talk to her? Kirke quirked a smile at her little brother. Sometimes people still surprised her. Maybe half the surprise came from anyone thinking she excelled at talking. Kirke tended to make up for lack of quality talk with sheer quantity, she knew, but still, that Aeëtes would even bother with such steps spoke well of him. Maybe for the whole of the benighted Silver Age.

"I don't suppose I could introduce you and you could talk to the woman yourself?" Her brother stared at her as though she had just given birth to a horse. Through her mouth. "No?" Too much to ask for. "Yeah, I'll talk to her for you."

6

PANDORA

623 Bronze Age

"You have given him guest-right," Pandora blurted while King Proitos continued to bellow for his guards.

The king spun on her, face quivering. Why had she even gotten involved? If Bellerophon had done what Stheneboea claimed, he deserved whatever wicked punishment Proitos could dream up. But ... but something had seemed off about the queen from the moment Pandora arrived. About her jealous intensity and questions about Bellerophon ... Because she wasn't worried about Pandora seducing her husband, she was worried about her seducing their young guest.

But if Pandora were to tell the king his wife had been the one to pursue Bellerophon—and find rejection, unless Pandora missed her guess—he wasn't like to believe her. Indeed, such accusations might see her become his enemy as well.

"You have given Bellerophon guest-right," Pandora said, trying to keep her voice steady. "Any action you take against him now violates that sacred bond. You think the Olympians frown on kinslaying? How do they look upon those who violate the precepts of guest-right?"

King Proitos sputtered, falling back and waving his hands.

The queen, though, took a threatening step toward Pandora and opened her mouth for an impending tirade. Her words faltered when the summoned guards burst into the hall, spears bristling and swords drawn.

Seeing no one save Pandora—and the queen staring at her with naked loathing—several of the men actually pointed their weapons at Pandora as if she were some threat. Amusing, but she was no warrior.

After a moment's hesitation, Proitos waved them off. "No, no. I think ... I had too much wine, Seleukos. Drunken fears seized me for a moment. Leave us."

The guard he addressed hesitated, glancing from one occupant of the room to the next. When the king raised a brow, the man finally nodded, then motioned for the rest of his men to follow him out.

After they had done so, Proitos turned to his queen. "You too, Stheneboea. I will see to it Bellerophon pays for his crimes, but Pandora has the right of it. I cannot simply kill him in my own house."

It was a flimsy argument, in truth. Zeus and his kin took little interest in what went on in the homes of Men, or they had in Pandora's day, and regardless, if Bellerophon had attempted to ravish Stheneboea, any claim he had on guest-right was forfeit.

"Does this whore control you?" Stheneboea spat at him.

Whore? Did she know about Pandora's past? But no, the queen no doubt meant it as a more general insult than a specific one. Funny, how even women wanted to shame other women for any hint of sexual autonomy. The Muse Thalia would have called it a result of societal indoctrination.

"Out," Proitos groaned, slumping down upon his throne with a resigned sigh. "Leave me with her. I would speak to Pandora alone."

With a sneer so full of disdain her face seemed apt to crack apart,

Stheneboea stormed from the hall, back stiff. This was a woman whose pride had been offended by rejection. Now, Pandora was certain of it.

"So, then," the king said when the queen had left the hall. "You point out guest-right but offer me no solution to this dilemma. I cannot strike against the man, nor can I allow my wife's impinged honour to go unavenged. You seem the clever one, so tell me."

Pandora's mind whirred a moment. Bellerophon could certainly not remain in Delphi. Sooner or later, Stheneboea would succeed in getting Proitos to act against him. On the road, though, a demigod like himself ought to be able to handle most any danger, shouldn't he? "You cannot directly harm him, my king," she ventured. "You can, however, send him into potential danger that might lead to his death."

The king folded his hands, his mind clearly trying to work its way through his intoxication. "Stheneboea's father Iobates is king of Phoeba. I will send Bellerophon there and the man may deal with him as befits one who violated his daughter."

Pandora suppressed a wince. That hadn't been quite what she'd had in mind.

DID warning Bellerophon make her guilty of betraying King Proitos, a man who had proved naught save an ally to her and was helping her find Perseus? This question danced about in Pandora's mind for hours on end, even while Proitos composed a missive to his father-in-law explaining the situation.

In the end, though, the king had latched upon her idea of sending him into danger, and if ill befell Bellerophon because of it, some portion of the blame would fall upon Pandora. She *could* have tried to convince the king his wife was lying, but did not do so, out of fear for herself.

The guilt of that had her gut in knots, even as she sought Bellerophon out in the early morning. She found him down by the sea, staring into the deep as though he saw aught denied to people like her. Did Poseidon's blood rise in him, whipped into a frenzy like storm-tossed waves?

"Proitos will send you to Phoeba today," she ventured. No matter what she did, she betrayed either Bellerophon or Proitos, but, in the end, she had her answer to what was right, didn't she? "He will ask you to carry a sealed message to his father-in-law, who is king there. And the message will accuse you of attempting to force yourself upon the queen."

Bellerophon jerked up from his examination of the sea, gaze roaming over Pandora's face as if to search for deception. "Damn that woman," he rasped. "I told her I would not so dishonour her husband when she came to me ..." As Pandora had surmised. "But I cannot refuse a request to carry a message on behalf of the man who sheltered me and absolved me of my crimes, either."

Oh, Hades damn men and their sense of honour. Further indoctrination, in fact, not that Thalia had written of that side of it.

How many times must Pandora save these people from themselves? "Fine, then. Make yourself King Iobates's guest, as well. Once he's feasted you and befriended you, he won't be free to take your life, either."

Bellerophon looked at Pandora, a smile beginning to creep across his face. "You have Hermes cunning in you, Heliad."

Not hardly.

TRUE TO HIS WORD, Proitos arranged a ship to take her to Neritum, one that planned to make port in Argos first. As Bellerophon needed to sail around the peninsula before he could make for Lydia, he joined her, and Pandora found she could not leave Delphi behind soon enough.

What would happen if Stheneboea managed to sway her husband or if Proitos thought through the flaw in her guest-right argument? Both Bellerophon and Pandora herself might be in grave danger.

Standing at the gunwale and watching the port recede, Pandora could not help but release a sigh of profound relief. This world, this time, was not her own, and she could not afford to forget that, nor to become distracted from her true mission.

Lost in a moment, a person could fail to see the coils of the ouroboros encircling them, binding them to the weave of Ananke. Her eyes must remain open.

"I believe I owe you a debt," Bellerophon said, his sandals slapping the deck as he plodded up behind her. "I suspect I might have lost my head in Delphi were it not for you."

Pandora glanced back at him. "Think naught of it."

"I'm sorry I was not the demigod you sought."

So was she. A shame the other Pandora had not sent her directly to Neritum. It raised all sorts of questions. Was even that future Pandora's control of the Box imprecise, such that she could only get but so close to her desired destination? Or, rather, had the future her decided to ensure her own past by sending Pandora to exactly when and where she herself had been sent? If so, did that loop have any beginning, or had it *always* played out thus, both cause and effect, one more symptom of the encircling ouroboros?

That being the case, wouldn't future Pandora have stood here, wondering these same questions before deciding to fulfil the loops anyway? How many times had she had these *same* thoughts?

"Are you all right?" Bellerophon asked.

"Hmm?" Pandora shook herself. "Yes, sorry. Lost in musings."

The demigod drummed his fingers upon the gunwale. "Ah, well, I may have a bit more for you to think upon. If this Perseus you seek is the grandson of Akrisios, you'll wish to know more about the King of Argos. You see, Akrisios and Proitos were twins, with Proitos born first. According to the tale I heard, they fought even in the very womb of their mother—if you can credit such a thing. Either way, when old King Abas died, Akrisios exiled Proitos, denying him any inheritance and claiming the whole of the western peninsula for himself.

"Proitos, in his wanderings, came to Lydia, and married the daughter of King Iobates, our dear Stheneboea. With that backing, he returned and threatened war. To avoid it, Akrisios agreed to grant Proitos rulership of Delphi while he himself retained the throne of Argos. Maybe he was willing to give up Delphi because he didn't like the prophecy he'd been given." Bellerophon shrugged. "Either way, remember this is a man who cast out his own twin, imprisoned and later tried to drown his daughter, and would not hesitate to murder a stranger."

Indeed, Akrisios sounded like so many Titans. "I've no quarrel with him, though. I've no doubt he's a wretched man, but Perseus is in Neritum, not in Argos."

"Well enough, then. Just remember, you go looking for help from that demigod, you're like to find yourself embroiled in his troubles, as well. And, so far as I know, almost all demigods have our troubles, as well you have just seen of mine."

For certain she had, and a twinge of sympathy ran through her. She laid a reassuring hand upon his forearm. "You'll find your way."

THE SHIP ARRIVED IN ARGOS, and while Pandora had heard the city had no walls, still it came as a surprise to see such a major polis unprotected. According to legend, the Argosians relied solely upon the well-earned reputation of their warriors for their defence. While most Elládosi armies were raised by kings in times of strife, composed of farmers and tradesmen levied for a season, all Argosian free men served in their army until they died or grew too old to do so. Their vaunted, endless training produced soldiers so fierce they were the equal of any three men elsewhere, or so the gossip on Atlantis had held, six centuries prior.

Perhaps that warrior tradition had endured, for upon disembarking, Pandora saw armed Argosian men about the harbour and no other sign of protection for the polis.

"We'll be making for Neritum in a few hours," the captain shouted after Pandora as she descended the gangplank.

She waved back at him in acknowledgment, then accepted Bellerophon's hand to help her down onto the pier.

"I'll be looking to find passage east, myself," he said. "So, I suppose this is where we part ways."

Funny, Pandora found herself reluctant to bid him farewell. He was the only person she knew in this time, after all, and when he left, she would once more find herself alone. That, and she could say almost of a certainty she would not see the demigod again. Once she found Perseus, she would set out to rescue Prometheus from Tartarus, and then, she hoped, have the chance to return to her own time.

"Be careful in Iobates's court, Bellerophon." It was, admittedly, banal advice he had little need of. Better had she admonished him not to go at all, but he would not have listened.

"And you in Neritum," he returned, and that was that.

How oft people came in one's life for but moments and faded like dreams, she mused as she strolled the polis. Should she mourn the passing of a relation or cherish the memory all the more for its transitory nature?

The city lay along the banks of the Bomycas river. Running alongside those shores, she found vendors of various Elládosi foods. For an obol, she purchased a purse-full of nuts and olives, which would serve well enough to hold her over until supper.

Tossing a few pine nuts in her mouth, she continued to stroll. Across the riverbank she caught sight of naked boys training with— what she assumed to be blunted—spears while a grown man corrected their stances and forms.

Passing further into the city, she peered up at the acropolis. Scholars in her day disagreed as to whether Hera herself founded the polis or her disciples did so in her honour. Either way, the acropolis was dedicated to the Olympian, though the city was ruled by a line of Tethid kings. By Akrisios.

How strange to think the king of this city was descended from the same ancestor as Europa, a thought that clenched her stomach. Stranger still to imagine the horrors Akrisios had wrought upon his own kin. She doubted a mortal king lived upon the acropolis, but he would no doubt have a palace somewhere in the city, perhaps beyond the agora. A minuscule part of her imagined storming in there and demanding to know who that bastard thought he was, casting his daughter into the sea.

Was some such story how Pandora had wound up fostered by Europa?

But aught she said or did here might jeopardise Perseus. Sooner or later, Akrisios would learn his grandson lived, and Pandora could only imagine he would strike against him. Better if Pandora did not speed the process.

After passing through a forum and taking in the city, she doubled back, making her way to the harbour. Already the merchant crew had finished unloading their ship and were prepping for the voyage on to Neritum.

"Got something to eat?" the captain asked when she made her way back up the gangplank.

She hefted the bag of nuts and olives in answer, then settled herself upon the gunwale, watching as the sailors made ready the ship.

When at last they left they made good time, the crew singing a shanty while Pandora gazed at the passing waves. Then there was the island, rising from the sea like a rocky crag, beckoning her forward.

As they drew nigh, she caught sight of marble towers jutting up from the tallest hill upon the isle. There, she would find the court of the petty kings. There, she would find Perseus and the way forward.

The way to change the hand that Ananke had dealt to her.

7

ATHENE

1587 Silver Age

While Athene could not have cared less about Minos's wedding to Pasiphaë—one of Helios's more insipid Nymph brats—she'd not have disrespected her father by missing her half-brother's ceremony. Of course, Father himself disappeared off with one Nymph after another, almost enough to make Athene wonder if the whole wedding was but a pretence for him to arrange yet more extramarital affairs against Hera.

Not that Athene bore more love for her father's wife. Her stepmother had vinegar for blood instead of ichor. When she spoke, she spewed such vitriol she could have blighted entire fields. Her eyes held within them the sum of all denigratory thoughts a parent might ever hold toward a child. Only her father's sheltering gaze, when it fell upon her, had spared Athene the beatings and reprobations, and only for brief respites.

Instead, she found herself walking alongside Mother, out to the balcony. Athene had never fathomed the complexities of her mother and father's relationship, but Mother had remained ever more aloof in the wake of Zeus's binding of Prometheus. Once, in an atrabilious fit years ago, Mother had confided in her that Prometheus was, in fact, her own father. Athene had gasped to think him her grandfather, but, as Mother had pointed out, that title was one earned by word and action rather than by seed.

"When had he ever taken direct intercession in your life? In Kirke's? He holds himself apart from his grandchildren for reasons of his own. Seeking familial bonds from him is not like to avail you, daughter."

"Did he hold himself apart from you?" Athene had asked back then.

Though Mother had not answered, the pensive set of her shoulders left Athene to wonder if, in fact, it was her, not him, who sundered the bonds she spoke of.

"And my grandmother?" she asked.

"Is Rhea." Kronos's erstwhile lover, lost during the Titanomachy. Of Hekate's own mother, she never spoke.

Now, Mother leaned against the balustrade. From the acropolis, Athene could see the ocean, moonlight glinting off the dark waves in dreamlike undulations. The muted expanse of the Thalassa stretched out forever from here. Maybe, were she closer, Athene could have apprehended some truths in the hypnotic patterns formed by the sea, though still waters more oft triggered her Sight.

That and ...

"You still crave it," Mother said. Had she read Athene's mind? Was that possible? Or perhaps she judged her state through the stiffening of her posture. On her return from the Underworld, Mother had divined that Athene suffered from some sort of addiction but had allowed Athene her time in admitting the truth: that Kirke had brewed Nectar and that Athene had imbibed it for years, trying to rarify her Sight.

And it had worked, even if the price had proved higher than she'd have wished.

An inkling of insight tickled her, even now, and she looked over her shoulder to spot Kirke spying on them from just beyond the balcony. Athene forced her face to impassiveness. Her older sister withered under her regard and retreated into Helios's palace.

Mother sighed, no doubt having gathered the import of it all.

"What?" Athene demanded. "Her actions jeopardised Pandion's authority by damaging relations with Mnemosynia."

"Or perhaps you judge too harshly. Both your sister and yourself."

Athene folded her arms over her chest. She didn't need to hear this.

Mother said it anyway. "You must find it easier to blame Kirke for your perennial need for what she provided, as if she forced it upon you, as if you yourself are not culpable for your choices. But in the shadowed recesses of your soul, you already know that, daughter, and thus you languish under your guilt as much as your loathing for your sister." Mother paused. "Absolve yourself, and her along with you. The self-deception of boundless strength, that need to project an amaranthine façade—it ruins us, abrades our hearts one poisonous deceit at a time."

She scoffed. She had to because she couldn't well swallow what Mother offered her. "Is that the sum of your wisdom, Mother? Forgiveness? Shall I offer it to Hephaistos as well?"

The look on the woman's face made plain her thoughts on the matter, for they had debated this oft enough.

Athene threw up her hands. "I can't. I won't."

Not even if Mother was right about Kirke. Not even if she had wisdom. Some things she could not endure.

WHEN ATHENE HAD, in a fit of malice, first accused Kirke of poisoning her with Nectar, Mother had told her that Kirke's life had never been an easy one. "She has not endured Hera's scathing ire, true, but she too grew up unloved and out of place, and since then, suffered her share of heartbreaks."

Sometimes, Athene thought Mother saw more of herself in Kirke than she did in Athene. Sometimes, in dolorous moods, Athene could not help but think it because Mother had trained Kirke in the Art while refusing to teach Athene. The two witches shared the damnation that seemed to accompany the uncovering of forbidden arcana, and though she knew it for madness, even that bond sparked a hint of jealousy in Athene.

Still, as her mother had said, she could not well blame Kirke for all her woes. Thus, she sought out her half-sister and found her rising from a divan where she sat with some Nymph in obvious fellowship. An old friend, perhaps, though not one Athene knew.

Kirke's gaze fell on Athene as she rose, and her sister turned away, making to slip out through the columned exit into the courtyard. Quickening her steps, Athene moved to intercept her.

"Wait," she said, raising a hand to forestall the Nymph once she managed to get ahead of her. "Wait, I just want to talk."

"Sure, talk is fine and all. Though I tend to prefer it when it doesn't involve me getting castigated or exiled. I mean, if we're taking votes on the course the conversation ought to follow."

Athene led the woman into the courtyard, though Kirke had to pause to offer some greeting to her half-sister Phaethusa. Helios's beautiful bastard daughter met them halfway, stalling them with inane pleasantries Kirke navigated with more poise than Athene might have managed.

At last, when Phaethusa moved on, Athene and Kirke settled beneath a cypress tree.

Kirke folded her hands in her lap. "So, it's nice to see you and all. How's life, how's Pandion, and just how much Nectar is it you need now?"

"Y-you have it on you?" Athene flinched, both from Kirke's accusation and then the realisation of the words that had slipped unbidden from her own mouth.

With a wan smile, Kirke withdrew a tiny ceramic phial from her peplos, though she kept it in the palm of her hand. Sweat began to bead between Athene's shoulder blades and under her arms. "I usually charge five tetradrachmae for this much," Kirke said. "Yeah, but, for you, I think ten. Hmm. Everybody wants something, right? Come to the witch and she'll solve all your problems. Oh, yeah, then you can scorn her for those same talents. Only fair."

Athene wheezed. "I'll send the money to your house." She shouldn't ... but already her fingers reached for the amber relief hidden behind the fragile clay. Relief, and clarity of thought and vision that came no other way.

"Hmph." Kirke pushed the phial into Athene's palm. "Yeah, for a moment, I thought maybe you wanted to talk to me, you know, for me. I don't know why I thought that." Her voice cracked a little as she pushed herself up.

"Wait ..." Athene said, her own voice a whisper now, as she reached for Kirke with her free hand. She *had* come to Kirke to try to make amends.

But the Nymph had already fled back into the palace.

Athene should go after her. She should try to explain, try to say something. She should ... do something other than pop the stopper out of the phial. Yet she found herself inhaling its rich, fruity aroma. So sweet and intoxicating.

A shuddering warmth and a slight burn rushed through her as she downed it. Sparks coruscated through her veins, setting the whole of her being tingling. Her mind expanded like unfurling flower petals, even as Athene dragged herself over to the fountain, watching its burbling flow and the tantalising promises lurking within.

Artemis huffed, arms folded over her chest like a petulant child despite having millennia of life behind her. "So quick to chastise me over the boar, as if your hands are clean, sister. As if Medusa did not writhe in torment at the curse you wrought upon her."

Athene shut her eyes in acknowledgment. Blood and ichor indeed stained her fingers, such that they might never wash clean. Was the petti-ness, the wrath, the all-consuming vitriol a side effect of the Ambrosia they all so craved? Did the very source of Titan immortality and puissance corrupt even as it fortified, thus sending them spiralling into depravity?

Over the centuries, she had seen so many of her kind fall to it, wracking suffering upon mortals and Nymphs because they could. Or did she, in seeking to blame the Ambrosia, simply seek to abrogate her own culpability for a faulty character?

"In the end," Artemis said, perhaps following her line of thought, "we are not so different from Man."

"We are gluttonous beasts, grown corpulent on feasts of power, whilst looking upon our fellows as lions look upon prey."

WANDERING the aureate halls of Helios's palace, inchoate images danced about the guests, intimating salacious encounters, lurid pasts, and winding futures. There, the bride, repining over the inevitable infidelities of her husband, and him, gawking in rapt horror at his own monstrous spawn, a horned and deformed abomination mewling in blood-stained blankets. The wretchedness of the sight had Athene spinning, cursing her addled mind for parading such macabre fancies before her eyes.

Was it, in fact, nightmarish delusion born from her muddled state? Or had she beheld some fell, dark future, a world beset by monsters?

Still shaken and a bit bilious, Athene stumbled toward a crowd, this one gathered around a radiant Nymph who pranced amid the hall, her beauty a whip cracking upon the attention of every male within two dozen paces. Indeed, Hephaistos's fiery-haired daughter Medusa had let slip the shoulder of her peplos so low as to reveal a hint of areola, though the girl affected ignorance to her state.

Her eyes lidded, Medusa trailed a finger along a man's forearm, tittering her insipid laugh. She looked at them as her prey, her tongue flitting between her teeth like a snake's before licking her lips. Every sway of too-perfect hips a sashay calculated to drive them all to distraction.

The girl, born to Hephaistos's mercurial siren wife, Aphrodite, had the too-perfect figure of her mother, lithe and stunning. Perhaps Medusa caught Athene's regard, for she drifted over with such flowing grace Athene had to fight a creeping sneer. "Oh, Mother, welcome to the party," Medusa purred.

"Mother?" So taken aback, Athene found she couldn't hold her scowl.

"Oh, well, Father told me he had asked for your hand." That coy smile. "If you would have favoured him with more than a night, it would have made you my stepmother." That chittering laughter like a swarm of scorpions running across Athene's face. "Wouldn't that have been grand, Mother?" That simpering wave of her hand to accompany her giggles.

It might have spoiled Minos's wedding if Athene had punched Medusa in the throat. Nevertheless, she could not shake off the mental image of the Nymph lying on the floor, gasping for breath that would not come, hands around her collapsed oesophagus. Rather than answer, Athene forced a mirthless smile to crease her cheeks.

Before she could decide whether to make a retort or beat the insolent brat, a commotion rose from the courtyard.

"You never did aught to get her back," Demeter spat at Zeus, her words slurred with drink and rage. The king had emerged from wherever he took the last Nymph, and now offered Demeter a disinterested glance. "You think with naught save your shrivelled cock."

Ooh. Athene winced. The Inumiden Titan should have left off without the 'shrivelled' part.

Athene's father came alert, head swivelling around and darkening gaze crashing in on his former lover.

"Your memory has begun to falter," he growled. "Perhaps you need a closer look at my divine person."

Drunk enough to have overstepped, but not so drunk as to not realise it, Demeter quavered.

It was too late, of course, and Athene set her jaw, her stomach churning, knowing Father would unleash his wrath.

Indeed, a single fulguration crackled overhead, thunder rumbling not so far off.

"Get on your knees and give it a thorough evaluation," her father demanded, spreading his legs and hiking up his khiton in the middle of the damn courtyard.

With a groan, Athene turned away. The last thing she wanted to see was someone pleasure her father, and the king would force the issue, she had no doubt. As an Olympian, Demeter should have known better than to challenge their king's pride. The Titan woman had never gotten over Hades abducting her daughter—Athene's half-sister. But confronting Father here, in public, meant he would shame her in public too.

Still, Athene grimaced in disgust with the whole affair. When she found Mother, the woman was back on the balcony, watching the moon. Maybe she knew what went on in the courtyard—Mother oft knew many things—but she did not speak of it.

Athene pressed her back against the balustrade so she could look into her Mother's golden eyes. "I've thought of a fitting fate for Medusa, assuming your Art can handle warping of the flesh."

Mother's mouth twitched, perhaps in distaste, but if so, Athene was in no mood for it. Mother had promised her she would help her extract her vengeance upon Hephaistos and his kin, Medusa included. That the Nymph was a haughty bitch only made it all the sweeter.

"Curses can achieve such things, but not with ease, and the cost will be high, for the both of us, Daughter." A pause. "Perhaps better to slay her and spare us all."

No, too easy. "I will take from her that which she values above all else: her precious, vaunted beauty and the pride she derives from it. I will make her a monster. Whatever the price, I'll pay."

"Only those who do not fathom real cost can claim they would pay any price." Mother swallowed, lips pursed. A long time she held silent before looking at Athene. "I will do as you wish. I even know a wretched hold to which we can send her to pass the ages. But Athene … this is the sole time I will use the Art thus for your retribution."

Fair enough.

"Get me some of her hair."

Oh, Athene would enjoy ripping a chunk of those fiery hairs off the woman's head.

8

HEKATE

226 Golden Age

The aureate irises meant the babe Hekate cradled probably had Heliad blood, though she supposed the child could have gotten those from her. Sweat and afterbirth drenched the linens upon which she reclined in her chambers within the Lodge of Whispers. Given the night of conception, perhaps she'd never know for certain whose daughter this was, but she was guessing Helios.

With a contented sigh, she leaned back, allowing her daughter to nurse. Fingers languid, she twirled the girl's few hairs.

Incipient visions danced before her half-lidded eyes, an auburn-haired child racing about the golden halls of Helion, beautiful and vivacious. Perhaps a prescient confirmation of the girl's parentage.

It was sometime later when the rapping came on her door. She thought she might have slept, for she had some vague recollection of further fevered images. Whether they held any portent or not, she could not call them up again. Sloppy for an oneiromancer, and

Morpheus had been training her to plumb her dreams over the past year.

"Enter," she said, rubbing at her eyes and shifting the babe upon her chest.

After peeking a head in the doorway, Keuthos stepped inside and came to sit beside her. "How are you feeling?"

"Like I just made a person and then had to squeeze her out through my nethers. Maybe you should try that. Any other questions?"

The man blushed. He had probably deserved better. He'd been a friend to her all year, helping her with studies and, as her delivery drew nigh, eager to assist any way he could. She had thought of him as a boy, only to learn his Hyperborean features made him seem younger than he was, as Keuthos was actually a year older than her.

Yes, he might have deserved better ... but he probably should have also *known* better, and Hekate was too exhausted to do more than let the remonstration lie between them.

After a moment, Keuthos cleared his throat. "I'll leave you to rest, then."

"No, wait." Hekate grunted in discomfort, trying to shift to find some way to lie that would soothe the aches. "Someone needs to tell Helios the child is his."

Her friend settled onto his arse with a *huff*. "You tell him that, he might try to claim her."

"I know." The words lanced through Hekate like shards of rock through her veins. They tore her insides apart and left her hollow. But what did she know of being a mother? When she'd learnt she was with child, her instinct had screamed at her to brew a tonic to loose the babe from her womb. Even in keeping it, she'd known she could not do right by the babe. "I never knew my mother, either ..." Her voice cracked, damn it. She would *not* weep in front of him.

"But why?"

"Because I am tainted, by nature and by action. I am consumed by a pursuit of knowledge I cannot turn back from—I know myself, and I know to bring a child along would only endanger her. If she grows to adulthood in the golden halls of her father, she will want for naught in this world."

"Save a mother."

Hekate winced as if he had twisted a knife in her gut.

"Will you even name her?"

Well, her mother had managed that much at least, even if Hekate no longer used that name. She supposed she must do no less. "Her name is Kirke." Hekate swallowed the painful lump in her throat. "Now, find her father."

As HEKATE HAD KNOWN he would, Helios gladly claimed Kirke for his ever-growing brood of Heliads. She would by reared in the resplendent halls of Helion, a golden princess primed for a life of luxury.

That Hekate had sobbed for the whole of a day when Helios had taken her away, that she had wept until her voice was but a rasp and her eyes burned as if on fire, it mattered little compared to Kirke's future. It was what she had seen for the babe, and Hekate could not have offered a tenth so much to her. Or so she told herself in the nights that followed, arms wrapt around her sides just to keep her heart from spilling out and the core of her from rupturing. Such was the comfort she offered herself while rocking herself to sleep with lachrymal tremors.

The days passed and passed, and the hollow became another scar carved upon her soul, even as she occupied her mind with translations of the Sefer Raziel. This book she had seen in her dreams, hers and hers alone, and that thought tormented her.

It would be hers. It must.

Some nights, she called up ghosts of forgotten ages to draw upon their wisdom, seeking any clue that might lead to the unraveling of the grimoire. For thus she had taken to calling the tome, a record of spells and secrets about the nature of the cosmos, hidden just out of reach.

A thousand, thousand bits of arcana there for the grasping if she could only unlock the key. It was a purpose, a striving after all knowledge unjustly denied to Man and even Titan.

The Circle kept the grimoire chained to the pedestal in the library, bound by indestructible orichalcum chains that ensured no members could remove it or claim it for themselves. Thus, Hekate had begun spending nigh all her time in there, sitting on the floor or standing over the book, waiting for it to unlock its mysteries.

When it came to her, a revelation like tumblers clicking into place, it sent her scrambling forward, frantically scribbling notes upon a papyrus scroll. Her neck ached from bending over the grimoire, then her knees hurt from dropping onto the floor to record her mess of observations. In her haste, Hekate sent a phial of ink toppling over and hissed at the mess she had made. With naught else to clean it, she dabbed it dry with her peplos, then dove back into her scribing.

Because if this was accurate ...

"Hekate?" Keuthos asked, apparently having made his way into the library. "It's past dawn, Hekate. Have you been at this all night? Have you taken no rest?"

All sorcerers knew the night was best for working the Art, and thus many in the Lodge tended to work until the wee hours of the morning and sleep late. Her friend's concern might have been touching, had Hekate had any mind to spare for such things. "It's out there," she rasped, instead. "It's out in the desert, I know it is."

Was that, too, why her dream had shown her shifting the sands?

"What's out where? You're not making any sense."

"On Kumari Kandam, one of the lost cities of ... of ..." Hekate lurched to her feet, mopping her hands upon her ruined peplos to make sure she didn't risk staining the grimoire with ink. Then she thumped the page that still stood open upon the pedestal. "Gorias, a city of Dark Faerie."

Grunting, Keuthos folded his arms. "Of what now?"

"Nigh as I can tell," Hekate said, grabbing his arm and dragging him over to peer at the book, "in the Time of Nyx—or even maybe before it, if you can believe that—grand workers of the Art raised four great cities, one on each of the continents. Maybe the sorcerers weren't Men but something else, something more akin to spirits." She knew she was rambling, talking too fast for him to follow, but couldn't hold back the flood of her epiphany now that it had come. "All the secrets—these arcana—we seek about the true nature of the cosmos and a means to control it, may lie buried beneath the desert of Kumari Kandam, hidden in Gorias."

Keuthos clucked his tongue. "If these people—beings, whatever —knew all the secrets of the World, why did they fall?"

Hekate opened her mouth, then spread her hands, empty. "I've no idea." Now she swayed, waves of fatigue finally catching up with her. "I don't know, but whoever this Raziel was who wrote this tome, he records all this like history he witnessed firsthand."

"Assuming your translations are correct." Keuthos peered at the tome and her notes. "And you seem to have partially translated only a small segment of the tome. Perhaps you should finish before we even consider—"

"It's not all in the same language."

"What?"

Hekate thumped the book. "Multiple authors, multiple hands, and in fact, there are empty spaces in the tome, as if places were left for further recordings. Pieces of this are Supernal. There are diagrams and invocations and such. Formulae for potions, instructions for Soulforging orichalcum ... So much knowledge in one place. I think this Raziel may have visited Gorias and the other cities, may have been one of these people. But I ... I can't translate it all. Not with what I have here. We need to find the city to understand more, Keuthos. I *must* have the answers."

The Hyperborean shook his head in resignation. "Will what I have to say on the matter make a difference?"

Hekate snorted and clapped him on the shoulder. "You know me better than that by now."

"Indeed." Keuthos stroked his brow with thumb and forefinger, looking like he might object anyway. Instead, he shrugged. "We'll need supplies, preparations. Gaia alone knows what we'll face in Kumari Kandam."

Oh, that was true enough. They would need a great many things, including the power to defend themselves.

"Tonight, I will evoke a lampad," she admitted. "I will bind it to myself to give us what we need."

Grim-faced, Keuthos only nodded. "Then, I suppose I'll be arranging a ship for the next morn." He hesitated. "Are you planning to inform the rest of the Circle about your intention?"

"Not hardly. If they believe us at all, don't you think one of the Inner Circle will try to take this from us and claim it for themselves? No, Keuthos, we can trust only each other." A twinge of regret shot through her. A wish that Artemis had returned. Maybe all friendships, all relationships were ephemeral things. Not even bonds of the heart could survive the shifting currents of Ananke.

THE CIRCLE OF GOETIC MYSTERIES provided members with several conjuring chambers for practicing the Art. Each chamber was a secluded, windowless room dug out beneath the main compound, with wards engraved into both the bronze-banded door and the stone walls encircling the space. Hekate first set a series of oil lamps around the circumference of the summoning circle, then examined the geometric patterns of the carved circle itself.

While proficient enough, she suspected she could have improved upon the design cut into the floor, given what she had learnt from the grimoire. As it stood, however, the existing circle didn't accommodate changes, so instead, she began making notes on which glyphs she would set within the boundaries. There were spaces left within the vertices and intersections where a conjurer could mark their chosen sigils to make certain they invoked those spirits most needed.

She had spread several sheets of notes scribbled on papyrus in accessible locations and paused to review. Everything had to be perfect.

The chamber door opened with a braying cry, and Keuthos dragged a reluctant goat inside by a rope. While the animal could not have suspected what lay in store for it, it must have felt the perverse Otherworldly energies that pervaded the room.

Poor creature. Blood was strongest, and its scent called out to the denizens beyond the Veil.

After dragging the creature close, Keuthos held it steady, while Hekate fell into a Supernal incantation, calling up shades first, to build the foundation of her wards. The discordant syllables reverberated inside her skull even as they pierced the Etheric membrane separating the Mortal Realm from the beyond. Embracing the Sight, she peered into the shadows and the whole of the Penumbra shuddered beneath the weight of her cant. The Penumbra was a Realm of shadow and thought, prowled by the endless dead and entities older than history. To look into its chill depths was to turn from colour and warmth and welcome in the breath of the grave.

Though the animal could not see the results of her incantation, still it bucked in Keuthos's arms, revolting against the unnatural touch which now brushed against their world. Still incanting, Hekate drew a knife from her belt. Keuthos set a bowl beneath the goat's head, then forced the animal down, closer to the floor. With a single swift jerk of the blade, Hekate sliced open its throat, releasing a sanguine cataract.

She allowed herself a glance at the notes she had made on her papyrus, then dipped her first two fingers in the bowl of blood and began to paint the glyphs she had selected into the circle. As she worked, her cants increased in tempo and volume, the echoes inside her head—inside her *soul*—growing so powerful they felt apt to send her shuddering to pieces.

With the Sight embraced, she saw them approach, the hordes of frayed dead drifting about the ambit of her circle, forming a moaning sphere of damnation. Soon, greater forces joined the procession, carried upon nether winds, lurking on the fringes. A furious harpy, crackling with lightning, vexed at being cajoled by a mortal, even as it served to reinforce the circle against Hekate's true target. And a scowling, rocky kabeiros pantomiming crushing her between its granite palms. Still, its power served to check that of the harpy.

The hair on her neck stood on end at the regard of so many eidolons, all eager to slip inside her flesh and claim it as their own. But it was the billowing cold that wafted in from somewhere farther off that she sought. Carried in on an icy brume, pulled out of the frozen netherworld of the Spirit Realm, this one she called by name.

"Khione ..." The famed Snow Queen had been drawn into the depths and become something greater in death than even in life. The dead had told her so, when she had called upon them, night after night, prying loose secret whispers the living could not and would not hear. "Khione ... Lampad Khione."

Summoned, the mist freely pierced her circle, flowing inward in great rippling clouds that must have concealed a pale-skinned maiden. The brume twisted about Hekate in unnatural whorls, tendrils bent into exotic spirals that became twisting vortices, closing ever inward. Toward her.

A sudden moment of doubt seized her, her heart hammering. What if she had miscalculated? A misdrawn glyph, a misspoken syllable, a faltering of the will, and the spirit—

The mist engulfed her, poured in through her mouth and nostrils, filling her up, freezing her from the inside out. Shuddering, soul-crunching cold washed through her, sent her stumbling to her knees, her cants forgotten. Hekate tried to curl into a foetal ball, but her limbs refused her commands. Agony and terror blended into a miasma of torment.

What had she done?

Mine.

Of its own accord—or rather of the lampad's—Hekate's body pushed off the floor. Her Sight had winked out, leaving only the flickering oil lamps to see by and a stricken Keuthos backing away, raising hands that would not protect him from the Otherworldly power of Mist.

No! No, her body was her own. Her will collided with Khione's, sending tremors through her form. She doubled over, unsteady and anguished, but refused to back down. If she surrendered now, the Mist spirit would have her. With a growl, Hekate hurled all she was—the essence of a girl, a daughter, a sorceress—at the entity now sharing her body.

Doing so redoubled the cold, left her wanting to retch. To tear apart her own skull to relieve the pressure building inside her head.

Bits of herself were flensed away. Her childhood and the person that had arisen from it chipped, pieces seized up by the spirit and devoured like a delicacy.

Then she felt the ice holding her crack, a spiderwebbing of the lampad's will.

With a pained gasp, Hekate collapsed onto her back and lay on the floor, moaning. She couldn't say when, but a layer of rime had crusted the stone here. Upon the cold floor, Hekate combed her mind, trying to remember what ephemeral aspect of her soul she had lost.

She knew something was gone, but whatever it was, whatever bit of the essence of her she had traded for this power, she could not even identify it.

"Did you think the Art would come without cost?" Morpheus had asked her.

She hadn't known what she'd lost back then, either. Had it been … had its loss been how she got here, now?

No answers came to her.

෴

"We need the book," Hekate said.

"It's madness," Keuthos objected. "They will come for it. They will come for us."

"Perhaps," Hekate admitted. But still, if she was to translate the greater arcana of Sefer Raziel, she needed to bring it with her to Gorias.

And she had seen herself with the book there.

They stood in the library, staring down at the tome, and she saw no point in further debate. Keuthos might argue with her, but he would not stand up to her, and she would have her way.

"Anyway," her friend continued to protest, "the orichalcum chain binding it to the pedestal is indestructible."

"Of course it is. But the pedestal isn't." Before he could object further, she grabbed the stone slab and willed the icy force of Khione's power into her palms. The Mist spirit latched onto her when called, feasting upon Hekate's Pneuma. But in the process, Hekate gained access to the Art of Mist.

Bitter chill seeped into the stone, pouring from her hands. Wafts of mist rose into the air like tendrils of steam. She felt it as ice formed inside tiny pores within the surface. Growling, using the Pneumatikoi of Potency to increase her strength, Hekate snapped off the top of the podium. Frozen chunks tumbled around her.

With the podium shattered, she simply unthreaded the orichalcum chain from the book, and began to wrap it for safe-keeping in case she ever—

"What in Tartarus are you doing!" a girl shrieked.

Hekate and Keuthos spun to see Deino there. Reflexively, Hekate jerked her hand up. A hundred icy razors hurtled from her fingertips at Deino, and the woman fell screeching, clutching her shredded face. Blood seeped between fingers over Deino's eyes, and Hekate's stomach fell with the sudden realisation ice shards had shredded the delicate orbs.

Oh ... fuck. What had she done? Was that her? Had she willed such a thing to happen? Had Khione used Hekate's body for such violence?

Keuthos grabbed Hekate's elbow and dragged her forward at a dash. "We have to move! We have to go before anyone realises what we've done." He flung open the library door.

He was right, of course. Hekate followed him down the hall, out through a vestibule full of confused sorcerers; some few had risen to go see what the commotion was.

They fled out into the necropolis, where the sunlight stung her eyes, and beyond. Toward the secrets she had so desperately sought.

INTERLUDE: BELLEROPHON

623 Bronze Age

King Iobates of Phoeba was the kind of man whose chins danced with his mirth, such that Bellerophon could have imagined extra smiles hid within the folds of his oily beard. In the same vein, he fancied he now saw at least three scowls peeking out from the mound of flesh as the king read the papyrus Bellerophon had given him.

Oh, Bellerophon knew well enough what it said and the reason for the king's growing distress. In the message, King Proitos of Delphi asked Iobates, his father-in-law, to kill the bearer of the message. Since Iobates himself had only just broken the royal seal of Delphi, the king could not have suspected Bellerophon had the least inkling of the letter's contents. But a friend had warned him, and even now, it took an effort to keep a mischievous smirk from creeping upon his face. Iobates was trapped, even as Proitos had been before him. Bellerophon had partaken of Iobates's hospitality for the past ten days, and no man could turn on his own guest and hope to escape punishment by the Erinyes. Tales claimed those frightful Furies would haunt dreams, driving transgressors to madness, unfurling snaking paths of self-destruction that must end in ruination. What man would chance such a fate by violating guest-right?

Mayhap Proitos had even charged Bellerophon with attempting to force himself upon Stheneboea, his wife and Iobates's daughter. The sordid truth was the two of them had, in fact, lain together once. But Bellerophon had declined further liaisons after realising—when not so drunk—what would happen if the king sheltering him learnt Bellerophon had cuckolded him. Stheneboea took his refusal like an assault upon her pride and had accused him of having tried to force himself upon her. Whilst Bellerophon may have relied upon honeyed words—outright lies about running away with her, even—and might have laid a hand upon her arse before she had strictly granted permission, he certainly had not *forced* anyone to his bed.

And by Zeus's beard, a woman ought to realise that just because a man sought her flesh once didn't mean he intended to bind himself to it forever. No romp in the sack was worth being parted from one's head.

Iobates was fighting a losing battle to control his temper now, and Bellerophon almost pitied him. The king ran the back of his meaty thumb along his brow as if he could squeeze an answer out of his bloated brain thus. Perhaps it even worked, for a slow, self-satisfied gleam crept into the king's shadowed eyes, and he drew a deep, snorting breath. "Well, my dear friend Bellerophon." His phlegmy cough bespoke a man who'd enjoyed far too much wine for far too long and now reaped the consequences. How many years did Iobates have left to him? Not so many, Bellerophon suspected. "Lydia finds itself beset by a particularly vicious chimera of late. Surely it can only be by the will of Ananke that I find myself a friend in a demigod son of an Olympian. Who better than Bellerophon, son of the great Poseidon himself, to slay such a foul beast and liberate our shores?"

"A chimera." Bellerophon fought to keep any inflection from his voice. He might have pointed out that he'd never met his father. He might have reminded the king that, so far as Bellerophon knew,

Poseidon only ever saved Men from sea monsters he himself had threatened them with, and only if they offered him whatever tributes he demanded. He might have also asked whether Iobates had pushed his brow so hard he'd popped his brains out like pus from a swollen pimple.

He might have said any number of things if honour did not demand he, as a guest of Iobates, acquiesce to the request of his host. How could he claim to be a demigod and refuse to hunt a monster? It would, he supposed, serve to further carve the bedrock of his legend and thus ensure himself welcome in some other polis if Phoeba turned against him as Delphi and Korinth had.

For a moment, Bellerophon wondered how it was he managed to vex the kings of every city he happened upon. Was he a foul man? Ah, mostlike it was the will of the Moirai, weaving greatness from his hardships. Fate had driven him to kill his foster brother, even as Fate —or wine—had gotten him into bed with Stheneboea. He could hardly be blamed for following the designs of the Moirai, could he?

"I can refuse you naught, my friend," he said at last. "Tell me of this chimera."

THE BEAST BELLEROPHON had so hastily agreed to slay could, in fact, *fly*. Wise Men avoided chimeras and the lands they haunted. When the abominations prowled too close to poleis, kings sent out cries for Artemis to come and save them. Or sometimes, Bellerophon had heard, Athene would arrive unbidden—as if she knew when Men suffered and died—and strike down the monsters. Chimeras were most oft foul amalgamations of two animals.

One tale claimed Athene had speared a creature, half bear, half frog. Another claimed Artemis had shot a wolf with a scorpion tail.

Iobates, however, had sent Bellerophon after a creature with the forequarters of a lion, the hindquarters of a goat, and drakon wings. The beast, if tales could be believed, had a snake-like drakon head in place of a tail, and lion and goat heads bursting from its shoulders.

Best of all—and Bellerophon admitted he found this hard to credit—
the creature was said to breathe fire from one or perhaps all of those
godsdamned heads.

He was not certain whether to laugh or weep at the patent absur-
dity of the task before him. He might flee from Lydia altogether,
though to do so after agreeing to aid Iobates would redouble his
shame. Indeed, he'd mostlike never be able to show his face in Elládos, Lydia, or Phrygia again.

On the other hand, if he sailed for Phoenikia, Men would not
know him, and he might call upon his distant Tethid kin and find a
place there. The descendants of Io yet reigned in the great
Phoenikian poleis, even if their heyday had faded into the mists of
antiquity.

Yet Bellerophon found himself wandering the wilds of Lydia,
hunting for the chimera. How he was meant to find, much less
pursue and slay, a monster that could fly, he could not say. If the beast
took note of him at all, it might well spew its flaming death upon him
from the sky, giving him not the least chance to come within spear
range. Besides which, was he to search for tracks upon the firmament? Should he seek monster spoor in the clouds?

Iobates had chosen well a task to doom Bellerophon. Either he
would never find the chimera and thus must flee in shame, or it
would kill him before he could land a single blow. But why, he asked
himself not for the first time, would the Moirai weave such an ending
to his grand tale? Surely the Fates meant him for greater ends than
this? Bellerophon was the son of a god, blessed with strength,
stamina, and agility ordinary Men could not match. He could leap
farther, swim deeper, and hurl a javelin with more accuracy than any
man he'd ever seen. He could wrestle champions and pin them in the
dust.

How was he to accept an ignominious end? Why would the Fates
abandon him?

Huffing, he slumped in the shadow of a rock overlooking a spring.
After pausing to drink and wash his face, he dozed, allowing himself
a time to seep in the tepid comforts of self-pity. The mocking face of

his foster brother, Deliades, rose in phantasmagoric visions, casting his silent aspersions.

"You cannot blame me for following the course Ananke wove for me," Bellerophon spat. His protestations had as much effect upon the phantom now as they had in the past. If Deliades had any counter to the logic of Bellerophon's argument, the image did not offer it.

Then, of a sudden, a frightful sound erupted from the shade's mouth, something akin to a horse's whinny, but tinged with an almost Otherworldly tenor that raised every hair upon his arms. Before Bellerophon's eyes, the image of his brother broke into mist, and through it strode grey-eyed Athene, clad in burnished panoply that glinted in the moonlight. Behind her, a black pegasus scuffed one hoof in the dust, its wings at rest and yet somehow still stirring the air.

"G-goddess," Bellerophon rasped, uncertain whether he yet dreamt or had now woken to behold the most mysterious of all Olympians before himself. Either way, he pushed himself to his knees.

"Now is not the time for rest, Bellerophon." She drew the pegasus forward by a halter attached to a golden bridle.

"Have you come to slay the chimera?" Perhaps he ought not to have asked so impertinent a question, but it burst from his lips before he could think better of it. And besides, if an Olympian slew the beast before Bellerophon found it, Iobates could hardly blame Bellerophon for that.

A hint of a smile creased her face that, had he not known better, he might have called pained. "Do you know why I oft send Men or demigods to slay monsters, Bellerophon, rather than undertake the tasks myself?"

"Uh ..." Well, that was a damn fine question, but if his former outburst was not brazen, to ask such as this surely was. No Man, so far as he knew, had ever dared voice such wonderings. "No."

Athene whispered something into the pegasus's ear, and the animal tromped off to water itself at the spring. The goddess then reclined on the rock beside which Bellerophon knelt and, thankfully, motioned for him to sit and give his knees some respite. "What would happen if Men required Titans to solve all their problems?" Bellerophon shrugged, and Athene's face fell a little, as if she had expected a better answer. "When a Man, even a demigod, protects his fellow Men by overcoming dangers, that Man becomes a hero. A symbol of hope and courage behind which his kind might rally and believe that, in truth, this World is theirs, as well." For an instant, she looked like she might say more, but she abruptly cut herself off. "Perhaps one day you might understand. I bring you the pegasus that you might slay this great chimera and inspire Mankind with your valour, as once did Kadmus, and as even now Perseus strives for. You'll find the beast lairs in the Arad Mountains, north of Phoeba." A slight pause. "But for you, I have seen a danger perhaps greater even than the monster. So, I bid you, be wary of overmuch pride."

"What does that mean?"

"I ..." Athene shook her head. "Sometimes Oracular insight reveals a future clear as pellucid waters glittering in the midday sun, but oft enough, it is more intimation and instinct. A feeling, a fear, that, if you trod without due care, you might well become the wrong sort of symbol for your brethren. I'd have you be a beacon, not a warning."

She patted his knee, and for an instant, Bellerophon was tempted to try his charms upon her—few women resisted those any better than Stheneboea had—but before he could make up his mind, she rose and clucked her tongue. The pegasus tromped back over and neighed in his face, ruffling his hair. By the time Bellerophon blinked away his shock, Athene had vanished.

Despite Athene having gifted him the pegasus bridled and ready to mount, Bellerophon found himself surprised the beast did not throw him the instant he dared to clamber onto its bare back. Pegasi served as steeds for Olympians and their most favoured of Titan followers. To even think to ride such an animal would earn a Man the displeasure of the gods. But it was a goddess who had provided this ebony stallion, so surely it meant the Moirai intended such an honour for Bellerophon. Who was he to argue with the Fates' design?

So, atop the glorious steed, under Hyperion's amber light, he soared for the Arad Mountains. Fingers wrapt in the animal's mane, legs clutching in a death grip, he held to his mount, a spear in his right hand held tight to his side. The wind tugged at his clothes and made his hair billow. Long had he clung to the pegasus, and ever and again, the sense of his own smallness crept upon him.

Was this the hubristic danger of which Athene had warned? That if he was not careful, he'd plummet to his crashing doom so far below? Ah, but such a disgraceful end would not prove his destiny. The Moirai weaved greater tales for Men like Bellerophon. For him, bards would compose their masterpieces.

He would not be small.

Over the mountains he flew, Hyperion's last rays singeing his retinas. Bellerophon hefted his spear, saluting the sun. But still, he saw no sign of the chimera. And at last, twilight crawled its way over the mountains, smearing the sky lavender and staining the peaks in flames.

"Where are you?" Bellerophon shouted into the gathering darkness. He had not flown so far, upon such a majestic steed, to find himself thwarted by reluctant prey. "Are you not the monster Lydia so fears?"

Perhaps his taunting words reached the creature, for a roar split the gloom. This bellow seemed to utter not from the throat of any earthly beast but from the very bowels of Gaia, as though she herself rose to his challenge. Despite himself, despite his bravado, Bellerophon's stomach dropped. Animal dread seized his guts and squeezed so tight he scarce kept from shitting himself.

The World convulsed, unable to bear the approach of so foul an abomination.

He saw it then, a shadow rising from between two peaks. The flap of its leathery membranes bent the air, heralding its approach with foreboding equal somehow to that of its roar. Nigh as large as the stories of Kemetian elephants claimed, this creature hurtled through the air. Its goat-like head craned around, a carmine gaze latching onto Bellerophon's eyes, holding him there.

His grip on the pegasus's mane tightened until his knuckles ached.

The chimera came about so a second head could peer at him. This one, a lion's, had eyes black as Nyx's bosom. Its maw opened, exposing fangs like scythe blades.

Bellerophon flicked the spear to reverse his grip, intent on hurling it.

The goat head reared back, its ruby eyes turning incandescent. Smoke curled out of nostrils in twisting fingers. All this in a heartbeat, before that head lurched forward. A stream of liquid flame erupted from the goat, naphtha bursting skyward. The blaze turned clouds to hissing steam. It scorched the air, leaving it tangy.

The pegasus banked so swiftly the spear tumbled from Bellerophon's fingers, and all he could do was fling himself against the animal's withers and pray to Zeus he would not join his weapon. For the spear had vanished into the blackness of some sylvan valley far, far below. A curtain of heat washed over him, but the pegasus, in self-preserving instinct, kept turning, ever evading any further blasts of fire.

Had the chimera managed to get above them, Bellerophon doubted even his ebony steed could have avoided being reduced to smouldering bones pitching out of the sky. As the pegasus turned about the chimera, Bellerophon dared release one hand to grab at the javelins dangling from his hip. Their position had his bag hanging too far below, and he could ill afford to lose those weapons should they spill from his case. His fingers brushed one, and he grabbed it and yanked it free.

The chimera, snarling, turned. Great beats of those leathery wings carried it upward, closing in. The lion gnashed its teeth as though incensed on behalf of the goat that any might evade its wretched flame. It was the hissing, darting snake-drakon head of its tail that inspired the most horror, however. Glistening venom dribbled from its curving fangs, even as that head swivelled about with uncanny agility.

The pegasus apprehended their danger without Bellerophon needing to speak of it and climbed upward with each beat of its own feathered wings. Still, the chimera closed the distance between them too quickly.

The whooshing wind made careful aim impossible, even if Bellerophon could have managed it over the maddening pounding of his pulse in his ears. Still, he lined up the javelin as best he could with that lethal drakon head and let fly. The snake-thing jerked to the side, easily evading his hurled projectile.

"Ares's arsehole," Bellerophon spat at it, fumbling to claim another javelin.

He'd never hit such a target. Not like this.

The goat head reared back once again before belching another torrent of bilious flames into the sky. The black pegasus dove under the stream, but dribbles of it rained around Bellerophon and his mount, and he found himself screaming in horror.

Naphtha sizzled where it spattered the pegasus's wings, and the animal flung its head from one side to the other in agony. Bellerophon clung on, close to his mount.

"We can only do this together," he shouted at the horse. The beginnings of an idea tingled. "Can you understand me? I need you to line me up for a throw. Provoke the damn goat head, Pegasus!" Pegasus, he decided, was a good enough name for a pegasus at the moment.

Though the chimera's powerful wings could hurl it across vast distances faster, Pegasus was more agile and managed to come up under the abomination. Pegasus, perhaps in understanding of Bellerophon's plan, or perhaps simply not wanting to close with the other heads, kept just out of range. Until, once more, the goat head's eyes turned incandescent. As it reared back, Bellerophon hurled his javelin at its throat.

The projectile took the monster through the neck as it tried to spew its bile upon Pegasus. The goat's throat burst apart in a grisly explosion of smouldering bile. Its goat head ruptured, and a rush of sizzling lava-like fluid sprayed over the lion head as well. The chimera stalled, convulsing in midair, its wings twisted out of position with the spasms of its pain. Like a meteor, it hurtled earthward.

Then, with a cloud of dust and a crash like an earthquake, it was smote upon the lower slope of the Arad Mountains.

For a time, Pegasus circled, panting even harder than Bellerophon.

He supposed they would have to go down there and make certain the beast was dead. On the off chance having one of its heads explode and the other drenched in lava-vomit didn't kill it. Still, he was fair certain what he'd find, and that it ought to have proved himself to Iobates.

Allowing himself a proud sigh of exhaustion, Bellerophon patted Pegasus's neck. "What a team we make, you and I."

PART II

<hr>

While the Ouranid League was irrevocably shattered, its vestiges remain in the aristoi bloodlines, the genē. Every genos traces its descent to one of the founders, from Atlantids to the Heliads. Their Titan descendants now rule the world, and mortal kings alike are distant scions of the demigod bastards of Titans. Six genē make up the Elládosi world, and the legacy of the Ouranids endures.

— Polyhymnia, Analects of the Muses

9

———

PERSEUS

623 Bronze Age

When the summons had come from his uncle, Perseus had feared it but one more sideways attempt at wooing his mother away from his stepfather. As it turned out, though, King Polydektes had called all his friends—well, friends was a stretch since some of them would have sooner spent an evening drinking wine with a three-legged goat than the king—to announce he would ask for the hand of Hippodameia. Lounging on a fur rug, four cups of Argosian red in, Perseus had finally worked up the courage to ask someone who Hippodameia was.

"Daughter of King Oinomaos of Ithaka," one of the other guests said, a man with a beard that had probably last been groomed by the man's mother when he was still in swaddling clothes. "Makes her a descendant of Ares himself," Tangle-beard said.

Because if Perseus was looking for marital bliss, the first place he'd look was with the brood of the ill-tempered god of war.

Perseus raised his cup in salute. "Demigods abound." Since his mother persisted in claiming Perseus the son of all-powerful Zeus himself, that would actually make Hippodameia some kind of cousin. What kind? Perseus didn't much bother himself with such things. Considering extended relations when drunk made his head spin and worrying about them when sober drove him to drink.

"Friends!" Polydektes announced to no one in particular, unless he had an invisible friend in the centre of the hall. "Now we are all well lubricated, I should announce I am gathering contributions for my marriage offer to Oinomaos. Imagine the prestige and importance that will flow into Neritum if Ares's granddaughter becomes our queen!"

"Hear, hear!" Tangle-beard bellowed, though since his gaze was locked on his cup, Perseus imagined he was toasting the wine itself, rather than the king. Fair enough, as the wine deserved it more.

Still, Perseus supposed he ought to do his part to get these rich merchants and aristocrats offering up some drachmae. He couldn't pledge much, true, but if it meant his uncle gave over any further misguided attempts to steal Mama away from his brother, Perseus would gladly help Polydektes marry a princess. He'd help him marry a casserole if it would get Uncle to leave them in peace. "Uncle, I make the first pledge for your offering, and let our gathered friends take full heed. Little though my means are, I would deny you naught at all. I give you my word, but name the prize and I'll retrieve it—if it lies within my power."

Polydektes grinned wide enough his face seemed apt to split in half. "My nephew!" he said, raising his cup in Perseus's direction. "Indeed, and you, divine-blooded, could deliver prizes sure to awe even wealthy Oinomaos." Huh. Maybe Perseus had enjoyed the wine a bit too much, but the look on Uncle's face was a bit disconcerting. Somewhat akin to a cat who had cornered a mouse and was deciding how to eat it. Perseus was fairly certain he didn't want to be eaten by a cat. "I can think of one trophy that could not help but achieve the desired effect, nephew. You have heard of the famed Gorgon, the monster Medusa?" Somehow that grin spread wider, seeming now almost sharklike to Perseus. "Fulfil your oath by delivering her head to me, that I can send it to Ithaka."

Scattered laughter spread through the lounge, and for a moment, Perseus too thought maybe his uncle jested with him. But the man's eyes glinted with such perverse glee he clearly thought Perseus snared in his net. Which meant Perseus could either break his oath or leave Neritum in search of a legendary monster said to turn men to stone. Neither much appealed, but breaking an oath was unthinkable.

"It shall be yours, Uncle," Perseus said, his mouth suddenly thick and dry, despite the abundance of wine he'd thrown back.

Moments later, others began to pledge drachmae or fleeces or silver tributes. Maybe they feared if they didn't make their own offer, Polydektes would next ask for Zeus's own stones. Perseus excused himself, swaying slightly as he made his way out of the lounge.

A golden-eyed, black-haired Heliad woman pressed a hand against his chest when he stepped into the courtyard. Blinking, he looked her up and down. No women had been allowed in the lounge for Polydektes's announcement, but a fair number had lingered out here. Some were serving girls, though this one didn't have the air of such, and her clothes were those of an aristos.

"I don't suppose you're Medusa?" he asked.

"Indeed, and I've come to offer my head," she retorted, straight-faced. Perseus decided he was going to like the Heliad. "Your uncle seems to place high worth on familial bonds, sending his nephew to hunt a monster."

Perseus shrugged. "Technically we don't share blood, so I suppose there's that."

"Because Zeus is your real father?"

Perseus had the distinct impression this woman had him at a bit of a disadvantage, he just wasn't sure whether that was a problem yet. "Um ... I'm Perseus and I'm certain we have not met. Even were I drunk enough to have forgotten my own name, I think I'd remember yours."

"No doubt. I'm Pandora, and I've come to Neritum to find you."

She grabbed his hand and drew him to sit beside a fountain in the courtyard. "I need your help to free someone I love, and an Oracle told me that you and you alone have the power to save him."

Perseus had enjoyed too much wine. Or not enough. Either way, he probably should not have attended to Uncle's summons after all. In one night, he'd been sent to slay an unkillable monster and found a stranger showing up demanding he undertake a daring rescue. "Much as I've oft fancied myself the hero type, I generally imagined my adventures, ah … in succession rather than all at once. Creates a more coherent narrative for the bards, you know." His sudden burp carried the distinct aftertaste of mediocre wine.

"Your uncle just sent you on a suicide mission," Pandora said. "An utterly unnecessary one, so I'm guessing he simply wants you gone. Why? Does he have some designs on your mother?"

How in Hades's dark domain had she figured that out so quickly? "Uh …"

"Either way, he seeks only to be rid of you, which seems to mean your hastily spoken oath to him amounts to naught. What I ask of you, on the other hand, is to save a man from the worst imaginable fate. You dream of heroism? This is your chance."

Perseus shrugged. "Well, see, the thing is, if I did aspire to hero-ism, I *would* be bound even by hastily spoken oaths. That's how tales go, isn't it? Our daring heroes spout off promises without having the first clue what they might entail. You have heard of, ah, stories, right?" He grinned, though despair had begun to wash over the Heliad's face. "They go like this, you see. I, Perseus, promise to help you in whatever you need, Pandora, the moment I fulfil my oath to Polydektes."

Pandora groaned, then folded her arms across her chest. "Don't think the air of self-effacing foppery fools *anyone* save fools, Perseus. I can see damn well you know I'm right, and you know your uncle has entrapped you with all this."

Yes, well, the World was so oft peopled by fools, and that was as it should be. He patted her knee indulgently just to see if he could get a rise out of her. And, indeed, her eyes narrowed in irritation. "You just wait here, my dear, and once I've achieved one impossible quest, I'll be ready to undertake the next."

Perseus started to rise, but Pandora fair leapt to her feet, snatching his wrist. "If you insist on following through with this madness, then I'm not letting you out of my sight."

"Uh ... you want to go with me on a 'suicide mission'? Need I point out how those most oft culminate?"

"You have no idea what I've been through of late, and I'm not losing any chance to help my love."

Perseus shrugged again. "I suppose a hero needs a witness. Ah ... Hmm. Do let me know if you want me to flex my muscles or something. We should make sure to find the best pose for any future statues they carve of me."

"Not fooling anyone," Pandora repeated, drawing him out of Polydektes's courtyard.

Perseus was rather certain he was fooling *someone*, but that hardly seemed to be the point, and anyway ...

Pandora drew up short as they left the palace, and it took only a moment to see why. Standing just outside was a grey-eyed Titan woman, clad in the purest white khiton, and eyeing the two of them. Grey-eyed ... Athene!

Perseus prostrated himself before the favoured daughter of almighty Zeus. Only on his knees did he even consider that she might be his half-sister. Consider it and dare seek a quick look up at her face and those distinctive eyes.

Beside him, Pandora had also knelt, albeit far slower than him, and was staring hard at Athene almost as if she knew her.

The goddess, however, had focused her gaze upon Perseus. "Rise," she commanded.

Perseus did so, finding his heart ready to beat right out of his chest, take flight and zip around her like a butterfly. "My Lady," he said, inclining his head.

"Enough, Perseus," Athene said. "I've come to help you in your quest." Help him? An Olympian was going to help him? Well, that seemed to confirm his parentage, didn't it? "To slay Medusa, you will need special weapons forged of adamant. Such tools were hidden in the Garden of the Hesperides following the Gigantomachy. Follow the river to find the garden, then dig beneath the shadow of the owl-shaped rock to uncover the weapons. Once you have claimed them, you must find the Graeae. They alone can tell you where to seek for Medusa."

Much as he wanted to ask why she was helping him, questioning the Olympian seemed impertinent. Normally, Perseus considered impertinence his favourite kind of pertinence, but there were times—blessedly few though they were—even he decided it best to keep his mouth shut.

"The Garden of the Hesperides," Pandora said. "On Atlantis."

Athene cast a glance at Perseus's companion, her eyes roaming over the woman in apparent consternation, before offering a nod in answer. Then she was off, drifting into the night and leaving them alone.

PANDORA, as it turned out, knew a great deal more about Perseus's birth than even his own mother had told him. The woman had the tale from King Proitos of Delphi, and while Perseus guided the tiller of their small ship the next morn, she regaled him with details about just how he and Mama had come to wash up on the shores of Neritum. That Akrisios would lock his own daughter away, first in a prison, then in a chest tossed in the sea, seemed almost too cruel to be believed.

Yet he had to admit, on hearing the prophecy he would cause the death of his grandfather, an ill feeling had settled in his stomach. Small wonder Mama had seldom wished to talk much of her past and had bid him remain secluded on their small island. An isle that now seemed uncomfortably close to Argos.

He made sail for Atlantis, where Pandora assured him this Garden of the Hesperides was located, though Perseus knew precious little of the fabled place.

"You've been there?" he asked.

"To the garden? No," she admitted. "But I spent many years on Atlantis, and I know the general location of where it lies. According to tale, a great drakon that never sleeps watches over the garden, ensuring none dare approach the Tree of Life."

"Ah, well, then it's fitting we should be the first."

"Mmm." She studied him a moment. "Are you all right?"

Perseus shrugged. "Well, since you mention it, I could do with a massage and perhaps a bowl of soup, if you're offering."

"I'll get right on that. Shortly after I conquer Olympus and proclaim myself queen of Elládos."

"I wouldn't trouble a queen for soup."

Pandora quirked a smile. "But a massage?"

"It would be rude to refuse such an offer."

She leaned back against the gunwale, fixing him with her golden gaze. "It weighs upon you, as it must."

He couldn't say it much pleased him, learning all that had happened with his grandfather. But what was he to do about it? Part of him wanted to show up in Argos, stomp his foot, and demand his grandfather deal with him. A smaller part wanted to kick the man black and blue, then bring him to his knees before Mama to beg her forgiveness. Maybe it was best he stay as far away as possible and thus avert the prophecy. "I doubt the massage will be so heavy I'd call it a burden," he answered, not really looking at Pandora.

Out there, across the sea, lay Atlantis and the first step in this quest he'd gotten himself into. Despite his pretences—well, and maybe no small desire for adoration—heroism wasn't quite something he'd aspired to. Certainly not like this.

"How is it your stepfather is a fisherman and your uncle a king?" Pandora asked.

Now he did glance back at the Heliad. "Polydektes was the elder and inherited the throne. Father never seemed to mind, though, least not that he let on. He took me out on long trips all day, sometimes even into evening, hunting after the best spots to cast the nets. It was a good life, I suppose."

"Even if you weren't born of him, he's still your father."

He offered her an absent nod, though she spoke like someone who knew such things from personal experience. "Tell me of your lover, then, Pandora. Even a hero must sometimes indulge in fanning the flames of jealousy. What man has won your heart?"

She hesitated, tapping a finger upon her lip. "He's wise and kind, with the sharpest intellect I've ever encountered and a soul that seems old as the World. When he speaks, there is a depth to it, as if the ocean moves beneath his words, and when he grasps my hand, I feel the bulwark of mountains supporting me."

Huh. The depths of the passion in her voice, in her words, left her seeming raw, as if she flensed away her flesh and exposed her beating heart before him. It left him struggling for a rejoinder. For a moment. "But can he cook?"

A light snort of feigned exasperation escaped her. "As it happens, yes."

"All right, my dear, you've convinced me."

"Oh?"

"I am no longer jealous of him. Now I am jealous of *you*. There's naught for it—we shall fight for his hand in marriage."

Pandora chuckled. "What in Hades's dark domain did your mother feed you as a child?"

"Mostly fish."

"Anyway, I'm not much of a fighter," she admitted. "Or, rather, you might say I fight more with words than weapons."

After checking the tiller, Perseus fixed her with a heavy look. "You plan to fight a legendary monster with a sharp tongue? I'm fairly certain that's the worst plan I've heard since Galenos challenged me to try to pin an octopus with a pankration hold." With practiced ease he navigated the boat to the hold and drew forth two of the spears he'd packed, tossing one to Pandora.

Despite her claims of not knowing how to fight, she caught it with only the barest hint of a fumble.

"Hold it like this," he said, demonstrating the proper grip. "Good. Now look at my feet. A proper stance is ninety percent of the battle.

Yes, good. The other half of the battle is all in the thrust. Hmm. I hope your lover won't take it amiss if I show you my thrusting technique."

Pandora rolled her eyes. "How long have you been waiting to work that one in?"

He shrugged. "My dear, I'm always trying to work my thrusting in whenever I can. Not always with success, mind." He cleared his throat. "Now, watch."

For hours, he demonstrated the most basic of moves. A spear was an ideal weapon for her, after all, as the reach meant she could keep opponents well away from her, and the manoeuvres were not as multifaceted as swordplay. In which Perseus was, admittedly, less experienced himself.

Despite her claims of ignorance in the arts of war, Pandora proved a remarkably quick study, able to master almost aught he demonstrated after seeing it once or, at most, twice.

"We'll make a fair warrior out of you yet," he promised.

Something passed over her face, but whether it was pride at her accomplishments or some anxiety he couldn't see, that he could not guess.

10

HEKATE

228 Golden Age

For nigh unto two years, Hekate and Keuthos had wandered the expanses of Kumari Kandam, the southern continent. They had scoured the ancient records of timeless Nineveh, hunting any mention of forgotten Gorias. Though Nineveh—itself dating to the Time of Nyx—held records of lost cities aplenty, none had proved to be the fabled wonder Hekate sought.

They had consulted a wandering wizard, delighting in his spell-songs that reshaped the very World to the beauty of his voice, but all he knew of Gorias was a whisper and a dream, a threat of those who worshipped Flame and became one with it. A place not even the mighty dared to tread.

At last, after following fruitless trails and a hundred false leads, they had to come to the Empty Desert, where legend said even gods came to wither and die beneath the effulgent sun. Their footsteps across the unending dunes washed away in the ceaseless, biting winds, and Hekate despaired. How could anyone track a trail in a landscape that flowed like the sea? As the days and moons wore on, they sought out oases, found hints of comfort—and always one more rumour.

After yet another abortive day of searching, Keuthos pitched their tents in the comparative shelter between two great dunes. The months here had first burnt, then darkened the Hyperborean's fair skin, and though he clearly misliked the heat, he complained little of it. Keeping her gaze upon the grimoire and her translations thereof—she had taken to making notes in the margins now—Hekate surreptitiously regarded Keuthos.

"You weary of this search, I'm certain," she asked, taking care not to let him realise she watched him.

Keuthos grunted, settling upon his elbow across from her. "I can hardly allow you sole credit for such a discovery when we finally make it." His voice stumbled over the unspoken volumes between them, and it took all her will to keep from favouring him with a smile. Thus far, he had proven a true ally, yes, but she had made the mistake of trusting others already—not least, Artemis—and had learnt the hard way to rely only upon herself.

As if she failed you, Khione's sibilant voice intruded into her mind. The searing sun tended to drive the lampad into dormancy, but twilight set her stirring in Hekate's mind. A constant chatter it took an effort of will not to answer aloud.

Did it matter if Keuthos had fallen for her? Would it stop him from betraying her if the Circle had set him to do so all along? She would not put it past Morpheus or the others to have let her elude capture this long on the dim hope she might succeed, and they could then claim both the grimoire and the lost city. Ever so oft, she felt the other oneiromancer probing at her dreams, seeking a means of ingress.

She had inked their skin with tattoo wards designed to block scrying, but stopping an oneiromancer was not so simple. Each night, Hekate meditated before bed, steeling her mind against intrusion in case that night would prove one of his assaults. Morpheus had, perhaps, taught her a little too well, and thus far, she had managed to keep him out of her dreams. Still, the effort of forever guarding herself meant her sleep was less restful than she might have liked.

As for Keuthos, though he said naught of it, she could not help but notice the lingering looks he cast her way as they trekked. Maybe he had always looked at her thus, but in the dark of the Lodge of Whispers, she had been so driven by purpose—or grief?—that she had barely seen him. Now, with naught around for miles save sand and one another, it had become increasingly hard to ignore.

"We'll share whatever acclaim comes from this." As they must share in the infamy the treachery against the Circle would have engendered for them among other sorcerers. If they returned to the Elládosi world, in success or failure, would they find themselves ostracised? It would not be the first time Hekate had been left a wandering exile.

Now she did cast a glance at Keuthos. Maybe she should have trusted the Hyperborean, but she could not take that chance. Not with her mission, and certainly not with her heart. "Return to your own tent, Keuthos. I must fortify my mind for sleep, and you should do the same."

The man rose without complaint, though she fancied a hint of disappointment crossed his face. Maybe she ought to have lain with him. If his loyalty to her was born of desire for her, perhaps allowing him some chance to consummate it would secure it. She could do so without truly opening herself to him ... The thought had occurred again and again, and always she demurred, even when she could not assure herself of the reason. It had felt ... a defilement of something sacred.

You lie to yourself, Khione mocked, her wispy laugh hateful.

When Keuthos had left, she continued making notes in the grimoire. Little by little, she had eked meaning from the tome. Holding it was like holding history in her hands. A sense of profound time, stretching down through generations. At first, making her own marks in such a work of art had seemed profane, but repetition had a way of transforming the basest of crimes into the banal. Now, she scribbled away with little regard for propriety. If she solved the riddles of this codex, generations of sorcerers would owe her for the wisdom. If no one decoded it, it was useless anyway.

When fatigue crept in on her, she forced herself to set the grimoire aside. Best get to the meditations before she risked falling asleep during them.

A CONTORTION BENT *the night air, an invisible perversion so intense Hekate held up her hand to silence Demeter. The Titan sputtered in indignation a moment, but then she too, though no sorceress, must have felt the violation of nature that so blasphemed the World. A thousand scorpions crawled along Hekate's skin as she strode toward the steps leading atop the wall.*

The ground trembled before she reached them, lurching in protestation. A glance back, and Demeter had grabbed young Persephone, desperation having replaced loathing upon the Titan's face. To see that, to see her look to Hekate with such dread and the hope that Hekate, of all of them, might somehow save them from whatever impended—that more than aught else tied the noose around Hekate's throat. She couldn't breathe.

Blinking, in shaking steps, she ascended, having to steady herself as the tremors wracking the land grew more insistent. A roar of grinding rock. A convulsion of Gaia that alluded to pangs of birth, though Hekate knew, in truth, whatever lurched into reality was not born of the Earth.

Then she crested the wall and found herself clutching the rampart, wheezing weak, pathetic breaths through her nose at the panoply unfolding. The bucking, heaving of the land, as an abomination yanked itself free from Gaia's womb, grasping hands the size of horses latching onto rocks and hills, yanking a flowing, amorphous bulk out from a colossal rent splitting the hills. Hand after hand, a dozen. Two dozen. Three.

Arms bifurcated at elbows, each branch large enough to sweep away buildings, each acting as if possessed of its own fearful intellect. Arms acting as legs, dragging forth a flowing, shifting mountain. A chittering erupted, screeching over her brain, as dozens of Etheric heads formed and unformed upon a vaguely arachnid body, eyes bulbous wells of black.

And still it continued to heave itself free, a bulk that would dwarf the hills around their town. A mass of limbs and heads and unspeakable, ever shifting revolution her very soul rejected.

⁊

A PRESENCE PUSHED AGAINST HER, not so unlike when Khione had first intruded into her mind. Hekate jolted awake from the nightmare, casting off her blanket and thrashing about a moment. Her heart hammered; her palms were clammy. The assault was less graceful than Morpheus's, different in flavour.

Was someone else after them now?

She quickly draped on her peplos, then ducked from her tent and lifted the flap to her companion's. "Keuthos," she hissed.

The Hyperborean shifted in his sleep but did not waken. Dammit. Hekate crawled inside on her hands and knees, grabbed the man by his shoulder and shook him. "Keuthos, wake up. Someone has tried to penetrate my dreams." Still, the man did not rise. What in the depths of Tartarus? "Keuthos?"

"He won't wake," someone said from behind her. "I had not expected you to, either, but I suppose that's no real burden."

Casting about herself, Hekate spied Keuthos's dagger and snatched it up, before ducking outside.

A dark-haired Kimmerian man waited to greet her, far from his homeland. Hypnos had those gentle, hooded eyes that made him seem always groggy, made those who conversed with him feel placid and lethargic.

"What have you done to him?" Hekate demanded.

"Did you think Morpheus showed you every possible use of oneiromancy in the few months you trained with him?" Morpheus's other apprentice shrugged lazily, his smile coy and infuriating for being so damn disarming. "There are so many more depths you could have learnt, had you lingered with us, rather than following your perfidious route." His voice was a cat's purr, a lullaby singing her to sleep as Papa had done so very long ago.

No!

Hekate thrust her hand forward, forming up ice crystals to launch at Hypnos.

Except naught happened. No surge of cold, no swell of mist, and certainly no frozen blades flying at her opponent.

"Oh ... Even spirits can be induced into sleep, you know. Even the dead can dream, my beautiful darling." He raised one finger to his lip and pointed at her with his other hand. "Shh."

The dagger tumbled from her limp fingers the instant before Hekate collapsed to her knees in the sand. Her eyes had begun to close of their own accord, her vision dimming. She needed but a few moments of rest, then she would ...

Of a sudden, the power affecting her abated. Hekate blinked to find Hypnos convulsing. A blade had burst through his chest, incarnadine rivers streaming around it, pouring from his mouth. The blade slipped back out, and Hypnos slumped over to crash down and stain the unforgiving desert.

Behind him stood a man she did not know, black-bearded and of indeterminate origin. In one hand he grasped the blood-drunk knife. The other he held up between himself and her in a warning against violence, as if he had not, this very instant, murdered a man.

Hekate gasped, snatched up the dagger, and reached once more for Khione's power. She felt the lampad stir within her soul, but the spirit had not yet fully risen from the torpor Hypnos had induced. "Who the fuck are you?" Hekate demanded. "I mean, not that I'm not grateful ..."

Though in truth, she'd not have wanted to murder Hypnos. She had rather enjoyed some of their long conversations before the hearth in the Lodge. He had spoken in some detail of the wild nomads of Kimmeria, so much she almost felt as though she had seen them herself. He had woven tales of far-off lands and the monsters that lurked in hidden places, and always she had ended such evenings drunk and happy.

And now he was dead in the middle of nowhere.

"I am called Mithra, and you, I assume, must be Hekate."

"How do you ...?"

"I am well acquainted with Enodia, and she knew you would be here." From her own dreams? Had she sent this Mithra to save her from Hypnos? More pressingly, would Hypnos have actually slain her for what she'd done? Perhaps he would have. She had betrayed the Circle, and they would not take kindly to it … but she had dared to imagine another recourse.

She had also thought she would feel more dismay at Hypnos's loss. More than this vague disappointment. What was she becoming, that she found herself simply stepping around the corpse of a man she'd known and liked? Did it besmirch her character that she could move past murder itself just as easily?

"You saved us from him," she said, still uncertain what to make of that. All she could do was stare at the stranger. "What is it you want?"

Mithra withdrew a small cloth to clean his knife, taking his eyes off her as if certain she'd not move against him. "Oh, Enodia wants you to find that which you seek, you know. In fact, I think she knows you will find it, but *I* have seen the ruins. Perhaps a glimmer of direction would not be amiss?" His gaze flicked to her for a moment. "Some miles north of the jungles of Nysa, you'll find the Nagarahara Oasis. There is a small, fortified town there you cannot miss. Were you to trek a day and half northwest from there, buried in the sand, you might find your destiny."

Damn, but she wished Keuthos had woken. Any move she made to wake him would seem suspicious at best, though. "If you know where to find the lost city, why haven't you claimed its treasures and knowledge?"

The stranger snorted lightly. "Treasures? I have all I need from that place, sorceress. As far as knowledge, some knowledge is best shared, some guarded jealously from those who cannot abide it. You will understand, I think, one day."

"I understand you have an agenda," she said, not bothering to hide the distrust from her voice.

"Another way of saying I have goals in life," he admitted, spreading his hands in a mockery of innocence, especially considering one still held a murderous blade. "What dolts do not? But take the advice or disregard it, as it suits you, sorceress. We shall see each other again, in time."

Though part of her wanted to detain him and question him further, no pretence for doing so sprang to mind. He had possibly saved her life, offered her information she sought at no charge, and given no real offence save for the possession of an air of mystery so common to many who sought the arcana. A sorcerer perhaps, but not an enemy, so far as she could tell.

Thus, when he began to slip away into the night, she ducked back inside the tent to wake Keuthos and tell him they had a new destination.

11

PANDORA

623 Bronze Age

*D*espite the long years she'd lived here, despite having only left some few days ago, Pandora could not help but feel a profound foreignness when Perseus brought the ship into Atlantis's harbour. It was the same city, and yet not. Perhaps beholding a single location in three different ages must necessarily bemuse the mind and render the known strange.

Perhaps every paradigm shift, every change within the self, effectively altered all that had preceded it.

The last time she'd been here, sometime in the future, the island had been ripping in half, with the city itself thrown beneath the waves in the cataclysm. Centuries ago, as a child, she'd been brought here as a slave and sold to Tantalus.

Round and round, the ouroboros went, in perverse circles that had her stomach roiling, with so little desire to walk these streets again. This had not been her home in ages, literally. Her home was with Prometheus on Ogygia, and Pandora would do aught in the World to return to it.

Perseus paid the harbourmaster a fee to watch his boat, then looked to her.

She pointed up to the Evenor Mountain that dominated the heart of Atlantis, this time blessedly free of storms. "We have to head there," she said when she was sure no one would hear them. "I think the Garden lies in a valley beyond the mountain, formed by the lesser peaks around it. Grab some supplies in the harbour district, then we'll have to set out through the fields and the wilds. This is a forbidden place, Perseus, so be discreet."

"My dear, discretion is one of my three best qualities."

She was afraid to ask what the other two were. The man had a strange charm to him, and a manner that made him easy to talk to, though she had avoided revealing too much about herself. Besides the fact no one was like to believe her if she claimed to be a time traveler, she had no idea how famed Prometheus was in this age. What would Perseus even say if she asked him to rescue a Titan imprisoned by his own father centuries ago? Stranger still, Pandora could not stomach the thought of Prometheus suffering for all those centuries, so she would need to convince Perseus to go back in time with her and help her in her own age.

The weight of it all might have crushed her, save the demigod remained by her side, holding her buoyant simply through his vivacity. If they could slay this Medusa, maybe he could, in fact, brave the depths of Tartarus for her. Naught seemed to hold him down for long, and she needed that tenacity.

When he had gathered a few days' food and water, they set out from the city, passing through wide fields of wheat. Miles and miles of the golden grain, all harvested to feed the ever-increasing population of the polis. Scattered farmhouses broke the otherwise homogenous landscape, though even those grew fewer in number as they drew closer to the soaring peak of the Evenor Mountain.

As they walked, it grew to claim the horizon, until naught save the mountain remained. By evening, the flat lands had given way to foothills, and fatigue gripped her hard while Perseus kindled a small fire for them.

"Not many people come out here, though the mountain itself isn't forbidden like the valley beyond. Still, I think after tonight we may want to forgo any fires." She didn't even want to imagine what the Titans would do to mortals—even demigods—they found sneaking anywhere nigh to the source of their precious Ambrosia. The story was, the Tree of Life sprouted golden apples, and the Titans had discovered some means of brewing their draughts from that fruit. It gave them their immortality and enhanced their Pneuma.

The Ouranid League had guarded the Ambrosia jealously in the Golden Age. Since then, Zeus's possessiveness of the stuff had reached levels heretofore unknown. Anyone who dared even think of tasting it outside of his channels was flayed or worse. The madman had slaughtered the whole of the Pleiades when he thought them complicit in the propagation of Nectar, and that was a pale imitation of real Ambrosia, from all Pandora had gathered.

"I find it considerably more difficult to cook the dried fish I brought without fire," Perseus said. "I could, perhaps, try my smouldering gaze, but I don't know if that will give it quite the same taste."

Pandora folded her legs beneath herself, the spear Perseus had given her resting lightly by her side. While it served as a convenient walking stick, there was an oddness about traveling with a weapon, as if she might ever stab someone with it. But then, wasn't that exactly what Perseus had been training her for?

"What is this Medusa you've pledged yourself to kill?" she pressed, while Perseus was about placing the fish on a spit.

He didn't answer until he'd set the spit, then he leaned back on his haunches and stared at her. "All I have are the tales sailors brought to Neritum, and if you believe those, every man at sea has bedded Poseidon's granddaughter Triteia, and half of them have seen sea serpents in the depths during storms. I, of course, believe every last word that comes out of sailors' mouths, but you must judge for yourself.

"I've heard it told Medusa was mortal once, or perhaps a demigod daughter of Hephaistos, and that she incurred the wrath of Olympus and was thus cursed, transformed into some kind of snake monster whose very gaze could turn men to stone. Admittedly, I have met a few women who seemed capable of turning me hard with a mere look, and thus I know when to flee."

"You might be doing it wrong," Pandora said.

"What's that?"

"Life. How did Medusa earn the wrath of Olympus?"

Perseus grunted. "Given that I fail at life, I cannot say that my word should count for much. Should you wish to take it for what it's worth, stories vary." He cleared his throat. "A common tale is that uh ... she spurned the advances of Poseidon."

Pandora groaned. How predictable. "So, the Titan couldn't have what he wanted and made certain no other man could either."

"Well, er ... actually, in this version of the story, he pursued her into Athene's temple where she thought she'd be safe. He, ahem, well, he took her anyway, and the goddess was so disgusted at having her sacred place defiled she cursed Medusa to make sure she would never again tempt a man."

Pandora balked. "That ..." The sheer outrageousness of it, to hear that the goddess would punish a victim for what was done to her, so rankled Pandora she actually felt ill. A surge of dizziness gripped her, and she had to steady herself. "The very Olympian who sent us here?"

Perseus frowned. "It's one tale, though not otherwise consistent with most stories about Athene. Of course, most of the tales do seem to involve Athene in Medusa's plight, so who knows. Somehow, the woman seems to have offended the goddess."

"When was all this, anyway?"

A shrug, then he set to turning the spit. "Centuries back, long, long before my time."

Pandora wondered if she even had an appetite anymore. "It seems to me as though we have set out to hunt someone who rather deserves our sympathies."

"Maybe, then, don't swallow sailors' tales whole. Either way, I made an oath, Pandora. I cannot renounce it."

❧

THE GOING PROVED HARDER the next day, forcing them to wend around hills or climb increasingly steep paths as they closed in toward the mountain. By the next gloaming, they had reached the rocky slope of Evenor Mountain itself and made camp amid the scattered poplars and fig trees on the lower ridges.

She helped Perseus set out their bedrolls and immediately regretted her earlier protestations against a fire. It had seemed a good idea at the time, but somehow in the moment, the thought of lying on the ground without the warmth of flame, of eating cold fish, rankled. Though she'd have looked a fool, she found herself almost tempted to recant and tell him to kindle another fire.

Perseus, though, didn't press and handed her the very dried fish she did *not* want to eat, claiming one for himself, though without much relish.

"I think I changed my mind after all," he said, while she forced herself to eat the tasteless rations. She looked up to find him staring at her. "Maybe it is your lover I am jealous of."

Pandora hardly knew what to say to that, though he no doubt meant it as a compliment. "One day I'm sure you'll find someone who makes you feel the same. Who makes you feel you have a home."

The man laughed and waved her comment away as though it all meant naught. As usual, he was fooling no one save, perhaps, himself.

❧

THEY SKIRTED the edge of Evenor Mountain, and when they caught sight of a rough footpath running down toward the valley beyond, they gave it a wide berth for fear of encountering any Titan guards. According to Perseus, Zeus's daughter Hebe now ruled this island

and oversaw the distribution of Ambrosia—she had to assume he'd given her Atlantis after murdering the Pleiades—and Pandora had absolutely no desire to run afoul of another Olympian. Or rather, she might well have liked to see the lot of them cast into Tartarus themselves, but she had no illusions about her ability to challenge them.

Fortunately, the forest grew denser as they reached the far side of the slope, a blanket of green covering the whole of the valley. Rising from this blanket like a sheltering roof spread the boughs of the famed Tree of Life. It towered over the rest of the forest as if in challenge of the very mountain peaks, and Pandora could scarce fathom the scale of it, though she had heard legends of the colossal Tree as a child. Given that it sprouted the golden apples, she had expected an apple tree, but in truth it looked more like a hybrid of a hundred species. Or perhaps, rather, as if every breed of tree spread across the land had sprung from this one.

Perseus, for once struck speechless, gaped at the Tree before casting a wary glance back at her.

What was there to say in front of such majesty? Thus, Pandora descended into the valley herself, her sandals occasionally skidding over loose scree, forcing her to direct her gaze to her immediate vicinity rather than to continue gawking at the Tree.

Once they passed into the forest proper, the canopy concealed sight of it anyway. They plodded on for quite some time before she became fair certain she'd seen that oak tree before. "Are we headed in a straight line?"

Perseus cocked his head to the side, looking about. "I'm not an expert woodsman, though I explored as much wilderness as Neritum had to offer ... Ah, hmm. I think I hear running water. She said to find the river."

That sounded like a better plan than wandering around at random. Perseus led them and, soon enough, they reached a river that burbled along, cutting a swathe through the heart of the valley. She had to assume it ran down from one of the other mountains, as she hadn't seen it from Evenor's lower slopes. Both quiet, they trekked along the riverbank. From here, the lower canopy broke, giving them a view of the higher one created by the Tree of Life that sheltered this whole garden.

Already, the sun had begun to dip lower. Pandora did not fancy lingering in the garden after dark, but neither did it seem wise to leave without what they'd come for. Spending the night back on the slope only increased their chances of being discovered.

Perhaps Perseus thought the same, because he increased his pace, the river guiding them ever closer to the mountainous trunk. As twilight loomed closer, the banks grew mushy, as if the river demarcated a boundary of a marsh on this side of the wood. Mud sucked at her sandals as she pressed on but, though she heard the *plop* as he pulled his feet free over and over, it seemed to trouble Perseus little. Demigod strength and stamina had distinct advantages.

Of a sudden, though, he drew up short, holding out a hand behind him to stop her as well. When he looked back at her, his mouth was slightly ajar, eyes wide. She was about to ask what had disturbed him ... but she could feel it in the air. A sense of an alien presence, something momentous saturating the valley, filling it up almost as thoroughly as the Tree itself. A weight had begun to press upon her chest, a chill to creep its way up her limbs.

"We have to keep going," he whispered.

Funny, but Pandora would have given almost aught imaginable to turn back now. Something dwelt here, ancient and unknowable, vast and terrible. No doubt sensing her distress, Perseus grabbed her hand in his own and offered a firm nod. His casual foolery melted away in an instant and his face became a determined mask, strength radiating into her through his iron grip.

Wasn't he frightened? Did he not feel the heart-rending, soul-crushing dread that had settled upon them in the valley? Or did he feel it and merely push through, denying its presence, even to himself?

They continued onward, deeper into the wood, closer to the Tree and its fabled guardian, and Pandora felt fair certain it was this drakon, Ladon, whose mind brushed against hers. Or rather, it felt like a hundred minds bombarding her with searching tendrils, encircling her like stalking predators.

The blurry, blind terror of nightmare.

Her chest felt heavy, unable to draw enough breath to sustain herself. Her hand was clammy in Perseus's, and he must have felt it, but he gave no indication of noticing. Now, the *plop* of their sandals sounded like clarions announcing their presence in the garden. Not even the rumble of the river could smother such sounds. They had intruded where they did not belong, and something was watching them.

Though she could not make out aught beyond the tree line across the river, she felt again and again the weight of an eldritch gaze upon her, peering through her flesh and into her soul. A profound violation that threatened to crush her. Unshed tears turned her vision watery, and she wanted to curl into a ball and beg for this all to go away. Perseus remained a rock, holding her up. Maybe, without him, she'd have broken already. Have crumbled into a heap, unable to move forward or backward, trapped forever in this descending terror.

Then, when next she looked, she caught sight of slithering saurian bulks behind the trees. Not a single mighty serpent, but many, writhing overtop one another before vanishing in the tenebrous depths of the wood.

Perseus squeezed her hand, guiding her onward. The river twisted around a bend, and rising from the midst of that curve jutted a leaning stone. Someone had gouged the edges to resemble feathers and carved the highest point into the likeness of an owl's head.

They didn't have to cross the river. They didn't have to pass into the same space as the monumental serpents. Were they spawn of Ladon or aspects of the drakon? She didn't know, and for once, Pandora wasn't sure she even wanted the knowledge. Perhaps some mysteries were so crushing that to know them was to be consumed by them.

With a final squeeze, Perseus released her hand and crept forward, toward the owl rock. Pandora dropped into a crouch and watched him as he sifted through the dirt. It looked drier up there, elevated above the marshy area she found herself in, so maybe whatever Athene had hidden there yet remained despite the passing of centuries.

Had the goddess buried these weapons there knowing they would come here? Was that Oracular insight—or merely a convenient hiding spot where no one would look, and she could keep buried her treasures until she had need of them? Moreover, did Athene now help them out of some guilt for the curse she'd laid upon Medusa?

A great number of questions plagued Pandora, and occupying herself with them kept her from dwelling upon whatever draconic abominations lurked between her and the Tree. She had a feeling that, if they swam that river, serpentine maws would converge upon them as though they were rats fallen into a nest of snakes. The mental image had her quivering once more, even as Perseus rose, bearing a wool-wrapt bundle.

The demigod cast a furtive glance over his shoulder, no doubt pondering the same umbral horrors in the woods, then scrambled over to her.

"What is it?" she asked.

He peeled back the wool to reveal a round shield and a xiphos, both forged from some slate-coloured metal she had to assume was stronger than bronze. Wavelike patterns coloured the sword, beautiful and hypnotic. The shield had clearly once been polished to a mirror sheen but now was dimmed by dust and smudges.

"I imagine this is what we needed," he said.

"What, you don't think some other Olympian hid Otherworldly weapons beneath an owl-shaped rock in sight of the Tree of Life?"

Perseus scratched his chin as if considering it. "I think ... we should leave."

❧

By tacit agreement, they pressed on even in the dead of night, though the double canopy made wending their way through the wood nigh impossible. Still, neither of them much wanted to linger in the valley, and neither seemed willing to speak of the perverse, encircling will they felt pressing in upon them.

Following the river downstream eventually led them back into the mountains, and Pandora let loose a weary sigh before collapsing on the ground, not even bothering with setting her bedroll. Perseus plopped down beside her, rested his head upon his satchel, and was snoring in moments.

In her dreams, darkness spread around her, an enormity from outside of time slithering unseen, ever closer. Perhaps she wept in her sleep, for she started awake when Perseus's hand clutched her own.

Pandora jerked away from the contact, then regretted the reaction. He'd only been trying to help, of course. But there were few people in the World whose unexpected touch she would welcome.

Maybe she should apologise?

Before she could decide, a form dropped from the tree not five feet from them. In the moonlight, she couldn't make out features. The figure stood, revealing Titan height and build, and Pandora's heart froze. They had found them.

Her mind whirred, trying to think up any remotely plausible excuse as to why Men would have business in these mountains.

Before she could even open her mouth, the Titan strode forward, even as Perseus scrambled to his knees.

"Enough of that, little brother," the Titan said. Brother? "I am Hermes. My sister sent me to observe and see if you survived your foray into the Garden."

Hermes, Zeus's son by the Pleiad Maia, which made the Olympian a half-brother to Perseus. Despite his words, Perseus remained kneeling. Perhaps that was the source of the smirk on the Titan's face.

"I survived," Perseus said, his usual demeanour now subdued.

"Barely, it would seem. Are you so certain you want the Grey-eyed One for a patron, demigod? You could do better than my sister." So Athene had asked him to watch over them—was she unable to do so herself here?—but he was trying to usurp her hold on him anyway. No loyalty among the Olympians, then.

Perseus hesitated, clearly afraid to speak one way or the other. "I have already pledged my trust to her and cannot revoke it."

Hermes snorted, his smirk not faltering. He glanced in Pandora's direction. "I don't know why you're here, but stay away from Zeus's children." With that dismissal, he took off running, a gust of wind following in his wake, tugging at her clothes. Hermes moved so quickly he vanished into the darkness in an instant.

Had he recognised her from somewhere? For a moment, when he'd looked upon her, she thought she'd seen such on his face. Had he been there, on Olympus, when Zeus imprisoned Prometheus?

When she looked to Perseus, he was rubbing his hands together, shoulders taut. No man desired to be torn between two Olympians. That was a good way to get ripped in half.

12

HEKATE

228 Golden Age

*A*s Mithra had promised, they found the Nagarahara Oasis a few days north of the edge of the jungle realm of Nysa. Beside a modest, palm-encircled watering hole had grown up a sandstone fortress, shimmering in the late afternoon sun. The gate stood open during the day, though she imagined they closed it every twilight to avoid risking anything wandering in from the desert.

After so long trekking the sands, she and Keuthos resembled dust-covered shambles more than people, and the gate guard turned up his nose at them but did not bar their passage. A few obols bought them a chance to wash and straw mats to sleep on by the hearth of the only guest house in the town.

Sitting in the corner, bowl cupped between her hands, Hekate sipped at watery soup that had, perhaps, once looked at a carrot in envy. No civilised person would have called this good—few would have even termed it food, in the strictest sense—but the heat alone was welcome at the moment. Back against the wall, Keuthos slid down to rest beside her. The Hyperborean groaned in contentment, probably relieved to be off his feet, then offered her a cup of beer.

Which, as it turned out, was about as strong as the soup.

"In the morn, we set out to find it," Hekate said, not mentioning the place by name. This close, locals would have heard legends of the lost city. Nor did she want to make it any easier for the Circle to track them. By now, they would have learnt what had befallen Hypnos. Now, she had not only stolen from them—and blinded Deino—she had murdered a member of the Inner Circle.

Retribution was coming for them, and she had no desire to speed it along.

"Hekate ..." Keuthos began. "If they find us ..." Clearly, his mind followed the same track as hers. "I want you to know, I—"

"We're going to find it," she interrupted before he could say something they might regret. "Once we do, once I unlock the power of this grimoire, not even Morpheus or Isis would wish to challenge me."

Keuthos grunted, not seeming convinced. But she would show him. She would find a way to make this all worth it.

MAYBE, if a sandstorm had not forced them to take shelter in a valley, they might have overlooked the half-buried ruins lying within. Maybe, had the stinging winds not uncovered the tip of a stone spire, they'd have wasted days or longer doubling back on themselves to find this place. As it was, Hekate and Keuthos paced about the valley, peering down at the protruding vestiges of the upper-most reaches of the buried city.

From what she could glean, they looked at a series of towers, each carved from glinting golden stone, bedecked with graceful arches and buttresses, carved with such delicate flourishes she imagined it must have taken a thousand masters a thousand lifetimes to create such a work. The jutting spires resembled thin mountains, or perhaps a forest of trees, with the inset recessions not so different from bark.

Some of those towers had windows through which rivers of sand had found ingress into the interior city. She and Keuthos had dug away at one, enough to see they'd find no easy way through from there. Not with mountains of sand they'd have to excavate one handful at a time.

"I have to clear more of the city itself," she finally said when the two of them stood staring at the ruins, plastered in sweat and grime.

"Should I fetch a shovel at the oasis?" Keuthos asked. "A bucket might help too."

"I have to direct the winds," Hekate answered, not deigning to acknowledge his foolery.

Keuthos, however, grabbed her biceps and spun her to face him. "You want to summon a Storm spirit? Out here?" He waved his other hand to indicate the expanse of dunes. "How are you going to form a proper summoning circle in *sand*? One that would survive the winds you intend to conjure?"

She shook her head. "I'm not." Without the circle to ward her and bulwark her will, she would find herself forced to reckon directly with the Storm spirit—the harpy—but what choice remained to her? She would not turn back now.

Besides, she had seen this in her dreams, had she not? The sense of prescient fulfilment settled upon her like a physical weight.

"You will get yourself possessed like that," Keuthos objected. "You call it across the Veil without precautions, and it will ride you like a mule. It will wear your face as it traipses around Kumari Kandam sating its Otherworldly lusts and perverse desires. It will delight in revenging itself upon you for the hubris of trying to master it." He meant it would come after those she cared about. It would hurt him.

"I won't allow that to happen, Keuthos. I'm strong enough to call it for this one service without letting it claim me."

The man's dubiousness was writ plain across his face, but he snapped his mouth shut, having seen naught remained to be said.

Waiting for nightfall, she settled herself to meditate and fortify her will against what she knew must come. The secrets of the grimoire, those she had uncovered thus far, would help her in this, but Keuthos was right about one thing. The Circle of Goetic

Mysteries considered what she intended utter madness and would probably have executed any sorcerer they learnt of following such imprudent paths. For how few could ever hope to vie with the Otherworldly will of a spirit?

She knew it for hubris, yes, but she could not turn back. Not having come this far.

Thus, when the moon rose, she rose as well, grimoire in hand. To draw the spirit's attention, she dug its glyph in the sand, a trough that would serve to bring it closer though offer no assistance in commanding it. Then, rising and taking a few steadying breaths, she began the incantation to evoke a Storm spirit.

Supernal words once more reverberated inside her mind and sent her soul shuddering in a blurring of dread and ecstasy. The world-rending power of it rushed through her, even as she embraced the Sight. Color and warmth bled from the world, and she beheld the desolate shadowscape of the Penumbra. Here, nether winds already whistled about her, but they failed to stir the sands of the Mortal Realm.

At first. Then, a whisk set the desert twisting in a dozen whorls. The howling intensified, reaching into both Realms. In the Etheric sky, iridescent lightning crackled overhead, offering hints of colour in the otherwise blue-green Penumbra. The winds became a gale, whipping the desert into a frenzy that spun about her like a maelstrom. The sands lacerated her exposed arms and legs, but Hekate forced herself to ignore the pain—she could not afford to direct Pneuma to suppress it—to continue her incantation.

The spirit drew nigh, and she could not falter now. It came, plunging through the firmament, feathers coruscating with lightning as it plummeted to crash before her, an avian mockery of a woman. The harpy landed in a crouch, taloned feet digging rivets in the sand as it slowly rose, head cocked too far to the side while its onyx eyes remained locked upon Hekate's face and soul. Blood dripped from rubescent wings as the spirit spread them overhead.

"Summon the winds," Hekate commanded in Supernal. "Summon the winds to clear away the sands burying Gorias."

The harpy cackled, the sound like knives in the brain, one of its great talons taking a menacing step forward. "I shall flense the flesh from your bones with a single grain of sand, arrogant mortal." Its voice was an eagle's cry. "You shall spend the next century watching your life drain even as your mind is swept away in a typhoon of agony."

Dimly, Hekate wondered if Keuthos had embraced the Sight and could see or hear aught save swirling winds and her Supernal words. The Hyperborean was not as strong with such abilities as herself. Almost no one was.

"Summon. The. Winds." Hekate commanded. "Free Gorias from its prison within the Earth, and I will release you."

The harpy cackled again, the blades of its laughter stretching from beyond Hekate's mind and into her soul. A monstrous alien will sought to bleed her dry of her essence, and it took all she had to remain in place, teeth gritted against the mental assault. Without warning, the harpy lunged forward, a wing swiped across Hekate. Razor-sharp feathers gouged her face and arms and chest, shredding her peplos and sending her screaming, tumbling over backward.

The moment she fell, the harpy was atop her, those taloned feet pinning her thighs, digging into her flesh like lances of flame. The harpy leered at her, leaning closer, opening a maw that seemed some profane amalgam of beak and tooth-lined jaws.

Instinct screamed at Hekate to hurl ice at the spirit, but drawing Khione's power would deplete her Pneuma and leave her even closer to possession.

"Summon the winds," she shrieked, focusing all her effort not on escaping the physical clutches of the entity, but upon its will. "Summon them, wretch!"

And the harpy faltered against her mental assault. In evoking it, she had built a connection between them, a bridge that flowed both ways. But could she overmaster the will of such a creature with no wards, no invoked spirits in a self-reinforcing circle? No, Keuthos had been right, and she had damned herself.

The harpy remained frozen in indecision, perhaps unable to close in and consume her, but too strong for her to command it. They would find themselves trapped thus until fatigue weakened her, and then ... all Keuthos had predicted would come to pass.

"You would waken the hateful stones of Gorias once more," the harpy rasped. "You cannot fathom the war that sundered the world between these cities. You pathetic, mortal worms have forgotten the deeds of your forebears. The lengths to which they went to bury this past ..." The harpy snickered, even as a seed of doubt crept inside Hekate. Did this spirit know the lost history of Dark Faerie, or did it merely taunt her ignorance without possessing the whole truth itself?

Maybe it did not matter. Whatever mistakes Man made so long ago, she needed the power buried here. She needed answers about the very secrets the harpy mocked. She needed Truth, and one way or another, the harpy could provide it.

"Serve me now," she gasped, "and I will freely offer Pneuma in return."

The harpy licked at its beak with a distended purple tongue. "I shall have your Pneuma and a tithe of your soul in the process."

"No!" Keuthos shrieked, clearly having heard it after all.

What was a soul, really? "Take it," Hekate answered before her companion could interfere.

The harpy's mouth closed over Hekate's own in a mockery of a kiss. A rough, violating tongue probed at her teeth and gums before scraping over the roof of her mouth, making her gag. Then the harpy began to inhale, the sucking feeling apt to yank Hekate's stomach out through her oesophagus. No, she realised as the horror of it drowned out even the discomfort, not her stomach. Some vital, immeasurable part of her was wrenched loose.

A thousand precious memories flitted through her mind and lost their substance, the heart of them turned to vapour and dust, devoured by the ravenous hunger of the creature atop her. Ephemeral thoughts vanished even as they tried to form.

Convulsions of defilement seized her body and sent her thrashing, but even those grew weak as bits of her Pneuma drained away.

The harpy gorged itself such that Hekate only half noticed when the typhoon winds turned themselves upon the buried city.

Much as spirits lied, they did not break their word.

Still, as the harpy took flight, Hekate collapsed, too drained to even lift her head. The life of her had been sucked out, and it would take days and more of rest and meditation to begin to replenish the Pneuma she'd lost.

Dazed, she half felt Keuthos heft her in his arms and blinked as she watched the swirling sands being hurled aside as centuries and millennia melted away to reveal the unfathomable stone city so long buried. Like a coral reef, it stretched, and what she had taken for separate towers were in fact connected by bridges, as if the whole of the colossal city were a single structure, each tower a tendril of flame dancing in the air.

"You have paid too high a price for this," Keuthos said, his voice distant, almost inaudible over the roaring winds.

There was no price too high for the knowledge she sought.

IN THE GREAT stone halls of Gorias, staring at the vaulted ceiling supported by intersecting buttresses, Hekate bucked beneath Keuthos's thrusting hips. Though she could not remember making the decision to lay with him—couldn't remember much at all—it felt right, like something she had denied herself too long. For the life of her, she couldn't imagine why they had not done this sooner.

Gaia, but she had needed someone.

She moaned beneath him.

His hands closed around her throat and squeezed. Hekate's eyes popped open, wheezing, struggling to tell him she had no desire for this sort of thing ...

"This is what you dream about, apprentice?" Morpheus asked, continuing to thrust inside her. "I cannot say I mind such an invitation."

Hekate could neither move nor breathe, all her strength gone from spent Pneuma. Shadows closed in around her.

"Where are you?" Morpheus purred in her ear, rhythm increasing. "Where is this strange place, Hekate?" His hands eased off her throat and she drew in a rasping breath, air scorching her throat. "Tell me," he said, his grip switching to her shoulder.

Hekate opened her mouth as if to speak but willed herself into wakefulness instead. Perhaps Morpheus had not expected her still strong enough to even try, for she felt her mind slip through his grasp and lurched awake with a gasp.

They indeed lay within the same stone hall, her rasping breaths echoing off the cavernous ceiling. Hekate glanced about but saw no sign of Morpheus. The Hyperborean slept beside her, fully clad and having clearly not shared the intimate moment with her she'd thought. Numerous lacerations marred her flesh, the worst of which Keuthos had apparently wrapt and packed with poultices. Everything hurt, and she barely had the strength to sit up.

Tremors shot through her, and she hugged herself. She wanted to retch, but her stomach remained painfully empty.

Fuck.

Hekate rubbed her face, surprised to see no tears had wet her cheeks.

Fuck.

Just trembling rage and despair. Why couldn't she weep? What was wrong with her, that she could endure the ravages of the harpy and the violation of her dreams and not ...

A tithe of your soul ...

Fresh shudders claimed her. What was she becoming?

And beyond that, how much had Morpheus gleaned? The truth was, she was damn lucky to have slipped his grasp. An oneiromancer that powerful could have locked her in the dream until he had peeled her mind apart piece by piece. Only his having thought her broken and helpless had given her the chance to escape.

She had fallen asleep without fortifying her mind against intrusion, and she could not afford to repeat that mistake. Not ever.

§

So many of these empty halls centred around cyclopean fire pits, such that Hekate wondered, in exploring the ruins with Keuthos, if its inhabitants had worshipped flame. What must this place have looked like before its fall, thick with a population that may or may not have been human?

"I find myself coming to believe the rumours these cities might be older even than the Time of Nyx," Keuthos said.

She had not told him of her dream, neither about him nor about Morpheus slipping into it and stealing his place. How could she share such a thing?

She could not say it, could not even look at him now, without the reminder. And he had begun to sense the rising distance between them. But some gulfs were unbridgeable.

"There's so much here for us to explore," she said instead. "It will take years."

"Hmm." The Hyperborean nodded. "Well, perhaps splitting up will make it faster."

"Perhaps."

But when he left, when she found her sandals echoing off lonely halls without any company, she was left to ask herself the same question over and over. What was she becoming?

So many of her childhood memories had faded now, blurred, with missing pieces. But one came back to her. A warning, Papa's voice ringing in her head: *"You must turn back from the path you have set yourself upon. The Art has broken entire civilisations. It has rendered death on a scale you cannot conceive, blanketing the land in night. I beseech you to give over any further pursuit of this."*

What was she becoming?

13

KIRKE

1587 Silver Age

Father's summons, when it came, carried with it the usual connotations of a demand and the absolute certainty of obedience. As Kirke made her way through his golden halls, her heart galloped ahead of her, running wild with the thought of him having found out the truth of her alchemical pursuits. Always, always that fear lurked around every bend. What if someone broke into her home and spied the lab? What if someone managed to trail her through the shadows when she sold her batches, though she always concealed her face with her himation.

What if, what if, what if ...

"Aeëtes and that Nymph of his shall wed in a fortnight," Father declared when Kirke approached his throne, though, of course, she already knew that. Her little brother had managed to secure his marriage a month after Pasiphaë's, though Aeëtes's would never prove quite so grand an affair.

Kirke inclined her head. Where was her father going with this?

The Titan drummed his fingers upon his armrest. "You had something to do with it, yes?"

"Oh." Was that bad? "There was that. My little brother came to me at the party, all, 'you have to help me,' and I mean, who was I to refuse? So, yeah. I may have whispered in a few ears." Idyia's, rather. "An ear. It would have been weird if I had to say the same thing in both of her ears. Yeah."

Her father rolled his eyes. "The Nymph descends from Koios."

It took a moment to even realise what he was on about. "You mean from Phoebe. She's a Phoebid. The genos is named after her ..." Kirke trailed off when her father's visage made plain what he thought of her correcting him. Even if it was with the obvious.

"She's not a Phoebid." Oh? "*Koios* founded the city of Kolchis in his years apart from Phoebe following the Ambrosial War, and during that time he had a lover. The girl comes from that line, which means she's heir to the throne of Kolchis, which yet remains unclaimed."

Kirke opened her mouth to point out the throne was unclaimed because Kolchis was now run by a Senate, the people having ousted their last king a decade ago. Given how Father had reacted to her last bit of insight—which turned out wrong, but whatever—she decided to keep it to herself. "Sure ..." she said instead.

Maybe if she went to grab some wine, by the time she got back, he'd have gotten to the part where this had something to do with her.

"Through his new wife, your brother can thus claim the throne of Kolchis."

"Yeah, that will go over well. 'Excuse me, Senators, but we're going to have to ask you to leave.'" Kirke chortled, then realised, based on the darkening of Father's face, she maybe should have kept that to herself too. "Ahem."

"I know you helped Athene secure a throne for her bastard demigod son in Kronion."

"It's Athenai now ..."

"*Kirke*," Father growled, and she winced, deciding not to mention that whole affair had not, in fact, ended so well for her. "You are to ensure your brother's ascension to Kolchis's throne, bringing it into the fold of our empire." All for the glory of Helion, huh? Hyperion forbid he ask her to do something for Aeëtes's benefit.

"Right. Sure, I will ... do ... that. Uh, huh." She hoped her smile didn't reveal the bilious turning of her stomach.

A FORTNIGHT after the couple were wed, Kirke found herself aboard a trireme bound for the Axeinos Sea and the nigh-mythical polis of Kolchis. Father had granted Aeëtes the crew of the ship, enough men-at-arms to protect him, though certainly not enough to overthrow a city.

Ixion led the warriors, and even now, he clung to Kirke's brother like a remora. The man approached his duty to protect the prince with such fervour Kirke could only assume Ixion was the one wiping Aeëtes's arse when the time came, and perhaps even sitting in the couple's bed at night, offering helpful guidance.

The guard captain saw her grinning at him as she passed toward her brother's cabin, and he glowered, his expression growing darker still when she favoured him with a wink. Discomfiting the self-serious offered its own small rewards.

When she entered, Idyia lay reclining on the divan, Aeëtes kneeling beside her, stroking her hand, his expression wobbling between excitement and disbelief. "We're to have a child!" the man blurted.

Huh. "Well, that was fast," Kirke said. "I mean the pregnancy, not the conception. I mean to say, not that you were fast, separately. Just ... uh, fast together. Mutual ... quickness." She cleared her throat, her own flush responding as Aeëtes looked away, blushing. "So, congratulations."

"Thank you," Idyia answered, the other Nymph's smile so sweet maybe she meant to offer gratitude to Kirke for having arranged the wedding in the first place.

Strange, despite her long life, Kirke couldn't recall too many instances of having done real good in the world. When was the last time someone had thanked her for aught she had done?

On leaving the cabin, she offered Ixion another wink, this one filled with a touch of lightness.

Though accustomed to long voyages by ship, Kirke could not say she much *enjoyed* them, and here in the Axeinos Sea, the waters seemed darker than those of the Thalassa, more like to conceal benthic terrors in their fathomless depths. From a porthole in Aeëtes's cabin, she watched the slap of murky waves against the hull, certain an implied threat lurked behind each breaking of the water.

Or perhaps it was the knowledge of their intent, with Kolchis drawing nigh. The deposed king, as it turned out, had been Idyia's uncle. He and her parents had all perished, though loyalists had smuggled her out of the polis during the coup.

Though the girl wore a brave face, Kirke could see the roil of emotion behind her eyes. The dread at returning mingling with the desire she feared to acknowledge to reclaim her due. Had Father pushed her toward this path? Kirke felt certain he had. And now Idyia could well see the time to demure had long passed.

Which meant Kirke got to watch the rise and fall of her resolve, though she had no real words of comfort to offer the girl. Any of them—all of them—might well find themselves meeting the same fate as Idyia's kin for this. And Kirke could not shake the feeling that behind the ambition lay not the benefit of the couple, but that of her father, with Aeëtes's fortunes an ancillary concern at best, and Idyia's not even that.

"We cannot enter the city openly," Kirke said, glancing back at the couple. The pair of them sat upon the divan, hands clasped, while Ixion leaned against the cabin door, affecting boredom Kirke doubted he felt. "We must conceal our identities until we have in place a plan to overthrow the Senate."

"We kill them," Aeëtes said with a shrug. "Break into their homes and drive them off, the way they did Idyia's family."

"Sure, and when the populace finds out, we get to see what that looks like firsthand. Yeah, brother, I don't really think these Senators ousted the royal family without the support of a lot of soldiers and a fair portion of the common folk. We have no allies here and not half enough men to go in there and set the pair of you up as tyrants. You know, if you even wanted that sort of thing." She fixed a hard stare on her little brother. "If you want to be king for longer than it takes to eat supper, you and Idyia need to come in as saviours, protecting Kolchis from a threat the mortal Senators cannot face."

Ironic, given how much effort Kirke had put into perfecting Nectar to advance the cause of Man, that now her plans hinged upon showing Man inferior. But Father had given her little choice, and challenging his orders would avail her little.

Kirke glanced back at the onyx depths encompassing them. Beneath them might lurk serpents vast enough to encircle the ship. Whales that could capsize them on a whim or even by accident. Other colossal spawn of Echidna, squirming on the shrouded ocean floor. Beasts of which even she, an immortal daughter of Titans, might feel an innominate dread.

"We need something … monstrous."

14

PANDORA

624 Bronze Age

When Athene had come to them on Neritum, she had mentioned that only the Graeae could tell them where to find Medusa. Pandora remained somewhat dubious that Athene herself did not know the location of the woman she had cursed or could not have found that location more easily than sending them to hunt for these other beings first.

Perseus, though, had insisted whatever Athene did, she did with reason. Perhaps he sought to convince himself as much as her of his faith in the goddess. Pandora, though, suspected that Athene's reason, if she was not simply amusing herself at his expense, might have to do with fulfilling Oracular visions. Circular prophecies she carried out simply because she had seen them unfold a certain way, and thus she sought to fulfil them that way, in much the same vein as Prometheus upholding the loops in time the Box had created. As Pandora herself would one day do, she supposed.

Were, then, all Oracles trapped by the ouroboros? All chasing their own tails, creating their self-fulfilling prophecies?

Either way, for months she and Perseus had sought after these Graeae, chasing rumours around the Thalassa. Stories came to them of ancient sorceresses, blinded by their hubris, turned feral, become like evil spirits haunting the wilds of Phoenikia. Then came the tale of the broken Lodge of Whispers, a sorcerous cult that had once lurked in the fringes of Byblos.

A deep sense of malaise settled upon her as Perseus tied their boat in the harbour of the Phoenikian city-state. Pandora had never thought to return to Phoenikia. Oh, as a child, she had dreamt of it oft enough, but such dreams had withered and died with each rutting thrust Tantalus made while holding her down. She had buried any such desire when she resolved to build her life as a hetaira and had nigh forgotten these thoughts entirely when she made a home with Prometheus.

But Byblos, in her day, had been ruled by Pandora's favourite uncle Phoenix, along with his wife. Pandora had been so little ... Kassiopeia, that was her name. Kassiopeia's family had held Byblos for long before that, but Phoenix had married her and united the two great city-states of Phoenikia in peace.

Perseus exchanged a few words with a dockhand, then looked to her. "It seems one must pay tribute to Sirsir in order to moor in Byblos these days."

Sirsir? Here? Pandora had last seen the mer thousands of years ago, in the Golden Age. Was there a chance he would recognise her after all this time? Frowning, she pulled her himation over her hair to shadow her face, though she dared hope anyone would think it a mere hood against the bright sun and blazing heat of Phoenikia.

"The boy said this Sirsir is an agent of Poseidon who has worked out some sort of trade arrangement with King Kepheus."

"He's a mer," Pandora said. And apparently Phoenikian domination of these waters was slipping if Poseidon had laid claim enough to demand tribute from all who came here. Back in her own age, the locals had worshipped another mer, Dagon. Had Poseidon usurped his place? Were they allies now?

Perseus cast a wary glance at her, suddenly more on edge for hearing he would deal with a benthic deity rather than a mortal man. He led her to where the dockhand had indicated, and they descended a wood staircase to a lower pier. Across from this, in the shade of the main dock, a mer sat in the shallows. Hints of gills flapped beneath his hair, and when he looked at them, his eyes occasionally nictitated. He was *not,* however, the same mer who had saved her from the sea by Ogygia in the Golden Age.

Perhaps this one was named for the ancient one? Sadly, there were far too many unknowns about the denizens of Pontus. Either way, Pandora kept her face shadowed and held back while Perseus tossed a few drachmae to the mer. "We're on dock B."

The creature flashed sharpened teeth and a too-wide smile but otherwise said naught.

Perseus glanced back at Pandora, who nodded, and they both climbed back to the upper level, all too eager to be out of the mer's sight.

"As a fisherman's son," he said when they were well away, "I had not thought I was like to have to pay the fish."

"I'd count myself fortunate the price was in drachmae and not something of greater value."

"You seem to underestimate just how much people tend to value drachmae."

Pandora frowned. "There are higher prices."

Though Pandora had spent her earliest years in Tyros, not so many miles south of here, Phoenix had never gotten the chance to bring her to see Byblos, and Pandora found herself somewhat revelling in the sights. It was a place she had heard a hundred tales of as a child, and now, walking these streets, a faint dreamlike wonder had replaced her earlier disquiet on returning to Phoenikia.

Wandering the city, they came to the great spring Phoenix had once told her about. It lay within a crater some twenty feet below street level, accessible by a winding stair cut into the perimeter. Her uncle had said that, according to legend, the spring had no bottom at all. Anyone who ever tried to reach it had given over and been forced to swim back up, and a few had even drowned trying to prove themselves.

Nigh to the spring, Perseus found them a lodging house and within they took a hot meal of lamb and olives, washing it down with spiced wine. It had been a while since Pandora had enjoyed a Phoenikian vintage, and she savoured it, peering around the crowd in the dining hall. Many were locals, but she spotted the deep wheatish skin tones of Nusantarans, too, and others, perhaps out of Kumari Kandam. Others had a touch fairer skin and mostlike hailed from Elládos or Phlegra. So many people, all taking a reprieve from the midday heat.

A serving girl refilled Perseus's cup, then Pandora's as well, and she found tension unfurling from her shoulders like streams of water in the rain. She picked at the lamb, noting Perseus had already devoured his meal as if a starving man.

"What?" he said, noticing her regard. "Talking to fish gods is stressful. Poseidon alone knows how many of the man's kin I might have caught in my nets."

"Perhaps best if Poseidon does *not* know."

Perseus raised his cup in acknowledgment of her point. "Either way, we should be about finding this Lodge of Whispers."

Perhaps he spoke incautiously, because Pandora could have sworn the conversations nigh to them at once dwindled. She had a feeling that, despite everyone deliberately not looking in their direction, a dozen eyes now watched them.

Grimacing, she waved a dismissive hand at Perseus.

"Yes, hello," he said. "We've met, you know."

"Leave it," she whispered under her breath. "We'll talk later."

The demigod shrugged, nonchalant, downed the last of his wine, and rose. "If you'll excuse me, I've a pressing appointment. Ah, insofar as my bladder is being pressed, at least."

Pandora rolled her eyes then scanned the room. Those adjacent to their table continued to point their gazes anywhere but at her. All save a Nusantaran man sipping wine alone by the hearth, whose eyes met hers for an instant.

After one more swig of wine for courage, Pandora pushed up from her table and sauntered over to the man, settling down across from him. "Good afternoon," she said in his own language.

The Nusantaran started. "You speak my tongue?"

"Some." She was a bit out of practice, but she had a gift for languages and trusted it to come back to her. "They are afraid."

"Some fools endanger only themselves, and we laugh at them. Other fools endanger us all, and it is not so amusing."

Pandora tapped her lip. "The Lodge of Whispers somehow poses a danger to all Byblos?"

"That, I cannot say, Elládosi."

"I'm Phoenikian," she interrupted.

"Then shouldn't you know the answer?"

Yes, and why had she felt the need to assert her identity thus? "I've been long away, and I wasn't from Byblos, regardless."

The Nusantaran looked about but seemed satisfied no locals here spoke his tongue. "I know only the tales told in port, most oft late at night, and after sailors have had too much wine." As if to prove his point, he took a long draught of his own cup before clattering the empty vessel back on the table and looking pointedly at it.

Pandora motioned for the serving girl to fill it.

When she left, the Nusantaran sailor continued. "As I have heard it, thousands of years ago, when the World had first emerged from a time of eternal night, men and women sought to harness the Dark whence we came. They delved into secrets no man ought to know and sang songs that shook the bounds of the heavens, leaving reality bleeding from the echoes. They gathered in the shadows and shared profane rituals in their lust for power and forbidden knowledge.

"Two of these sorcerers founded a lodge for others of their kind, naming it the Circle of Goetic Mysteries. Byblos was there, even before night broke, or so the tale goes, and its dead extend for untold generations, bloodlines tracing into primeval darkness. At the fringes of the inner city lies the sprawling necropolis where the innumerable fallen lie interred. And within the necropolis, within an ancient cave temple at its heart, the Circle built their infamous Lodge of Whispers.

"Would-be sorcerers came to them, creeping out of the shadows of the World, fair salivating for the very lore that would damn them. No one knows for certain just how many they were, but as I heard the tale, they accepted nine masters and nine apprentices. For centuries, they delved into the dark of the Art, seeking the wisdom of spirits and ghosts, of gods and demons. One can only assume that delving was the very thing that destroyed them.

"Long before the Titanomachy, some nameless obscenity crawled its way into their Lodge and rent the sorcerers asunder. Some say it ate them whole, and that was the end of it. Some say it dragged the tattered remnants of their souls screaming down into the shadows of the Underworld. What is known by the people of this city is a simple, awful truth. Whatever fell upon them, something of it survived, enduring within the vestiges of the Circle itself. It warped and blinded the sorceresses, turning them into pitiable wretches. They call them the Graeae, the 'Grey Ones,' for they have gone pallid, withered by time but unable to die. Forces we cannot know or comprehend entomb them within their former refuge, but sometimes, in the darkest night, the entrance cracks open, and one hears their lamentations ringing through the necropolis."

As the Nusantaran finished his story, Perseus returned, bearing two more cups of wine. Hardly looking at him, Pandora took the cup. Her hand shook, sloshing crimson liquid about, and she could do naught save stare at it.

The sailor noted her distress, and a wicked grin spread across his face. "Well, men in their cups like to talk. But then, who truly knows what happens inside cave temples where none have dared venture in millennia? None who returned at least."

"It sounds rather like you discovered something," Perseus said.

Pandora took her cup in both hands and chugged it. This all meant naught. The horror of the tale paled compared to what they would face to brave Tartarus. It meant naught.

Or so she kept telling herself, all the way to their private rooms as she worked up the nerve to relay the tale to Perseus.

❧

"IF THE TALE HOLDS TRUE," Perseus said, lamp out before him as he wended between the grave markers in the necropolis, "we may only be able to access the Lodge of Whispers at night."

Perhaps he said it to reassure himself they were not mad for venturing here after sunset, because they had already argued this point well beyond Pandora's liking. In truth, she misliked everything about this adventure and had to ask herself once more if Athene had arranged all this for her half-brother as some sort of amusement for the gods. True, perhaps it was more test than entertainment and she wanted something more of Perseus, but the Olympians so oft seemed fickle that Pandora wasn't sure she'd have credited any of them with such grand designs.

Of course, she had heard of the Circle of Goetic Mysteries before. Some of their records had found their way into Prometheus's library in his Aviary, and it was those very treatises she had relied upon when trying to understand the nature of Tartarus. Now, she knew those same studies that had allowed them to write the treatises may also have led to their demise.

The Art. Such a simple, unassuming name for practices that bent the laws of reality and shredded the cosmos. As if sorcery and other arcane disciplines had aught in common with painting or music.

Spear in hand, she stuck close to Perseus as he navigated the necropolis.

"I don't think there's much to fear," he said. "The horrifying parts lie *within* the Lodge, not out here."

"It's good you're here to let me know when to panic. I'd hate to miss my chance."

"Ah, my dear, even if you did, I can almost certainly promise you more opportunities in the future."

The lamp failed to illuminate more than a few feet in any direction, causing the looming shadows to dance and flit about her periphery. Despite the oppressive necropolis, Pandora managed to keep her breathing steady. Maybe that was thanks to Perseus, too. The steady way he scanned the region, the coiling and uncoiling of his muscles, his graceful walk—all bespoke a predator at her side. More than once, she had found herself almost wishing to see just what he was capable of if he truly unleashed all that suppressed power.

Now she was afraid the opportunity would come too soon.

Amidst the necropolis, surrounded by jutting obelisks that pierced the night, they came to a rocky hill. Perseus paused before it for only a heartbeat, then began a circuit, seeking after some entrance, for surely this must be the place they sought. It was too dark to say whether they had reached the centre of the necropolis, but she had to assume so.

After a few moments circumnavigating the hill, Perseus strode forward, raising the lamp to illuminate a stone arch cut into the rock. Within this archway lay double doors carved from sandstone and engraved with geometric patterns that almost seemed to move as the lamplight flowed over them.

The doors stood ajar, just a crack. Pandora leaned forward to see if she could make out anything within the umbral recesses. As if answering her interest, a faint sound emanated, of women weeping or groaning in despair. Lamentations of the damned.

It had her skin crawling, her fingers clenching and unclenching. It had her trembling, falling backward involuntarily.

Perseus cast a concerned look at her, then wedged himself into the crack and slipped inside.

Oh, well damn it. If he was going in, she supposed she had little choice. Cold stone from the door brushed against her back as she slipped within the cave. In here, the light from Perseus's lamp bounced off the walls, illuminating a tunnel choked with dust and cobwebs. The place stank of stale air that had Pandora suppressing a cough, and the moaning had grown louder.

Perseus advanced, spear point levelled in front of himself and lamp held by his head. His sandals slapped the floor, which was worked smooth stone, if not completely level. Pandora found herself trailing, both hands clutching around her own spear. Despite her best efforts, her mind seized upon every shifting shadow, conjuring up a passage into the caliginous depths of Tartarus. Was this what she would see? What she would feel descending into the darkness beyond the World in the hopes of saving her lover?

Motion on her periphery caught her eye, and she spun but only saw a glimpse of something dark skittering along the wall before it vanished behind a maze of webs.

"*Hehe ... hehe ...*"

The cackle traced the lines of the cave temple, emanating from all sides, even behind her.

She saw the muscles in Perseus's back grow tighter, but his pace didn't slow.

"I see you ..." a female voice whispered; the sound retched up from the darkness.

The passage opened into a wide vestibule with a ceiling too high for the lamp's light to reach its recesses. The space around her melted into greater darkness without walls for the faint light to bounce off. Instinct demanded she press close to Perseus, trust in his skill and speed to protect her, but drawing too nigh might impede his ability to manoeuvre and fight.

A fresh cackle reverberated through the open chamber, as if the gloom itself mocked their presence here, feasting upon her growing dread.

"Show yourselves!" Perseus demanded.

"He wants us exposed," a female said, her voice cracking and ancient. The figure materialised from cobwebs, pressing through them as if unaware of their presence, though they clung to her otherwise nude form. Her flesh was withered and wrinkled, so gaunt and decayed Pandora could scarce believe the woman yet lived. Spiralling tattoos marred her desiccated grey cheeks, and above them stood two gaping voids where her eyes ought to have rested. Between two fingers, she pinched an eyeball, which she held out before her.

Two more figures followed at her heels, hands upon her shoulders. Their eyes were gone as well, and they seemed reliant upon the first to guide them. Like the first, twisted spiral tattoos lined their faces.

"He comes to sate us?" one of the back ones asked.

"Oh, hehe, let *me* see him then." The other witch snickered and roughly seized the wrist of the one holding the eye. For a brief instant, the two struggled over it, then the back witch claimed it and waved it in front of her face, as if that somehow allowed her to see Perseus and Pandora.

From the gap-toothed grin that spread over her wretched face, Pandora had to imagine she *could* see them. Black drool dribbled from the rotted ruin of her mouth, and a purple tongue that should not have been half so long lolled out. "Tasty ..."

Pandora hefted the spear, quite certain she didn't want to know whether the witch meant that salaciously or in fact intended to feast upon their flesh.

"My dears," Perseus said, his nonchalance obviously affected. He cleared his throat. "Can one of you tell me where to the find the Gorgon, Medusa?"

Fresh snickers passed among the Graeae, and they continued to draw closer. A vile stench emanated from them, like putrescence and faeces. She bobbed the spear threateningly as they approached, but Perseus pushed the edge down with his own, a silent admonition that they needed these sorceresses.

Chortling, one of them closed with her and traced a clammy finger along Pandora's forearm. The witch's long, claw-like nails left a faint scratch upon Pandora's flesh. It took the sum of all her will to hold still under such ministrations.

"Let *me* see," another said, and there erupted another minor scuffle for control of the eye.

Perseus moved so quickly Pandora barely saw aught. He dropped his spear, shoved Pandora back, and his hand darted forward like lightning, snatching the eye from the two witches as they struggled for it.

A collective wail erupted from all three at once, as if, while completely blind, they sensed exactly what he had done. With an arm over her chest—the one holding the lamp, the clay of which pressed against her—Perseus guided Pandora to back away from the Graeae.

"Now," he said. "I do hate rudeness, but then it rather perturbed me to not receive an answer to the question."

"What question?" all three shrieked at once. One of the witches fell to her knees and began casting about the stone floor, as if she might find the eye there. Another advanced in the general direction of Perseus, her hands grasping at shadows. The last kept turning about, sniffing.

"Where do I find dear Medusa, of course," Perseus said. "We have a pressing engagement, and I cannot be later than I already am."

The one stumbling toward him groaned, that distended tongue lapping at her lips once more. "Return the eye, lovely boy. Let us look upon you."

"Perhaps I'll keep this. I imagine it will make for a fascinating topic of discussion if I ever attend a symposium."

The one on her knees wailed, and Pandora thought she might begin weeping, assuming she could still make tears.

"Of course, if I had Medusa, I could talk about her, and I would have no need to let the eye leave the Lodge."

The closest witch hissed at them, then deflated. "The cursed one dwells in the ruins of the Circle's refuge upon Sarpedon."

"Where is it?" Pandora demanded.

Another hiss answered her. "An island some thirty miles from here, wretched girl."

"Ah," Perseus said, "see, now wasn't that easy? Catch!" He hurled the eye amid the three witches and almost at the same moment snatched Pandora's wrist, yanking her along behind him.

It took her a moment to realise he'd caught her up with the same slimy fingers that held the eye, and by then he'd pulled her almost back to the great double doors. "Best move before they finish squabbling over that," he said.

Pandora didn't need another invitation to leave this place and squeezed back outside the Lodge, followed by Perseus. Perhaps the Graeae truly could not leave the confines of their hold, but Pandora broke into a run anyway, not stopping until she passed outside the necropolis. There she faltered, hands upon her knees, panting.

The demigod, though, seemed not the least winded and was actually grinning. "So Sarpedon, then?"

Pandora had to admit the temptation—however slight—that came upon her to tell him to go fuck himself.

15

HEKATE

277 Golden Age

After fifty years spent wandering the breadth of Kumari Kandam and then Mu, Hekate was at last returning to the Thalassa world, her small ship pulling into the harbour of Helion. The mouth of the harbour was now straddled by a hundred-foot-tall statue of Helios, an army of sculptors slaving away beneath the scorching sun to get the details just right. While Helios's pretension ought not to have surprised her, nevertheless, Hekate found herself gawking at the construction. And not for its grandeur.

"He thinks well of himself," Keuthos said from behind her.

"He thinks the sun shines from his arsehole," she answered without looking at her friend.

While the Circle had spent decades hunting for her—and Hekate had killed three members of the Circle and five times as many of their hired mercenaries—Helios himself had not proved fool enough to come after her. Or if he had, he'd never managed to get close enough, but true, she had ventured so far beyond these lands as to have entered realms of legend.

A wizard in the Sumeru Mountains had taught her more of the spellsongs of Kumari Kandam than even the Circle seemed to have mastered. She had dwelt with a tohunga in the Dreaming Desert, smoking their exotic herbs and letting her mind jaunt into spaces others could not have conceived of. She sailed the waters of Nusantara and watched the sunrise upon the peaks of Hawaiki.

Insipid, Tithorea said in her mind. The host of her bound spirits became a chorus in her head at night, but most dozed beneath the sunlight, giving her moments of reprieve. None of them much cared for the light of day, and Hekate could not say what had prompted her desire to watch the dawn that day, but it had earned her a cacophony of protests. The dryad was, however, less affected by the sun than most of the others.

They made port, and Keuthos tied off their ship while Hekate scanned the city. It had grown since the brief stopover she had made here with Artemis, a lifetime ago. For a moment, she stood in repose. What had ever happened to her old friend? Moon spirits such as the bear inside Artemis blended with the host rather than one becoming the master. Perhaps the process had driven Artemis mad, though she hoped not. Funny, until this moment, Hekate had not even considered that Artemis was Kirke's half-sister. Would the two of them have met, here in their father's court?

As though you so care, Tithorea taunted. *You, who cast her aside like chaff the day she was born.*

"I did not cast her aside!" Hekate snapped.

Keuthos looked sharply at her. No matter how much practice one had in conversing in one's head, it was all too easy to be drawn into arguments with spirits and ghosts that would, to outsiders, seem bouts of madness. Of course, Keuthos had bound his own lampad, and he knew what was happening. It did not stop him from lecturing her—at tedious length—about the dangers she invited by having bound multiple eidolons inside her body and soul.

But Hekate could also not turn from the diversity of power such entities offered her. It was *her* power that had saved them, time and again, from hunters sent by the Circle, from chimeras haunting the wilds they had wandered, or even simply from bandits thinking them easy prey.

You lie to yourself with practiced ease, the dryad said. *Your self-deceptions balm what remains of your abraded soul, allowing you to pretend you are not the wretch your erstwhile companions take you for. Even whilst you wade through rivers of blood and visit your horrors upon those who stand in your way.*

"Shut up," she growled through gritted teeth.

Tithorea snickered in her mind, satisfied at having provoked Hekate.

Keuthos clucked his judging tongue at her, but her scowl warned him off any further admonitions. For now.

They took lodging in a guest house intended for wandering merchants. "We'll call upon Helios in the morn," Hekate said, and the look Keuthos shot her carried a full measure of judgment. "I weary of this," she snapped at him when he lingered at the threshold of her room. "These bound spirits slow our ageing, but we need Ambrosia to be true Titans. Helios is a member of the Ouranid League and can grant us all we require and more."

Your daughter, Khione said.

She wants her back now, Okypete teased.

Regret ... Mormo rasped. The wraith's voice was the most mind-rending of them all, the most hateful. A dead sorceress herself, the power she offered was more than Hekate could pass up, but still, every tattered, wispy word felt like being dragged through tar.

She cannot regret ... Tithorea mocked. *Her capacity for it withers with the putrefaction of her soul. How long before she, in her perfection, alone exists?*

The Circle's teachings warned that sorcery abraded the soul. That a risk, of one pushed too far into madness, was giving in to solipsism. And those entities swirling about her soul knew its secret fears. The lanced them like pustules and forced her to look upon them. To squirm as they held the mirror up to her eyes.

"We need Ambrosia," Keuthos admitted. "You're mother to one of his children. Just ask for it."

IN THE BRIGHT-COLUMNED great hall of Helion, the golden Titan sat upon his golden throne, peering down at Hekate as though she were some specimen of filth he found smeared upon his sandal. Beside him—or rather just behind—still as marble, sat Leto, his wife, in her gleaming white peplos. The queen's gaze seemed locked upon the floor, as if she'd not dare to look upon her husband's guests.

"I require enough Ambrosia to last me and Keuthos several decades," Hekate said, hands by her sides. She could match Helios's haughty pride measure for measure. "Full draughts, not the paltry pittances you dole out to Nymphs."

A tittering rolled through the court, as no few Nymphs lurked among those columns. Helios knew well what he denied them, offering them barely enough of the precious liquid to retain their youth, and not a drop more.

"You are a Nymph," Helios said dismissively. "I have a counterproposal, you pompous cunt. Turn the Sefer Raziel over to me, beg my forgiveness, and I will not have your eyes gouged out before leaving you to beg on the streets." He spoke so evenly she could almost believe his blood not up.

Hekate allowed herself a grim smile. "You do not realise where we are."

Now Helios rose, chuckling. "We stand in the very seat of my power." His sandals fell heavy upon the marble floor as he trod closer.

"No," Hekate replied. "You are in the seat of mine."

An effort of will and the sun streaming in through the high windows vanished, day turning to night, the full moon now providing the only illumination in the room.

"What?" Helios gasped, turning to look up at the changed firmament in stultification.

"Do you know why mighty Heka gave over his attempts to find me and walked away from the Circle? Why Phobetor, self-proclaimed master of fear, no doubt still cowers at the mention of my name?"

"Heka *walked* away?" He seemed surprised. "You have destroyed the whole of the Circle!"

Hardly. "I left them be once they ceased hunting me. You, however, continue to vex."

Helios's gaze darted to the columns, where tendrils of blood began to seep through the ceiling and run in sanguine troughs.

"What is this …?" Helios demanded pointing an accusing finger at her. The flesh of the offending digit sloughed away like motes of dust, swirling about the hall, even as Helios moaned in abject horror. The bone of that finger crumpled, snapping off. The Titan lord raised both hands to his face only find the whole of them flitting away, his limbs those of a desiccated corpse.

Hekate allowed herself a grim smile as she strode toward him. "You're going to give me what I want, Helios. It gets worse from here."

He fell back, stumbling upon the marmoreal floor of his throne room. An inarticulate moan escaped him as he opened his mouth. Rivulets of blood spilled out, followed by his teeth, clattering upon the floor one by one.

Clink. Clink. Clink.

The lord tried to call for his guards, but his tongue had become a dead lump in his mouth, unwilling to respond.

His men snapped into motion regardless, striding forward, only to convulse. Scales sprouted from their necks an instant before they slithered from their armour becoming a writhing nest of serpents covering the floor. Helios scrambled back up onto the dais, looked to Leto, his obedient wife to save him.

She greeted him with a too wide smile. Her flesh and peplos ruptured, split down the sides. Her skeleton crawled out from its meat casing, streaming blood even as it reached for him, thumbs closing in on his face.

"Gouge out my eyes, hmm?" Hekate said. She cleared her throat to be heard over his voiceless moans. "Well, sweet dreams then. I'll be here in the morning for the Ambrosia."

❦

WHEN THEY ARRIVED in the flesh in Helios's aureate palace, the seneschal escorted them to see Leto sat upon the throne. The king did not receive them, but the queen beckoned a servant forward. The man plodded toward them, arms weighted down with a filigree-decorated chest.

"A gift from his lordship, Helios," Leto said, her voice calm but eyes revealing her confusion. Helios had no doubt ordered her to present them with the Ambrosia but could not look Hekate in the eyes. Which suited her just as well.

She popped the clasp on the chest, and indeed, within lay eight phials of amber liquid. She inclined her head to Leto. "We'll need rooms in the palace."

"See to it," Leto said to the seneschal, her curiosity apparently not extending into questioning events. The Nymph was more like a whipped dog than a person. Hekate could not help but feel her sympathy sliding into disdain at how Leto no longer even tried to live her own life.

A broken toy, Tithorea mocked. *Even as you may have broken her proud husband.*

Hekate ignored that. "Is Artemis in the city, by chance?"

Leto looked up for once, a bare hint of vitality limning her features. "She's not been here in five years."

A shame.

The seneschal escorted her and Keuthos to guest chambers. The moment the door was shut, Hekate licked her lips, her hand pushing against Keuthos's chest. They said Ambrosia drove men and women into bouts of prurient frenzy so profound as to be life altering.

Keuthos caught her wrist and pushed her back. "You haunted Helios."

"What?"

"I asked you to first request the Ambrosia from him, but you stalked his dreams before we ever entered this place."

Hekate scoffed. "I asked him in his dreams. His response was as petty as it was predictable."

"The wild gyrations of a mind asleep are not the same as actions taken in the waking world." His words were almost a growl.

"Helios is a pig who cannot see a use for a woman save when he has her on her back! You'd have me come here, upon my knees, and chance his wrath? What do you imagine I'd have had to do to this court *in reality* should he have sent warriors after us? Can you envisage the slaughter?"

"You tortured a man because of what you thought he *might* do!" Keuthos snapped.

Hekate folded her arms. Keuthos had no idea how perilous was the ground upon which he now trod. Was this jealousy that her power so outstripped his own? Was it fear of her gifts as an oneiromancer, that most dreaded of disciplines? "I did naught that Morpheus has not done to me."

"Perhaps you ought not to use the dream stalker as a model for morality."

An urge to wrap her fingers around his throat arose in her, powerful enough to clench her gut in knots.

Kill ... Mormo rasped. *Feast upon his weakness ... Feed me his soul ...*

"No!" she snapped at the wraith, but still her fingers curled into claws. No, she'd not harm him.

Then drag him screaming to your bed, Okypete demanded. *Sate us all upon his helpless manhood.*

Hekate pressed a palm to her temple in a vain attempt to silence the cackling spirits. "Just ... take your share of the Ambrosia and go, Keuthos. I weary of your reproaches."

Suddenly, he looked taken aback, as if he had not seen this coming, despite his endless berating, his refusal to accept the necessity of their position. "Hekate, I—"

"Go!" She flung open the chest, snatched half the phials, and shoved them against his chest. "Get the fuck out of here!"

Precious containers cradled in his arms and face stricken, Keuthos backed out the door. "You do not know the path you follow." He swallowed, pain creasing his mouth. "I would help you if I could ..."

"You want to help me?" she snapped. "Send in someone with a working cock!" she screamed into hall, heedless of the gaping servants staring at them. Then, she slammed the door in his face.

❧

KIRKE SHE FOUND in the modest library Helios maintained, squinting in the candlelight, poring over scrolls spread across the floor. Knowing the Titan lord, Helios probably had his own private collection of scrolls, ones he'd not share with his offspring nor anyone else. Perhaps that was where the lord now hid while Hekate stalked his halls.

Your claws sunk deep into the tender reaches of his mind, Okypete purred.

Oh, she rent his soul, even as she did Heka and Phobetor before him, Tithorea said.

The World itself spirals in decay and depravity ... Mormo said, cackling. *And we but stir the cauldron ... Til we might sip from the putrid dregs of our labor ...*

She wonders if the Hyperborean is right, Khione offered.

Oh, she won't wonder long, Tithorea said. *Such misgivings are for those burdened with unvarnished souls weak enough for self-reflection.*

"Stop it," Hekate snarled, and Kirke abruptly looked up at her.

"Who are you?" the sandy-haired woman demanded. Some fifty years old now, and still the golden-eyed child had a youthful mien, more than mere Titan blood would have accounted for. She'd at least sipped a partial dose of Ambrosia, of that Hekate was certain. Well enough, as it meant Helios had not wholly neglected her, and the draught would have fortified her Pneuma.

"Your mother," Hekate said, settling down cross-legged in front of her daughter.

Kirke stared at her a moment. "Yeah, no, I'm pretty sure the person who had a claim on that title surrendered it a while back. You know, what with abandoning me and never looking back and all. Maybe you'd think Leto would've been a mother. Hmm, but guess how much she liked having her husband's bastard Nymph daughter chasing around after her skirts, begging for a scrap of attention?" Kirke rubbed her ribs. "Did you know even a Nymph can kick a six-year-old hard enough to send her crashing through a plastered wall? Go on, then, ask me how I know that? Go *on* ... You know you wanna ask, don't you?"

The child putrefies in glorious petulance, Tithorea intoned, her voice a moan of pleasure.

Hekate folded her arms across her chest. "I did not know my mother, either." Saying it no longer even hurt.

The lies we tell ourselves taste the sweetest, Khione offered.

"But unlike myself, she never returned for her daughter. I am here now, having traveled across the breadth of two continents and delved the arcana mortal Men cannot fathom."

"Sure, yeah, and I'm gratified to know you were enjoying yourself while I was getting harassed and beaten. Makes it all worthwhile. Honestly, I even got you something to thank you for it. Hmm." She patted about her peplos, appearing to search for whatever it was. "Huh. Where did I ...?" Kirke withdrew her hand from the folds of her dress to expose an obscene gesture. "Oh, there it is! I knew I had this somewhere."

Charming child, Khione cooed.

Hekate sighed, forcing down her irritation. Or at least trying. "I have returned here to offer you the chance to learn the Art from me. If this foolery continues, perhaps I will withdraw the offer."

A wash of emotions rushed over Kirke's face, and the girl huffed. "You'll show me?"

"Your father never did, I'm sure."

Kirke shook her head.

Hekate leaned back. "I met someone when I was but a girl ..." Enodia had shown up only a handful of times in the past decades, offering vague directions to where Hekate could learn more, improve her Art, and then vanishing again for years at a time. But maybe it was because the sorceress knew Hekate had progressed beyond the need for her instructions. "Someone who helped me make my start, as I will help you make yours. In time, you may seek out other tutors, but the deeper secrets of the cosmos—the arcana—those you will have to uncover on your own, as we all do."

Her daughter managed a slight smile. "Deal."

INTERLUDE: PROMETHEUS

Silver Age

Thunder rumbled in the caliginous upper reaches of Prometheus's prison, and sporadic crackles of lightning fulminated high above. It was coming back.

Bound in orichalcum, naked, and alone atop the bloody walls of Tartarus, he found it best to let his mind drift into his palace of memory, staving off madness for one day longer. Or another hour, at least. Always a bit longer. He would escape this ordeal eventually, but would he still be himself?

In desperate need to affirm that, he twisted, trying to peer into the swirling depths of the fiery twisters that roamed the far side of this cavern. They had bound him here, on the threshold of Khaos, and sometimes he could not help but look—even knowing he ought not—into the atramentous expanse that fell away below him. Within that absolute darkness slithered and squirmed abyssal enormities, ever grasping at his mind and soul.

Watcher ...

The demon's voice was somehow both a gong and a whisper, worming through his brain and shredding his attempts at distracting himself, as it so oft did. Or maybe it was not always the same entity that spoke to him, for he felt as though legions of the hateful abominations lurked within the Khaos bounded between the two walls of Tartarus.

"I am not that," he grated.

Change is illusion ...

"I am not *that*," he insisted. Those few who persisted in the title persisted in self-delusion, preferring to hold to even the most momentous of lies rather than admit to themselves they had based their reality upon so egregious a misapprehension.

The answer that welled up in him was a maelstrom of oily sensations caressing his insides. A violating intrusion he took to be the entity's amusement.

No, he needed to focus. Within the depths of the conflagrations that lit the greater cavern, he could see patterns. Patterns in flame were all he needed to call up pyromantic visions of other times and places, to push his mind outward ...

You know what's coming ...

No!

No, he had to keep his mind elsewhere.

That narrow shore that took shape in his mind, that pass through the mountains, guarded by Elládosi warriors. And beyond, an endless stream of invaders—Kandamians?—trying to push inward. A sea of bristling spears crashing forward like waves ready to break upon the pass. Did he know that pass?

What was this moment he beheld, where a few hundred Elládosi would try to hold off so many invaders?

A brighter flash of lightning ripped through the firmament, snapping his mind out of the trance.

And it was there, crouching upon the lip of the wall, a fell wind whipping around it, setting its feathers trembling even as it leered at him. Prometheus instinctively flinched away, stretching the limits of his fetters, though he had not far he could pull back.

Not again.

The Storm spirit feasted upon his dread as much as his flesh, and it leaned forward, flapping its eagle-like wings. It dropped down with hands upon the ground, breasts and hips swaying as it approached, in a mockery of human sensuality. The harpy's legs ended in birdlike talons, its face a vile amalgam of woman and bird, including a beak for a nose.

No, no, no. Not again ...

Or turn to us ...

"No," Prometheus snapped aloud. Even the harpy was better than the demons. At least, he had to hope he had the strength to keep making that choice. Probably not even they could actually kill him, but they could do *worse*.

With blinding speed, the harpy launched itself at him, one of its hands pinning his face to the black wall of his prison. Its monumental strength allowed him not the least chance to move, not even as it traced one of its talons along his gut.

Lances of fire shot through Prometheus, and it took all he had to choke down his screams. Then the harpy rammed its free hand inside him and wriggled its fingers around in his innards, and the scream ripped out of him. On and on, until his throat was scraped raw. Tears blinded him and, as he did daily, he mentally begged for a death that could never come.

The spirit yanked his liver free and gnawed on in right in front of his face, splattering him with blood and gore.

For a moment, things grew dim. Shadows welled up and darkness closed in. Could this truly be the end? An idle fancy, of course.

As the harpy released him, blood began to seep back *into* the gaping wound its talons had opened in him. Temporal currents flowed about him, ravaged him, even as they reformed a liver in the air. Dimly, Prometheus wondered if it vanished from the harpy's stomach in the process. Such musings were another distraction from the—

"Aah!" he shrieked as the liver jammed its way back inside, hurting almost as much as it had coming out.

Agonies shot through him like flash fires as his flesh reformed.

The last of his stamina gave out and the blackness rose to greet him, offering a final glimpse of the harpy licking its fingers before taking flight.

YEARS OF TORMENT AND TORTURE, and neither the harpy nor the demon tired of the game. Sooner or later, his mind would crack from the strain, this he knew. He but delayed the inevitable with his visions of the future and the reliving of long-past memories. That, and a final distraction that churned within his breast.

Another spirit dwelt there, claimed by him long ago from Phlegethon and its smouldering master. It was a piece torn of a greater whole but given life and thought and power all its own. It had come to him with incipient awareness that had grown and grown— Surtr, it named itself—until it had become an entity complete unto itself.

A piece rendered an individual, as the spark of one flame might give birth to another. Pieces of that spark had passed on to others, yes, to create his Firewalkers. But then, what if he could take more than an ember? What if he could form something more fateful and give rise to that which he had so long sought after? After learning of the entity, he had become obsessed with finding its source, having it ready for her when the time came.

The irony was, it had taken him so long to realise this last pyrogenic creation would not be found by him, but wrought *within* him, and perhaps thus he could temper Surtr's spark.

Ananke fed upon irony, and he knew that better than any other.

So, Prometheus waited, nurturing an as yet fragile ember in the depths of his soul. Because the future was still coming. Because she would need it.

PART III

The Olympians are, of course, Titans, yes, no different than their forebears save in the title the claim for themselves. And yet, the rise of their reign over the world does demarcate a substantial shift in history. It is the first time Titans demanded worship by Men. Through them, we enter an Age of Gods.

— Thalia, Dialogues of the Muses

16

PANDORA

624 Bronze Age

The wooded cliffs of Sarpedon seemed nigh impenetrable to Pandora as Perseus guided their boat around the circumference of the island. As the Graeae had told them, the island lay a few miles off the mainland, about halfway between Byblos and Tyros. A part of Pandora had teased herself with fancies about pushing further south to check in on her old home. But even had they made port in Tyros, more than six hundred years separated her from her own time, and *that* time was twenty years after she'd left. There was naught for her there and never would be again.

"I see an inlet," Perseus said.

"Where?" Pandora asked, peering at the woods but catching no sight of whatever he'd spied.

"My dear, trust me, I'm an expert at finding ... inlets."

She rolled her eyes. "Must you?"

"Perhaps not," he said with a shrug. "But I enjoy it nonetheless."

As he'd claimed, though, there was a narrow cut leading into the interior of the island, which was well, as Pandora had *not* relished any thought of trying to scale those cliffs.

Perseus made for the inlet, reducing sail to guide them with care.

"I don't suppose you've changed your mind about this madness," Pandora asked, already knowing the answer. "You're hunting a cursed woman to satisfy the vanity of a man who wants you dead."

"Not so heroic, eh?" Perseus grunted. "I made an oath, Pandora. What would the world come to if Men could no longer trust in oaths? Next we know, we'd have people dancing naked in streets while poleis burn around us."

"Because I'm certain you swore an oath not to dance naked."

He flashed a grin. "Of course not, I'm no fool."

No, and perhaps he had *some* point in claiming the foundations of civilisation, the structures that separated Men from animals, lay in the ability to trust the words of other Men. It was, after all, in the self-interest of all concerned that promises hold weight and lies be condemned, for without this, commerce and cooperation would crumble. But did upholding a dangerous oath one had been manipulated into fall into the same line as the normal valuations of honesty? It seemed to her these conceptions of honour bespoke more of pride than of integrity.

Singing under his breath—not a song she knew, but hardly surprising given the centuries that separated them—Perseus guided the boat through the inlet. The declivities that formed the outer banks of it gave way as the land sloped inward, as if the whole of the island were a caldera. Dense forest overhung the waterway, creating a canopy that shrouded their passage and seemed to swallow outside sound. In fact ...

"Stay silent a moment," she said.

"My dear, if you don't like my singing, well—"

"Shh." She held up a hand, focusing her senses. "I don't hear any birdsong." For that matter, she didn't hear the buzz of insects or any other sound save the gentle lapping of the water and the swaying of leaves in the wind.

"Maybe they feared to compete with my voice," Perseus offered.

The breeze carried on it an acerbic taste that had her grimacing. Maybe the sheer cliffs where not the only reason no one had tried to settle upon this tiny island. She cast a wary glance at Perseus who nodded sternly, not half so oblivious as he liked to act.

Wordlessly, he pointed at something just beyond the tree line. Up ahead, set on a shelf of level ground, she spied a crumbling stone structure. Vines enwrapped the sandstone columns and lichen had almost swallowed the better part of the whole building.

Perseus couldn't bring their ship, small as it was, right up to the bank, so they had no choice but to jump the side and swim to shore. The water washed over her, warm, but too thick, seeming to cling to her skin even as she climbed free of it. For a sick moment, Pandora stood upon the muddy bank, staring at her arm, watching the liquid bead and dribble off like honey. With a shiver, she flung the excess off her and caught Perseus doing the same.

"Something has saturated this place with a foulness," she said.

"Hmm," he answered. "Can't imagine why those sorcerers abandoned it."

When he had wrung himself dry, he slipped the adamant shield from his back and drew the xiphos, taking a few practice swings to loosen his muscles. Pandora planted the butt of her spear in the loam and watched the demigod warm up, knowing she should do the same, but seized by a reluctance to even move.

A foulness indeed, in the air, in the water. It made her skin crawl and the hair on her arms stand on end. Huffing, she forced herself into motion, pushing through a handful of exercises he'd shown her in training. Slow spear forms, but enough to get her blood flowing once again.

After a moment, she caught him watching her and fell still. Without a word, he pointed his sword at the tenebrous entrance to the ruined structure. Rather than a mere absence of light, a palpable darkness seemed to radiate from the sandstone archway leading inside the ancient Circle refuge. The whole place stretched further into the jungle than she'd at first thought, like a forgotten temple to some blasphemous god.

Words could not even express how much she did not want to take a single step inside there.

But could she leave Perseus to do it on his own? If he died, not only could she not save Prometheus, she wasn't certain she could navigate the ship away from this accursed isle. Grimacing, Pandora set about wrapping an oil-soaked cloth around a stick to create a torch.

Once it was lit, she fell in behind Perseus, who waited at the threshold. She hadn't really trained much at using the spear one-handed as warriors in a phalanx would have. It felt awkward and heavy thus, but with Perseus carrying sword and shield, she was the only one who could hold the light.

The demigod blew out a breath, then plodded gently into the dark space ahead of them, his sandals shuffling on the stone. An ocean of dust greeted them, whipped into a frenzy by their passage. The shadows choking the vestibule retreated from her torch, but barely, and with the aspect of insects skittering away from an intruder.

A balcony rimmed this entry chamber, though Pandora's torch failed to illuminate aught above them. Great columns supported the upper level, and Pandora moved to inspect one. Cracked and faded paint bedecked the pillar. Had this once been a place of colour and beauty before whatever obscenities the Goetic Circle had called up had tainted this island? Had people laughed and smiled in these halls in ages long since past? No doubt they had, unaware of the doom they would cast upon the whole of Sarpedon.

Beyond the column rested a cracked marble statue of a warrior, arms raised in warding, face a rictus of shock. A statue ... Pandora reached tentative fingers to brush over the warrior's lifelike face. Age had weathered the stone, but it was too perfect. Because Medusa was said to transform men who met her gaze to stone.

With the air of a stalking cat, Perseus crept through the cyclopean shadows, skirting the perimeter of the vestibule. At an interior arch-way, he beckoned her closer and she moved to his side, shining her torchlight down the new hall. Once more, darkness scrambled away from the light, almost seeming to hiss at its intrusion. Down this way lay a corridor rimmed with side rooms. Sleeping chambers perhaps, though she couldn't be certain without plodding down the passage to check. And in front of one of them, on hands and knees, another statue.

Another victim ... Fuck, they shouldn't have come here. Fool pride would cost them both.

Perseus seemed more inclined to continue exploring the main vestibule, though, as he turned back, then froze in place, hefting his shield up, the sword above it poised for a thrust.

Slithering scales scraped over stone in the distance, as if something had crawled down from above and now occupied the darkness beneath the balcony, watching them, concealed by the columns. Pandora crept forward, whipping the torch around to try to catch a glimpse of whatever had made that sound, though her hand holding the light trembled furiously and her heart felt apt to explode. Despite the heat, a chill crept over her and with it an almost irresistible urge to make a break for the faint daylight reaching in through the front archway.

Had the creature been above them this whole time?

Sword and shield locked together, Perseus took a small step into the open space. Then another. And another. "My dear, if you can understand me, trust me when I tell you it should be better for all concerned if you come out now for the slaying. Have you not suffered long enough, Medusa? And if you've never tried being slain, perhaps you'd even like it. Almost no one I've ever slain has complained once they've gotten used to it, you know."

A hiss answered him, as of a dozen serpents disturbed.

Pandora wanted to weep but she forced herself to ease her way forward, bringing the torch out ahead in the hopes of catching some glimpse of the creature they hunted. Instead, she saw only the shifting of shadows and, within, the overwhelming sense of something slinking through them.

"She sent you to end it at last ..." The voice was warped, both by pain and inhuman sibilance. "Or maybe you are like the othersss."

"I might be a bit different," Perseus rejoined, advancing toward the hissing sound.

A snarl answered him, and a lunge, the creature launching itself from the shadows. Pandora saw Perseus dive to the side, shield raised over his head even as the monster soared above him. She barely had time to shriek before a serpentine bulk collided with her, stealing her breath, slamming her up against a sandstone column. The torch and her spear tumbled from her grasp, and her vision refused to focus for an instant.

When it did, she found the abomination staring at her with a cocked head. In place of legs was an enormous, drakon-scaled tail. Upon Medusa's head writhed a nest of hissing, spitting snakes, half of which fixed upon Pandora with their awful yellow gazes. Boar-like tusks jutted from her lower lip, and aureate wings shredded the air around the monster. The Gorgon held her aloft by the throat but had not cut off her air, instead peering into her face.

She was dead.

The thought raced through Pandora's mind. But no, she did not turn to stone, and Medusa just stared hard at her.

Perseus roared, flying through the air behind the Gorgon. The monster spun, flinging Pandora at him like a missile. They impacted midair and tumbled to the ground, and Pandora knew naught save pain and hissing, tumbling, aching madness.

She heard a *thwack* of something solid upon flesh, then Perseus was off her, launching himself in a whirlwind. As Pandora turned, his xiphos darted in and out in a blur, slashing at Medusa. Rather than look at the Gorgon, he was watching her in the reflection of his adamant shield. The strategy may have kept him from falling prey to her lethal gaze, but it was awkward. The Gorgon's tail snared his legs and sent him toppling to the ground.

Fast as an arrow from a bow, Medusa surged above him, hissing and rearing brazen claws ready to rip him apart if he refused to meet her gaze. Pandora lunged for her fallen torch, caught it, and flung it at Medusa. The Gorgon snarled, but Pandora hadn't waited to see if it connected. Rather, she scrambled to catch her spear and spun, thrusting straight out.

Its point scraped over those draconic scales upon Medusa's lower half, failing to draw blood and feeling more like she'd struck metal. Before she could recover from her attack, those coils slammed into her, sending her hurtling through the air to smack into a column.

Everything faded.

WHEN PANDORA CAME TO, it seemed only a moment had passed. Perseus was roaring, flipping through the air in a blinding whirl. As he landed, his blade cleaved through the Gorgon's neck. Medusa's head tumbled from her shoulders and smacked upon the sandstone floor with a *thwop*. The serpents of her head continued to hiss and writhe for several more breaths, while her torso flailed about before finally collapsing in a heap.

"Don't look!" Pandora wheezed, finding her breath still short. The room swayed unevenly, and a dark haze still loomed at her periphery. "The head might yet have power ... if you meet the eyes."

Perseus stood peering at the Gorgon through the reflection in his shield, but he grunted. When the serpents finally stopped slithering, he snatched the head up by one of them and plopped it into a sack. "So. That was the most awful thing I've ever witnessed. How about you?"

An image came to her, unbidden, of the man she loved beaten and dragged down to Tartarus for eternal torment. Of a family sundered by an impossible gulf of time. Of herself, forced to abandon her daughter for the desperate chance to save Pyrrha's father. "I've seen worse."

Perseus knelt beside her, easing her up. "Can you walk?"

"I think so."

"Ah, my dear, then perhaps we should make back for Neritum."

Pandora's head felt like it would split apart and spill out all her thoughts. "Let's stop for the night in Byblos. I could use a warm bed."

"Just one?" He winked.

"One for me. You can sleep in the stables."

Perseus shrugged. "The burden of heroes can be great."

Oh, he had no idea. When he delivered the Gorgon's head back to Polydektes, she would ask of him something that would make all this seem mere games in comparison.

17

PERSEUS

624 Bronze Age

The Thalassa had grown perturbed as they made sail back toward Byblos, the sky darkening as if the death of Medusa had angered Poseidon. Depending on what tale one believed of Medusa, perhaps the sea god *did* resent what Perseus had done on Sarpedon. One could never judge if decapitating a drakon-snake-woman would upset anyone until after the fact, Perseus supposed.

Exasperated waves slapped the hull, even as his ship drew nigh upon the harbour.

Struggling to help with the lines, Pandora grunted. "It wasn't this bad heading south."

"No," he admitted.

The ship bucked, the prow riding too high a moment before crashing down. Perseus kept his feet, but Pandora pitched forward, smacking her shoulder against the gunwale while blessedly remaining inside the vessel.

After tying down a line himself, he offered her a hand then

helped her up. "If I didn't know better—and I rarely do—I'd think something has vexed the sirens of Pontus."

"Pontus?" Pandora hesitated. "What ever happened to Dagon?"

"Not familiar with the local mer of these waters, but I'm fair certain Poseidon and his brood control this area and push almost to the shores of Neshia." Or that was what Papa had always said of it. *The hand of Pontus reaches ever outward from the Aegean and will not rest until all the seas lie within its domain.* Poseidon would one day, no doubt, claim rulership over all the oceans.

Despite the turbulent waves, Perseus brought them into port at Byblos. To his surprise, the whole of the harbour seemed abustle with people rushing, screaming, and as whipped into as turbulent a frenzy as the sea. Amid the turmoil, unperturbed, stood a pegasus, an island of calm.

Line in hand, Perseus vaulted the gunwale, tied the boat down, and charged into the throng. "What in Hades's dark domain is going on?" he demanded from no one in particular. The bigger the demand, the better it was to not direct it at anyone who might take offence, he'd found.

A dark-haired, short-bearded Tethid pushed through the crowd at his words, standing tall enough he might have been a Titan, or perhaps a demigod. The man looked Perseus over with a cursory glance, then took in his boat. "Poseidon is sending his pet sea serpent upon the town. Ketus, they call it, and claim it large enough to inundate a polis."

"Because of Medusa?" Perseus asked. He'd have credited Poseidon making the seas rough to show his ire at them slaying the Gorgon. He'd not have imagined the Olympian would go so far as to turn another monster upon an entire city.

"What? No. *Queen* Kassiopeia provoked the ire of the Nereids. So, they got Poseidon involved, and now he's going to destroy the city unless King Kepheus exposes the princess to the monster."

Nereids ... daughters of Nereus, a mer related to Poseidon, unless Perseus missed his guess.

"You're connected to the queen," Pandora said from behind Perseus's shoulder.

He suppressed a start, not having realised she'd come up on them in the commotion. And she was no doubt right.

The Tethid glowered. "I'm Aiolos. Kassiopeia is my daughter. Which makes Princess Andromeda my granddaughter."

Aiolos ... the name of a demigod, Perseus was fair certain, though he knew little of his parentage.

Perseus stole a glance back at Pandora who was already shaking her head. "I hear rescuing princesses tends to make fine tales for would-be-heroes. Gets the bards all worked up. Fortunately, my companion agrees, and thus it would be my honour to save said maiden."

"You'd act against the will of Poseidon?" Pandora asked Aiolos.

The Tethid's frown deepened. "I doubt I could slay Ketus if I tried, and no, I cannot risk such a thing."

Perseus shrugged. "Just get me close. I love risking things." He waved for the other demigod to follow him back to the boat.

He'd not gotten far when Pandora seized his arm. "What do you think you're doing? We had a deal. You'd help me as soon as we returned Medusa's head to Polydektes."

He flashed her a grin. "As the head remains in a sack on the boat, I cannot imagine Polydektes yet has it."

"Your honour was a pretence, then?"

Her vitriol struck him like a blow. "What? No, but ... I ... Pandora, a girl is going to die if I don't act."

Her face softened a hair, some invisible war going on behind her eyes. "A girl? Would it matter to you so much were she just a girl and not a princess?"

"If I have it in my power to save *any* innocent life, I must do so. If I stand by and ignore their plight, then some culpability for their end falls upon my feet."

Pandora's hands dropped to her side. "You've read Urania's Dialogues on morality."

"I, er, have *had* a few dialogues. With people. From time to time."

He turned to find Aiolos had not only boarded his boat but led the pegasus onto it as well.

When he looked back, Pandora's face was set, mouth a grim line. "You're right, of course. If we can save anyone from Titan wrath, we must do so."

ONCE THEY HAD CLEARED the harbour, Aiolos took a gourd from his satchel. The fruit was dried, though it resembled goods Perseus had seen imported from Kemet on the rarest of occasions. Sometimes, desiccated, hollowed gourds were used for storage by Kemetian sailors. Aiolos's had a cork in it.

The demigod made his way to the back of the ship. "Might want to brace yourselves. We're going to need a burst of speed to reach the cliffs before Ketus claims Andromeda."

"Ah, indeed," Perseus said, grabbing a line. "But I'm not certain throwing fruit at the sails will actually make us go faster. I mean I haven't tried it, mind, but I imagine—"

The moment Aiolos uncorked the gourd, a gale erupted from its lip. The force of it sent the other demigod's sandals sliding backward over the sodden deck. The wind caught the sails and flung the ship forward like a stone from a sling, riding too high over the waves.

All Perseus could do was guide the tiller and hope the mast could handle the strain Aiolos was putting upon it as wood creaked in protest.

When he looked, he spied Pandora clinging to a line with one hand and holding her spear with the other. Her long black hair streamed behind her, obscuring her face when she looked to meet his gaze, though he could still register her shock.

"Imagine what he could do with a vegetable!" He shouted at her.

The Heliad offered no answer, however, seeming lost in her own thoughts. Perseus hadn't meant to chastise her on morality, though she seemed to have taken it that way. Nor did he think himself wrong.

Whatever her mother had done to provoke the Nereids, Andromeda was innocent, and Perseus would see her safe.

The sea grew more turbulent as they closed in toward the cliffs where Aiolos said Andromeda had been bound. The waves lashed his ship, the vessel suddenly seeming slight and unmatched to the mercurial fury of Poseidon. Beyond, upon the rocky bluffs of the land, the waves broke even higher, stretching up thirty feet or more before raining back down in great showers.

Perseus peered at those cliffs, searching for any sign of the princess. There, fettered upon a shelf high enough the crashing waves cast their spray only over her legs, stood a dark-haired girl. They had bound her naked in perverse sacrifice, and Perseus felt his ire rise that her father could have done such a thing, even to preserve the life of all those in his city. But then, Perseus's own grandfather had done worse with his daughter, and for less reason.

"I've got to get to her," he shouted, even as Aiolos replaced the stopper in the gourd to abate the winds. "I'll free her from those chains before the monster even arrives."

"You do that, and Poseidon turns it upon Byblos!" Pandora said.

Well, damn logic and all that.

"Perseus," Pandora said an instant later, pointing at something over his shoulder.

Which was *never* good. He turned, even as the behemoth shadow emerged from the deep, water sloshing off its saurian bulk, all frills and spurs. Its passage heaved their little ship once more, sending them riding high before crashing down before the serpent. The aquamarine monstrosity gleamed in the evening sun. Its incandescent eye fixated upon them, as if daring them to run, to do aught save worship its awful magnificence. And then it bellowed, exposing sword-like teeth. Its roar reverberated off the bluffs, carrying across the water like an endless gong, drowning out all other sound, all other thought.

Pandora fell to one knee but didn't lose her grip upon the spear. Slowly, she stood, pointing the weapon at the serpent as if she might slay it from here.

But this fell to Perseus, didn't it? Because Pandora was right. If he didn't kill the serpent, people would die. There was no way around it, no trick and no rejoinder that would abrogate his need to fight Ketus. Thus resolved, he grabbed the pegasus's mane.

"I hope you don't mind," he said to Aiolos. Since he could barely hear his own voice over the ringing the monster had left in his ears, perhaps the Tethid couldn't hear him either. Regardless, no one tried to stop him.

He leapt astride the pegasus. The moment he mounted, Aiolos's steed kicked off the deck, flinging them into the air. The animal's momentum sent Perseus skidding backward, only his fist tangled in the mane kept him from pitching back onto the deck. Which would *not* have been the kind of thing he'd want a bard singing about.

Even as he scrambled to retain his perch, the pegasus soared higher and higher. Wind stole his breath and whipped his hair behind him while he focused upon Ketus. Everything came down to focus. Balance. Reflexes.

The monster craned its saurian neck around, tracking him, but it seemed to move as if in a mire, languid and ponderous. Perseus slid the adamant blade free from its sheath. It had served for the Gorgon; it would serve for this drakon-spawned abomination.

"Down, closer," he commanded the pegasus. With intellect beyond any horse, the animal dove, wings streaking like a falcon. Perseus's arse continued to slide about the horse's haunches, forcing him to rely on his hand in the mane for balance, even as he raised the sword higher.

The serpent lunged at him, its bulk like a surging mountain. Though no doubt fast as a striking snake, even its movement slowed with Perseus's Pneumatikoi active. The pegasus ducked down, coming up under the crashing coils as that maw slammed back into the sea. Perseus swung overhead, his blade shrieking as it careened over rock-hard scales. A shower of seawater rained down over him and the pegasus, and then they were past, banking even as the horse climbed skyward once more.

"Woo!" Perseus bellowed. "Woo! Again! Come at it again!"

Ketus, however, did not seem amused. Rather than try to catch the pegasus a second time, the serpent flung itself against the cliff-side. It hit like an earthquake, shattering the rock face, pulverising otherwise obdurate stone in a downpour of dust and debris. The pegasus banked once more, but with his Pneumatikoi enhancing his reflexes, Perseus caught sight of Andromeda. Of the tumbling cataclysm of earth plummeting toward her.

Even if the immediate debris missed her, the whole of the cliff was collapsing, and she remained fettered to it. Screaming in defiance, he stood upon the pegasus's back, watching the boulders tumble down in slow motion. Watching death crash upon him and the woman he'd come here to save.

Perseus kicked off the pegasus and flew through the air, landed upon a falling boulder. The surface spun beneath him, his adamant sword scraping along it until he came around facing the land, then he kicked off once more. The motion sent him flying into the cliff, and he ran along it for a dozen steps. He'd never managed this far before … and his foot began to slip, forcing him to kick off again, bounce against another falling rock, then back to the wall.

The shower of earth became a cacophony, burying his screams in its roar. The dust meant he could barely see, but he kept pressing forward. He slammed into Andromeda swinging his adamant sword at her burnished fetters even as he collided with her. The miraculous sword sheared through the chains, and the pair of them pitched off the cliff, the sea sweeping up to claim them. Waters rushed over his head, subduing his senses, limiting even the impact of his enhanced reflexes.

As he twisted around, the woman in his arms, great shadows closed in from above. Boulders plummeting down from the bluff as the landscape itself rebelled against Ketus's assault.

A larger bulk surged through the depths, the serpent no doubt coming around to claim them both. But the maw never came into sight, the serpent launching itself skyward, something else having drawn its ire.

Andromeda broke free from his arms and swam for the surface, and Perseus followed. He burst into air and gasped down precious breaths, body shaking from exertion.

And Ketus's gargantuan maw closed upon the ship. It splintered like kindling, exploding in all directions. For an instant, Perseus's heart stopped in abject horror. Pandora. Pandora?

But then he saw her already in the water, having apparently leapt free after whatever she'd done to draw its attention away from Perseus and Andromeda.

The princess had already begun swimming to shore, so Perseus followed. They caught the side of a water-slicked rock rising from the sea. The quakes had abated, but the cliff continued to collapse just beyond them, all structural integrity now eroded. Trying to scale it would be a manoeuvre of utter madness.

Which was one of his favourite kinds, of course.

Drawing upon his Pneumatikoi, Perseus raced forward, running up the sliding, crumbling bluff and leaping to the closest outcropping. "Pegasus! Pegasus!" he shouted, hoping the horse could hear him over the roar of battle.

It must have, for the animal banked back toward him. Perseus took a running jump and caught the pegasus's side. Awkwardly, as the animal turned, he managed to remount it. "Drop me on the serpent's head!" he shouted. Which was, admittedly, not a line he had expected to utter today.

The pegasus swooped down once more, giving Perseus a chance to jump upon Ketus, sword-point down. The adamant blade punched through drakon scale as he landed, sending up a hot spray of acidic blood and drawing forth a pained bellow. Perseus hissed in shock at it even as his sandals slipped and skidded over slick scales.

His foot caught upon a barb that rose from a frill, and for an instant he was dangling before an enraged, incandescent eye. "Ah, sorry," he breathed. Then he ripped the xiphos free, kicked off the frill, and landed higher up on the head.

Standing here, the serpent couldn't eat him, so he supposed that was well. He rammed the blade into the monster once more. Another roar, and the serpent bucked, lunging beneath the waves. The sudden impact threatened to tear the blade from Perseus's grasp, water surging past him. Everything became a blur.

Perseus managed to wedge his hand inside a wound to steady himself, then yanked free the xiphos once more. Again and again he struck, until the whole of the sea seemed filled with steaming draconic blood. He wedged the blade deeper, tearing through flesh, carving into skull and the pulpy matter within.

The thrashing abated. It *had* to be dead now. Lungs apt to burst, he kicked off, swimming desperately for a surface he couldn't even see. He broke free, sucking down precious breaths, unable to manage much more than treading water.

Then, Pandora was swimming for him, caught him, and drew his arm around her shoulders, helping him swim to shore.

"Feeling heroic now?" she asked, though panting herself.

"What exactly did you *do* to it?"

"I threw a spear at it. I had hoped maybe Medusa's head would turn it to stone."

"Didn't work, I take it."

She grunted. "Oh, it did. Those last few moments you were battling a statue."

"Explains how I worked up such a sweat."

The two of them managed to reach the rock where Aiolos and Andromeda stood. Her grandfather had draped her in his cloak and was now extending a hand to help Perseus and Pandora out of the sea.

Perseus collapsed onto his back and lay there a few moments. "I truly hope someone got a good look at that. I want the bards to hear the best parts, you know."

"A feat worthy of a saga," Aiolos said. Perseus was too exhausted to be sure whether he was being humoured or mocked.

"Makes me a hero," Perseus wheezed, raising a triumphant finger. An entire fist seemed like too much to manage. "Ah, I'm pretty sure heroes get to marry the princess. I heard that somewhere."

Aiolos craned his neck down to look Perseus in the eyes.

"Andromeda is betrothed already, I'm afraid." He did almost sound disappointed.

Perseus had been about to open his mouth to say what a shame that was, when Andromeda spoke for the first time. "You mean to an uncle who couldn't be bothered to raise even his voice against my fate, much less his sword? You mean *that* engagement, Grandfather?"

Hope lived on, it would seem.

Perseus allowed himself an exhausted smile.

18

HEKATE

2386 Golden Age

The arcana of a hundred civilisations filled Hekate's grimoire—for it was hers now, though once it had been the Sefer Raziel. For two thousand years she had wandered the world, drawing out the secrets of dead workers of the Art. She had transcribed runes, summoned the shades of shamans, consulted the ghosts of witches, and taken counsel from spirits. She had smoked sacred weeds with medicine men of the Rainwoods of Hy-Brasil, explored serpent-infested ruins in the Jungles of Kush, and paddled the rivers in the forbidden east of Yueshang.

Even, she had traveled to the lost island of Hyperborea, where some small part of her still sought after Keuthos. But her erstwhile friend had not returned to his homeland, and she had seen little sign of him over the passing centuries.

And for more than two thousand years, Hekate had pushed her limits, scraping beyond them, silencing—for the most part—the chorus of voices in her head even while mastering every form of the

Art known to Man. Her grimoire was flush with secrets no other could have fathomed, and she dared believe no sorcerer alive could contend with the breadth of power she wielded.

And still, she sought more. Ever more, for there were things she did not yet understand. Fearful intimations that even the compelled dead could not or would not speak of. Insinuations of greater Truth, of what lay beyond the Mortal Realm. Of the true reach of purpose of the Elder Gods whose tendrils wrapt around all ambit of the World, squeezing it like a plump fruit.

No, Hekate would not give over her search until the cosmos surrendered up their last secrets. Until she knew what lurked in every shadow, every hidden corner just out of sight.

Thus, she made her way toward fabled Thule, an island far north of even Hyperborea. Her stop in Kronion would allow her provisions for a return to Keuthos's homeland. It was a long trek there, but immortality had taught her the value of patience. What matter the months or even years spent trekking, where every step brought her closer to the power and knowledge she sought? She had time.

Passing through the market, she spread her drachmae with little care. Coins, like so many contrivances of the Mortal Realm, represented transitory value. The dead held on to naught, and the immortal could always attain more, given time. That was all coins meant, really. Time—years of labor whittled away from mortal lives, traded for things they prayed would make their remaining years more palatable.

Quirking a smile at the sad rush of humanity shoving their way through the market, Hekate paused to examine a fur cloak. Given the warm weather and the garment being out of season, she couldn't imagine the merchant would hold much hope for selling it, but she'd need such garb where she was going. To reach Hyperborea, she'd have to navigate the mountain passes north of Illyris that most mortals considered impenetrable.

When her satchels were brimming with warm clothes and food-stuffs, she made her way back toward the harbour. Already, evening closed in, though, and she'd not find anyone keen to sail at night, much less to take her to Salon in Illyris. Before that, she supposed it was best to find lodgings with local aristoi. Surely one or another of them would have an estate close enough to the port to make her inquiries easier.

After a short stroll, she picked a manor and was about to announce herself when she felt eyes upon her. Turning slowly, she peered about. Within the shadow of trees decorating the estate, she saw a hooded figure which seemed to watch her.

For a moment, she held the viewer's gaze, then turned to reach the gate.

"Evening, my lady," the doorman said, sweeping a bow. He couldn't have had more than twenty years behind him. The man had a delicious smile, but he looked at her with a hint of desire creasing his eyes.

Hekate might well have reported him and seen him dismissed, maybe even beaten ... though he might also have provided a pleasant diversion later if she let his demeanour slide. "Tell your master the Titan Hekate has come to seek lodging."

The doorman's eyes widened, trepidation overwriting his lust, and he scrambled away to obey her orders.

He'd barely taken five steps when Hekate slipped inside the gate and strode toward the figure who had been staring at her. Though she, as ever, concealed her face from the light, it was certainly Enodia.

"Are you here seeking me?" Hekate demanded. "I hardly have further need of a mentor."

Enodia rose with a grunt of discomfort. Though immortal, perhaps age had ravaged her body somewhat before she'd gotten enough Ambrosia. A twinge of pity—just a twinge—shot through Hekate.

One would not want to feel overmuch for others, Okypete crooned.

Enodia scoffed. "Who was it, do you think, who broke the Circle of Goetic Mysteries and freed you from their hounding pursuit of their stolen prize?"

Had she been the one to finally destroy them? Hekate had heard it that Oizys and her sisters, after joining the Inner Circle, had summoned something they could not control and those of the rest who survived the onslaught had foresworn all connection with the Circle. "Either way, I doubt they would have dared challenge me much longer, witch. I despoiled the minds of three of their number, slew dozens of hunters, and killed several of the Circle with my own hand."

"Mithra slew Hypnos."

A moment of shock ran through her. But then, Mithra had admitted to knowing her. "He told you thus."

"Did he also tell me you plan to make for fabled Thule?"

Hekate folded her arms. "You're an Oracle." Which explained how the sorceress had always been able to find Hekate when she wished. Had she been playing out her visions all these centuries? Had Hekate been but a piece moved along her board?

"I have seen things," Enodia admitted. "Some of them involve you, as well I think you now guess."

Well, Hekate certainly owed Enodia enough for her early training. She motioned, and the older sorceress led her deeper into the estate grounds. Perhaps the doorman would return with an invitation and wonder where she'd gone. The thought brought a quirk of amusement, but no more.

"What would you have of me?" she asked, listening to the chirp of insects. "You did not seek me out here for pleasantries."

"Hmm. We were never the sort to be pleasant, were we?" Enodia leaned against a tree, exposing a hint of a sallow, diseased hand. If this was what all her flesh looked like, Hekate could understand why she always hid her face. "I will tell you what course you should take, Hekate, but you must do as you see fit."

Hekate spread her hands, sparing a glance back at the manor.

"You are familiar with Kronos's youngest son, Zeus."

"A petulant brat with a violent temper and delusions of grandeur, yes. I've met him." Unfortunately.

"You should seduce him."

Hekate snickered, shaking her head. "Yes, that's usually my response on meeting someone with their head stuck so far up their own arse they can see their liver. Naught gets a woman in the mood like a toddler in a man's body."

"He is flush with more Pneuma than most Titans could dream of, and you can siphon bits of it away from him in your bed, even whilst winning his trust."

"I could," she admitted. "But I can think of about a thousand men in this city I'd rather take to my bed." Including the damn doorman.

Enodia ignored her jibes. "Zeus will be the future. He will rule this world one day soon. Would you rather not be by his side than risk becoming the target of his wrath?"

Zeus would rule the world? Zeus would ... A rush of memory hit Hekate, and she stumbled back a step. A grey-eyed child ... a daughter she had given Zeus in a dream at Delphi, two thousand years ago, back before she even knew who the man was.

Another daughter ...

"You have also seen visions," Enodia intoned, not really a question.

It was so long ago, and she had not considered it in ages. But her dreams had so oft held answers, maybe even more answers than the dead. Maybe more than she would find in far Thule.

"Where is Zeus now?" she asked, the question sticking in her mouth.

"At his father's palace here in Kronion, as luck would have it."

Hekate grunted. Of course he was. "What do you get out of this?"

"Oh ... A child useful to the future."

PRACTITIONERS of the Art tended to view their sexuality prosaically, Hekate had found, and few would hesitate to use it as a weapon when necessary. Flesh was useful for bargaining with other sorcerers and even spirits, always filled with prodigious lusts. The idea of seducing someone with ulterior motive did not much offend, and she knew from her own prescient dream he would indeed father a child on her. Still ... still. He would not have been Hekate's first choice.

As a famed Titan sorceress, she received easy welcome in Kronos's palace, though the Titan lord himself was apparently away in the Olympian Mountains, of all places. Perhaps he sought solitude, solace from the pressures of ruling this polis for the last two thousand years. Perhaps it was something else. Either way, Kronos need concern her little for the moment, and his absence made Hekate's intentions easier to act upon.

Perhaps Enodia had planned it that way.

Zeus she found in one of Kronos's numerous lounges, sipping wine and leering at the ebony-skinned Titan who sat across from him. She was out of Inumiden, unless Hekate missed her guess. The sweltering land lay north of the Jungles of Kush, it too covered in large swathes of dense woodland. Hekate had spent some few years there in her wanderings of Hy-Brasil, and the Titan's vibrant garb was distinctive of those people.

Perhaps sensing her regard, Zeus looked up. She could almost see recognition working behind his pale blue eyes. "Hekate, be welcome," he said after a moment, motioning for her to join them. "Come, sit. This is Demeter, come to us from Hy-Brasil." He waved Demeter's origins away as if all lands beyond Elládos were the same. As if a thousand peoples did not call the massive continent of Hy-Brasil home.

Taking the invitation, Hekate settled down on a cushion adjacent to Zeus, closer than she might have chosen under any other circumstances. She flashed an easy smile and flicked her hair behind her ear. Fiery locks like hers drew attention, especially in the Elládosi world, and on some few occasions, that proved beneficial.

The Titan prince's gaze flitted back and forth between Demeter and Hekate, giving her the distinct impression he thought himself choosing what to buy at the market. Or perhaps, knowing Zeus, thinking he could come home with two prizes.

Demeter had no doubt come here thinking she could win herself a prince as a husband. And while Hekate would deny her that, she had to wonder if she was, in fact, doing the Inumiden a favour. Either way, the foreign Titan would have to be induced to leave.

Hmm. Perhaps a vicious rash would turn Zeus's eye from her?

A simple task, Tithorea confirmed. *Or you could make her skin peel off.*

No. No, Hekate would not take it so far unless forced to it.

⁊

IN THE END, Hekate had summoned another dryad to curse Demeter with boils. A mild case, and one that could be soothed as soon as she left this island. Which she had, given Zeus's mocking sneer for his erstwhile lover.

Sitting up in his bed now, listening to him snore, she wondered how Demeter had tolerated it. He might have proved a proficient lover, had he cared in the least for anyone's pleasure besides his own. But Hekate had become his pallake—his concubine—and she would need to endure his attentions a while longer.

At least until she gave him that grey-eyed daughter.

With a sigh, she rose and donned her peplos before slipping out the door. In the hall, another Titan stared at her, arms folded across his chest. He had a flaxen beard, with a long red scar crossing his nose and gouging his cheek. Hekate had encountered Kronos's elder son Hades only a few times, and never exchanged words with him.

Now, she met his gaze, daring him to offer her challenge.

"My brother's latest conquest emerges," the Titan said.

Well then. She forced down her retort, having to maintain the role a while longer. "Is there something amiss, Prince Hades?"

"Someone has come to see you."

Now she had to quirk a brow. Who even knew she was in the palace, save Enodia? Had the other sorceress come to seek her out? Had she come to confirm that Hekate had fulfilled her visions? A quiver of annoyance shot through Hekate at the thought. Next time, Enodia could be the one to lie beneath those inelegant thrusts.

"Show me the way," she said.

Hades snickered lightly, then turned on his heel and guided her through the palace. As they walked, a thought crept upon her, a strange wonder. What visitor would prompt a prince to bother acting as personal messenger?

When he led her to another couch-strewn lounge, she found her answer, as Morpheus rose to greet her. She had heard he'd survived the fate of the Circle but had never been so unfortunate as to encounter him again.

"My old mentor," she said, striding over to him.

"Hekate," the oneiromancer purred. "It's been an age, dear, and we have so much to—"

Her knee connecting with his stones abruptly cut him off and doubled him over. Hekate caught him with a hand on his cheek, thumb holding his jaw. Leaning in close, she whispered into his ear. "I've been dreaming about *that* for an age."

Behind her, Hades released a sharp breath, somewhere between gasp and chortle.

Hekate shoved Morpheus to the ground by his face, then knelt beside him. "You are the highest of fools to come before me, oneiromancer. That I did not seek you out does not mean I would not salivate over the utter ruination of your flesh."

The Titan flashed gritted teeth at her. "I serve ... Zeus," he rasped.

So, the prince had somehow retained the fallen sorcerer? What could he have possibly offered the ancient oneiromancer to get him to agree to that? If it was true, though, she couldn't exactly rip out his bowels without jeopardising her position in this court?

Moreover, Morpheus had said *Zeus*, not his father Kronos. That implied the prince had begun building his own cadre of supporters. Sycophants, perhaps, though she'd not expect Morpheus's loyalty to run deeper than the thinnest of veneers.

Her lip curling in distaste, she rose.

"Zeus wants to know what runs through the minds of those in his circle," Morpheus said, not rising.

For a moment, all she could do was stare at him. Such a violation of privacy perhaps should not have shocked, and yet she found herself struggling not to sputter in indignation, not only for herself, but for everyone else in this court. Would she have to submit to his probing of her dreams? If she did so, he might well devise her true motivation for sharing Zeus's bed. Which would undermine all she sought to achieve here. Besides, the idea of allowing him into her mind again left her clammy and feeling the need to bathe.

"You ever touch my mind again," she warned, "and the fate that befell the Circle will seem a reward compared to what you shall endure."

When she left, Hades was staring at her with eyes wide and brows reaching for his hairline. Hekate suppressed a slight smile at that.

&

"Zeus has been imbibing excess Ambrosia," Enodia said as they walked the long wall of Kronion one evening, some days later.

"What?" Hekate demanded. "How would he even get excess? The Ouranid League regulates what's available to all Titans. Is his father permitting this?"

"No, of course not. Why do you think he has gathered his little band of followers?"

Even knowing they were alone, that the closest wall guards were hundreds of feet away, Hekate found herself casting furtive glances around to make certain they were not overheard. "He's siphoning off the supplies," she realised. "He's using his influence and whatever authority his father gave him to steal little bits at a time."

"More, perhaps, than you think. Kronos is distracted with his fearful studies of the murky future and his dread apprehensions of what is to come."

"What fears should one of the rulers of the world have?"

Enodia huffed, a thin raspy laugh. "Ask your father."

"What?"

The sorceress stared out over the Strait of Korinth, not answering. "Zeus's followers are rewarded with more Ambrosia themselves, but still less than Zeus, who consumes many times his allotment."

Hekate shuddered. "That way lies madness." As if Zeus was stable before. But Ambrosia, taken long enough, eroded away at humanity and drove Titans to become self-absorbed. Overuse exacerbated the process, transforming them into madmen. The whole of the Ouranid League had probably taken too much for too long, but what Enodia claimed Zeus did went even further. "If I turned him in to Kronos, it would be the end of him."

"But we don't want to be the end of him. A war is coming, and Zeus will win. You need to help him, ensure he's had enough Ambrosia. We need a Destroyer fit to end an age and usher in a new one."

Hekate reeled at what Enodia implied. Consuming vast amounts of Ambrosia *would* fortify Zeus's Pneuma, make him a living god, if an unhinged one. "You want me to join his inner circle, to become a party to his conspiracy." Which would mean indulging in the excess herself, a thought that at once titillated—that rush of power and salacious energies!—and horrified. Had she not lost enough of herself through the Art?

"You want power? This is how you take it. This how the world changes forever."

19

PERSEUS

624 Bronze Age

With his ship destroyed, Perseus and his companions had no choice save to walk back to Byblos. They'd made camp for the evening, cold, wet, and with naught to eat, but all had agreed it was better than trekking through the darkness. Besides, Perseus was asleep moments after lying upon the ground.

After rising at dawn, they made their way back toward the city, Andromeda chatting amiably—the best kind of chatting, if you asked Perseus—all the while. So far as he could tell, Queen Kassiopeia had vexed the Nereids by flaunting the demigod lineage of her daughter and made some ill-conceived comparison to the beauty of mermaids. Perseus considered the destruction of an entire city—or the sacrifice of one's child—a bit of an overreaction for a mother's pride in her offspring, and Andromeda seemed to agree.

Rather, the princess blamed her father for not doing more to defend her. While Perseus suspected King Kepheus could not have done much save let Byblos drown in defiance, he understood her feelings. The betrayal of kin cut deeper than the sharpest of swords.

"From time to time, they send maidens down to the shore," Andromeda said. "Offerings to Pontus, stripped naked and served unto the lusts of the Deep Ones. I do not know if they murder them, but I can say none have ever returned."

"Offered to Nereus?" Pandora asked.

Perseus glanced at her, brow raised to inquire what she knew of it.

"He was a king of Pontus during the Golden Age," Pandora said, seeming lost in thought. "I did not realise he was still around until I heard mention of Nereids."

"They are sent to Pontus," Andromeda answered. "Beyond that, I cannot say."

Pandora tapped a finger upon her lower lip, face pensive as though working out some puzzle in her mind. The woman remained an eternal enigma.

❦

EVENING HAD COME upon them once more as they drew nigh to Byblos. Upon the shore before the city, a mer rose from the sea, striding naked onto the land to bar their path. He stood with webbed hands upon his hips, glare fixed upon each of them.

"Sirsir," Perseus said, sweeping a bow for the benthic god. "You honour us with your presence."

"You dishonour Poseidon in slaying a beast from his menagerie," Sirsir snapped. "Dishonour for which he might be inclined to unveil further oddities from his collection." His gaze settled upon Pandora, and he cocked his head. Beside Perseus, Pandora stiffened ever so slightly. "Do I know this mortal?" Sirsir asked.

"She was with me when I paid tribute in the harbour some few days ago." Perseus wrung his hands, not sure what to say to the mer. "Ah. Hmm. So, how might we appease Lord Poseidon, then?"

Sirsir's eyes nictitated as he turned his gaze back upon Perseus. Little fins upon his arms and legs flapped around, disquieting, albeit less so than gills pulsing on his neck. Mer remained capricious gods, more like to drown sailors than answer prayers, especially if vexed.

"Three young men and women in tribute, sent down to the shore within three days."

"Six sacrifices!" Andromeda blurted. "Six ...?"

In saving one life, had Perseus damned six others? The thought lanced his heart. He'd wanted to save innocent lives. What was he to do here? Challenge Poseidon himself?

"Feel free to occupy one of the places, Princess," Sirsir snapped at her.

"I'll pass the message on to the king," Aiolos said before Perseus could decide how to respond.

Maybe there was no way out. The whole of Man remained mired in the Titan trap. Every show of strength, every act of valour in defence of humanity would serve but to tighten the noose around their necks. And three of them here were demigods. How much worse for those with no Titan blood at all?

Sneering, Sirsir plodded off and vanished back beneath the sea. Pandora, Perseus noted, kept watching him a long time after he had gone.

Whatever had her mind awhirl, she kept it to herself as they continued into the city proper. Aiolos guided them to Kepheus's palace. As they passed the streets, men and women gathered, gaping at them, whispering in wonder and horror at those who had dared risk the further ire of Pontus.

Perseus walked with his head high but felt ready to wilt beneath their gazes. Shame coiled about his bowels, festering in his helplessness to truly make their lives better. These people, when they at last learnt what Pontus now demanded of them, would blame him and their princess both. Andromeda's name might well become a curse in Byblos, all for the crime of having lived. Or for the crime of having a mother who thought her daughter beautiful and dared to say so.

Such was the grace and glory of Poseidon, to visit terror amid these people. And if Zeus, another Olympian, were truly Perseus's father, was he any better? Was the King of Olympus kinder, more considerate toward Man than the Lord of the Sea? Perseus suspected allowing himself to believe such was but a pleasant self-delusion.

Andromeda's fingers twined with his own. A gentle squeeze. A reminder that, whatever else he had done, he had saved a life. A woman who wanted life. Maybe the rest fell to Kepheus to handle. Let him defy Poseidon or not, as his nature demanded. But Perseus had saved Andromeda, and he would continue to save her, by giving her a better home than this. A place where no one would look upon her and blame her for their troubles.

That much he swore.

When they arrived in the palace, Aiolos announced them. Almost immediately, an ageing man came striding toward them, arms spread. His face fell a bit when his gaze fixed upon Andromeda's hand laced with Perseus's own. Which probably meant this was her delightfully feckless uncle Phineus.

"Welcome stranger, and thank you for returning my bride," the man said, reaching for Andromeda.

"Yes, well, I *love* being thanked for things," Perseus said. "I mean it means more regarding things I've actually done, but I suppose I'll take gratitude for just about aught. I don't wish to appear ungracious." Appearing ungracious was almost as bad as *being* ungracious. Perhaps he could leave the last bit unsaid. Perseus clapped the man on the chest. "You, of course, forfeited any claim to any betrothed by failing to speak in her defence, but I shall see about finding you someone else for whom that won't be an issue." He shrugged. "A corpse, perhaps."

Phineus's eyes bulged as if he couldn't quite believe Perseus's temerity. Which was fair enough, as Perseus had enough temerity to count it as another Pneumatikoi.

Aiolos shoved Andromeda's uncle aside with more force than necessary and strode forward to address the king, a man even older than his brother, who was already pushing through the throng toward them. "I give you Perseus, slayer of the monster Ketus, saviour of Andromeda, who comes to claim her hand. Will you give your blessing, King Kepheus?"

The grey-haired king didn't answer his wife's father but rather swept his daughter into his embrace. Andromeda stiffened, at least for a moment, before softening as her father's tears fell upon her shoulder. Even if some things defied forgiveness, sometimes forgiveness wormed its way in. Then the queen was there too, arms around both her daughter and husband, all propriety lost in the moment of resurgent hope.

"The man who saved my daughter ..." the king wheezed, releasing his family, "shall have aught he ever wishes of me."

Perseus raised a finger. "Ah. Yes, wine, food, and a wedding." He paused. "To Andromeda, I mean." No sense in the king arranging someone else for him to marry.

KEPHEUS'S HALL fair overflowed with guests, the aristoi of Byblos, visiting merchants from Tyros, and even some few from farther abroad. The Neshians hailed out of Ugart, or so Perseus had heard, their long hair woven into a multitude of thin braids. From what he had heard, the last remnants of the etiolated Ugartian Empire had been annexed by Nineveh some years back, so these men were no doubt vassals of the great Ninevehan Empire, here by chance more than design.

The king of Byblos had laid out an aromatic spread across a cluster of long tables in the hall, the scents of hummus and simmering beef reaching Perseus, mingling with those of cod and other fish. At the centre of one table lay a platter teeming with octopus arms, their suckers seared pink.

Rather than indulge in gorging himself, Perseus merely claimed a handful of roasted pine nuts and wandered the halls, accepting the half-hearted congratulations of a hundred men whose names he planned to forget the moment he turned his back upon them. Not only was the crowd itself overwhelming, but one could hardly forget that these people looked upon him and his soon-to-be-wife with barely concealed loathing. They blamed them, perhaps not without cause, for the hardship that would soon be borne by the rest of Byblos.

His shame left him bilious, and he caught himself ever seeking out Andromeda, though as they were not yet wed, she remained hidden away somewhere in a pretence of propriety, the whole of the hall choosing to ignore that Perseus had rescued her when she had been chained naked and left to die alone. Try as he might, he found it impossible to pull himself out of his dolour. When drowning in the company of false friends, feigning smiles could cost more than the purest of silver.

"Perseus," someone said, her voice cutting through the clangour of the celebration. "Perseus." Pandora's hand fell upon his shoulder, and he looked to her. There were, admittedly, few women present here at the moment, and had she not been involved in the rescue of Andromeda, perhaps Kepheus would have denied even the Heliad access to the party. In truth, Perseus might owe her an apology for insisting she be allowed here.

"Are you well?" she asked.

For a moment, he stared into her golden eyes. Could everyone here see through his veneer of conviviality? No, just Pandora, so astute it seemed almost preternatural with her, as if she possessed some extra sense offering her insight denied to others. "I have a promise to keep, I know, my dear. They'll want to stretch the feasting over a few days, then we can be off. I'll take Andromeda back to Neritum with us, present the Gorgon's head"—he patted the macabre lump in his satchel—"and then we'll see about freeing your lover from whatever circumstances he finds himself in."

Before she could answer, a susurration ran through the hall, a muttering of the guests as though they had all become a burbling river, breaking and parting around newcomers.

Flowing through the crowd, Phineus strode in, a host of men streaming behind him, bearing daggers and xiphe. Phineus himself brandished a spear, its butt clanking upon the sandstone floor with each ominous step he took. When his gaze settled upon Perseus, he pointed the tip of his weapon at him. "You brought shame upon me,

Elládosi! Did you think I would not avenge the theft of my bride? Did you think you could come to our lands and intrude in our affairs without consequence?"

Perseus shrugged. "I rather did. I must admit, I took you for a limpet feigning manhood."

Predictably, that drew a snarl from Phineus, who pushed forward, spear-point first. Perseus reached for his xiphos, but he'd left it in his room, bringing only the satchel for fear of what would happen if someone dug through his things and found the head of Medusa.

"Brother!" Kepheus bellowed, rising from his throne and making his way toward Phineus. "Have you gone mad? You gave over any claim to Andromeda when you consented to her death, same as I. As I live with my guilt, you must endure your regret. Do not further sully this day with violence."

At that moment, Andromeda appeared, peering over her father's shoulder to level a cold gaze upon her uncle. For whatever reason, the princess chose to hold her tongue now—the hall full of guests, perhaps—but Phineus could not have missed her contempt.

The man growled in response, reversed his grip upon his spear, and flung it at Perseus. Time seemed to slow around Perseus as he drew upon his Pneumatikoi. He twisted to the side and watched the spear soar by. An instant too late he realised there were people behind him and reached for it, but not even his reflexes were fast enough. The shaft embedded in the gut of a Neshian merchant, and the man collapsed in a spray of red and a wet gurgle.

A quietude settled upon the hall, as if in the eye of a storm. Then, like the first breaking waves summoned by a tempest, the feast erupted into violence. Phineus's men, the only ones armed—for Kepheus's guards were at the fringes—surged forth, some driving back anyone who might attempt to intervene, almost a dozen others closing in on Perseus.

When he looked, Pandora had already vanished amid the throng, no doubt having seen trouble coming. Having no weapon at hand, Perseus raised his fists to meet the oncoming attackers. Only a fool fought twelve against one. So, what kind of drunken cretin imagined taking on twelve *armed* men with his bare hands? Perseus supposed he would find out. And, sad though it was, his best chance of survival might now lie in the fear all Men held of so-called demigods.

The first man lunged with a knife, his movements seeming languid, almost comical with Perseus's Pneumatikoi drawn. He dodged to the side of the blow and swung his fist. The impact rang through the hall, dislocating the man's jaw, spinning him around and sending both him and his teeth flying.

Already two more were on him. He caught the arm of a swordsman when the attacker tried to skewer him. A swift yank pulled him into Perseus's punch. The man's sternum collapsed under the blow with a sickening crunch of bone, then Perseus had to duck aside, dodging an attack from another man.

They swarmed over him, too caught in their bloodlust to notice, or care what he'd done to two of their numbers. Even with his reflexes, it took all his concentration to keep dodging blows and avoid getting slashed or impaled. Mounting a counterattack became impossible.

Someone tried to grab him, but Perseus was faster, snatching his wrist first and vaulting over the man, then kicking off his back. The attacker went skidding one way while Perseus flew to a column in the opposite direction, bounced off it, and landed with it at his back. At least here they could not surround him.

Phineus's ruffians raced toward him again but could not close all at once. Perseus dodged the first attack, his fist connecting with the throat of the man. His attacker dropped his knife and Perseus snatched it from midair the instant before another man tried to run him through. A dodge, and a swipe, and his newest attacker was clutching severed tendons in his elbow, shrieking.

They were closing upon him again, but wary now, eyes tracking his blood-slicked blade. Perseus allowed himself a grim smile. "Sheep ought not stalk a wolf, lest they actually manage to corner it."

Indeed, they hesitated, and Perseus lunged forward, wading amid them with speed they could not match, weaving a pattern of gouges, shallow cuts, and mortal wounds unto these curs who dared attack unarmed guests at a wedding. No, they deserved no mercy.

"Enough!" Phineus roared, no doubt distraught to see his friends lying in sanguine heaps upon the floor.

But Perseus had tolerated too much from this wretch already. Growling, he drove his blade up under the chin of another of Phineus's companions.

"Athanas!" Andromeda's uncle shrieked, voice seeming apt to break. When Perseus looked to him, the man had Pandora with one hand snared in her locks, the other holding a knife to her throat. Phineus visibly steeled himself, his gaze scanning over the carnage Perseus had wrought. The death Phineus had *forced* Perseus to unleash. "Drop the knife," Phineus rasped, his blade nicking Pandora's flesh, dangerously close to an artery. "Drop it, Elládosi!"

Perseus's eyes met Pandora's. What choice did he have? He could not allow harm to befall her.

His stolen dagger clattered upon the sandstone.

"Now bring me my bride, and I'll leave you."

Andromeda pushed around her father. "Release the woman, Uncle. You cannot think this will end well."

Perseus saw her from the corner of his eye, but it was Pandora's wink to draw his attention. The almost imperceptible twitch of her finger, trying to tell him something. To remind him ... to use the last weapon at his disposal. Which would not affect a woman.

"You shall have a wedding present from me," Perseus said, slowly reaching into his satchel. The clammy, rough touch of dead snakes upon his fingers churned his stomach, though not half so much as his intent. As what he would do now, even to a man who had earned it with his perfidy and craven attack. "A monument to this day, Phineus, and if you still wish for Andromeda after the gift, you have but to say so."

"What could you possibly offer me that I would—"

Perseus yanked the gruesome head from his satchel, brandishing Medusa in all her awful visage. Phineus gaped at the sight a moment, then convulsed, his muscles seeming to seize up. Pandora used his agony and shock to wriggle free. The same instant, flesh calcified, until naught save a marble statue remained, face a rictus of torment.

Before anyone else might chance to look upon the severed head, Perseus shoved it back in the satchel. But all eyes were locked upon Phineus, now become an eternal monument to folly.

20

HEKATE

2390 Golden Age

Hekate cradled the grey-eyed babe, dabbing her finger against the newborn's hand in hopes of getting her to grab it with her own tiny digits. The girl stared at her, wide-eyed, hand half closing around her finger.

"Aww. That's it, Mama's got you. Mama's always got you."

Her midwife moved about the plush chamber around her, gathering up rags and towels. "Are you well, my lady?"

Hekate was perfect and graced the midwife with a smile. "Well enough, Eileithyia. Well enough, for certain."

The door was flung open before Eileithyia could say aught in answer, and Zeus billowed in, his platinum hair flowing about him.

"Well," he demanded.

"A beautiful baby girl," Hekate said, beaming.

Zeus, though, seemed to deflate, and he shook his head. "A girl." Was it scorn in his voice, or just disappointment?

Either way, Hekate frowned at him. "What should we call her?"

Zeus shrugged, apparently beyond all care for the birth now. "Whatever suits you."

The Titan departed, followed by Eileithyia, leaving her alone with her child. Which little bothered her. Hekate stroked the babe's cheek. "Well, then, we'll call you ... Athene." It had a nice ring to it.

The child stared at her with such rapt attention, Hekate could almost have fancied Athene understood her circumstances. The open curiosity in her visage could have broken Hekate's heart. Maybe it had.

Four years she had spent beside Zeus, helping him steal Ambrosia from his father. Even when his wife Hera had shown up, Hekate had lingered on as his pallake. Of course, she had already been several months with child by then, so where was she to go?

She had asked herself, then, if she still would have seduced him if she'd known he was married to that bitch back then. In truth, it would have made it more appealing, just to spite the Titan who had so long tormented Hekate. She had stayed on as Zeus's pallake, watching Hera squirm in impotent rage.

It was in Tethys's court in Thebes she had delivered Athene, while Zeus visited the home of his in-laws. Another man might have thought it poor taste to bring his pallake to such a place, but Zeus could do no wrong in his own eyes, which meant aught amiss was invariably someone else's fault.

Besides, this was where Hekate had always been for the birth. After so many centuries, the vision of this moment had faded into the haze that swallows all dreams, but now, it had arrived, and sense of it, of fulfilment, had seized her with glorious violence. Hekate had known Athene more than two millennia before her birth, though she had not known the name until now.

Maybe ... maybe she could do better by this daughter than she had by Kirke. Certainly, she would not make the mistake of training another child in the Art. The knowledge that ought to have empowered Kirke had only served to further divide her from those around her. Despite her parentage, Kirke was condemned to live forever with the title of Nymph, for her Pneumatikoi proved too weak. The taste of puissance Hekate had given her with the Art had only led to further dissatisfaction with that lot, and she had watched her child grow bitter and lonely.

Not again, not this time.

A SURREALITY HAD SETTLED upon Hekate on first returning to her childhood home in Thebes, as if she moved through dream-woven halls. As if she waited for the amorphous nightmares of her youth to stalk free from behind every column and caryatid. Even that unease faded in time, though. It was, after all, just a place.

"Oh," Hera said when Hekate strolled the water gardens, carrying Athene around so the babe could admire the fountains. "I see the whore has finished whelping."

Hekate forced a placid smile and inclined her head while imaging using Mormo to devour the bitch's soul, leaving her desiccated corpse floating between statues of sirens. She could almost see those glassy eyes staring up at the pitiless firmament, wondering how she'd gone so wrong in her life.

Sadly, even if Hekate could have gotten away with murder—and perhaps she could have—it would have weakened Zeus. For better or for worse, she had cast her lot in with him and his band. Enodia had promised he would become the most powerful man in the world, and thus far, her Oracular insight had never failed Hekate.

It meant, for now, Hekate would endure Hera even as she endured Morpheus. For that matter, she cared little for snooping, sneering Hades, Zeus's sadistic brat Ares, or his simpering daughter Hebe. In fact, one of the only members of Zeus's entire faction she could even stand was modest, introspective Aidos, always eager to hear about the exotic places Hekate had visited in her journeys. The Nymph had tired of her status, relegated to naught save breeding stock, and had thrown in with Zeus in hopes for a different fate.

"This is Zeus's daughter, Athene."

"Daughter?" Hera scoffed. "To hear him tell it, he created her with the sweat of his brow and the strength of his will."

Hekate's smile turned wicked. "I recall him sweating, yes."

Hera curled her lip and strode off without another word. A twinge of sympathy for the woman ran through Hekate. After all, her husband had the loyalty of a reptile. Not more than a twinge, though, because Hera was, after all, a noxious snake herself.

"You win friends everywhere you go," Hades observed, stepping from the shadows.

Though she tried to suppress it, Hekate knew she had started at his appearance. He was always lurking and seemed to take perverse joy in catching her unawares. With affected disinterest, she looked him up and down, not for the first time wondering how he'd gotten that scar. "What do you want?"

Uninvited, he reached over and poked at Athene. "To see my niece, of course."

His unwelcome attentions had the babe bursting into tears, her sobs echoing through the garden. Hekate jerked the girl away, which only broadened the smile upon Hades's face. "Aww." He feigned offence, then stalked after Hera, chuckling.

Maybe Enodia was right. Maybe the ritual the sorceress had suggested—however profane—would be worthwhile simply not to have to look at one more member of this wretched family. The true irony lay in Hekate helping Zeus betray Kronos who, unlike his children, was affable if mysterious, driven more by intellect than vanity. Still, something weighed upon Kronos, and Hekate saw signs in him of budding paranoia. The questions he asked, the way his gaze lingered a bit overlong upon his sons.

It boded ill.

Whatever future impended, it would arrive all too soon.

IN THE END, perhaps that—the ever-descending future—was the real reason she came to Zeus, ready to share Enodia's proposal. Or the parts of it the prince needed to hear.

They met, not in the palace itself, so thick with Tethys's spies, but in the woodlands outside the city. Those woods had changed much since her childhood, even the river having somewhat shifted course. Changed, yes, and yet somehow the same.

Maybe it was Hekate that had changed, for now the foreboding of twilight no longer thrilled or frightened her. The ghosts that had tormented her were bent to her will, coming and going as she commanded. Such was the gift of a necromancer, especially one so powerful as herself.

"What are we doing out here?" Zeus demanded as Hekate guided him deeper into the woods.

She led him to a glade where she had prepared a ritual circle, having moved great standing rocks to demarcate its boundaries, then painstakingly carved glyphs into those surfaces.

"What the fuck is this?" the prince blustered.

"Your power waxes," Hekate said. "But it can grow further, beyond all bounds. Beyond this life and even unto the Underworld."

That had his attention, his icy blue eyes suddenly locked upon her face. "I can rule the Underworld?"

"Via proxy, yes, for I do not think you wish to take the path into the dark. It flows but one way."

"What proxy?"

"Someone you trust enough to enforce your will even in the deepest gloom. Control the king of the dead, and you control the dead themselves." Hekate hesitated for a moment. The Ambrosia had driven Zeus into ever greater spirals of megalomania, but there was always the chance some semblance of filial loyalty remained in him. "One's own blood is the most powerful. The greater the sacrifice, the greater the effect we can generate from it."

Zeus scratched at his beard, scowling. "Out with it."

The moment of truth ... "Can you think of none of your kin you could set with the task?"

Folding his arms, the prince leaned against a tree. "Not Ares. No, not one of the children ..."

"A brother then?"

Zeus grunted.

In truth, Hekate had no idea what Zeus had told Hades to get him to come to the circle. It would have boggled the mind to imagine anyone would have willingly marched here to his own death, so perhaps Zeus had convinced him he would bodily enter the Underworld to become its king.

Either way, the two brothers arrived sometime after twilight, while Hekate knelt in the grass studying the grimoire and the notes she had made in it after her conversation with Enodia. Naught in the Sefer Raziel prepared her for this exact operation, true, but there were rituals relating to transferral of power.

In a way, this was similar. She would need to imbue Hades with a fraction of her necromantic abilities but do so in a way he would retain them even in death. From there, he should be able to devour the souls of the dead to enhance those abilities and create a kingdom for himself in the Underworld. A kingdom loyal to his brother—for Hekate should still be able to exert some control over the sliver of her own power she would infuse into him.

"Take off your clothes," she said, not looking up from the book. Despite using the grimoire, despite advice from Enodia, Hekate was, in essence, creating an entirely new ritual, one that altered fundamental laws of reality. None of them could afford the least mistake.

The crux seemed to lie in using a spellsong to blend in with the ritual. Obviously, she couldn't sing and incant at the same time, so she would need to call up ghosts with the invocation, then switch to the song. Unless ... should she prime the area with her song first, and thus weaken the Veil?

Should she ... Hekate looked around to check the circle only to find both brothers had stripped naked and were staring at her.

Grimacing, she ran her tongue over her teeth. "Zeus, you can continue wearing your clothes. Hades, sit in the centre of the circle. I need to paint glyphs upon your flesh."

The brothers moved to comply, and Hekate took a bowl of deer's blood over to where Hades sat. One by one, she traced sigils over his back, chest, biceps, and thighs. The prince shuddered at her touch, whether from the cool night air, the blood, or fear, she didn't know. Or much care.

When she had finished, she rose, wiping her hands upon her peplos. It mattered little if she ruined a few garments for such an accomplishment as this. Her actions here would change the World, would redefine conceptions of what was possible with the Art. The thrill, the momentousness of that, it had her shuddering, her heart palpitating.

The very forest around her seemed to teeter in fearful intimation of her purpose.

In far Mu, sorceresses danced to harness their Pneuma, even as the spellsongs of Kumari Kandam focused it into similar shapes, congealing the breath of life into thought forms they called tulpas.

The heartbeat of the World itself had begun to thrum through Hekate, and mesmerised by it, she found her body had taken on a will of its own. A gentle sway, her fingers parting her peplos to let it fall from her shoulders. Her voice rang out, unsteady for but a moment before rising to caress the treetops with a song of passing ages.

A song of glorious cities that defied all known laws of physics, bending the Earth to their wills. A song of war, when Men, in desperation, called to the Moon and made beasts of themselves in the prodigiousness of their need.

She did not remember kicking off her sandals, but some part of her mind registered as her bare feet scraped over twigs and lichen, as loam squelched between her toes. If any had asked her, she could not have said whence came the wild dance, her hair flung about as if in a tempest, her arms heaving one way and the next.

Of their own accord, her eyes slipped into the colour-muddling vision of the Sight, revealing the hordes of gathering shades. The membrane separating the Mortal Realm from the beyond thrummed with each note she sang, as though someone plucked it like a harp, its melody ricocheting through the whole of the cosmos. She stamped her foot and lines of Etheric flame shot out in arcing parabolas, flaring through the Penumbra. They struck the bounds of her summoning circle and raced along its perimeter before rejoining one another in a whorl.

The men back in the Mortal Realm gasped, blind to the wondrous unmaking of reality around them, yet feeling its snapping threads, nonetheless. Its fraying would scrape their souls, leave them reeling with innominate thoughts they would never fully parse, and the accompanying dread of knowing something beyond their ken unfolded just out of sight.

Her voice soared, ripping order to shreds, leaving the World trembling, begging for release before it bent too far back upon itself. The forest lurched inward, becoming a sphere enclosing them, until the only aperture from the wood was directly above, a space filled up by a suddenly too large full moon.

Possessed by fell instinct, Hekate allowed her song, her lamentation of the tragedy of Dark Faerie, to blend into a Supernal incantation. She invoked all the ghosts in hearing range.

They came to her, the manifold dead drifting in like an Etheric flood. They came, reaching inward toward the focal point where she had directed all her Pneuma. Toward Hades, sitting stock-still upon a rock, trembling—though with the Sight embraced, Hekate could not make out the details of his face. Dilapidated, cadaverous fingers clawed at the membrane, worming their way in as though digging through threadbare silk.

And the men gasped again, a moan of inarticulate dread escaping Hades.

For he must have seen the grasping claws of a hundred ghosts dragging themselves into the fragile sphere he found himself at the centre of. Perhaps some part of him began to apprehend what now unfolded. Perhaps, in the crawling approach of the damned, he fathomed his own impending fate.

Ceasing her cant, Hekate whirled over to him, grabbed his jaw, and breathed into his open, gaping mouth. Her breath carried with it Pneuma—for Pneuma was the breath of life—and with it, a tether to those bound dead she called up.

The Titan prince convulsed from the influx of her energies, pitched over backward from the rock, landing upon his back in the grass. Seizures claimed him, his head slamming again and again upon the unforgiving ground. Blinking away the Sight, Hekate beheld him, looked hard at him, for she owed him at least that much. She owed him, bearing witness to the rictus of pain and horror he felt, as a hundred ghosts began to close in upon him.

A strand of flesh flayed away above Hades's ribs, followed by another and another.

"Fuck," Zeus exclaimed.

Bones abruptly burst apart, thrown wide as unseen spectres wormed their way inside the Titan's chest.

Hekate heard Hades's brother fall over, gasping, but paid him no mind, eyes locked on Hades. His convulsions had such a hold upon him they strangled even his screams. Sanguine rivers trickled down both sides of his mouth, painting his neck crimson, even as further invisible claws began to tear at that as well.

A gut-wrenching sound, flesh being ripped away whilst more and more of the dead climbed into their new host. She had compelled them inside Hades.

"I didn't know this would happen," Zeus complained.

Hekate didn't deign to respond. He had consented to the death of his brother. Did he demure now upon seeing it was messy? Did witnessing the agony change aught?

Abruptly, Hades's chest and neck imploded, compressed into gristly, distended mockeries of the human form, all jutting bone and pierced, weeping flesh.

Vertigo claimed Hekate, the most profound exhaustion she had ever experienced seizing her from the expenditure of so much Pneuma all at once. The World snapped back into place, leaving the ruined corpse in the glade. Hekate slipped to her knees, words failing her.

It was done.

Darkness teased its way in around her.

&

"Fucking epic," Zeus said, when Hekate awoke. The Titan fair rushed from one spot to another, abuzz with nervous energy. "The power of it ... like naught imaginable!"

Yes, the Art always carried with it a frenetic intensity, a coruscating thrill running through the veins, as of having wrapt one's fingers around the stuff of the cosmos. But to derive such obvious pleasure—indeed, she saw a bulge beneath his khiton—from the death of one's own kin bespoke such profound derangement as to defy words.

The prince continued to gush about the experience, even as they returned to Thebes, and for days afterward, despite Hekate's warnings toward caution. Caught in the throes of his triumph, Zeus had no doubt bragged of it to his wife and children. Perhaps Morpheus knew, perhaps the whole of the band.

Hekate, for her part, focused on trying to exert control over Hades's ghost. A tinge of madness brushed against the wretched soul now, and when she sought him, he radiated pain and a palpable sense of betrayal. Still, he too revelled in the power he wielded, building his own kingdom out in the Underworld.

For night after night, Hekate summoned Hades, demanding he report upon his progress. The dead flocked to him, as she had imagined, but with each time he came before her, she felt the push of his own obdurate will against hers.

It forced her, once, to imbibe an extra dose of Ambrosia—Zeus provided without question, as always—before she sat, trembling, calling the prince's dead brother. She needed her Pneuma flush, overflowing, to exert dominance over the ghost king.

Such things took the sum of her attention. Perhaps that was why she had not seen it coming. Why her oneiromantic dreams failed to surface and offer any forewarning before Kronos burst into Tethys's palace in Thebes.

The sudden clang of the doors thrown wide sent a reverberation of shock running through her, and Hekate found herself stumbling to rise from where she reclined in a lounge with Zeus. Gaping at his father, the prince fumbled his wine goblet, managing to drench his khiton rubescent.

Fists clenched at his sides, Kronos stood in the doorway, trembling with a rage that resounded off the marmoreal columns. It sucked the air from the palace, replacing it with a choking miasma that obliterated any question about what he knew. "Your own brother …" The Ouranid lord snarled.

Even as he spoke, Styx flowed around him like water, eyes darting around the room to take in all potential threats before fixating upon Hekate. "Had one asked me, I'd have not imagined the passing of even so many centuries would have returned you to Thebes. Like the most wretched of bitches, you slink back, tail between your legs, whimpering for the whip of your old master."

How could mere words eviscerate twenty-two centuries and leave her a quivering child once more flinching before the ill regard of an older girl? How could Hekate stand there, unable to form words, withering under that gaze? Such thoughts redoubled her shame.

She needed to do something, but her muscles refused her commands.

A tattered doll, Khione taunted her.

Her will falters, Tithorea said.

Then one of us will soon claim the tiller of this vessel, Okypete cooed, voice mocking, though the harpy's laughter paled before the insane cackles that erupted from Mormo.

Zeus had still not quite risen to meet his father. In great strides Kronos crossed the room, seized Zeus by his hair and hefted him the rest of the way to his feet. For an aching instant, the two men stared at one another, and Hekate watched Zeus's visage harden into his habitual sneer. The son opened his mouth to speak, but his father's fist slamming in between his eyes silenced him, sending him hurtling backward. Zeus smacked into a column, the marble splintering beneath the impact. Plaster rained from the ceiling, caking the prince even as the palace trembled.

"You ripped him apart!" Kronos bellowed. "You allowed your own brother to die in agony the likes of which you cannot even imagine! I should have you thrown bodily into Tartarus for that!"

Could he do that? How would he reach a prison said to exist even beyond the Spirit Realm?

Having slithered closer, Styx lunged for Hekate. Reflex drew Hekate from her stupor and summoned ice crystals from the depths of her soul where Khione yet lurked, even as she caught the woman's forearm. Styx faltered and shrieked as a thick layer of rime encased her arm up to the elbow. Wailing, Tethys's daughter collapsed to the floor, clutching her frozen limb, staring at it in incomprehension.

Hekate allowed the woman a bare instant of pity before tapping Okypete to call forth the Art of Storm. Billowing winds swept in from the windows and open doorway, whirling about Hekate to form a vortex that sent her peplos and hair whipping about her. With a growl, she poured Pneuma into those winds. Faster and faster they spun, reaching outward to drive back Tethys's guards as they had begun to flow into the chamber.

Her violent gales sent Styx careening along the floor, and even Kronos had raised an arm against the torrent. As Hekate screamed, flooding yet more Pneuma into her storm, the Ouranid lord's sandals skidded over the marmoreal floor, forcing him back.

It wouldn't be enough, though. They'd not escape the whole of Thebes this way. Mind whirring, Hekate made her way to Zeus, expanding the eye of her storm to encompass him as well. Men and Titans kept trying to push in at her, teeth gritted and faces grim, though they could not close in past the raging winds. A warrior hurled a javelin, but the projectile splintered, becoming debris within the whirlwind.

Only one way out remained to her, one path she had chanced only for brief sojourns, and never with another. A power drawn from the wraith bound to her soul. One hand upon Zeus, Hekate reached for Mormo within herself. Cloying darkness filled her senses, a wretched choking taste in her mouth that had her gasping, even as the impression of oil washing over her skin seized her. She pushed forward, feeling the viscous membrane of the Veil trying to hold her back.

Then it gave way and she and Zeus passed into shadow. The vibrancy of colour fled from her sight, replaced by the blue-grey shadowscape of the Penumbra. The world twisted, bent back upon itself. The columns of Tethys's hall warped, becoming spirals jutting at illogical angles. The ceiling turned concave, even as chill mist seeped in from the windows and the lamentations of the damned came to her on nether winds.

Those around her, save Zeus, faded to distant shadows, though greater vibrance radiated from the stronger Pneuma in the Titans.

She had pulled them into the Underworld.

Even as the incipient thought took shape, Mormo's assault began. The wraith's tattered, tenebrous shape began to peel away from the flesh on Hekate's hands, its skeletal claws crawling out of her fingers. Shrieking, Hekate hurled all that remained of her will at the ghost.

The Ambrosia had so fortified her Pneuma that even Mormo shuddered, retreating into her flesh with a squelching sound. This time.

Zeus heaved her to her feet. "Get up. We cannot remain in the palace."

Passing through the Underworld presented extreme danger, but she saw no alternative. And then ... "Athene!"

Zeus hesitated a bare moment. "You can get word to Morpheus, and he can slip out with her."

Though his lack of emotion for his daughter had her wanting to throttle the prince, he had the right of it. They needed to flee before someone figured out how to reach them, or before ghosts or spirits converged upon them here. They needed to get somewhere safe so she could pull them back into the Mortal Realm.

And they needed to do it fast.

21

PANDORA

624 Bronze Age

While the other guests remained fixated upon the grim fate that had befallen Phineus, Pandora could not help but notice the not-quite-concealed tremors that ran through Perseus. The ordeal had shaken something deep within him, almost as if he had not, until this moment, truly appreciated the horror of Medusa's curse. That a man, flush with the vibrance of life, however vilely lived, could become stone—alive one instant and irrevocably altered the next. Was it worse than death? Had the transmogrification destroyed the Ethereal part of him, denying him even the Underworld?

Indeed, Kepheus's guests gaped at the surface horror of it—the shock, rather—but Perseus, Pandora could tell, apprehended the deeper obscenity of what had transpired here.

Thus, the greater twinge of sympathy she felt was for Perseus, rather than Phineus, who had deserved whatever had become of his soul. She slipped through the crowd, took Perseus by the elbow, and guided him to sit—to collapse, in fact—upon one of the couches off the side of the hall. The demigod didn't look at her, seemed unaware of her as she patted his hand. "I'll find you some wine."

"It's a wretched thing," he mumbled.

Pandora was not certain whether he meant Phineus's fate or Medusa's head, but either way she nodded. "Wretchedness abounds where the lives of Men and gods cross." Athene's curse had wrought this. One more Titan who flung power about like a little boy seeing how far his piss could fly, caring little for anyone or anything sprayed in the processes.

The only Titan Pandora had found with a trace of humanity was Prometheus, and Olympus had stolen him from her. Soon, she'd need Perseus to help save him, but the demigod could help no one until he found his own footing once more.

Drifting away from him, she caught up with the serving girl. "Where's Andromeda?" she asked.

The girl, no more than ten years old, shuddered a little at being addressed. "She ... The princess went into the courtyard garden with her handmaid."

Thanking the servant, Pandora wended her way outside, onto a sandstone portico. Beyond it, she spied Andromeda strolling amid gladioluses, hand clutching that of another young woman. Because, of course, Andromeda too would soon leave her home city and never return. Perseus planned to bring her to Elládos, and given the circumstances, Pandora could not disagree with the need to do so, but still.

The sudden ache in her soul forced her to lean upon a pillar. Tyros was not so far from here, and she would never forgive Hekate for dragging her away from there, sobbing, begging for a home stolen from her right along with her innocence. Zeus had swept in, a squall of chaos and pomposity, rending asunder her World. Her nails scraped at the stone, almost feeling the Olympian's throat beneath them.

The force of her rage felt apt to split her in twain, to set her bursting aflame. It could immolate continents. Zeus and his ilk had taken everything from her, over and over, and for that she had been willing to murder his childhood self. Not that she'd managed it. Not that it wouldn't have destroyed all she had if he *hadn't* existed, with her love and her child predicated upon his torments.

Lest she break apart from dwelling on it, Pandora pushed off the pillar and intercepted Andromeda.

On seeing her, the princess patted her handmaid's shoulder and ushered her on.

"I know too well the trepidation creeping up upon you," Pandora said. "I've nigh drowned in it myself."

Andromeda started, though her expression quickly returned to neutrality. "These people left me to feed a sea serpent. They cheered as I was carted off to the cliffs, and now a fair many of them resent me for living through the ordeal."

"And still a part of you fears to leave it behind."

"No," the princess protested, though the lie hitched her voice and danced across her face.

Pandora forced a smile. "Perseus recoils in shock at what he did to your uncle. Perhaps a kind word might draw him from himself."

Surprise ran over her visage a moment. "Those men all deserved their deaths."

"I am quite certain he knows that. Still, there was something more unsettling about the manner of Phineus's death. The obscenity of it, the perversion of nature, it has imbrued his soul as surely as the blood of those men imbrued his knife." And maybe there was comfort for the two of them in each other.

When Hekate had taken Pandora away from Tyros, she was all too soon separated from Europa, forced to face her new reality alone, bereft of anyone she might draw strength or solace from. Andromeda and Perseus would have one another, and that must count for a great deal.

Catching her meaning, Andromeda inclined her head and made her way back into the palace.

Blowing out a breath, Pandora wandered the garden. The flicker of oil lamps dangling from bronze poles offered scant illumination to revel in the flowers here, though they must have seemed vibrant in daylight.

Beauty obscured by darkness. She imagined the Muse Thalia would have written fair poetry on such things, though naught came to mind.

Soon, they would sail for Neritum, perhaps again by way of Atlantis. She was so very close to Tyros, part of her almost longed to stop at the other polis and see how it had changed. But such thinking was facile, for she could not afford to leave Prometheus lingering in torment just to indulge in idle fancies that had no bearing on her real life. That life was with him and Pyrrha.

"Pandora," a voice called, one that had her jerking around in shock and incomprehension.

Because there he was, drawn from the shadows of her musings, standing in the light of a lamp pole, crystal blue eyes gleaming.

"Prometheus ..." Pandora took a faltering step toward him, mind reeling. How was ... How was it possible? "You're here." She knew her voice faltered. She knew the line was idiotically obvious, but still the words slipped out and she could find naught else to say as her heart lurched from such a profound change in the space of her reality.

And then she was running, dashing into his arms, casting herself against the rock-like surface of his chest. Tears welled in her eyes as she slapped a fist upon his shoulder over and over. He drew her close and held her like that, time stopping around them. All the palace had melted away and left them alone upon their private island.

With such tenderness he held her at arm's length to look at her, laid his palm against her cheek.

"How?"

"You saved me."

Again, a shifting of her World, the ground beneath her seeming to undulate as her mind accommodated the information. "Not yet. Not for *me*." But if he was here now, in Perseus's time, it meant she had—she *would*—travel back once more and secure his release closer to her own time. "So, I can take Perseus back with me using the Box."

Prometheus's face seemed haunted, she realised. Burdened by the weight of unfathomable torments rendered unto him and the pressure of the thousand things he dared not voice. Time and Fate made them all playthings, and he could not risk bucking the rules of the game for fear of unraveling the whole of their lives. "It's not Perseus who frees me, Pandora, it's his great-grandson Herakles."

She gaped at him, her legs going weak at the implication of his words. No. No, that would mean she'd have to go forward, get Herakles, then bring him back further in time and … No. When would this boundless madness end?

"Pandora, listen. I wish I could tell you—"

A shriek split the night sky an instant before a golden meteor crashed down beside them. The impact sent the both of them tumbling to the ground, Pandora landing upon her arse, and Prometheus catching himself upon hands and knees.

The meteor rose, lamplight glinting off aureate armour shrouding her head to toe, wings rising behind her. Nemesis.

"Fucking bitch," Pandora groaned, trying to rise.

"No," Prometheus growled. He shoved off the ground, flipping around sideways to land upon his feet before the agent of the Fates. He came up swinging with an open-handed strike at the winged woman. She blocked it on a vambrace, but Prometheus followed with another and another.

The pair of them fell into a dance so fast Pandora couldn't even track it, couldn't say who was attacking or what was happening, save that both seemed to be continually pushing the other's hands away. Their attacker kicked out at Prometheus, caught his knee, and drove him down to the ground. She had his arm, twisting it behind his back.

"Pandora, flee!" he bellowed at her.

Nemesis growled at him, her armoured fist crashing into his face. A spray of red erupted from Prometheus's lips, and he toppled.

"No!" Pandora shrieked but was already backing away as Prometheus had instructed. She had to trust he knew what he was saying.

Would Nemesis try to take the Box from her? Could she afford to take any chances? Should she attempt to hide here, in Byblos? No. She knew damn well she needed to find this Herakles and get him back into the past. There was naught for her here, naught for her any time until she had fulfilled her promise to save Prometheus from Tartarus.

And he had been here, free. Which meant she would succeed.

In a mad scramble, she dove behind some bushes and pulled the Box from her satchel. Desperate, she twisted the gears. She'd studied this device as much as she could over the past year, and she was fair certain she could adjust whether she moved forward or backward based on the positions of concealed inner tumblers connected to the gears.

So. Forward, to find this Herakles and put an end to the madness.

She activated the Box and the World pulsed.

THE DISORIENTATION from the time shift seemed somewhat diminished, though it still sent her spilling into the dirt of some dark alley. Gasping, Pandora landed on her hands and knees, sparing a mere moment before sweeping the Box back into her satchel.

She tried to rise, but the medley of emotions she'd been holding back latched onto her gut as if with fangs, and she swayed, caught between a sob and a scream of inexpressible frustration. She braced herself on the wall, then smacked her fist against it sideways. He'd been right *there*! He'd been in her arms, safe and ... and no different than if she had remained with him in Thebes during the Ambrosial War. Refusing to move forward, to find the way to save him, it was the same as damning him.

She needed someone to shriek at, to throttle for the innominate fury that had her trembling. But there was no one, save the gods-damned Fates themselves, to whom she might complain. No person in the whole ambit of the World that could fathom the burden she bore in flitting through time, seeking a solution that always seemed one further step away.

She had wandered into a maze, and every path forward was a step deeper into the puzzle.

The ouroboros was *crushing* her.

Drying her cheeks, she forced herself to make her way out into city streets. Here, the afternoon was about to set, and she could see the hints of twilight peeking out across the sky. In the distance, she thought she could hear the faint roar of a waterfall, the sound familiar. As were the streets. She knew this place.

Thebes. She was in the upper city of Thebes.

Dazed, she wandered the polis, coming at last to the agora she had first seen walking beside Tethys. The agora remained abustle with folk heading about their business—even if that was probably cutting through town to find cheap wine in many cases. The urge to grab someone and demand to know what year it was passed through her, bringing a faint smirk to Pandora's lips. And why not? They'd think her a madwoman, but she wasn't even certain that would be wrong.

A rough, clammy hand seized her elbow and spun her around. "It is you," a mer said. Though his features had changed somewhat, he perhaps resembled the Sirsir she had known during the Ambrosial War.

Which meant she had moved backward rather than forward, and maybe by millennia. Which meant ... *fuck*.

Pandora stilled her face, only half certain none of those thoughts had revealed themselves. "Sorry, have we met?"

"Tethys will wish to deal with you herself, spy," Sirsir said, exposing hints of sharklike teeth in his maw. The mer tightened his grip on her arm and yanked her after him, pulling her up the steps of the acropolis with such haste she twice stubbed her sandals on the stairs.

It did, however, give her mind time revolve around his words. Tethys still ruled here, which meant she was back in the Golden Age, because the Titan had fled the Thalassa world following the Titanomachy. Sirsir had physically changed from his appearance during the Ambrosial War, appearing in the third guise she'd seen him in. Taller now, with stronger cheek bones. A different body …

A sickening thought welled up inside her mind as she considered. Was that why the sirens of Pontus demanded human tribute from Byblos and other places? Was that what Tethys had offered to gain the service of the Telkhines in the first place? Because the mer were —appalling though the thought was—some kind of parasite inside Men. Sirsir took a mortal host and slowly transformed his features to match his own image, but not completely. Vestiges of the original host's appearance remained, which meant he appeared different in different times. Because he—*it*—was in other men.

Had her mind run away with her in her distress, or was such a thing even possible? Her stomach roiled at the thought, and suddenly, the clammy webbed hand holding her seemed so impossibly alien she would have paid any price to be able to flee as far from this creature as possible. What in Gaia was this *thing* that rode Men like horses? Worse than that, for they wore their faces, held their very essence hostage.

And Tethys knowingly worked with them. Surely the Ouranid lady knew what she had bartered away for their services. But she had made the pact and secured control of the seas through Pontus—and no doubt considered it a worthy bargain.

Sirsir guided Pandora back to the palace that had once been her home, then into not Tethys's grand hall, but rather through the marmoreal maze of the inner palace to reach the water gardens. At first, she wondered how he knew where Tethys was, but when she looked, she noticed him checking subtle cues from the servants, each cocking their heads in the right direction. No doubt they were as eager to be away from the alien god as she was.

Without preamble, Sirsir flung Pandora to the ground before a fountain she had oft visited when she lived here. Tethys paced around the fountain and exchanged a few words with Sirsir that Pandora did not catch while she was brushing herself off and rising to her feet.

"I remember finding more welcome here when last I came,"

Pandora said, taking the chance to scan the gardens for signs of aught familiar. But, save Tethys and Sirsir, she saw no one she knew. Even most of the mosaics painted upon the walls had been redone.

To Pandora's relief, Tethys dismissed the mer, then strode to stand before Pandora, glaring down at her with those deep blue eyes of hers, her black hair rustling in the gentle evening breeze. "That was two thousand years ago, *mortal*. More than that, in fact. How are you even still alive?" Before Pandora could answer, Tethys seized her by the chin and hefted her up so that Pandora's dangling sandals just brushed the cobblestones. Her neck protested, felt apt to yank right out of her torso, and all she could do was moan. "Did Prometheus give you Ambrosia? Do you have any idea what fate he would suffer for such a transgression?"

Flailing, Pandora slapped at the Titan's wrist, but she might as well have tried to pry loose the arm of a marble statue.

Abruptly, Tethys released her, and Pandora dropped back to the ground with a groan. For a heartbeat she stood there, massaging the crick in her neck. Little shots of lightning ran down her arms at the abuse she'd suffered, and she stared daggers at the Titan who had once hosted her. How quickly these creatures could turn on a person. "It's a long story," she rasped.

"I don't have time for long stories," Tethys snapped. "Tell me true, or I'll hand you over to the Telkhines and they'll have the answers from you. Are you a spy for Zeus, girl?"

"Zeus?" Oh. The Titanomachy. Zeus's rebellion against Kronos and the Ouranid League had begun. Which meant Pandora had now landed clean in the middle of the worst war in history. "Why in the name of Gaia's mossy arse would I possibly help a Titan you know damn well tried to kill me?"

Glowering, Tethys looked her up and down. "That was long ago. Your lover has sided with him, or at least with Hekate who serves that ingrate cur, amounting to much the same thing. Because of them, war has spilled over Elládos and Phlegra, and Kronos has us all hunting for his wayward son." She paused a moment as if to emphasise her point. "If I learn you know where to find him and have not revealed it, I will feed you to a drakon while you yet live."

"I'm not lying." So, Prometheus had already sided with Zeus. It was … inevitable, as he believed he had to follow the course of history as he had foreseen it. Pandora had told him, thousands of years ago, he would do so, had admonished him not to side with Zeus, not to make the same choice. But he had to, so as to ensure Pyrrha was born. So damn him and damn Ananke. "There is no man in the scope of history I loathe more than Zeus." She hesitated a mere moment. "And as for you and me, I was your guest. If you act against me without my having broken faith, does that not violate guest-right?" It had, after all, worked for Bellerophon.

Tethys sneered. The Titan had more anger in her than Pandora remembered. But then, she had known her before her beloved Okeanus had died in the Ambrosial War. Maybe some wounds not even time could heal—or at least could not erase the scars memory left upon us. "So be it. I free you with this warning. Should you happen upon your lover or Hekate, convince them both to abandon Kronos's perfidious son. If they are in his company when the League finds them, you and they will share Zeus's fate."

Why in the depths of the Underworld Tethys thought Pandora could convince Hekate of aught, Pandora couldn't guess, but then, she was just as glad to be out of the palace that clearly held no further welcome. As for Prometheus, no, he would not abandon Zeus, she suspected. He felt bound by invisible chains of history, forced to fulfil sick circles of the ouroboros that closed in around them all. But she would try because what else was there save the effort?

She would find him and try to get him to walk away from Zeus's rebellion. Maybe the whole of history would owe her for that.

INTERLUDE: BELLEROPHON

647 Bronze Age

The balcony of Bellerophon's megaron in Phoeba offered a view of the Aegean. The dying light of the evening sun glinted off the water like a field of diamonds. That ought to have induced a prideful smile, for, since old Iobates's death, over this grandeur Bellerophon had ruled supreme. And yet, he found his face twisted into a grimace as he cast a surreptitious glance back at Athene, where she stood within the shadow of a column.

"Or perhaps you find the glory of even Phoeba pales before the majesty of fine Mykenai," he said, daring the goddess to contradict him. Once, some years ago, Bellerophon had called upon Perseus in his great city, determined to prove himself not less than the famed slayer of Medusa. Vain Perseus had refused Bellerophon's challenges for pankration matches.

"Perhaps the king of Mykenai has grown craven beneath his soaring halls," Bellerophon had accused Perseus then, drawing a most satisfying scowl from the other demigod. Before all the gathered onlookers, Perseus had doffed his tunic and cast aside his sandals, conceding to wrestle that very moment.

Bellerophon might have had him, too, had the king of Mykenai not wriggled with the agility of a godsdamned lizard. The rank bastard had then feigned humility and called Bellerophon a worthy challenger.

But was he? Standing before the sea, Bellerophon had demanded answers from Poseidon. As ever, his father offered not the least acknowledgment of his existence.

"Your jealousy does not become you," Athene said, the Olympian's voice so soft it barely carried over the evening wind.

For a bitter instant, Bellerophon saw himself hurling Athene over the balcony to pitch down upon the stones of the acropolis far below. Would such a fall break a Titan? Worse ... could the goddess read his thoughts? If so, she gave little indication of it, and he pushed the vile impulse down into the shadows of his soul, where such things belonged.

"And yet, you come to call, time and again, upon great Perseus and his descendants. How oft have you graced *my* hall, Goddess, over these past decades? Perseus slew a monster, and I did the same. Yes, yes." He waved away the obvious objection. "I know about the sea monster too. But I fought more than my share of battles. More than him, for certain. But it is Perseus whose name graces the lips of bards and Olympians. Perseus who slew Medusa and Ketus. Perseus who built great Mykenai.

"But where are the tales of Bellerophon and the chimera? Where the songs about how Iobates sent me to overcome the whole host of the Solymi and secure his borders? When last did you hear about how I ventured against the Amazons who had ridden into Phrygia, to send them fleeing back to their wooded homeland?" He thumped the balustrade for emphasis. "How about when I overcame a score of bandits sent to ambush me? Did such even matter to you, Goddess? Why have I not earned so much favour as dear Perseus!"

He realised, belatedly, he had just bellowed at an Olympian, his voice echoing through the hall of his megaron, where no doubt the servants now cringed at his rank temerity.

"That is not what truly vexes you," Athene said, her voice still as damnably calm as before, not even deigning to take offence at his outburst. Instead, she strode from the shadows to hover over him, laying a hand upon his bicep in a meaningless condolence.

He gripped the balustrade tighter. He imagined his fingers scoring the marble. He saw, for a moment, the stubborn stone crumbling beneath the force of his wrath. And yet it remained obdurate and immutable, so like the weavings of the Moirai. "Why did you let him die?" His voice was a rasp, but he imagined it scything through the Titan like a blade, so sharp was his grief.

Athene squeezed his arm. Her attempts to comfort only further inflamed his raw nerves.

When Bellerophon had slain the chimera, Iobates had challenged him with seemingly impossible task after task. And when Bellerophon had conquered every enemy before Phoeba—and then slain would-be assassins he'd always assumed Iobates himself had sent after him—Iobates had found himself with no choice save to name Bellerophon a favoured son of the Olympians. He'd married Bellerophon to his other daughter, Philonoë—Bellerophon had oft wondered whether Iobates had known he'd induced the girl to spread her knees before that but had never quite been so brazen as to ask his father-in-law—and soon named him co-king of Phoeba.

Philonoë had given him sons and a daughter, and for them, Bellerophon had raised the megaron of Phoeba greater than ever. And when, some months back, the Solymi had once more risen in revolt against his rule, his eldest, Isander, had begged him for the chance to prove himself. And now the boy lay within the royal tomb, his body brought back by what remained of the men under his command.

Oh, Bellerophon had vented his rage upon the Solymi as though he himself had become the very chimera from his greatest victory.

Upon Pegasus's ebony back, he'd flown high above his foes, hurling javelins into the chests of Solymi princes and generals. In his wrath, he had crashed among their commanders and slain them to the last man. And still, Isander's shade wandered the banks of the Styx, and Bellerophon could do naught for him.

"That I sometimes see some of the tapestry of the future," Athene droned, "does not mean I see the whole picture. I did not know your son would die, nor even that you would send him against the Solymi."

Jerking his arm free, Bellerophon whirled upon Athene. It was madness, the threatening step he took toward the Titan. The sort of madness only a bereaved parent could muster, birthed from a place where rage alone kept one from drowning in grief, and only just. "What kind of *god* pleads ignorance and impotence in the face of the needs of those who offer you worship?"

"Bellerophon ..."

"Tell me!" He was shrieking now. But if blasphemy and hubris were the order of the day, then let them unfurl from his lips untrammelled at last. Surely, she had earned such by now. "Were you too busy watching over the Perseids to spare a thought for my children, Goddess?"

Athene flinched. "We're not gods," she blurted. The moment she said it, he saw plain upon her face she regretted it. Before his eyes, the great daughter of Zeus faltered. He could almost see words failing her. "The others have claimed such status, but I do not, Bellerophon. Immortal though I be, I ... I do not see all things. I'm a person, with limits ..."

A person ...? Gods ... Even his own invocation was nonsense, wasn't it? *Gods.* Men called Titans gods, especially the Olympians. Her words had him staggering backward until his arse brushed the balustrade. For an instant, he could see himself pitching over it, plummeting to his doom upon the very rocks he had moments ago imagined casting Athene onto.

And there she was, trembling, reaching an uncertain hand for him. Of all things, an unshed tear glistened in her grey eyes. "I'm trying ..." Her voice now a whisper, laced with such uncertainty.

She was just a woman. Bellerophon's hand went to his mouth, though he wasn't certain whether he sought to stifle a laugh or a scream. If Athene, daughter of almighty Zeus, was but a woman, then her father was but a man. Immortal, yes, powerful without doubt ... but not almighty at all.

What difference then, really, between the half-Titan demigod children of the Olympians and full-Titan children like Athene? Mentor to heroes? Bah! Athene was little more than an elder cousin to him.

He jabbed an accusing finger at her. "If you will not give me my due, then I will have it straight from the source! The blood of Olympus runs through my veins, as well. And I, and my remaining children, are as richly deserving of immortality as any upon that mountain."

"What?" A slow horror dawned upon Athene's face. "Bellerophon, you cannot think to—"

"Do not presume to tell me what I can or cannot think, *woman*! I see the truth all too plainly now. You play at supporting demigods, but you lack the will to see us receive our true birthright. I, too, shall live forever, and never again bury one of my children." He turned to the balcony. "Pegasus!" he roared. As if his faithful steed had already sensed his need, he saw those ebony wings approaching, rising up from the fields of the acropolis.

"This is madness," Athene protested, grabbing his arm.

He shoved against her, but she held firm, her grip like iron.

"Will you physically restrain me then?" His fist clenched at his side. Were she not a woman, he'd have pummelled her. "Shall we remain here, the two of us, locked in conflict the rest of my life? Or perhaps you'll strike me down, Mother of Heroes?"

Abruptly, Athene loosed her hold, and he jerked his arm away.

"I never claimed to be your mother, Bellerophon. Rather, I saw the failing of character wrought from my own pride, painful though it was to spot, and sought to rectify it. I wanted to help you become someone other Men could look to and have hope."

He sneered. "They will look to me when I sit my throne upon Olympus."

With that, he vaulted the balustrade and leapt onto the back of the waiting Pegasus.

"Don't do this!" Athene shouted after him. "You cannot imagine what punishments they will inflict upon you! Please, Bellerophon, please come back! I'll do aught in my power to aid you; just come back to your grieving wife and other children." Open weeping strained her voice now.

But Bellerophon had no time for her simpering this night. A long flight lay ahead, and when it was done, he would have immortality for himself, Hippolochus, and Laodamia.

LIGHTNING RUPTURED THE NIGHT, a moment of brilliant illumination filling the darkness beneath Olympus's roiling storm clouds. A peal of thunder presaged the touch of Bellerophon's sandals upon the slopes of Olympus.

Pegasus alighted within the agora, and what few men he saw about gaped at the coming of an unknown man upon such a majestic steed. Did they realise a nascent immortal had arrived among them?

"Brothers!" Bellerophon roared to the heavens. "Brothers and sisters, I, Bellerophon, son of Poseidon, have come among you now. I am here for my birthright! I come to claim my due!"

Another fulguration, and a man stood before him. Though Bellerophon was no small man himself, this newcomer stood head and shoulders above him, a Titan for certain, and one girt in glittering panoply. Based on the sword and helmet encrusted upon his cuirass, Bellerophon took him for Ares, the God of War.

"It is forbidden for Man to ride a pegasus," Ares said, though not with anger. Indeed, his face seemed lit with welcome, almost glee. For surely the immortals had long awaited a demigod with the courage, the *valour* sufficient to come and speak for himself and join their ranks. The Titan approached.

Bellerophon spread his arms. "I am Bell—"

Ares's fist slammed into his sternum. It sounded, to Bellerophon, like meal ground beneath a mill. The force sent him hurtling backward a dozen feet or more. He smacked down amid the cobbles, only then realising he could not draw breath through his collapsed torso.

Yet he opened his eyes and Ares already stood above him, though how he'd closed the distance with such speed, Bellerophon could not begin to guess.

"It's hubris for Men to rise too high," Ares said, giggling like a toddler with a new toy. The Olympian stood over him, then dropped, his knees slamming into Bellerophon's gut. Had he had air within, it would have blown out of him. As it was, Bellerophon could summon naught save an ever-deepening well of dread.

He gasped, hoping to catch a breath, to explain, to reassure Ares he belonged here.

"Hubris," Ares giggled. The God of War punched his fist into Bellerophon's open hand. The blow shattered the cobbles, pulverising Bellerophon's knuckles. Bellerophon could not even scream. "Hubris! Hubris! Hubris!" Ares cackled, slamming his fist again and again into Bellerophon's hand and forearm until both were but bloody smears upon the agora. "I *love* hubris!"

Dimly, some part of Bellerophon's brain registered that Ares had developed a severe erection. The Olympian leaned in close and gnawed on his lip and snickered. "Heh. I'm going to gouge out your eyes with thorns from the bushes overgrowing Demeter's temple. Heh heh. Ah." He smiled as though they shared some secret between them. "Oh, but worry not, I'll leave your legs intact. That way, you can wander the face of Gaia and tell your kind what happens to Men who get above themselves. Men need a good warning from time to time."

Bellerophon caught just enough air into his lungs to moan. It was impossible. The Moirai would not weave such a fate for him. He would not become Ares's warning …

Ares patted his cheek indulgently. "Would you like to pick out the thorns yourself?" With a hand tangled in Bellerophon's hair, Ares rose, yanking him up. "Heh. I like that idea. You're going to pick the thorns now. And if you don't, I'll keep breaking bones until you do." Another girly giggle spilled from him. "Let us get this started, shall we?"

PART IV

... thus did Zeus lead numerous younger Titans in open rebellion against the Ouranid League, attempting to seize control of the Thalassa world and of the Ambrosia, the lifeblood of all Titans. For ten years the war shifted across the lands, staining the seas red and gold with the blood of Men and Titans.

    — Kleio, Analects of the Muses

22

HEKATE

2391 Golden Age

For nigh to a year, Hekate and Zeus had fled from the combined wrath of the Ouranid League. Hades's command of the dead provided enough insight to allow them to remain a step ahead, if no more. Armies of Men and Titans hunted them everywhere they went, passing through Phlegra and into Phrygia, taking refuge in wild places, but ever fleeing from the superior numbers of their foes.

As now, when they lurked in a cave in the Arad Mountains some miles east of Ilium. The Titan lord Menoetius, brother to Atlas, seemed aware of their presence, for his patrols pushed out farther and farther each day. One day soon, they would have to abandon even this paltry shelter.

Something tickled her mind, some memory of Menoetius from so long back she could not place it, no matter how much thought she gave it.

Zeus had managed to summon the better part of his band to his side, but that only meant Hekate had to endure Hera, Hebe, and Ares, as well as Morpheus. Then there was Zeus's bastard son Hermes, got on the Pleiad Maia, who now served as messenger to those few Titans around the Elládosi world still loyal to Zeus. Hermes had brought with him twin sisters, Iris and Arke, perhaps his lovers, though Hekate cared too little to find out.

"We should leave the whole of the Thalassa world," Hekate suggested, knowing her advice would never be heeded. Zeus thought himself the rightful king of these lands and would settle for naught less than total dominance. For a man such as him, the very idea of failure seemed incomprehensible. His mind could not parse a reality where he did not come out on top. "There are vast lands in Kumari Kandam or Hy-Brasil where Kronos and the Ouranid League hold no sway. In Nysa or Kush we could bide our time and gather our strength."

Zeus waved away the idea, glowering. "And where would we get our Ambrosia? This world is mine, and I'll not let anyone steal it away from me." The Titan bared his teeth. "No one takes what's mine."

A temptation welled up in her to walk away, abandon the whole of Zeus and his cadre. In the recesses of the shadows, Aidos was watching them, so Hekate instead moved to join the other woman.

"We can't win this?" Aidos whispered when Hekate settled down beside her, their backs against the cool stone wall.

Hekate thumbed her brow. What was she to say? The truth? Zeus's petty uprising would have had little chance against Kronos alone, but the pompous oaf now thought to bring down the whole of the Ouranid League. He claimed, since Tethys had supported Kronos's attempt to arrest him, they were now all his enemies. A reality his words and mindset had helped effectuate. "Our position is not strong." In case Aidos missed the implication of them hiding in a cave, raiding caravans, and trying to annoy the League to death. "We are ... ants nibbling at the heels of the great feet plodding among us. Sooner or later, we must elevate our tactics or find ourselves squashed to pulp."

Aidos sighed, rubbing her knees. "I remember when the Ouranid League rose ..."

How long the Nymph had suffered. How desperate she must be to turn to Zeus and think *him* her saviour?

"Tell me about Hy-Brasil," Aidos said in an abrupt change of topic.

How many times should she relate such tales? But Aidos needed something, aught that might distract from the impending dolour, and Hekate could give her that, at least. "The greatest kingdom on Hy-Brasil is that of Kemet, land of the self-styled Sun God Ra. As pharaoh, he rules from the city of Memphis, as he has done since before the Time of Nyx. Some say the pharaoh is a literal child of the Sun itself, though I cannot attest to that one way or the other." Hekate could not help but smile at the wonder and even the hint of hope that limned Aidos's face. "One day, I'll take you to see the ancient kingdom there, and perhaps even to look upon the pharaoh."

Hera passed them by, sneering at both Hekate and Aidos. Whether Zeus's wife held true bitterness toward the Nymph or had instead swept her up in her loathing of Hekate, that she could not say. Either way, the woman never missed a chance to cast her wrathful eye upon the both of them. Maybe it was Hera whom Hekate should have had possessed all those years back, instead of her brother Poseidon. Maybe a mermaid tail would have softened her disposition.

Night crept in once more, and Hekate slept.

THE CREAKING FERRY SHUDDERED *as it moored at the derelict pier, not tethered by lines but rather by grasping skeletal arms that jutted free from the living vessel and seized the dock. The whole spectacle unfolded without a word from towering Kharon behind her, forcing Hekate to once more wonder if the ferry was, in fact, not some extension of the shrouded abomination itself.*

Though she had no desire to look back, to gaze once more upon the seething mass concealed beneath the tattered shroud, Kharon reached forth a bloated hand wide enough to have encompassed her skull, pointing his putrefying finger forward, into the writhing expanse of the Roil.

Moaning shades flowed from the ferry in a hiccupping stream, drawn ever toward the rising gloom ahead, though she doubted any of them could have said why, had she asked them. Hekate, too, climbed from the umbral vessel—vestiges of it teased her shins, as if imploring her to linger—and hopped onto a pier that groaned beneath her weight. For a gut-wrenching instant she thought the planks would give way and pitch her into the inky black current of the nether river, but the wood held. Not wanting to press her luck, Hekate scrambled onto the—comparatively—solid ground of the path the shades followed.

The nebulous expanse of the Roil around her ebbed and flowed like a languid sea, but the winding path held. Beneath her sandals the ground gave in too much, pliant as flesh. Down, into timeless paths of shadow she pressed on, whilst the chill nether winds ruffled her hair and clothes and the whole of the Realm closed in upon her, promising damnation.

For the living, the very World warned her, had no business treading through the Underworld.

☙

"Someone approaches." Arke's hissing warning jolted Hekate awake, though the sick feeling in her gut—the profound sense of Otherworldliness—lingered like clinging filth.

Scrambling to her feet, Hekate crept up to where Arke now watched from the cave's entrance. Like her twin, Arke had become a scout for them, always watching for patrols or seeking out ambush targets they could raid for supplies.

Hand on the woman's shoulder, Hekate peered into the darkness. She couldn't make out the moon but gauged the night perhaps a few hours before dawn, for the blackness seemed too complete, and they dared not light any fire now.

Footsteps slapped upon packed dirt nearby, and ice crystals formed in Hekate's other hand.

They faded the moment the flaxen-haired interloper appeared before the mouth of the cave, blinking into the gloom.

"Keuthonymos," Hekate breathed, rising to meet the Hyperborean. Of all the places she might have expected to see him again—though she had begun to fear he no longer lived after so long—she had not imagined finding him in Phrygia.

Still, she could not release the tension in her arms or fingers. "Who have you come here for?"

"I encountered Ares in Phlegra," he said. Indeed, Zeus had sent his son there to gather troops, promising aught imaginable to those who would dare rise against the hegemony of the Ouranid League. Using dreams, Morpheus relayed Zeus's commands and passed back whatever intel Ares gathered to the west. "He told me I'd find you here."

If Ares had, in fact, revealed their location, Keuthos must have earned his trust. Of course, Ares was a fool. Perhaps her concern lay writ plain upon her face, for Keuthos reached over to stroke her cheek.

Hekate flinched from his touch. Worse, he withdrew his hand and she cursed herself for her reaction. After so long ... could she have him back? Could she have a true, loyal friend once more?

"I wish we hadn't ..." the Hyperborean began.

"Said those things ..." Hekate agreed.

Fuck it. Fuck Zeus and anyone else watching. Hekate seized Keuthos and pulled him into her embrace. "I'll keep you by my side from this moment forth," she whispered into his ear. "It ought not to have ever gone that way."

The tension melted from his shoulders as his tentative hand went around her back as well. "Time inflicts such wounds, does it not?"

Yes, such.

❧

KEUTHOS, as it turned out, owned an estate upon the island of Khios. While Khios was a tributary to Helion, Keuthos assured them Helios took too little interest to have any idea of the guests Keuthos had brought. Thus, they came to the crescent-shaped isle, which to her eyes seemed a mountain that had tried to pull itself from the sea but only managed half the job. A few foothills rimmed the peaks, and upon one of these, Keuthos had his quaint dwelling.

"A rustic hovel," Zeus grumbled.

"You led us to live in a cave," Hera snapped back, though she too turned up her nose at the space.

Keuthos had moored his tiny ship in an inlet before guiding them up the hill to his home. Considering the trouble he'd gone to in bringing them all here and granting his estate for the use of this rebellion, he could have chided Zeus. Not that it would have gone over well. Zeus could do no wrong in his own eyes, which meant aught that spewed from his mouth, however excremental, must surely aurify upon touching the air.

Perhaps Keuthos intuited as much, for he let the boorishness pass without comment, instead leading them inside the gates and into his hall. The Hyperborean had a single servant—a Lydian, Hekate thought—who greeted them, offering wine while promising he had fish casserole almost ready in the kitchens. Keuthos thanked the man before seeing to settling his guests in their rooms himself.

Iris and Arke would share one chamber, as would Hera and Zeus. Hekate kept Athene with her, and Hebe, after a bit of simpering, agreed to sharing a room with Aidos. Morpheus and Hermes received solitary chambers, perhaps because not even the son of Zeus felt comfortable sleeping in the same room as the oneiromancer.

When they had eaten—the casserole fresher and more wholesome than aught Hekate had enjoyed in months—Keuthos invited her to stroll with him upon the mountain. After entrusting Athene to Aidos, they climbed up the rocky escarpment. Loose scree meant she had to watch her footing almost as much as the view, and Hekate spared but few glances at Keuthos.

"Helios does not come here at all?"

"On the rarest of occasions. The Nymph Neaera rules the island, though from the other side of the mountains. She had an affair with

Helios long ago and bore him two children. Much as Leto dares not challenge her husband, I think she manages to express enough ire at his indiscretions he takes some care."

A while more they walked, until they reached an outcropping that jutted over a gully. Keuthos pranced to the edge and dangled his feet, careless and free. While he did not instruct her sit beside him, Hekate felt compelled to by his nonchalance, as if physical strings tugged her along.

Once there, swinging her feet over the void, the air felt thin, everything too light. A moment of vertigo claimed her, but it passed with a few deep breaths.

For centuries, Hekate had imagined the thousand, thousand things she would say to him. How she would regale him with the depths of her study, with her unwavering journey toward the Ontos, or with the breadth of her travel across the face of Gaia. Yet when the moment arrived, she found herself silent, revelling instead in the perfection of stillness that crept up between them. Some relationships, perhaps, defied time and space, refusing to admit the least distance.

In the west, the sun had begun to limn the sky in purple streaks, its burning light stinging her eyes in a moment of searing perfection. Something to remember.

THE MONTHS STRETCHED BY, with Morpheus relaying Zeus's plans to strike against Kreios and Phoebe, whom he had convinced himself were the weakest of the Ouranid League. Though Hekate feared that, should he succeed in slaying one, Kronos would only sweep in and seize the spoils, Zeus hatched plot after plot to draw his targets out into the open.

None of his raids, piracy, or provocations produced the desired results, and no targets presented themselves for assassination. Sometimes, the prince listened to the advice Hekate or Morpheus offered, and those raids more oft proved successful. They had seized a shipment of Ambrosia bound from Atlantis to Phoeba and, using it, had drawn others to their cause with the promise of the precious tonic.

Still, things drew on, with no end in sight. How could she hope they might overcome Kronos or Tethys now, much less Atlas enshrined in his island?

After supper, Hekate reclined with Keuthos in his sitting room, poring over her grimoire by candlelight. The tome held manifold secrets, more than she had uncovered even in the passing of so many ages. She might go back over the same passage a dozen times and garner new import with each perusal. A subtle mind had woven threads of arcana into the tome, and even unlimited lifetimes might not unravel the depth of such a masterpiece.

"Watchers?" Keuthos asked, tapping a scribbled note she had made in the margin of an odd reference.

"Winged emissaries of the Elder Gods some time during—or perhaps before, even—the Time of Nyx," Hekate answered. That much she had guessed, though never had she gleaned much more. So many aspects of this puzzle lacked linear ordering. Perhaps the author wished to test the intellect of any who even managed to translate it.

"More foul witchcraft," Hera sneered from the doorway. "You taint the very air we breathe with your perversions of Gaia."

A hundred such jabs had rolled off Hekate in the time she'd been forced to endure living with Hera. This one, however, stuck in her skin and flensed her nerves, forcing her to rise. Maybe it was the vague, tattered memories of a little girl tormented by one who should have been more big sister. Maybe it was a dog's broken spine. Either way, Hekate no longer gave a fuck if Zeus wanted to keep his wife.

She rose, Mormo's soul-devouring grasp welling up inside of her. "If you think I'm going to tolerate any further—"

The wall behind her exploded in a rain of plaster and splinters, a muscled form plowing through it shoulder first. Kratos, Styx's massive son straightened himself, debris tumbling off him as he flexed.

The first notes of a shriek began from Hera the instant before

Kratos crashed into her and Hekate. The big man caught them both by the heads and Hekate's vision whirled. An impact tinged everything white, left her ears ringing, and she could not gauge up from down.

Before her vision had cleared, a heavy foot caught her in the ribs. They cracked under the blow, and Hekate flew weightless a bare instant before slamming into the ceiling. Then the floor again. Her senses fled, swallowed by a maelstrom of agony.

Waves of torment, every breath sent lances of flame coursing through veins. Thoughts flitted through her fingers like motes of dust. She reached for Pneuma to block the pain, but it blew away from her.

"Run!" the hoarse cry seemed far away though it broke through her stupor.

Hekate tried to breathe but found herself gagging on warm blood, her mouth filling with the taste of liquid metal. A sputtering cough, spraying her life over the floor.

"Hekate, flee!" This time, pain cracked the words with desperation.

"I'm going to rip out your spine!" someone roared.

Blinking, the swirling haze of her vision filled with too many colours. She tried for her knees. Swayed. Blinked again, the room solidifying around her.

Keuthos on his hands and knees, ichor pouring from his dislocated jaw and the ruination of one of his eyes. No! Kratos, storming toward Hekate. The big Titan's hands closed upon her shoulder and hefted her up, slamming her against the wall.

"Flee," Keuthos gurgled.

Hekate managed to claim the Pneumatikoi of Steadfastness, making her flesh hard as bronze the instant before Kratos's fist slammed into her face. Her head cracked back through plaster. Her skull felt apt to cave in. Had she not held the Pneumatikoi, his blow would have pulverised her bones.

An inarticulate roar escaped Keuthos the moment before he collided with Kratos, arms wrapt around the bigger Titan's waist, bearing him down. A paroxysm of rage had seized the Hyperborean, his fists raining upon Styx's son in a blinding shower of blows that split the marble floor.

Staggering, Hekate pushed off the wall to help him.

Before she could act, Kratos caught one of Keuthos's wrists. Snarling like an animal, his other fist crashed into Keuthos's chest. The blow rang like a gong and sent Keuthos shooting upward as though flung from a sling.

Hekate summoned ice crystals around her fingers and thrust her arm at Kratos, intent to impale the bastard on icicles the size of spears. Someone else slammed into her and her frozen barrage flew wide.

Zelus, Styx's daughter leered at Hekate with a manic gleam in her eye, driving her back against the wall, one hand upon each of her forearms. Cackling, Zelus reared back and slammed her forehead into Hekate's own. Only calling up Steadfastness once more kept Hekate conscious.

Chuckling, Kratos stalked over. He grabbed Hekate's right hand from his sister and laced his fingers through hers in a perverse mockery of an intimate gesture. "For mother," he purred. Then he jerked his hand the wrong way. Despite the Steadfastness, all Hekate's finger bones snapped under his prodigious strength.

They released her and she tumbled to her knees, gaping at the whole of her hand, fingers bent backwards, wailing in the agony of it.

As Zelus broke into mad giggles, Kratos stomped over to where Keuthos had fallen and grabbed his ankle, dragging him back before Hekate. The Hyperborean groaned, tried to rise. The fall of Kratos's sandal crushed his throat.

"No!" Hekate shrieked. "No!"

Instinct demanded she strike back, slaughter these wretched sadists. But a last inkling of self-preservation had her instead reaching for Mormo's power before one of them touched her again. Hekate pulled herself through the Veil, choking over the cloying darkness that filled her throat, writhing against the membrane that tried to hold her in the Mortal Realm. Then she spilled into the muted, twisted gloom before Keuthos's corpse, it only an echo without substance.

Her friend, however, stood there now, doubled over in pain. His flesh had begun to slough off, a slithering darkness oozing out through the split seams of his essence. His fingers became skeletal claws he held before his face in rapt horror. The space between his ribs widened, exposing a seething caliginous mass.

A tattered shroud took shape, formed up of the shadowy essence of the Penumbra itself. Lashing out like a wounded animal, Keuthos lunged at the shroud, drawing it about himself until his features vanished within its billowing folds, giving only the sense of infinite void lurking below.

Keuthos, his soul abraded by long use of the Art, had become a wraith.

Hekate wept. She started to reach for him.

The shadows behind Keuthos began to bleed, burbling like an onyx fountain. A dark shape lurched up, out of the Roil beneath the Penumbra, and met her gaze. Hades stood there, chest and throat the ruin she had wrought of them, scarred face spreading into a malevolent grin.

Shit.

The pain, the loss, it had ripped her dominance of him from her

...

Without warning, the shadowscape of the Penumbra heaved, bending in upon itself. Etheric hands surged up, snaring Keuthos's tattered essence, and yanked what remained of her friend's soul down, into the nebulous non-reality of the Roil.

Cackling, Hades stepped back, vanishing into shadow, until only his mocking laughter remained, carried to her on eternal nether winds. Until the whole of her world chortled at her shrieking horror, on her knees in a Realm without light or hope.

23

ARTEMIS

2391 Golden Age

Crouched in the shadows beneath the hill, Artemis watched the flicker of oil lamps in the window of the estate. With her Perspicacity, she could hear the grumble of voices within, even make out bits of the arguments, though she and her band remained too far out for her to sense the Pneuma of those within or gauge their numbers.

Father had commanded she hunt Zeus, and thus she had stalked across the land before a lead finally brought her to Khios. The irony that their prey hunkered in the very shadow of Father's glorious island brought a smirk to her lips. He liked to think himself so wise, to claim he saw all that transpired beneath the sun, but he missed even what unfolded upon his doorstep.

Still, he had ordered her to find Zeus, and Artemis would bring the rebel in. She almost dared to hope it might earn her some measure of respect. Almost ... Though she'd probably have to grow a cock for that to happen.

Behind her, Zelus ground her teeth. "What in the dark of Tartarus are we even waiting for? We know they're in there. *She's* in there." Artemis cast an expressionless glance at Zelus. Pyrrha, yes. Or Hekate now. "Mother lost half her fingers thanks to the bitch's ice," Zelus complained. "All rotted flesh turned black and putrid. It was fucking nasty."

Father had also insisted Artemis lead Styx's children in the hunt. Artemis had done that too. She did everything he ever asked in the shallow, faltering hope it might somehow matter. It never did.

She held up a hand for silence and cocked her head to the side, judging positions based on the conversations within the estate. "Hekate is within the east wing," she said, the words tasting like bile. Whatever had passed between them, handing over her erstwhile friend to Zelus churned Artemis's gut. She'd not have wanted to hand over her *foes* to the twisted bitch. "You and Kratos assault from that side. Bia and I will break in from the west and hunt Zeus. Do what you must, but Zeus does not leave this place save in chains."

Zelus curled her lips, whether at the image of proud Zeus in fetters or in dismissal of any orders Artemis gave, she could not say.

Either way, as Zelus and her hulking brother climbed the eastern slope, Artemis passed on an order for Helios's mortal warriors to attack the front gate the moment the fighting started. While Men would struggle to combat a Titan, their presence would slow down any attempt to flee Zeus might make.

With the orders set, Artemis beckoned Bia to follow and climbed up the western side, toward a window. As she drew nigh, she could feel the pulsing warmth of strong Pneuma signatures within. A good many Titans dwelt in this place, some so flush with Pneuma they might have challenged even Father. Which meant a bitter fight ahead unless she caught them off guard.

"Use the window only once you hear struggles," she whispered to Bia.

She allowed the flow of Pneuma to open, powering the Pneumatikoi of Alacrity and Lightness, even as she took off at a sprint toward the wall. Her steps carried her up the surface, over the sloping roof of the outer house, and into the air. Turning a flip, she landed in the courtyard in a crouch.

A woman looked up at her, mouth opened to scream for help. She never got the chance. Wind yanked at Artemis's clothes and hair as she raced toward the rebel and, with the strength of the bear within, bore her down, slamming her head against the cobbles. Only then did she recognise Aidos.

Artemis's stomach dropped out at seeing her cousin there, ichor seeping from the head wound. She bent over her, but the Nymph still breathed. "Sorry ..." When this was over, she'd need to get Aidos out of here, pretend she'd never seen her cousin in Khios. She'd not let her pay for Zeus's crimes.

She needed to find Zeus and subdue him before anyone found her. Her speed carried her like a floating wind between columns, flowing around the light streaming from doorways and windows as she sought her prey.

A resounding crash echoed from the east wing, so violent Artemis cringed. Well, Zelus and Kratos would have their attention now.

Zeus's bastard son Hermes raced through the courtyard, headed for the commotion, his own speed at least as fast as hers. The Titan drew up short, however, glancing around. He'd sensed her, no doubt with Perspicacity of his own.

Slipping a dagger from her belt, Artemis kicked off the ground. Lightness reduced her weight, allowing her to glide through the air at Hermes. The bastard turned at the last moment, jerking his wrist up to parry her own. Artemis bounced from the impact, floating backward up to catch herself on the rim of the courtyard roof.

A single bound sent Hermes racing toward her like an arrow from a bow. His fist smashed through tiles, pulverising them while Artemis flipped over him, drifting back to earth. Even as he jumped for her again, she kicked off, flying back at him. The pair of them collided in midair. Her knife snaked in for his flesh again and again, but his blocks came in at blinding speed. He caught her forearms and spun her round an instant before they hit the ground.

Artemis managed to flood Pneuma into Steadfastness just before his sandal connected with her gut, sending her careening backward. She had to release Lightness to have enough weight to steady herself, swinging her arms round in wild gyrations for balance. Before she even had a breath, he'd closed in upon her in a blur.

Growling, Artemis clipped his shoulder with her knife before his other hand sent the blade spinning from her grasp. Then she was falling back, blocking attacks from his good hand, him trying to grab her. But he had only one working arm. She darted toward his bad side, her fist catching him in the ribs.

Two women raced from a doorway, each holding a xiphos, charging blade-first at her. Drawing Lightness once more, Artemis ran up Hermes's side and kicked, sending him stumbling to the dirt while flinging herself up onto the roof in the same motion.

She had not gone far when both of the women—twins?—leapt onto the wall with Lightness of their own. Artemis ducked and wove amidst them, dodging thrusts and cuts from their blades. They were fast, but not as experienced combatants as she was.

A smile quirking her lips, Artemis twisted away from a thrust and snapped her elbow into the mouth of one woman. Her foe staggered and tumbled off the roof, Artemis paying her no further thought. She caught the wrist of the other woman and wrapt her in a pankration hold. With bear strength, she didn't even need draw upon the Pneumatikoi of Potency. She hefted her foe aloft to slam her back-first into the roof tiles. The force of the blow shattered the structure and sent the other woman crashing through the ceiling into the room below.

Even as Artemis rose, Hermes was on her again, having leapt to the roof. Artemis danced around the gaping hole, keeping space between them, but Zeus's bastard jumped over the opening. Artemis snapped her foot up, her sandal taking him in the midriff and hurling him away. She kicked the woman's fallen xiphos up into her hand. She preferred a knife, but this would do.

Hermes landed in a crouch, tiles breaking loose and crashing into the courtyard in a cacophonous rain as he skidded along the roof.

Winking, Artemis hopped down into the hole. Morpheus had begun examining the unconscious woman, but the oneiromancer's gaze fell heavy upon Artemis as she landed.

He raised a hand, tethers of power brushing against her mind.

Before he could draw her into sleep, Artemis thrust her hand out, flinging the sword like a dart. It wasn't intended for such a manoeuvre, but at this distance it flew true, punching through Morpheus's shoulder and sending him staggering backward into the wall.

Her senses flared as Hermes dropped down behind her and, on instinct, Artemis ducked his blow twisting around and flowing about the bastard like water. Her rising uppercut snapped into his jaw and sent him flailing backward. She surged upon him with a leap, her fist descending to catch him in the temple. It was like striking bronze, the impact ringing like a gong.

Perhaps she'd need Potency after all. Flooding a little Pneuma into that, she wrapt her fingers in his hair and seized the back of his tunic before hurling him sideways. Zeus's son spiralled through the air before crashing bodily through the wall and tumbling back into the courtyard.

"Artemis!"

She turned at the call of her name only to find Hekate out in the courtyard, cradling her right hand, bent double with pain. Perhaps it was the dark of night, perhaps imagination, but Artemis could have sworn shadows whirled within Hekate's eyes, her face shrouded.

"Artemis, stop," Hekate rasped. "Stop this ..."

Morpheus tried to remove the sword from his shoulder. A surge of speed carried Artemis to the oneiromancer, the back of her fist snapping into the Titan's nose even as her other hand grasped the hilt and jerked the blade free. He was, perhaps, too dangerous to let live. Morpheus had collapsed in a heap beneath her feet, and one stomp of her sandals could have ended him.

"Please," Hekate begged. "Please, if our friendship ever meant aught, please stop this."

Maybe she should have run the sorceress through. Maybe she

should have done something, other than let the xiphos hang by her side, limp and useless. "Our friendship?"

"I never meant for what happened to you to occur that way. You *know* that." Hekate took a stumbling, pain-laced step toward her. What in Nyx's darkness had happened to her hand? "I loved you as a sister, Artemis."

A sister? A sister ...

Days in a cottage in the woods. Nights of laughter in Phoeba. So very far away now, and yet some memories burnt through the haze of time, insistent. The essence of a life distilled into a thought. An emotion. Connections.

A scoff resounded behind Hekate, and Kratos stalked forward. "Witch didn't run far enough." The Titan looked to Artemis. "And you can't be fool enough to challenge the Ouranid League. Helios would have your head."

"He would, wouldn't he?" His own daughter, and he'd cast her aside in an instant to maintain his position. Artemis gnawed on her lip. A connection ran between her and Hekate, it was true, and maybe it went deeper than that with a father who had *never* accepted her. Not when she had helped him win the Ambrosial War, not in more than two millennia of service since. She favoured Kratos with a wry grin. "I think it best you leave now."

Kratos gaped at her. "*I'll* have your fucking head for this."

A tremendous bellow rang out, followed by Bia hurtling through the courtyard. It seemed Zeus had gotten the upper hand over her at last. The Kroniad came stomping after her, clothes torn, caked in ichor, a malevolent leer upon his face.

"I don't think it best you chance us all," Artemis warned Kratos.

The big Titan cast a look back over his shoulder, perhaps to Zelus. Then a growl, and he grabbed Bia and ran, making for the hole in the wall.

Maybe they would escape Zeus. Artemis didn't overmuch care.

Perhaps Zeus's rebellion was doomed, and yet, Artemis found herself dwelling upon how they might succeed. Hekate had thrown her support behind Kronos's son—had even given Zeus a child herself—and Artemis could not now turn her back upon the woman who'd named her sister.

Not cradling the grey-eyed child in her arms and running through old memories of happier times. Neither Helios nor Kronos nor any of the others of the Ouranid League—save perhaps Phoebe—had had a hand in her good memories. But Hekate held a few of them. Maybe that alone mattered.

Thus she found herself sitting across from her golden brother, weathering the patronising smile that peeked out from behind his wine goblet. "Styx claims you have betrayed the League," he said.

Artemis swished her own wine around in the cup without sipping. They sat just beyond his vineyard in the small estate he maintained outside Phoeba. Apollon had wasted no time in pointing out that the vintage they enjoyed had come from his own grapes and that demand for it had spread all the way to Byblos.

"Styx's brood lust after blood like leeches. They feast upon suffering and think themselves strong for it."

Apollon chuckled, raising his cup in salute. "Which makes them excellent enforcers for the League."

Artemis set down her cup so she could fold her arms and fix Apollon with a hard stare. "They're mad." His shrug dismissed that. So like their father, unconcerned by aught that did not affect him. "What if Zeus could win?"

Now Apollon too left his goblet on the table and leaned forward on his elbows. "The Ouranid League has endured for two millennia. We helped form it." *We*, he said. How fortunate a man had been around to claim the credit for her breaking Khione's siege and drawing Grandmother into Father's alliance.

But Apollon shared much with Father. Including pride. "And for all that, we remain in much the same position as before. What do we rule, brother?"

"What?"

Artemis spread her hands to encompass the modest estate and vineyard Grandmother had granted her twin. "You've got a few more places like this around, and not much else, hmm? While the six Titans we helped rise to hegemony remain the *entirety* of the hegemony. Zeus swears to elevate his most loyal supporters to rulers of the Thalassa world."

Her brother worked his jaw, leaning back. He lifted an amphora to pour more wine, though he didn't take up his goblet once he had. Oh, she had him.

"If Father wins, everything stays how it is. You farm grapes, I scout the world as his spy. Another few millennia flit away from us." She paused for emphasis. "If *Zeus* wins, we become part of the new hegemony, brother." Never mind what they'd lose if Zeus failed. Apollon wouldn't imagine failure.

Now, her twin did snatch up the goblet, sloshing wine everywhere before throwing back a long swig. "Let me sleep on it. Stay in the guest room and I'll have your answer in the morn."

While she might have liked to finish the discussion now, pushing too hard could send her brother in the wrong direction.

Long into the night she lingered beneath the moon. It pulled upon the bear spirit within her until she could stand it no longer and doffed her clothes to walk the woods in animal form.

Sometime before dawn, she returned, dressed herself, and awaited her brother. He rose early, bearing a bundle in his hands. Beckoning her over, he unfurled what turned out to be a map. "The town of Athyras upon the Axeinos Sea sits beyond the eyes of the Ouranid League. The locals have long chafed under the refusal of the League to provide Ambrosia. We might find allies there."

Artemis peered closer. "This is ... beyond the eyes of the League because Gigantes roam the wilds nigh to there." Eaters of Man-flesh, Titans unworthy of the name.

"As I said, the locals chafe under Ouranid rule."

Could Zeus truly recruit those monstrous Titans to his cause? If he did so, it might give him the army he needed to meet the League in open warfare. Still, Artemis misliked relying upon such creatures, much less promising them Ambrosia.

Her thoughts must have been writ plain upon her face because her brother scowled. "I'll not join a cause unless we can win. And we cannot win without warriors on our side."

So then, she would need to summon Zeus and the others to Phlegra.

24

———

KIRKE

1591 Silver Age

For four years, Kirke had worked in secret, perfecting the transformative potential of her Nectar. It had meant finding an out-of-the-way estate they could purchase beyond the gates of Kolchis. Then months cultivating moly and the other herbs she needed, designing her alchemical lab, and making arrangements, even before the ceaseless, neck-twisting study by oil lamp.

Neither Aeëtes nor Ixion had proved idle, however, both working the city to gather friends and supporters, by threat or bribe, or even— Kirke knew—by eliminating a few recalcitrant merchants and Senators. Twice, they had come to her asking for untraceable poisons, and she had given it to them, too afraid to ask what they intended. As if, if Kirke did not know who they poisoned with her brews, culpability for the murders could not find her.

Her dreams disagreed.

How, she asked herself, over and over, had she ever gotten into the business of king-making?

Much less the business of crafting monsters. And which was worse?

Either way, amorphous threats stalked the tenebrous spaces of her dreamscapes, mingling the horror of oneiromantic insights with the yet worse dread of her conscience. Sometimes, sipping wine alone on the portico, she would wonder what Kalypso would have said of all this. Was overthrowing a democracy—even a faltering one rife with corruption—to install a Titan king, not the antithesis of all they had dreamed of? Was this the better world they had striven for, bled for? Had the Pleiades died for *this*?

Sometimes, in the first flickers of impending sleep, she'd see Kalypso, crouched on the floor, clutching her knees, moans burbling from her in an unending river, calling for a mother she would never touch again.

Blinking away the thought, Kirke bent back over the latest batch of Nectar. Once she had turned a man into a bird by mistake. Now, she sought to make Men into monsters of her own will.

A gentle rap upon the door had her turning to see Idyia standing there, three-year-old Khalkiope cradled against her hip. "Auntie Kiki," the child cooed, reaching for her.

Yeah, when a three-year-old wanted up, it didn't matter if your work was urgent or the house was on fire. You picked up the three-year-old.

The child wended tiny fingers into Kirke's disheveled locks. "Nice hair ... nice ... orange hair." Khalkiope patted Kirke's head until satisfied, despite having made no progress in corralling the mess. "All better!"

Idyia so oft brought the child by to see Kirke in the midafternoon, after her nap. It served as a reprieve from the tedium of the lab, and perhaps Idyia realised that. By tacit accord they made their way from the house and out into the garden.

Once there, she deposited Khalkiope, who at once set about dancing and whirling. "Auntie Kiki, lookit! Do this, Auntie, do this, can you do this too? Do this, Auntie Kiki! Kiki, do this?"

"Maybe later," Kirke lied to appease the child. It worked, and the girl rushed about, chasing a butterfly, while Idyia and Kirke strolled.

For a time, silence reigned and Kirke found her gaze forever drawn back to the girl. Almost enough to make her consider having one of her own, giving over the contraceptives she took after any encounter.

"Sometimes I wonder if this rustic life should not prove enough," Idyia said.

"There's something to be said for the quiescence of tending a garden, away from the bustle of politics," Kirke admitted. "Not sure I'd want to spend forever doing it, but it has its appeal. I mean, sometimes you want a real person to talk to. Roots are terrible conversationalists."

"I have Aeëtes and Khalkiope and you," Idyia said.

"M-me?" Idyia spoke as though ... as though placing some import on these walks beyond the chance for Kirke to see her daughter and stretch her back and neck. "I mean, yeah, you have me. For ... you know."

"For now?"

Not what she'd meant. Kirke watched Khalkiope chasing a second butterfly, offering an excuse not to meet Idyia's gaze. Was she to say that she, most oft, found her welcome in places wore out after but a few years? That she forever seemed to drive away any who attempted to come close? "I, um ... Yeah, I mean, I'm making progress on the Nectar. So."

"Right," Idyia mumbled under her breath. Maybe the other Nymph didn't even want the throne now. Maybe she never had.

But their course was set years ago, and Kirke could not see turning from it now. Not unless her brother and his wife agreed together to make a different sort of life. Father would fume, but what could he do if they chose to retire to the idylls?

"I'm going to need a volunteer soon," Kirke said, looking at last at Idyia. "I mean, you can tell Aeëtes that. If it works, I guess I'll need a bunch of volunteers. If he's ... if you're ready to go forward with this."

"I'll tell him." Her voice had become a susurration Kirke could—almost—have imagined.

MAYBE IDYIA and Aeëtes did discuss it, debating whether to move forward with the plan that had brought them all here. Maybe the Nymph had never voiced her misgivings, or maybe he had overruled her out of his own desires or his unfailing sense of duty to Father. Kirke supposed she'd never know.

Either way, Aeëtes had come to her, Ixion in tow, some days later.

Not quite able to say why, Kirke found it hard to meet the warrior's eyes, instead finding her gaze pulled ever back to the small amphora set upon her worktable. To the silver goblet beside it, awaiting the blessed, damning draught she had prepared. The items beckoned and taunted, and Kirke found her skin tingled with the import of a moment from which there would be no return. A flicker of the Sight, perhaps, an incipient foretelling, or just open-eyed intuition as she trod down paths she knew she ought not to walk.

No one should, but they had all come here.

And she had *wanted* this. Wanted the chance to make her Nectar into the weapon she'd need to bring down Olympus. How was she to accomplish such ends without testing it upon the living?

Though it felt like yanking her own guts out, Kirke forced herself to turn, looking into Ixion's ochre eyes. The light from the brazier beside him glinted back at her. "This will change you forever," she warned, then swallowed. "There is more to the soul of Man than what we see. In the dark recesses we do not perceive lurks a bestial nature shrouded by the thinnest of veneers. Once you awaken that hidden vestige of yourself, you may not be able to shut it away again."

Ixion sucked spittle between his teeth and, for a moment, Kirke thought he might expel it on her workshop floor. Whether her expression dissuaded him or he hadn't intended it, she couldn't say. "While back, I found that beast part of me you speak of." The man winced, lost in the mire of his own memories while Kirke studied his face and Aeëtes stood in silence. Funny, in four years, she had never asked about Ixion's past. Maybe everyone had their torments, the secret shames plaguing their souls, the darkness that tugged at their periphery and threatened to make them something other than the person they envisaged themselves as. "I killed someone." Another pause, so long Kirke guessed he'd say no more about the how and why of it. "Maybe I'd have spent my life as an outlaw if not for Prince Aeëtes. So ... Aught he needs, that's his to ask."

The urge to grab the man and shake him rose in her. For the sake of loyalty, however earned, he would sacrifice something he did not understand. Even if it meant a subtle betrayal of her brother, of her own purpose here, didn't she owe it to this man to help him see what impended for him?

Kirke snatched up the amphora and held it before herself like a weapon. "If you take this, you will no longer be a Man."

A moment of hesitation, a flicker of the eyes reflecting the fear they ought to have held from the moment he walked into the room. "Seems a fair price for the years I had in between."

Well then, let the Moirai play their games with the living. After uncorking the amphora, Kirke poured the amber liquid into the goblet. It filled less than half the cup and, had it been wine, would have been more tease than draught.

Without another word, she handed the goblet to Ixion, then beckoned Aeëtes to her side, away from him. She couldn't know what would happen, but something about this moment held an eerie familiarity. A sense of fulfilment closing in.

Ixion threw back the tonic in one swig, gasped—perhaps from the strength of it—and tossed the goblet aside, the cup clattering off the stone. Once it stilled, the only sounds became the crackle of the brazier and Aeëtes's—and her own—irregular breathing. The anticipation had physical weight, all of which seemed to press down upon her gut.

Ixion stumbled, sinking down to the floor, but looked up at them a moment later, expression seeming to ask if that was all. She had ... expected more, in truth.

The man knelt in the shadow just beyond the brazier's light, his face concealed by the gloom. With a sudden convulsion, he pitched forward, catching himself on his hands. Aborted gasps escaped him, like he wanted to scream, but all he managed where pained wheezes. His flesh, what little the brazier illuminated of it, it rippled like waves, as if something monstrous flowed beneath the surface.

Nausea seized Kirke and she reached for him. The utter madness of what she saw flensed her, left her hugging herself in wordless horror.

The man fell forward, face smacking the ground, a moan building in his chest. Joints popped audibly within him. Then, the awful, gut-churning sound of muscle and tendons ripping apart.

"No ..." Kirke breathed.

Her victim screamed, his cries so long and agonised tears glistened in Kirke's eyes.

His hip snapped, breaking apart as something bulged within it. Desperately, he tugged away his clothes, casting the torn and ruined garments aside, even as the bulge in his hip ruptured. Flesh shred in a shower of gore as some new limb protruded, dragging its way free from his innards.

Stumbling backward, Kirke collapsed onto her arse, hand to her mouth.

The limb distended, until a hoof clacked upon the stone beside her.

Another followed, his hips broken into twisted spectacle as if a horse tried to burst forth from his nethers. Ixion shrieked again, toppling over, as the skin along his legs split down the middle and fell free in bloody chunks. More horse legs emerged from the ruination of his flesh.

The ravaging changes continued amid his cries—now become weeping as agony had overcome his masculine vanity—on and on. Until, at last, the creature that rose, hooves clanking, stood towering over them, head brushing the ceiling. He retained the torso of a Man, albeit one with a faint equine aspect to it, but from the waist down he had become a blood-slicked black stallion.

"Hyperion's light," Aeëtes rasped.

Kirke's voice spilled from her of its own accord, the numbness seizing her chest so complete she wondered that she even remembered to breathe. "We need more."

"What?" Aeëtes asked.

"One is not enough. Bring me ... a dozen more men and women. This new ... race will serve your ends."

What had she birthed?

Kolchis rang with the screams of the dying as Kirke's centaurs—for thus she named her small army of monstrosities—rampaged through the streets. Gutters ran red with the blood of the victims of her ploy, and Kirke watched from a rooftop, arms hugging her chest while she waited for Aeëtes and Idyia to show up and save the populace from the new monstrous threat. People would think the centaurs perhaps a new breed of Gigantes come in from the wild, and most like, none would ever imagine the truth.

For who could think such a thing, that the abominations charging down breezeways and alleys, hacking and slashing, had once been Men? Who could guess that a fallen royal line would turn to monsters for a last grasp at power? But maybe they should have known, she mused with a grimace. Maybe they should have realised that for those who had tasted power, no deed was too dark if it meant they held their thrones. Did she delude herself into thinking the Senators would not have done the same, had they the chance?

No, even these men the centaurs hunted had murdered their way into their positions and no doubt further murdered, extorted, and blackmailed to keep them.

The women slung over centaur shoulders, carried away screaming in the night, they were innocent, and Kirke did not like to imagine what Ixion's followers thought to do with them. There could be no good way, now, to sate their lusts, save on centaur females. And like a fool, Kirke had dared to believe that would prove enough for her creations.

But like grasping Senators, or desperate royals, or her own empire-building father, whatever lay before them was never sufficient. Conceptions of 'enough' must have seemed, to Men and monsters alike, quaint.

Though she hadn't realised she wept, a tear tumbled down her cheek and landed on her khiton. Irate, Kirke scrubbed her face. She'd no right to cry over this when she had wrought it.

No, once the Senate was dead—or most of them—and Aeëtes had shown up with his forces, Ixion would play his part and allow the centaurs to be driven off into the wild.

The grateful populace would proclaim Aeëtes and Idyia their king and queen, and maybe, just maybe, Father would look upon his expanded empire and say, "At last I am satisfied."

Maybe. But Kirke doubted it.

25

PANDORA

2392 Golden Age

Rumours flew like eagles, soaring above the breadth of the Thalassa world, carrying tidings that, on occasion, held grains of truth. Such rumours claimed Zeus's rebellion had begun raising an army in Phlegra, and thus Pandora made her way through the wild hills, skirting lofty peaks and fording great rivers until, at last, she came to the town of Athyras.

A wooden palisade protected the settlement, but before Pandora could even approach the gate, a rough hand seized her elbow, a woman seeming to melt up out of nowhere. Pandora turned toward her attacker but found herself gaping in horrified wonder when her eyes met the woman's.

Enyo, lover of Ares, whose murder in Atlantis would spark Zeus's rampage against the Pleiades. Now, very much alive, and snarling at Pandora as she looked her up and down. "Spy," the Titan fair hissed.

"I'm not—" Pandora began, only to have Enyo yank her forward, dragging her toward the gate she'd intended to walk through anyway.

The town had transformed itself—she assumed, for this state could not have long endured—into a war camp, the wall patrolled by armed warriors, all grim-faced. Smithies rang with the sound of hammer falls forging swords and breast plates, and in the agora, men trained with spears in loose formations. Everywhere she looked, broad-shouldered Titans paced about, attending to one preparation or another.

"Ares!" Enyo snapped at the entrance to a large house.

Before the man could emerge, however, another, more familiar voice rang out. "She is with me."

Pandora shut her eyes a brief instant to steady her heart before turning to see Prometheus, his crystal blue eyes glinting. Behind him stood a Titan woman Pandora did not know, fiery-haired and incarnadine-eyed.

Enyo grunted in obvious disappointment. Had she *wanted* to find a spy? Had she thought she could torture information from Pandora? Either way, Ares's lover released Pandora, threw up her hands, and walked away, grumbling under her breath about Prometheus bringing more strange women into camp.

"Pandora ..." Prometheus said, a hint of a tremor in his voice. How long had it been for him since last he'd seen her? Two thousand years, perhaps. She eased into his arms, the space as natural as breathing, and laid her head upon his chest a moment.

Wait, *was* the other woman his lover?

Perhaps her face revealed her concern, for Prometheus held her back a moment and motioned to the woman. "Pandora, this is my student, the Firewalker Hestia."

An Olympian. Because of course one of the Olympians had once been his student. It didn't really answer the question as to whether he'd taken her as a lover, but perhaps she ought to save that issue for a private conversation.

Other concerns pressed to the forefront at the moment. "What on the face of Gaia possessed you to take this path?" Did he aid Zeus solely to ensure the fulfilment of a future that would see Pandora sent back in time to mother Pyrrha?

Perhaps that too played out upon her visage. "Pyrrha is here, in service to Zeus."

"What? Here?" The words rang like a blow upon her temple. Pyrrha served Zeus? Her ... her precious daughter served that excremental blight upon the land?

"Give us a moment," Prometheus whispered to Hestia. The fiery-haired Titan nodded at Pandora, then headed off, joining a group of a half dozen Pandora realised had been watching them. More students?

Prometheus guided Pandora away, to walk into an alley formed by a smithy and a tanner. Between the stench of piss and the clang of metal upon metal, Pandora's mind refused to concentrate, to form a coherent question. "Pyrrha has borne him a child and they lead this rebellion together."

Pandora's stomach lurched. She wanted to retch. Pyrrha had lain with Zeus. Oh, fuck. Had the Titan lord forced himself upon her daughter as he had done upon so many other women? Tears of rage welled within her, though from the heat rising in her chest she wondered that they did not evaporate into steam.

"She ..." Prometheus hesitated. "She went to him by choice," he answered Pandora's unspoken question. "I do not understand her reasons, but I know this much."

Pandora slumped against the tannery wall, struggling to maintain her feet with the roiling of her emotions. Her heart threatened to rend her in two. A person could endure but so much agony without coming apart at the seams. "I ... I have to speak to her."

Prometheus gripped her biceps and leaned close. "She goes by Hekate now."

Pandora stared at him a moment more. Then her world dropped out from under her. The shape of Ananke slithered through her mind, the ouroboros constricting, and she choked on a scream of denial, managing instead a mere wheeze, open-mouthed. No.

No, no, no, no, no.

Unthinkable. Not even the Moirai could have imagined aught so cruel, so perfectly, circularly merciless. Her daughter had ... ruined her life. Abducted Pandora as a child, sold her into slavery. Acted as Zeus's *dog*.

Only Prometheus's stone grip kept Pandora from crumpling to the ground, from sinking into Gaia and fading away into oblivion. It could not ... be borne. Her eyes met Prometheus's, desperate, seeking some reassurance she had slipped into nightmare.

She found no such comfort, only pity.

No.

No.

He drew her into his embrace as the tears flowed free.

Her sandals felt apt to crack the Earth with each step they took toward the estate. Every footfall crashed with a cacophony that might forewarn her daughter of their coming. A chill sweat had built up between Pandora's shoulder blades, and her lover's hand in hers failed to abate the tremors that ravaged her.

According to Prometheus, Pyrrha had claimed the second finest abode in Athyras, a manse in the shadow of the town's small acropolis. If not for the wall, one could have seen the Axeinos Sea from the gardens, and salt air tingled on her tongue. Did the choice remind Pyrrha of the home they had once shared in Thebes?

Gods, her stomach heaved. The urge to rush to the bushes and retch up even the meagre morsels in her gut seized her.

A year had passed since she'd seen Pyrrha. For her. Thousands of years for her daughter. A blighted trail of anguish and abandonment that must, in time, lead toward the catalyst of Pandora's own tragedies. Hekate. The name rent Pandora to pieces.

Her mind could not wrap itself around the reality that she could not cradle her babe in her arms and rock her to sleep. Even knowing the vast gulf of ages that had passed, it remained unfathomable that her infant had become a grown woman. A two-thousand-year-old goddess. A tainted witch who delved into forbidden arts.

Still, Pandora could not turn away from her daughter, whatever she had become, whatever she must still become, ties stronger than Fate bound them.

On the portico, Prometheus hesitated, looking at Pandora. Waiting for her consent to move forward, to face the nightmare and dolour beyond the threshold. When she nodded, he pushed the door open, exposing a darkened vestibule. The only light came from an open courtyard beyond.

"Hekate?" Prometheus called out, peering not into the courtyard but into the gloom of halls breaking off the vestibule.

All too soon, footfalls answered, and Hekate came slinking down a passage, oil lamp in one hand. Her fiery hair, the set of her cheeks, her golden eyes ... On looking upon them *now*, knowing what she knew, Pandora could not help but see Pyrrha behind them. Could not help but wonder how she had never seen her before.

A sudden intake of breath drew Hekate's attention to her.

"Who is this, Papa?"

Prometheus squeezed Pandora's hand in reassurance, then ushered her all the way into the vestibule, shutting the door behind them. "This is ... your mother. Pandora."

The moment lingered on, Hekate staring at her in utter silence. Drenched in dancing shadows, her visage remained unreadable.

"Of course, I didn't know," Hekate snapped, turning her head a hair to the side. "No. No!" Her daughter looked back at Prometheus now, face accusing. "You told me we lost her in Kronos's attack upon Thebes."

"She was lost," Prometheus said.

What? Pandora pulled her hand free and turned to gape at her lover. He'd told their daughter she was *lost*, knowing full well the obvious implication that she had fallen in the attack. For who could imagine Pandora would become lost *in time*? A flicker of fury warmed her cheeks and she had to forestall herself from snapping at him. How dare he? But ... what was he to have told their daughter? The truth? Even disregarding the potential damage to the timeline, no child could parse such knowledge without it driving her mad.

Pandora forced her emotions down. Yes, Prometheus remained as trapped by all this as any of them.

"I was taken far away," Pandora managed. "Unable to return until now."

"Oh really?" Hekate snapped. At first, Pandora thought her denying what she had just said, but her daughter once more had turned her head as if speaking to some imaginary voice. "I hadn't considered that!" the woman spat, before looking back to Pandora.

A moment longer she stared, then stalked closer, so close her warm breath fell upon Pandora's cheek, as it once had when she'd cradled the babe to sleep at night.

"I don't know you," Hekate said, her emotionless whisper making each word a blow to Pandora's sternum. "I never knew you."

"Pyrrha ..." Pandora's voice cracked along with her heart. Along with the whole of her, trembling in her daughter's foyer.

Hekate sneered and stepped back. "There's no one here by that name." She shook her head. "And you are twenty-two centuries late to try playing the mother." After levelling an irate gaze at her father, Hekate stalked back down the hall she'd come from.

She'd ... walked away.

Prometheus had set his jaw, set his whole body, seeming to want to become a mountain against the agony he too must endure. Their eyes met, and he drew Pandora close to him. Not knowing why, Pandora beat an impotent fist against his chest, as powerless to move that as she was to alter the callous course of Ananke.

"Has she gone mad?" Pandora asked, wrapt in a blanket and huddled in front of the hearth in Prometheus's much smaller home on the edge of town.

"The dead speak to her, bombard her with words no one else can hear. And sorcerers bind within them eidolons from beyond the Veil, damning themselves to a cavalcade of voices in their own heads."

"You didn't answer the question."

"You of all people know too well that most conceptions of sanity are edifices of society created for the reassurance of the majority. They want to believe divergences from their life experiences represent condemnable deviances, something which we ought to fear."

Pandora scoffed and rubbed her face. And just as she could never expect anyone to understand her skewed perspective, jumping through time, the majority of people could not fathom the experience of one to whom shades whispered. What torment it must have proved for her precious, fragile child. A tearless sob wracked her. "I would have given aught in the World to spare her such."

Prometheus swallowed hard, suppressing tremors of his own pain. "I ... tried. I tried to save her, to guide her toward a different course. But the future has a momentum, undeniable and inexorable."

A sudden, sinking pit opened in Pandora's stomach. A memory, another symptom of the madness of her own existence that no others could fathom. "She might die in this. I ... I ... received a message ..." And how much could she tell him without compounding his own burden in time? So many things Ananke had forced him to hold tight within his breast. Prometheus believed neither could Fate change, nor *should* it, for doing so would risk the unmaking of their daughter. "From the future, I learnt ... I was told I have to convince Nike to fight alongside Zeus, against Kronos. That if I don't, Pyrrha would die."

Prometheus blanched before forcing his expression to placidity once more. "Who is Nike?"

Once more, her mind reeled. He didn't know? "A winged Titan who helps Zeus win the Titanomachy."

"*Winged*?" Some hidden emotion raged for a bare instant behind his eyes, some crack in the armour he had built for himself to conceal his thoughts and emotions. This day had worn even the ancient immortal thin, ravaged him. "You mean Nemesis." He hesitated. "In the Time of Nyx there were others, but she is all that remains of the winged ones, I think."

Nemesis? Was Pandora to recruit Nemesis to Zeus's cause? How and why? Every time she had encountered the Moirai's assassin, the creature had attacked her. Last she had seen Prometheus, in Perseus's time, Nemesis had locked herself in combat with Prometheus. "I don't know." She had assumed he would know who Nike was, not that she would have to go hunting for the woman. She didn't know aught anymore.

Prometheus reached out to clutch her fingers. "There are depths to your journey even I cannot fathom." Meaning, though he had made the Box, not even he could understand the whole of what it would unleash.

And if she had never opened it, would none of this have ever happened? Hekate never born, never able to kidnap Pandora, Prometheus never bound. Kronos never overthrown? Though she knew down such roads lay an infinite labyrinth of madness, still her mind wandered those paths, grasping at unrealities that could never exist.

THREE DAYS after Pandora arrived in Athyras, an Inumiden female Titan came to join them, clutching the hand of a five-year-old child and leading with her a trio of Cyclopes. When they entered the gate, Pandora had stood in the market, buying apples. Both she and the vendor forgot their transaction in a moment, gazes fixed upon the eleven-foot-tall giants who stooped to pass under the wall. Each one was a scarred mountain of grey muscle rising up to a misshapen head. Heavy brows shadowed an oversized single eye in the middle of their heads. One of them bore a great horn jutting from its forehead, and all carried clubs fit to smash Men into pulps.

The female Titan, Pandora soon learnt, was Demeter, and on Zeus's behalf she had negotiated an alliance with the Gigantes. The child, it turned out, was yet *another* of Zeus's bastards, Persephone, whom legend claimed Hades would kidnap as his bride. Seeing the young girl, so innocent, knowing her future, was one more flensing cut abrading Pandora's soul.

The Cyclopes led a mismatched army of the Man-eating brutes, and that army had gathered beyond the town gates, howling and slavering, eager to rain chaos upon the Ouranid League.

Prometheus beside her, Pandora dared to peer at the great throng.

Some had tails of serpents or eyes of wolves. Many had horns, fangs, claws. Their consumption of Man-flesh had turned them monstrous, more beasts than people, or so many seemed. Others looked almost like Titans, albeit too tall and brawny, among them she caught some few names: Pallas and Mimas and Niyros.

Monsters who feasted upon Men.

Such were the allies of Zeus, the despotic tyrant they had thrown their lot in with. Not for the first time, Pandora asked herself if Fate had forced them onto the wrong side.

26

———

PERSEUS

625 Bronze Age

"You know, my dear, when I left Neritum, it was in the company of Pandora," Perseus said to Andromeda, as their boat drew nigh to a home he'd left more than a year and a half ago. "I made her a promise."

"I know," she said, stroking his hand where it rested upon the tiller. Twilight impended, but with luck, he'd manage to tie off the ship her father had given them before the light gave out.

Of course she knew, for Perseus had lingered in Byblos longer than intended, searching for Pandora. How could he uphold an oath if he could not find the woman? Someone had attacked her, guests made that clear, and then she was just gone. No trail, no body—thank the Fates—and no means at all for him to make good upon his promise to her. Oh, how that had rankled. The sense of failure had crept upon him like a scorpion crawling over him in his sleep. The shame of his deficiency had robbed the sun of its brilliance, soured the initial bliss of his marriage, and left him so atrabilious he'd not have blamed Andromeda for abandoning him and returning to her father.

But rather than retreat, his wife had descended into the desultory bog that seized him and dragged him out by his heels. Had refused to allow him to wallow in despair for circumstances that, according to her, were wholly beyond his control. Maybe they were, and measure by measure, he had given in to her prompting. Her easy smile, when they were alone, had demanded he reciprocate—to do aught else would have been rude.

But Kepheus's court held no enduring welcome for them. Not when Sirsir came and pressed the claims of Pontus for tribute. Not when the king was forced to proclaim they would send down six youths in sacrifice to the siren depths. As the moons had passed, the ire of the folk for their princess and her rescuer had not mellowed but rather festered until, in the eyes of many, he and Andromeda somehow became symbols of all woe that had befallen Byblos.

Perseus had, in their minds, weakened the harvests of fish, had brought the bouts of pestilence that had ravaged the outer farms, and had precipitated the decline of trade with Neshia following the death of a merchant. When a child in a field died of a snakebite, that fell at his sandals, too, for Perseus carried snakes with him wherever he went, or so men claimed.

Outsiders were always the ones to blame for every woe—after all, there had to be *someone* to blame for the inherent inequities of life. Without someone to hold to account, a people would be forced to accept harsher realities about themselves and the World, to swallow truths too unpalatable to tolerate.

No, though he still had not found Pandora, when the season came again for travel, he was all too eager to be away, and Andromeda was of like mind.

"You have other things to attend to, do you not?" Andromeda prompted.

He laced his fingers with hers, delighting in her warm touch. "Ah, my dear, I cannot imagine what I might have done to deserve one such as you in my life, but it must have been epic."

"Besides slaying two legendary monsters and saving me from an uncle with the moral fibre of a mollusk?" She shrugged. "I guess it's that you're not a bad cook. With fish, at least."

"Life of a fisherman's son." They reached the docks and he tied down the ship, then helped Andromeda ashore. "It's not so far a walk to my parents' home. Just up this way."

Neritum must have seemed small, quaint even, to a princess having grown up in the grand courts of the King of Byblos, but Andromeda took it all in with a light in her eyes that left Perseus beaming. It made his heart feel too big for his chest. Made every dusty road and modest home seem fresh, even after his long sojourn into the wider world.

Fresh yes, but smaller, he had to admit. Maybe it was not only Andromeda that must see this place as quaint. Maybe ... maybe it could not quite ever be home again. Not as it had been, when his concerns tilted more toward which vineyard had the best wine, or where the fish were migrating. How did one return to a simple life after witnessing wonders abroad?

Being the unofficial head of the fishing village, his father—stepfather—owned the largest house, a cottage upon a slight hill, that one resting in the shadow of the greater hill where Serpo stood. In the morning, he'd have to venture to that town to see King Polydektes, deliver the prize, and hopefully win enduring peace for his mother.

For now, he just wanted to embrace his family, enjoy a hot meal, and get a good night's sleep. Side by side they climbed the hill, following the well-worn path to the summit. Perseus would have expected to see the flicker of an oil lamp in the window, as it wasn't so very late yet, but the house remained dark.

"Perseus ..." Andromeda whispered, clearly apprehending something amiss here.

"Mama?" Perseus called out. "Papa?"

No answer. He released Andromeda's hand and charged forward, closing the distance to the cottage with the speed of the wind. He flung the door open to find the caliginous interior completely abandoned.

"Mama!" He charged into his parents' back room, but the bed was set, no sign anyone had been here. A sudden, jagged ache shot through his chest and threatened to gnaw out his insides. "Mama?"

"No one's been here in days," Andromeda said. Perseus found his wife in the main room. She traced a finger along the hearth then held it up to reveal a thick sheen of dust.

"Cleaning wasn't always her highest priority ..." Perseus said.

"Maybe someone in the village knows where they went?"

"They fled to the Temple of Hera on the northern shore," a woman called from outside.

After exchanging a brief glance with Andromeda, Perseus's placed a hand upon the hilt of his adamant xiphos, and he eased his way outside. In the moonlight, he could scarcely make out the details of the tall woman lingering before his family home.

At least at first. But as he drew nigh, her bearing revealed her, even before he caught sight of her bronze helm and the grey eyes in the shadows beneath it.

"Goddess Athene," he said, falling to his knees. Behind him, he heard Andromeda mimic his gesture.

The Olympian laid a gentle hand upon his head. "In your absence, your uncle declared you dead, a failure, and has pressed his suit for Danaë. She and Diktys sought refuge from him in the temple, the one place he'd not dare violence. A priestess has been bringing them food, but even that cannot endure indefinitely."

Perseus winced. Pandora had warned him the whole quest for Medusa's head was a sham, and he'd known it well but had felt so bound by his oath of honour he'd sailed away, regardless. His need to keep that honour had endangered his parents.

"Polydektes has broken faith with me and, worse, has threatened those I love," Perseus said, daring to rise in Athene's presence. "With your leave, I will attend to him."

"Impetuousness is ... understandable, sometimes."

Was that why she was helping him? Had she, in fact, harmed Medusa thus, and now decided to make amends for whatever mistakes of her past? Could a goddess make mistakes?

"Of course, sometimes wrath is not impetuous in the least. Do as you must, Perseus, but when it is done, I will come for the Gorgon's head. It has wrought enough wickedness already."

So much, indeed, and he could not deny it.

"Stay here in the house," he told Andromeda. "You'll be safe."

"No. I'm coming with you."

"I could not do what I must if I fear for you. Please remain where I know no one will reach you, my love."

Maybe his wife would have protested further, but some look passed between her and Athene, and she lowered her eyes. It was, after all, hard to argue with gods.

Though he knew it for self-delusion, still Perseus could not help but feel the slap of his sandals upon the path to Serpo rang out louder than usual. Four watchtowers guarded the marble wall around the city, and at this hour, the gate was shut. They would admit none, which meant he ought to wait for morning.

But every hour Mama spent cradled in the arms of fear, huddling in the Temple of Hera out of terror of her own brother-in-law—every hour felt an affront to decency. It was not to be borne, so Perseus found himself pacing the length of the wall, clinging to shadows until he could find a place along the perimeter where the watchtower lanterns failed to illuminate. There would do. Or he hoped it would, as he had never attempted something quite like this.

Deep breaths, letting the Pneuma flow through him, breath infusing his limbs with lightness and speed, with power and the determination born from desperation. Then he took off at a wild sprint, dashing for the wall, wind whooshing behind him. As he reached it, he placed one foot upon the surface and vaulted upward, continuing his run. Upward, air rushing past him, tugging upon his tunic. Higher, twenty feet, almost, to crest the lip of the wall and soar skyward over the top of it.

Then he was falling, flailing his limbs as he plummeted down inside the town. He landed in a roll with a just a hair less grace than he might have hoped for, had anyone been watching. It would have made for a fine tale, had a bard heard of it.

Midnight shadows drenched the town, however, and none perceived him, at least that he could see. Concealed, he rose, cast about himself, then made for the palace.

It was not too late to turn back ... Would this make him a kinslayer? No. *No.* Just as Andromeda's uncle had broken all familial bonds and violated sacred trusts, Polydektes had done so as well. When kin transgress upon the foundations of kinship itself, they sacrifice any claim to the title. This he had to believe.

Polydektes's palace was modest compared to the grand halls of Kepheus. A pale imitation of the grandeur beyond these shores, really, though Perseus had never thought so before now. He found only a single, bleary-eyed guard watching the door.

Was this man an innocent? Perhaps, and yet, he took his drachmae from a man he knew ordered vile deeds done. The guard almost certainly had carried out some of those deeds himself. He knew he worked for an odious man who hurt others, but he considered the money he received from said man enough to assuage his conscience, if he had one. That made him culpable for the misdeeds, whether he actively participated or not.

Perseus charged from the darkness so fast the man had time neither to scream nor brandish his spear. With the speed of the wind, his fist crushed the guard's larynx. He allowed himself a moment to wince, to force himself to watch his victim asphyxiate because of his actions.

Then he slipped inside the palace. He had expected Polydektes to be asleep by now, but a clangour rose from the main hall, the very room where Perseus had once toasted his uncle's mendacious claims to seek marriage to Hippodameia.

So it seemed the Fates loved a bit of irony. They almost wrote the bards' tales for them in such circumstances. And who was Perseus to deny a prime setup served to him by the Fates?

He caught a young servant waddling into the room, arms laden with an amphora of yet more wine. "Find somewhere else to be, boy," Perseus said. "And call out any of your friends in there as well."

Wide-eyed, the servant set down the wine and scrambled off. Perseus hoped to obey.

After waiting a moment to give the child time, he dug Medusa's head out from his satchel. The loathsome thing had become a crushing weight ever at his side. Though it had not putrefied, still it reeked, and he would be glad to be rid of the accursed trophy.

Deep breaths. Mama needed him to see this through.

Steadied, he brazenly flung open the doors the servants had left merely cracked and strode through his uncle's hall. The man himself reclined upon a divan in languid repose, surrounded by a half dozen of his cronies. In the back of the hall, two guards stiffened at Perseus's entrance, snatching up spears they'd leaned against the wall.

By the time Polydektes even seemed to realise who he was, Perseus had crossed the chamber to stand not ten feet from the assembled glut of drunken curs.

"You sent me for a prize, Uncle," Perseus said, voice quivering with rage at what this man had done to him and his family. To his own family. "It's time you had it."

He hefted the Gorgon's head.

The effect took a breath to begin, just long enough for Polydektes to open his mouth and gape. Not long enough to form words before the pain shot through him. Perseus watched as the agonies ravaged his uncle, the man's friends, and his guards. They convulsed, thrashing for brief instants.

And then all that remained was a roomful of marble carvings, locked in poses of pain and terror. Testament to a sculptor with a warped mind and a talent for creating too lifelike work.

As promised, Athene awaited him back at his parents' home, and Perseus tossed the satchel at her feet. "I've no desire to ever wield such a thing again."

The goddess nodded as if already aware of the weight pressing down on him. She bent to retrieve the satchel and left without another word.

"It's over," Andromeda stated, rather than asked, from where she sat upon the cottage's portico.

"It's over," Perseus agreed. "Come with me to find my mother and father."

Andromeda rose, not protesting they had been up all day and all night. Just taking his hand.

"Will you claim the throne yourself?" she asked as they trod through the dark toward the temple Athene had mentioned.

Perseus sighed. "I think I will see my stepfather crowned. You and I ... we are destined for greater things than small islands and tiny villages, I think."

Andromeda snorted. "Glad to hear it."

Besides, there was another man who had wronged his mother worse than even Polydektes. And even that needed a reckoning.

So then, they would need to make for Argos.

27

HEKATE

2392 Golden Age

On the cliffs beyond the Olympian Mountains lay the polis of Thebes, Hekate's home in another lifetime. On the acropolis, in Tethys's marmoreal halls, she had run and played and wept at the petty cruelties Tethys's children had visited upon her. She had fled before the spite of Hera—the bitch now standing beside her—and her siblings, Styx, Poseidon, and Perse, while Tethys watched unmoved. Here, too, she had birthed little Athene, left now in the care of Aidos, back in Athyras.

And now the city lay aflame, a spreading conflagration that leapt between the streets, borne up by the raging winds Hekate had summoned. A crash of thunder rang out overhead, a bolt of lightning casting the night sky in brief illumination. Not even the incessant rain plastering her peplos to her body seemed able to arrest the blaze.

A ardent roar like an enraged lion, and a Cyclops crashed through a house, sending a storm of splinters and debris hurtling into the street. The brute swept his club almost at random, stumbling to a stop beneath the lightning, bellowing at the sky. Beyond him, Hekate could make out the gasping desperation of those within the building, surging for egress. With a rumble lost in the thunder, the home quivered and collapsed inward, a great tumbling pyre for the mountains of dead.

"This is what you wanted?" Pandora shrieked at Hekate, grabbing her elbow while hordes of Gigantes and Zeus's forces pressed forward like a flood sweeping over Thebes. They had breached the gates with sheer fury, Cyclopes smashing Telkhines to pulp before ripping mighty doors to kindling. During the Ambrosial War, not even Kronos had managed to break into the city proper in his assault, but naught could have prepared Tethys for the unbridled fury Zeus had unleashed upon her home. "This obscene chaos, this remorseless massacre?"

Hekate shoved her mother aside with just a hint of Potency, enough to send the mortal woman staggering backward several steps before Papa caught her. She had no time for the petty grievances of a heart that might bleed for strangers but had failed—for *two thousand years*—to find its way back to *her*.

Further down the street, Ares launched himself from one burning building to the next, each bound casting him like a hurtling meteor. He would land amidst scattered remnants of defenders, engaging ten or twenty at a time, his blade whirling so fast as to become invisible. Blood showered about him in greater torrents than even the downpour Hekate had called down upon this blighted city. Little though she loved Zeus's son by Hera, Hekate had to admit Ares had an uncanny talent for war, like an unstoppable wave on the battlefield.

Ahead, Zeus stood in the agora, blustering in inarticulate fury and paroxysms of bloodlust that had Hekate shuddering as she drew nigh. Their king—he had proclaimed himself such before the assault —had snared a Man by the ankles and used him as a flail, beating his fellows to death in a macabre rain of gore. At his side stood Demeter —the Inumiden had offered naught save glares to Hekate—and

Hebe, who watched her father's antics with a grimace, even as mud and viscera splattered her peplos.

Never in her two millennia had Hekate witnessed such a spectacle of slaughter. As if Gaia herself revolted against the rule of the Ouranid League and all the forces of the Earth converged to wipe Tethys and her brood from the face of history. The thought, however dire, brought a grim smile to Hekate's face.

Hera pushed past her, grabbed her daughter, and cried something to Hebe that Hekate could not make out over the cacophony of death and thunder.

Instead of lingering there, Hekate moved ahead to where Artemis and Apollon had taken the forefront. Their unerring arrows had felled what seemed to Hekate hundreds of men and women of Thebes. Warriors and guardsmen, citizenry defending their homes, even Telkhines, gods of the deep. If anyone could have matched Ares for sheer destructive ability, it would have been Helios's twins.

Of course, Hestia—Papa's apprentice—wielded fire as a weapon, igniting the initial blazes that swept over Thebes and sparked the panic, breaking the interior lines of her defenders. The Firewalker had strode forth, vortices of flame enveloping her forearms, dancing about her fingers. She led a small army of her kind, other Firewalkers out of Phoenikia and Neshia, all too eager to spread the flames while Men and Titans fled their fury.

Horror, Khione had called it. *Burning abomination.*

And indeed, Hestia had swung her hands outward, launching great sheets of billowing, exploding fire. A fervid conflagration that had ripped through Thebes's lines, leaving them flailing, charred corpses. It had not ended there, however. Hestia had hurled the flames up in curtains of burning naphtha, immolating stables with screaming horses inside, consuming smithies, even cracking stone masonry of the defensive wall. Under such a broiling assault, what force could stand its ground? No, Hekate had gaped, asking herself if Papa could have done such a thing or if only Hestia, glutted upon the Ambrosia Zeus had given her, had managed the dread inferno.

Another Cyclops lumbered forward, catching a man who had fled

Zeus around the waist. The Gígas tossed his victim in the air, then slapped him with the club in mockery of child's play, splattering the agora in further viscera.

There had only ever been one way this could have ended. Maybe it had been inevitable from the moment Tethys had banished Hekate as a child ... Though Hekate would not have chosen such an extreme vengeance given the choice.

Their slavering horde of Gigantes and Titans converged at last upon the acropolis. Ares and Enyo swept through a line of spearmen like the incoming tide. They moved amid lances, striking man after man, too fast and too strong for any to have a chance of countering, even could the mortals have pierced Titan flesh. Resounding cracks echoed as Pneuma-enhanced fists collided with armour, sending mortals hurtling left and right.

Another peal of thunder. More rain drenching them.

The last of the spearmen had fallen, and one of the Cyclopes—Steropes perhaps—roared, charging shoulder-first into the palace's double doors. A single blow and they burst inward, spraying chunks of wood over another line of defenders as hapless as the last.

Ares moved to subdue them, but Steropes lunged in first, his sweeping club taking men down three and four at a time. The Cyclops caught one defender up, hefted him to his mouth, and bit off the man's face, slurping down his macabre feast even as Ares and the others charged past him to bring down any remaining defenders.

Zeus and Hera followed behind their son, the king chortling as spilled entrails squelched beneath his sandals. "Revel in the glory of Zeus," he crooned to no one in particular.

Hekate trailed them, ice tingling along her fingertips, though she had needed to act little herself. It was well, she supposed, not to have to rely upon the spirits bound within her. Every time she used their power, she risked losing a bit more of herself to them until, at last, one of them would manage to claim her flesh as their own.

I will ... Mormo promised.

"You see," Zeus was saying, "the Ambrosial War will pale before the glory of this Titan war. The greatest, grandest victory in the scope of history."

"This way," Hera said, indicating a side hall in her old home. Hekate couldn't recall what lay down that path, but it was not the way to the throne room. Instead, Hera led them to a tunnel that bored down into the Earth.

Hekate had heard tale that Tethys kept a drakon lairing beneath Thebes. Did this connect to caves within the cliff? Hera had snatched up an oil lamp, and Enyo took another, the flickering flames glinting off the slick rock face down here. After a few moments, their path opened into a larder stuffed with crates and barrels and amphorae.

Ares and Enyo sliced their way through a half dozen guards, even as Tethys herself rose from bending over a table. Though she spared them an enraged glare, the Titan queen took off at a sprint, racing toward some recessed means of escape.

She made it only a handful of steps before a hulking form caught her and shoved her back toward Zeus.

"Kratos," Hekate gasped. Styx's Kreiad son had seized his grandmother and prevented her egress. Styx herself followed from the shadows, as did Bia. With them here, Zelus must too lurk nigh.

Of its own accord, the ice upon Hekate's fingers solidified, preparing to launch forth in killing shards. Kratos had murdered Keuthos, and for that, she would see him suffer.

"Forgive me, Mother," Styx said, "but my sister offered me a position I could not refuse."

Tethys rose, turning to look upon her perfidious daughter and grandchildren. Though Hekate could not see the Titan's face, after a moment, she saw Tethys's shoulders slump in defeat so all-encompassing that even Hekate could not help but experience a twinge of pity in her gut.

When the Ouranid lady turned back to face them, her eyes had become empty, devoid of all but a speck of life. This towering, monumental figure who had so long dominated this land—and the sea through her Telkhines—had in a single stroke transformed into shadow.

Sparing a glance at Zeus, Hekate caught him licking his lips as he strode toward Tethys.

Hera must have seen it too. "Remember our deal," the woman hissed at her husband.

Zeus stiffened, his hands clenching into fists at his sides. "You have failed, as you must, Tethys. Being supremely magnanimous, I ... I grant you the chance to live in exile." Yet his voice seemed to hope she would refuse, that he might make an example of her. Hekate did not wish to know what depredations he might visit upon the first member of the Ouranid League he had conquered.

"I choose exile," Tethys rasped, her voice as empty as her eyes.

No, no, no. If Styx wanted to join Zeus, well, Hekate tolerated Hera who was even worse. But Kratos had murdered Keuthonymos, and for that he must die. She would let Mormo devour his very soul.

Yes ...

She advanced upon the oaf but had not made it far when Hera shoved her back by the shoulder. Only sheer will kept her from lashing out, thrusting a frozen spike through Hera's arrogant smirk. "Styx and her children are welcomed into King Zeus's court."

"He murdered my friend."

Not even a faltering in Hera's face. "Our enemies have become our new friends. Old ones hardly matter."

Beyond the woman, Hekate looked to Zeus, who waved it away. "Yes, yes, they serve me now, as agreed. We cannot let petty sentiment guide our steps now." He turned back to Tethys. "You may go."

With a last sullen look at her daughters, Tethys turned and vanished into the same dark recesses she previously tried to escape down.

Seeing the Titan depart her city for the last time, Hekate could not help but feel something momentous had shifted. A change, a breaking of bonds that had held together civilisation and order.

Naught would ever be the same again.

28

ATHENE

1600 Silver Age

Crouched upon the lower slopes of Olympus, Athene watched the slavering horde of Gigantes approaching out of Phlegra. Many of the great battles of the Titanomachy had been fought in those lands, so perhaps it was irony—or Ananke—that the next great war spilled out from those wild hills beyond the Olympian mountains.

The ground rumbled in their passage, as if Gaia presaged their coming. Dozens and dozens of Cyclopes made up the greater portion of their army, though among them trudged some Gigantes even taller or more grotesque. Consuming the flesh of Man had warped them, and some had serpent tails in place of legs, while others had tusks like boars, and more still seemed fell amalgamation of bear and wolf and Titan. A mismatched sea of savagery, heights ranging from eight feet tall to more than twice that, though all of them larger and stronger than other Titans.

Man-flesh changed them, yes, but it empowered them too, and Athene could not deny that.

The tremor that ran through her and set her hands to shaking, it was not quite fear.

A hand alighted on her shoulder. "Demeter is with them," Artemis said, pointing off into the midst of the Cyclopes' horde, while Athene jerked her hand down to wrap around her sword hilt, hoping Artemis had not seen it while staring into the distance. The other Titan's eyes always astounded most Olympians with their acuity.

"Maybe it was always inevitable," Athene mused.

Artemis snorted. "Well, it was inevitable when Zeus made her suck his cock in front of a room full of people, I can tell you that."

Athene stiffened and shrugged free of the other woman. She knew damn well who her father was, but then, so had Demeter when she had come to challenge him. They had *both* lost Persephone, and what was Father to do, march down to the Underworld to find her? Mother alone seemed to have that power, and even she had not been able to save Persephone from Hades.

"The Olympian council is broken," Athene said, rising. "The bonds that held us together these sixteen centuries are severed."

"Hmm. You never saw the last war. These bonds were not so strong as you might have thought. Desperation and hope mingled to bring us together." There was something unspoken in Artemis's tone, some thought the woman feared giving voice to. Or perhaps she feared sharing it with Athene, daughter of the king. Did she, too, harbour some threads of disloyalty? Did she sympathise with Demeter more than she let on? Athene cast a sharp look her way, and Artemis shrugged. "The Gigantes fought for us then, and when it was done, we called them monsters and banished them to the wilds beyond our sight. Perhaps we could not stand to look at them for they reminded us of weakness lurking in our own flesh."

"You banished them because they preyed upon Men."

"So do we, even if we do not eat Man-flesh."

Athene didn't know what to say to that, but Artemis's words made her skin crawl. Either way, she and Ares had command of Olympus's defence, and she would see to it. "Take your brother and claim the high ground. Your arrows will slow their climb. Ares will guard the south slopes, and I will go to meet this force. Send me Hermes and Hestia, though, and what demigods they can raise."

Artemis might have objected, might have mentioned that she had, in fact, first trained Athene in the arts of stealth and battle. The other Titan did not say that, however, instead nodding and taking off to fulfil her orders. Her steps over the uneven escarpment and loose scree fell so sure Athene couldn't help but admire Artemis's grace.

And was the woman right? Had the Gigantes long been primed for rebellion against Father's rule, slighted by events Athene was too young to recall? It mattered naught, in truth. These creatures ate the flesh of Man and turned themselves into abominations, and for such crimes, they deserved worse than ostracisation: they deserved annihilation.

Soon, they would reach the slopes and she would wade into battle. Soon, but not yet. With a grimace, she held her hand out before her face. More tremors. Such would prove a liability in battle —if her spear shook, if her adamant shield faltered. Really, she had no choice ... Licking her lips, Athene withdrew a phial of Nectar from her khiton.

Just a small dose, enough to get through the battle.

STANDING BEFORE HER, Herakles clenched and unclenched his fists, shrugging his shoulders to loosen them. Nervous energy radiated off him in palpable waves, and Athene fought down the instinct to lay a calming hand upon his head. To indulge in such maternal adoration of him ... she had neither the right, nor would it instil in him the confidence he'd need to face Erginos and the Minyans.

"They'll be here soon," Herakles said, the young man fair dancing about the small house's atrium.

"And Thebes will suffer, perhaps even fall, if Erginos has his way. You have given him the excuse he craves to sack this city and claim its spoils. The only question remains now if you shall finish what you have begun."

"I cannot fight an army," Herakles objected.

Athene allowed herself a small smile. She had seen this moment so long ago, and with the disjointed sense of gratification that oft accompanied prescient fulfilment, she knelt at a chest and flipped the top to reveal a cloth-wrapt bundle. "You can lead one, Herakles. You are the great-grandson of Perseus himself, heir to his courage and his legacy."

When she handed him the bundle, he threw back the covering to reveal a gleaming adamant sword and shield, reflecting back his awed expression.

THEY CAME, howling and jeering, rushing over the defences of Olympus with sheer numbers and animalistic fury. Oh, Olympian arrows rained down onto the Gigantes, felling some and slowing others who, nevertheless, continued to surge upward, fletchings jutting from their flesh. Athene tried to direct her fellows, but the chaos of melee swallowed her vision. Two Cyclopes already lay dead, broken beneath her, corpses sent skittering down the escarpment, but more and more Gigantes kept coming.

Another closed in, Athene dancing up to meet it. The Gígas launched itself up past Athene, its torso a bulging, misshapen mass of muscle, its lower half formed from a trio of writhing serpents. The thing reeked of earthy musk and spilt blood, and it passed so close Athene slipped backward. The Gígas lunged at her in her moment of weakness, but Athene managed to jerk her spear up into position.

The point burst through its belly, splattering her with blood not quite gold enough to be called ichor. A foul stench erupted from its spilt innards. Despite being impaled upon her spear, the Gígas continued to drag itself toward her, muscles bunching with great heaves.

A serpentine neck wrapt around her ankle and Athene shrieked as it jerked her underneath the slavering monster. The Gígas's fist slammed toward her face.

She twisted to the side and the blow crashed into loose scree, sending the both of them careening further down the escarpment, toward a precarious ledge that might pitch them into open air beneath Olympus.

Now, the creature leaned in, roaring at her with teeth filed into fangs, spewing putrid breath over her. It meant to actually bite her face off.

Screaming, Athene twisted the spear in its belly. The Gígas's gaping maw twisted in pain.

Flooding as much Pneuma as she could into the Pneumatikoi of Potency, Athene heaved with her legs. Her attacker flew skyward five feet, enough for her to roll out from under it before it crashed back down onto the slope. Its momentum sent it skittering toward the precipice below. On her belly, Athene watched as it skidded over the edge, arms and serpents flailing in wild gyrations for a heartbeat before it dropped off into the mists.

More Pneuma. She needed to send more Pneuma coursing through her channels, into the Pneumatikoi of Tolerance to block the pain and get her moving.

Doing so, she had barely gained her feet before another shadow fell over her.

Oh, damn.

Athene dove to the side once more, an instant before the crashing form of another Gígas landed in the spot she had just occupied. The impact of its landing flung up a storm of loose rock, but it barely fazed the Gígas, who was already up, advancing upon her with a spear.

This one had legs and was barely warped by the consumption of Man-flesh. Only when she rose, her own spear between them, did she recognise its—*his*—face. Pallas, son of Kreios and father of Hephaistos, among other perverse spawn. His eyes had taken on a leonine aspect, and coarse hair had sprung up around him like a mane, but otherwise, he might still have passed for an ordinary Titan.

Still, he had joined the attack on Olympus. Which meant she was more than free to kill the bastard.

But this ... she had seen this moment. The revelation dazed her, left her reeling, even as she remembered it had in her vision.

His lunge, when it came, was so fast she barely saw him move. Even with her Alacrity Pneumatikoi flowing, he was a blur, his spear thrust more like a soaring arrow. Her own spear turned the point aside, barely, but not before it struck her cuirass with enough force to part the bronze, then gouge her bicep.

Stumbling backward, Athene gave ground under the furious onslaught, careening ever closer to the same ledge she had just sent the other Gígas pitching down. Pallas roared—that too more lion-like than human—and charged in, and Athene could see why some Men had called him a god of war like her brother, Ares.

Again and again, she deflected his spear with her own, only managing to keep up by continuing to give ground. She'd never defeat him like this, though. Internally, she shifted the flow of her Pneuma, draining even what she'd sent into Tolerance—and the pain hit her in fresh waves—to pour into the Pneumatikoi of Steadfastness, turning her flesh to iron.

His next blow she allowed to take her in the shoulder. It punched through her cuirass, drove through her reinforced skin, and sent her down to one knee with sheer force. But her own swipe took out Pallas's kneecap and sent him pitching over, tumbling among the scree.

White haze danced at the fringes of her vision, her stomach lurching at the pain. It forced her to return the Pneuma flow to Tolerance just to retain consciousness. Shaking off the delirium, she gained her feet.

Pallas had started to turn over. Athene couldn't use her left arm but managed a clumsy swipe of her spear blade, nevertheless, carving out Pallas's hamstring. The Gígas bellowed in agony, all pretence of leonine might cast aside.

This bastard not only made war on Olympus ... Worse, he sired

Hephaistos. What a father he must have been, to raise a son capable of such ... such ...

Panting, Athene dropped down, knees landing upon the Gígas's back. She cast aside the spear and pulled a knife, then wedged the point in between the creature's shoulder blades. "You know hunters claim lion skins as proof of their prowess ... I think I'm going to wear yours."

And she set to carving, his screams resounding off the slopes of Olympus.

DRENCHED IN BLOOD, dragging Pallas's skin behind her, Athene rose, surveying the landscape. It fair crawled with Gigantes and she could not see this battle ending before dark. Wending among them, to the south, a tall, muscular man—perhaps a Titan, though she did not know him—shot Gígas after Gígas with a massive bow.

Athene allowed herself a moment to remove her helmet and mop the sweat from her brow before replacing it. The man continued upward, trailed by a spear-wielding woman, though the man did most of the fighting. Any ally was welcome at this point wherever they had come from.

The man spotted her. She ... knew him. This was the man she had beheld in a Nectar-induced vision before the fighting began, though he looked older now, more worn. Herakles ... The name came up unbidden, but she knew it with the certainty of prescient memory.

At his side was the sword she'd given him, on his back the shield.

While she gaped at him, the man nocked an arrow and pointed it her way. What was he ...? Did he think her a Gígas? He loosed, and Athene flooded Pneuma to Alacrity to enhance her reflexes, throwing herself to the side. The arrow whooshed past her, aimed too high to have hit her at all. Instead, it slammed into a Gígas above her with a wet smack. The creature, concealed in the rocks, seemed to have been crawling about for an ambush, but now it pitched over backward to land hard upon the escarpment, an arrow lodged in its throat.

The man who'd saved her watched her a moment before trudging up to her level, pausing some distance off.

"Athene," he said, his breaths heavy from the fatigue of battle and thick with some emotion she couldn't name. Not a Titan, she thought, but perhaps a demigod. And strange he neither knelt nor offered any appellation of respect when he spoke her name. Considering he had slain the Gígas, she supposed she could let it slide.

"You are Herakles," she said, trying for all she could to make it sound as though she knew what was happening. Mortals, even demigods, they needed to think Olympians knew all and saw all.

The man glanced back at the woman behind him, a dark-haired Heliad who paused without closing the distance between them, perhaps intimidated by Athene's presence.

"I am," Herakles admitted, voice thick with an emotion she could not gauge.

A sudden certainty settled upon her, a knowledge that before her stood a demigod who would change their world. A champion she must find a way to guide, though he did not, at present, seem to seek guidance.

"What are you doing here?"

"I have to reach the summit of Olympus," the man said, casting another glance back at the Heliad. "I will slay any Gigantes who try to claim it." His hand rested on the sword hilt. *Her* sword, which even now also was strapped to Athene's side. How was this possible?

Athene swallowed and nodded. "Go then, and be blessed, ally of Olympus."

The Heliad woman had watched her with appraising eyes, though she averted her gaze when she noticed Athene looking her way. Herakles looked as though he wanted to speak, but instead just inclined his head.

The pair of them moved on, further up the mountain, and Athene had no more time to offer them as further Gigantes closed in around her. She had since lost her spear, so she drew the adamant xiphos. Her sword darted one way and the next, taking a Cyclops in the throat, carving out a Gígas's knees. Instinct guided her steps, and almost prescient awareness of where her foes moved. They fell about her in droves, misshapen corpses bedecking the foothills in macabre spectacle. Until, at last, only Demeter stood before her.

The Inumiden Titan's spearpoint drooped a hair, her visage warring between fear and determination. Athene might almost have pitied her, had she not betrayed them all.

"So you are, in the end, your father's daughter," Demeter said, trying to edge around Athene.

"I didn't know that was in doubt."

Demeter launched a probing strike and Athene deflected it. Maybe she could have ended this then and there, but the thought of seeing this woman—who had sat across from her in the grand hall—tortured and dragged screaming into Tartarus like Prometheus, rankled. Even if Athene could but delay the inevitable.

"Perhaps that's how you turn a blind eye to the monster that whelped you."

"Monster?" Athene scoffed, sweeping her sword around to encompass the hordes dead around her. Still more of the Gigantes had surged past her, she knew, and the others would need her help. Tarrying here endangered lives. She ought to end this ... "You brought the Man eaters."

"We are children of Gaia," Demeter said. Only then, when she opened her mouth a hair wider than necessary, did Athene catch sight of the first points of forming fangs.

"Y-you have tasted the flesh of Man!"

"Do you not feast upon all the bounty of the Earth?"

"Not on Mankind!" Athene shrieked. How ... how could an Olympian take such an obscene step? Could desperation alone prompt this vulgarity? Her stomach lurched at the thought of what Demeter had done. "Why?" The word ripped from her, stealing her strength, making her knees wobble. How could someone she'd known her whole life do this? Gigantes were *monsters*.

A sneer answered her, and Demeter clacked the butt of her spear on the ground, her timidity forgotten. The woman revelled in the horror she had engendered in Athene, didn't she? She made armour of the disgust her actions had summoned. "You have no idea who your father really is, child. The things he's done … and the things he has failed to do. He cares more for pride than kin. For the sake of his ego, he would let the world burn. He would set the kindling himself. Like a moth to flame, I flocked to the allure of his regal grandeur. I blinded myself then, even as you do now, to the wretched putrescence in the heart of that man."

"You speak of the King of Olympus!" Athene shrieked at her, her own weapon shaking now. How dare she, this defiler of their most sacred law, so defame her father?

"Your father killed his own brother," Demeter spat. What? Hades died and became the God of the Underworld … He didn't … Father wouldn't … "He and your mother murdered Hades, and when Hades returned from the grave for his vengeance, he took your half-sister and Zeus … did … *naught*. He waved his hand with impotence and assuaged his bruised ego by abducting and raping Princess Io of Argos. Until he could deny Persephone had ever existed."

Father had forbidden any on Olympus to speak her name …

Athene balked.

Snarling, Demeter lunged in, her thrusts savage but amateurish. Athene deflected two with the edge of her sword, then drove the point straight through Demeter's sternum. Golden streams of ichor burbled from the Titan's chest as she collapsed unto her knees.

It was a mercy far kinder than handing her over to Father. "Maybe you can find Persephone now," Athene said, managing only a slight hitch in her voice. She eased the other woman to the ground, watched the pain give way to resignation. And darkness.

She stared at the blade that had taken the life of a fellow Olympian. The blade this Herakles also somehow wielded.

A shudder ran through her, a desire to flee from this. Could all Demeter had accused Father of hold truth? The churning of her gut told her she well knew the answer to it. And still, she had killed Demeter. Struck her down like one more Gígas. What did that make Athene?

Part of her wanted to toss her arms aside. Part of her needed to scream at Dyaus and Hyperion above, to curse Ananke and defy the Moirai.

But up there, on the peak, more Gigantes were closing in on her home, on her kin. Whatever her father had or had not done ... Athene would not abandon those she had sworn to protect.

29

HERAKLES

715 Bronze Age

The high-pitched giggling of young boys rang through the house, drawing Herakles from his doze beside the central hearth. Rubbing his eyes, he grunted, looking around. No one in here. A day's work in the fields must have worn him out more than he'd thought, for he'd not planned to sleep.

With a stretch he rose, plodded over to the window, and peered outside. Stick in hand, Kreontiades chased his two brothers around the house under the eye of his mother, who stood upon the portico, humming while weaving a basket. They'd named Kreontiades for Megara's father, and though only their middle son, he tended to lead the pack of wild wolves Herakles and his wife had seemed to have sired.

Hooting and screaming, the boys tromped through the mud before disappearing once more from Herakles's vision around the corner.

Eh, well. They'd have a dunk in the river in their future. Head-first, if Herakles heard they'd vexed Megara overmuch. But then, who could ask for more in the house than the pellucid laughter of children? Contented, he collapsed back onto the divan, snatched up the amphora, and filled his cup.

Such days beat the fervour of battle, and any man who thought otherwise deluded himself or else missed the point of life.

After downing the cup in one swig, Herakles found himself staring at the goblet. That had ... tasted a little off. A bad vintage? He sniffed the amphora. Huh. The wine had some sort of fragrance mixed within. Almost like ... Ambrosia? Herakles had sampled the draught of the gods only once in his life, brought to him by Athene as a gift from his father Zeus. The only thing the king of Olympus had ever given him.

Perhaps it was all his imagination. Perhaps fatigue yet wore at him and he needed more sleep.

Staring at the amphora, he considered whether to allow himself one more cup. But if the wine had soured, he might well wind up tasting it a second time—when he spent half the night retching.

When he looked up, the sun had vanished behind the hills. Strange, he hadn't realised he'd spent so long mulling over the damn wine. Already the moon had risen, though it lay occluded by thick clouds blanketing the night sky.

The hairs on the back of his neck rose at the creeping sense of a presence in the room with him. Fists clenching at his side, Herakles turned but saw naught save the flickering shadows cast by the hearth. "Megara?" he called.

A raspy chortle answered, ephemeral and grating, as if the night itself mocked his sudden discomfort. Something Otherworldly brushed against this place, an Etheric presence that sent shudders running down his spine.

"Boys!" he bellowed. "Get inside!"

The dancing gloom at the fringes curled into unnatural shapes, almost like half-formed figures of men. Snickering and wailing, they flitted about, even as Herakles spun, trying to keep them in view. Chills wracked him, his heart pounding. Were these ... no. He knew these shades, their bent fingers thrust at him in damning accusation.

Erginos and his Minyan horde, all shrieking their lamentation, drawing closer and closer, decrying their deaths.

Herakles backed up until his arse brushed against the hearth. "You got what you deserved." His words lacked conviction, even in his own ears. As if he hadn't slain them more for his own glory than the fact they preyed upon Thebes. "You got ..."

One of the ghosts wailed at him in defiance of his words, lunging. Spectral claws raked his chest, shredding his tunic and slicing down to expose bone. A haze of white pain filled his vision, sent him tumbling to the floor.

The mass of shadows surged forward like a breaking wave, converging upon him from all sides, even as Herakles screamed. A moment of desperation, and Pneuma allowed him to block the pain. Push it down enough to drown it with rage. "You were murderers and thieves!" he roared into the darkness.

The fury had him, and he swung. To his shock, his fist collided with a ghost, though the blow only sent the shade rocking rather than dropping it. The entity hissed, however, as the impact sent it careening toward the flame. Bellowing in inarticulate fury, Herakles grappled with the nebulous darkness closing in around him, kicking and punching, driving the hateful shades into the open hearth.

If they craved the gloom, he would give them such illumination they had no choice but to leave him be. Again and again, he attacked, fists smacking into ghost flesh, scattering his attackers.

But the darkness that had seeped in grew too complete, pulled him to his knees. And, at last, sent him spiralling down into the blackness himself.

❧

A PAINED GROAN escaped Herakles as he pushed himself off the floor. Sunlight streaming in through the window stung his eyes. Something had crusted his face, his lip cracking with it as he moved. A swiped hand over his face came away caked with dried blood. What in Hades's Underworld?

Herakles blinked, looking around. Across from him, a moan. Its source, Megara, lying in a pool of her own blood, her head awash with it.

A pain shot through Herakles's chest, a horror beyond words or thoughts that held him immobile for a bare instant. Then he dashed to her side, reaching trembling fingers—his knuckles, too, burst and bloody—to check her pulse.

Alive, with a strong enough pulse she seemed like to stay that way.

What ... what ...

But he knew. A gnawing apprehension crept up from his gut, worming its damning way along his shuddering spine before settling in his brain. His wife ... his wife ... his ... his ...

Tears already welled in his eyes as he turned, looking for the boys. When he scanned the room, his gaze caught upon the hearth.

Upon the fire-blackened skeletons draped upon one another inside the pit. Upon the tiny, child finger bones brushing over the stone lip.

The shriek that escaped him was no sound Man made, but that of an animal in unfathomable anguish. Herakles's World imploded, collapsed in on itself, even as he toppled to the floor. A nightmare, worse than any conjuring of a fevered mind. A torment, complete and soul-devouring, leaving naught in its wake save ashes.

30

———

PANDORA

2392 Golden Age

*D*awn spilled over a ravished Thebes, pale light limning the smouldering embers of the polis in an obscene glow. Arms wrapt around herself—though the rain had abated and no cold bothered her—Pandora trudged through the ruins alongside Prometheus. Once she had witnessed the apocalyptic sundering of Atlantis, and while that destruction was more complete, this one tasted fouler, orchestrated as it was by the hands of people. By their own daughter and her wretched ally, Zeus, who had unleashed his monsters in the name of victory. By the very Men to whom Prometheus had given the Art of Fire.

The storm had made a foul sludge of the roads, choked them with a blend of shit and mud and viscera, with plaster and kindling and the ruination of lives.

"And still, you support him," she said, when the silence had taken on such weight it crushed the words from her lungs.

Prometheus grunted. "You and I, we have beheld this future, in the flesh and in the flame. It is the weave of history, the will of the Moirai."

"You mean this is all Fate."

"It is history. Your history, in compounding chains that underlay the totality of your existence and that of our family. That of our society, of our entire world."

The same argument, round and round, binding them in those same chains Prometheus spoke of. But Pandora grew tired of fetters, weary of impotence, and exhausted at the thought of enduring another moment of Zeus's violent tantrums. Setting her jaw, she grabbed Prometheus's khiton, pulling him to a stop on their way to the harbour.

Word had come of some summit to be held there, and though Zeus had not summoned Prometheus, much less Pandora, still both shared a tacit agreement they needed to know what would next unfold in this Titanomachy. But not yet. This proved more pressing.

"I refuse to believe Ananke rules every aspect of our lives." There had to be some way to escape the ouroboros.

"That is what makes it Fate, Pandora. All we are is predicated upon causal chains."

She patted her satchel. "I will find a way to use the Box to change it. To change everything, to make a better world for us all. You and I and Pyrrha, and everyone else. There has to be some path, some route not yet accounted for. Within the weave of Ananke, some loose thread I can pluck to change the whole of the picture. If I can pass through any point in history, one of those points must yield to my will rather than always the inverse. Otherwise ..."

"Otherwise, you fear your own will a self-delusion." He said naught more, but something in the timbre of his voice spoke of conversations held before. How could an Oracle not have doubts about the existence of free will? To see the future and be unable to alter its course must prove a burden beyond compare.

Sympathy warmed her, and she took his hand as they trudged onward, rubbing his fingers with her own. Who was she to judge his response to the weights pushing down upon him? Together, they made their way toward the great steps down to the harbour, the same ones Tethys had once escorted her up. Vertiginous waves passed through her, having less to do with the height than with the recurrent realisation that everything she experienced here—from meeting Hekate to once more climbing these steps—they represented much more recent memories for her than for those around her.

Tethys, Hekate, and Prometheus, too, had endured ages more than she could conceive since last they had seen her. She, who had lived but a few decades, could not grasp the depth or nature of their experience, save with the obvious: that a mind enduring so long must invariably find itself altered by the process. That to live without end while the world around you withered and died over and over, to persist like obdurate mountains or the eternal seas, must skew the thoughts, even as the compounding of memories began to suffocate.

She leaned on Prometheus for support in her vertigo, yes, but also because doing so would show him *her* support, which he would need. When she left here—and she would use the Box to try to create the better world she had spoken of—he would mostlike not look upon her again until their encounter on Atlantis, almost sixteen centuries from now. The Prometheus of this time would know that time lay ahead, but not when or what he must face between then and now. Could she tell him? Would it make aught easier for him?

They paused on the landing halfway down to the harbour, Prometheus watching the distant roaring cataract in rapt silence, staring at it with almost the intensity he used to stare into flame, though Pandora knew he saw visions only in fire. After a moment, she squeezed his fingers. "We don't want to miss whatever unfolds below."

A faint grunt answered her, and they pressed on, at last coming down to the sea. Upon the pier, Zeus waited with Hera, before them standing a mer. Though upon two legs, scales running up his limbs made his nature all too obvious.

"Brother-in-law," Zeus proclaimed, arms wide as if to embrace the mer, though he made no move to step forward and do so.

The mer favoured him with bared, sharklike teeth in what *might* have been a greeting.

"It's Poseidon," Prometheus whispered to her. "Hera's brother. Once possessed by Nereus, I have heard the two of them have reached a kind of symbiosis. I suspect Tethys, with her agreements with Pontus, helped negotiate that for her son."

Pandora's mind reeled struggling to parse the information Prometheus had dropped in her lap. Her earlier supposition seemed correct—that mer took human bodies like parasites and steered them. It made sense then, she supposed, to hear a mer had claimed Poseidon. How else did a Titan become a ruler of the seas?

"I came for my sister's sake," Poseidon said, gills flapping when he spoke. "But Mother claims you have banished her from Elládos."

Zeus scoffed. "Voluntary exile."

The king looked primed to spew forth more, but Hera cut him off. "A new order is coming, Brother. The League has already begun to fall. But if you join us, pledge the might of Pontus to us, we shall guarantee you a seat on the new ruling council when the war is over. You will not find such an offer from the League, nor do any remain with such bargains as Tethys made to Pontus."

The silence stretched on to uncomfortable lengths, and Pandora half hoped Poseidon would spit in their faces, though the shape of the future told her otherwise. Poseidon became an Olympian, this she knew all too well.

Indeed, the mer extended a webbed hand which Zeus took with some obvious disdain. Poseidon leaned in close, whispering something to his sister and brother-in-law. Pandora could not catch it, but knowing what she knew now, she had to imagine it involved tributes the land must soon offer the sea. More hosts for the sirens of Pontus, more obscene sacrifices to the Otherworld.

"You are watching the future you know take shape before your eyes," Prometheus observed, insightful as always.

But then, the time Pandora had come from, the time she knew, was not one which she much loved. How was she to look upon its inception and with aught save a grimace?

❦

"IT FEELS like we are always bidding each other farewell," Pandora said. Hekate had given them the same room in the palace she had shared with Prometheus when living in Thebes so long ago. Perhaps the sorceress meant it as a comfort, perhaps as a jibe. She oft proved hard to read and offered Pandora too little of her time for her to overcome her mysteries.

They sat upon the floor of the room that had once been home, and the sense of having lived the same instant choked her. Here, they had stolen moments upon a whale mosaic, knowing she would tear herself away from Pyrrha. Here, staring out this window, she had decided to use the Box to travel back to save Prometheus from the awful imprisonment Zeus had imposed upon him. Now, in Zeus's own court, she had to make the same choice a second time, and her world felt more sundered than ever.

Rather than bringing down the tyrant king, she strode along his retinue and watched as he began his ascension. As he claimed the very throne from which he would piss down upon the world. By her mere presence, by not acting against him when she knew the wretched deeds he would enact, she became culpable in those crimes.

"We are not given the choices we might wish," Prometheus said, stroking her cheek. Did he respond to her words or to the conflict playing out in her heart, given he so oft seemed able to read such things? "Oracles bear burdens others cannot fathom, and you, in wandering the twisting paths of history, must carry a similar weight upon your shoulders."

Or perhaps, his words meant *both*, twined in her as he had become.

"Break the chains of Ananke," she implored, knowing he neither could nor would.

His thumb brushed over her cheekbone in answer, his sapphire eyes glinting in the light of their oil lamp. He did not say that Fate still bound them. He did not need to, for she knew it well enough. Even her future self had warned her she needed to find Nike and ensure Zeus won, or Pyrrha would pay the price. But she had no idea where to find the winged goddess—though if Nike was Nemesis, trying the change the weave of Ananke might well conjure her up. Either way, her promise to save Prometheus in the future remained unresolved, and perhaps Pandora's own only hope for a life with him lay with *that* Prometheus, not this one staring at her with the damning muddle of longing and determination.

"I love you," she whispered, the words ripped out of her soul. Shouldn't they be enough? Shouldn't those words mean *everything*?

"I love you too," he said, such conviction in his voice she almost dared to believe this might yet work out. That it might, if she found the paths, resolve itself into some possibility of joy and family. That she might save him and herself in the process.

She had sworn to herself she would find a way to fix everything, and she meant to do so, Ananke be damned.

Before she could say aught more, he leaned forward, his lips brushing over hers. Massaging with need, admitting the waves of pain lurking inside his breast as well.

With a stifled sob, Pandora jerked away. She had to do this before her resolve weakened. She fished out the Box and began setting it.

Prometheus reached for it, and she handed it over. "I saw something in the flames," he said, twisting and sliding panels. "A setting I would make. Perhaps it will send you where you need to go to find who you seek."

This Herakles ...

When he returned the Box, Pandora examined the modifications. She needed to understand every possible working of this device if she was to have any hope of enacting her plan to right the World and free it from the ouroboros. Once satisfied with all he had done, she opened the top, embracing the sudden popping of her ears, the folding of light on itself, the vertiginous waves that engulfed her.

Every time got easier, she found. The period of distortion compressed. She found herself kneeling in a field—a farm?—and blinking, beheld a forest beyond it. As she rose, she saw a man, tall and burly-shouldered with curling brown hair, staring at something he had wedged into the mud. A xiphos, set point up at an angle.

Dread apprehension seized her. Herakles intended to slay himself.

Desperation leant her strength and speed, and Pandora hurled herself at the large warrior. Had his own suicide not so occupied him, she couldn't imagine she would have caught him unawares enough to send the both of them toppling down into the field, but she did, and the pair of them slammed into the loam, Pandora atop him.

Herakles landed with an *oomph* of breath blown out of him, giving Pandora enough time to scramble off him.

"Whatever you've suffered, whatever you've done," she panted, "you cannot believe taking your life will offer absolution."

The warrior rose onto his haunches, looking Pandora up and down. "Who in Hades's dark domain are you?"

Pandora brushed herself off and stood, looking down at him. "I'm Pandora. And Hades's dark domain is exactly where you were headed. What do you imagine awaits down there that might prove so much more desirable than life up here, Herakles?"

His brows narrowed. "How do you know my name? Did Athene send you?"

Athene. Interesting. It would seem the Olympian acted as some sort of patron to Herakles, just as she had to his great-grandfather Perseus. To what end, well that Pandora would still have to discover. She could not rule out the possibility Athene intended to bring weal to Perseus's line ... but one ought never assume altruism as a motivation for any Titan. Maybe not even for Men.

"She did not send me," Pandora admitted. "Someone else did, someone who needs your help."

His chuckle came out so forced Pandora almost winced at the pain lancing his very breath. "Help?" He waved a hand back at a farmhouse behind them. "I am a madman who beat his own wife unconscious and cast his children into the fire. I am not fit to offer succour to a leech. Wretches condemned to die would not welcome my aid if they knew the truth of me. You and your friend ought best to look elsewhere, Pandora, and leave me to my well-deserved end."

Well, shit.

Her mind whirred with indecision. She could not deny cringing at his description of his crimes. The thought of it churned her stomach. Why, oh why, hadn't Perseus proved the correct son of Zeus to aid her? The man overflowed with valour and compassion, where his great-grandson stained his hands with the blood of innocents and marred his soul with kinslaying. But still, Prometheus had told her Herakles had *already* saved him in Perseus's time, decades before the time she must have now reached. Whatever this man had done, whatever his reasons, if she could but nudge him in the right direction, she might yet reunite with her lover. And with that done, maybe, somehow, she could right the rest of the world.

All this played out in her mind in an instant while she struggled to keep her expression blank—lest he read her condemnation of him upon her features. With a low sigh, she settled down before him.

"Why did you do it?"

Herakles's pathetic laugh cracked halfway through, becoming a sob. "That's the worst of it ... I don't even fucking know. I saw ... I thought ghosts had come to drag me to Hades. I thought myself beset by Etheric foes. I thought ..." He swallowed and shook his head. "I am a madman, woman, and you had best stay well clear of me."

Sound advice. Given any choice, Pandora would walk away and never look on the murderer again. "I can't. It has to be you, Herakles. You alone can save one condemned to a fate worse than death." She forced herself to reach out and touch his hand. "I don't know why this madness beset you, but if you can save another, perhaps you may find redemption."

For a long time, so long her chest ached with all the fervour of her protesting knees, he stared at her hand upon his own. Weight sagged his shoulders, a despair so profound it seemed to mirror Pandora's own the day Hekate had kidnapped her—or the day Ananke had forced Pandora to abandon Pyrrha as a baby. The sort of burden that ground lives and souls to dust like a pestle.

But when she looked up, in those blue eyes lay a hint of something more. Something she had given him, Pandora realised with a flush of pride.

Something maybe she could, in time, give the whole of the World.

Hope.

EPILOGUE

2389 Golden Age

Atop the Aviary, Prometheus sat in a ring of braziers, the wind whipping his hair while he watched Hestia. His apprentice passed the flame back and forth between her hands with the ease of a natural. Of all those he had trained, his first student had still made the most progress. After three years, in fact, her demonstration was more spectacle than any need to prove herself.

"The Firewalkers have spread to Phoenikia and Phrygia," she said, gaze locked on the mesmerising dance of flame coiling about her fingers. "Mostly Men, though some Titans, as well."

Prometheus offered her a slight nod of acknowledgment. Yes, they had spread, and he had seen to it. The age of the Ouranid League was drawing to a close, and war impended, probably in less than a year unless he missed his guess. Man would need every edge possible to survive what would soon unfold. "Go to Neshia. Find the worthy and train them."

"Me?"

"Who better?"

Pyromantic insight told him she would get swept up in the coming war sooner or later. By sending her away, he might ensure it was later. His visions revealed so much death. So much carnage. Over and over. After a fashion, it all fell upon his shoulders. For it would have ended, had he allowed the World to dissolve in the first Era.

Hestia offered him a bow before she left. Always eager for his approval. It would do her good to be out there, making her own way. She had the talent and the will. Now, she required confidence.

When she had left, he crossed his legs beneath himself and settled into meditation, his respite from the strangling threads of the Tapestry. Or perhaps his self-inflicted torment, dwelling upon them.

It was just before midday when men climbed up to the terrace.

"Lord Prometheus," Kyril said. "We found this man approaching the village."

Prometheus did not, at first, open his eyes. He was drained almost dry with the knowledge of his part in starting the coming war and all that would follow. All that had preceded it.

"Loki," the newcomer said sharply.

Now, Prometheus opened his eyes to take in a strange old man. He bore a wide-brimmed hat, had but one eye, and wore clothes not of these lands. And that name ... Had Prometheus not heard that name in some prescient vision? "Leave me with him."

"But, my lord, we don't know if the king sent him. He could be a Titan."

Prometheus smiled. No, this man was something else, and he could guess what. "He's not a Titan."

When the others had left, Prometheus rose and paced toward Odin, pausing several feet away. "Who are you? Why do you call me that name?"

The man fell back a step, cocking his head. "This is the first time we've met ... for *you*."

Yes, a time traveler. Prometheus glanced beyond the stranger to make sure none of his allies had lingered. "You used the Box?"

The man groaned. "I have no idea what that means." He hesitated. "Titans ... you're at war with them. Jotunnar?"

"We're not at war." Not yet.

"They called you the Firebringer." The man shook his head. "You gave them the Art of Fire. Is this ... the first time?"

Yes, he could see it inside the man. Another incarnation of the Destroyer. He'd come through time somehow, though apparently not with the Box. The Time Chambers, then? "I'm called Prometheus, and yes, I gave the Art of Fire to Man to offer them a bulwark against the Titans and against other, darker forces."

The stranger nodded. "I'm Odin. And ... One day, we shall be blood brothers. Until you finally betray me."

Prometheus flinched. The directness of the statement—not even an accusation—struck him like a blow. He had always tried to serve as a guide to the Destroyer ... But then, he was always also sending him to his death, wasn't he? "It's you, isn't it? Yes, of course it is." Prometheus hesitated. Didn't he have a right to know? And, of course, Odin could not remember the choices he had made in prior lifetimes. "I believed we would *need* the cycle. I ... for whatever it's worth ... I'm sorry it has to be you, over and over. I didn't have the strength to do this myself ..."

Odin strode toward Prometheus and snared his tunic. "So you *did* create the Eschaton cycle. Why? Why have you done this?"

Prometheus looked to Odin's grip and considered knocking the presumptive Man backward. "I ... I don't know how much I can safely tell you. Not only for your sake, but because speaking it aloud might draw the attention of forces we need to avoid as much as possible."

"You mean the Norns."

"I assume that's just another name for the Moirai, but they're not the only powers we need to concern ourselves with ... Odin. They serve a function, holding together the timeline with their Wheel of Fate. But the greater threat comes from powers darker still, consumptive forces that feed upon souls and, if not sated, might burst forth and bring down the foundations of the World. Thus, the only solution, terrible though it was, seemed to be to initiate a cataclysmic struggle to overcome the rising tide of darkness. It ended the World but at least allowed a new World to rise from the ashes like a phoenix."

"A what?"

Something forgotten by the future then, but he had seen it, and it was real, of that he was certain. Prometheus waved that away. "The point is, the Moirai agreed, perhaps so wholeheartedly that the process became a cycle. It is a means of propitiating the Darkness, Odin. A bad solution, yes, but still the only one available to us."

Odin paled, looked almost like he might be sick. "You did this ... because you couldn't otherwise hold the World together?"

Prometheus fixed him with his gaze. He need not answer, for Odin clearly already knew the truth. He might have even glimpsed some fragment of the Ontos. And Prometheus's future self had clearly spared Odin the greater horror as long as he might.

Trembling, Odin sank to his knees, and Prometheus knelt beside him, hands on his shoulders, saying naught, just looking into his eye. Yes, he understood.

Odin, like so many other incarnations of the Destroyer, had to suffer. He had to fight, to strive, to die, and to rise again, over and over. Because it was all that kept the World going.

And time grew ever denser.

Author's Note:

"And he bound Prometheus with ineluctable fetters, Painful bonds, and drove a shaft through his middle,

And set a long-winged eagle on him that kept gnawing His undying liver, but whatever the long-winged bird Ate the whole day through, would all grow back by night."
—Hesiod, Theogony

WHILE ALL SEQUELS must invariably involve change or risk stagnation, I was still nervous about this one because it shifted some part of the focus from the "goddess" main characters to secondary demigod heroes (in this book, Perseus and Herakles). Myths, in general, often present the personalities of heroes as bare-bones at best. We know of Perseus's origins, his heroic deeds, and his more successful reign than most Greek heroes, yes. But what of his personality? His foibles and tastes, his fears and his dreams?

Gods and heroes are larger than life figures, and herein I hope to retain that aspect to a certain degree, while grounding them as flawed human beings. I hope I succeeded.

In the meantime, we also see Pandora and the other women's stories continue to unfold in parallel to one another. Their timelines sometimes overlap, but rarely mesh for more than brief spans, ships passing in the night. For Pandora, she's coming to grips with the reality that the knots created by these time loops are denser than she had ever imagined, and she's not going to untangle them as quickly as she might have wished.

In fact, it's only just beginning.

One more aspect I wanted touch on here is the genē and why they're divided the way they are, with, for example, many gods and Titans having their parentage changed to fit within these conceptions. I stumbled across the fact that most of Greek mythology followed a handful of noble families and developed this idea into the genē we see in the series.

My general philosophy in adapting myth and folklore follows a pattern of conversation of character and relationships. Namely, that if the story can be enhanced by having a character serve multiple roles or by a shift in the relationship between two characters, this is probably the right decision. In *Tapestry of Fate*, this led to significant deviation in the normal parentage of many gods and Titans.

While traditional mythology has, for example, Artemis and Apollon as children of Zeus, I opted to make them children of Helios.

Doing so not only connected the sun god Apollon with the sun god Helios, but created a more compelling narrative. Rather than a single father siring half the gods in existence, there were several bloodlines, allowing the narrative to be more about the interaction between a handful of families instead of just one.

If you've enjoyed this book, I encourage you to join the Skalds' Tribe newsletter and get access to exclusive insider information and your FREE copy of *The Moments of Kadmus*. **I generally send every week or every other; I promise not to mail more often than that.** No spam, no selling your email address to marauding warlords, none of that.

Join me here to grab a free novella and stay connected with me: https://www.mattlarkinbooks.com/skalds/

Thank you for reading,
Matt

PS Pandora's journey continues in the *Inferno of Prometheus* ...

https://books2read.com/infernoofprometheus

Join the Skalds' Tribe newsletter and get access to exclusive insider information and a selection of free books to kickstart your Matt Larkin library.

https://www.mattlarkinbooks.com/skalds/

ALSO BY MATT LARKIN

Tapestry of Fate

The Gifts of Pandora

The Valor of Perseus

The Inferno of Prometheus

The Madness of Herakles

The Threads of Theseus

Heirs of Mana

Tides of Mana

Flames of Mana

Queens of Mana

Gods of the Ragnarok Era

The Apples of Idunn

The Mists of Niflheim

The Shores of Vanaheim

The High Seat of Asgard

The Well of Mimir

The Radiance of Alfheim

The Shadows of Svartalfheim

The Gates of Hel

The Fires of Muspelheim

ABOUT THE AUTHOR

Matt Larkin writes retellings of mythology as dark, gritty fantasy. His passions of myths, philosophy, and history inform his series. He strives to combine gut-wrenching action with thought-provoking ideas and culturally resonant stories.

Matt's mythic fantasy takes place in the Eschaton Cycle universe, a world—as the name implies—of cyclical apocalypses. Each series can be read alone in any order, but they weave together to form a greater tapestry. Want a place to start? Check out *Darkness Forged*.

Learn more at mattlarkinbooks.com or connect with Matt through his fan group, the Skalds' Tribe: https://www.mattlarkin books.com/join-the-skalds-tribe/

For my family.

I want to offer special thanks to all the amazing people at Kickstarter who helped me bring this to life:

Regina Dowling, Rachel Strehlow, John Van Mulligen, Mary K Cordray, Dale Russell, Matthea Ross, Bryan Lash, Diane Youngblood, Dyrk Ashton, Jon Auerbach, Dan Zangari & Robert Zangari, yesterspectre, Shannon Leigh Broughton-Smith, Eskil, Juhi Larkin, Tristan Amant, Debbie Mumford, Suzan Harden, Rebecca Kellogg, Judy Lunsford, Kari Kilgore, Curmudgeon of Phoenix Rising, Lee Sharp, Rebecca Hiatt, Jon Wasik, Lee, Henry C Eggleton, Danny van Giersbergen, Ashli Tingle, Stuart renz, Brad, Joseph, Ron Arons, Al Burke, Caleb Monroe, Emilia Pulliainen, Michał Kabza, A.P Beswick, Thomas Colgrave, Jeremy Irwin, Connor Whiteley, Scott Smith, Bryan, Sarah Polk, Duane Warnecke, Govinda P. G. Embleton, FireflyArc, Jason Hays, and Braedon Bourassa.

Thank you all,
Matt

www.ingramcontent.com/pod-product-compliance
Lightning Source LLC
Chambersburg PA
CBHW061053190726
48286CB00006B/1731